The GUILD of ST. COOPER

The GUILD of ST. COOPER

Shya Scanlon

DZANC
BOOKS

5220 Dexter Ann Arbor Rd.
Ann Arbor, MI 48103
www.dzancbooks.org

Library of Congress Cataloging-in-Publication Data

Scanlon, Shya.
  The Guild of St. Cooper / Shya Scanlon.
    pages cm
  I. Title.
  PS3619.C266G85 2015
  813'.6--dc23

                                                    2014013418

First US edition: May 2015
ISBN: 978-1936873613
Book design by Michelle Dotter

Printed in the United States of America

10   9   8   7   6   5   4   3   2   1

For Erin

The **GUILD** of **ST. COOPER**

"The imagination loses vitality as it ceases to adhere to what is real."

— *Wallace Stevens*

"The more clearly one sees this world, the more one is obliged to pretend it does not exist."

— *James Salter*

"I have no idea where this will lead us, but I have a definite feeling it will be a place both wonderful and strange."

— *Dale Cooper*

Part I

DAY 1

MY BROTHER HAD LEFT, my wife had left, and Fred, the only neighbor left on the block, was packing. Even those who stayed were tired of waiting. Soon, the few stores remaining would close. The pharmacy. The grocery. Everything under a buck. What then? From my perch on the high porch I watched my mother gather blooms in the back yard. Her long white hair fell loose around her narrow shoulders, coating them with snow. It was hot. The sun smashed down on her back and on the upturned faces of the flowers and she clipped one—bright orange, many-petaled—then held her bouquet at arm's length and nodded, turning it slowly in her hands.

"Zinnias are from Mexico," she said, seeing me, and then, "Keep an eye out for Zane, will you? He's delivering some marijuana today."

As she walked to the edge of the porch and held up the bouquet, a shadow flickered across her face as a crow passed overhead. I took the flowers inside. Yesterday's flowers, only slightly faded, still filled a vase at the center of the dining-room table, and I replaced them, then joined my mother's masks in staring. Masks from all over the world covered the walls, staring impassively at whatever unfamiliar thing the room produced. Years ago they'd spooked me. I'd thought they were watching me, spying on me, whispering my secrets. Now I just felt bad for them, unwilling spectators at a strange and impenetrable ritual. I felt bad, and I empathized.

The emergency radio crackled like a dog eating bones, then fell silent. The whole house was silent. I stood in silence above the bouquet and stared out the window.

Across the street, Fred was lifting a large metal sculpture into the back of his van. It looked like he had it, but at the last moment his grip failed and the complicated, fragile thing crashed to his feet. He cursed loudly, and as though drawn to the noise I joined him outside. Fred had never been a very close neighbor, but with everyone else gone our bond had deepened. Since the evacuation, his once-intimidating body had grown bent with worry and suddenly with age. He leaned it against his van and rubbed its lower back with a frown.

"Damn thing," he said.

"What's the story?"

"Was given to me by a Russian czar for a job I did in Alaska."

Now in pieces, the sculpture had been of a chicken with fire shooting out of its mouth. I turned over one of the small flames with my foot and it made the muffled clink of pocket change.

"Why a chicken?"

Fred quickly gathered the pieces and hoisted them into the van, his back audibly popping, his face tight.

"Dragon," he said. He closed the van door and held out a massive, lumpy hand. "Well, I guess this is it. Give your mother my best."

In the three seconds our hands were clasped a slimy glaze slicked my palm.

"Given," I said.

He walked up the short, trimmed path to his steps, up his steps to the porch, and locked his front door. He tried the handle and put the key back in his pocket, then made his way back to the van.

"And please," he said, leaning out the window, "tell your mother to keep that gas tank secret. No telling who'd do what for it."

He gave the abandoned cars and fallen branches a wide berth on his way down the block, and paused at the end of the street with his blinker on. Then, with a small wave of his hand, he was gone.

I looked back at his house. He'd kept his property groomed, a polite rebuttal to the slow collapse around it. Looking at this house and only at this house, a person wouldn't suspect anything had changed.

Out of respect, I decided to give it twenty-four hours before breaking in.

Unlike Fred's place, my mother's had fallen into semi-disrepair since my brother had taken his family east. I did what I could to keep the trees back and maintain the drainage around the foundation like he'd shown me, but I wasn't quite up to the task, and my mother made it easy to neglect the place.

"It'll outlive me," she'd say with a shrug.

With the exception of her garden, neglect was a lifestyle decision at 939 NW 64th Street. It formed a bond between us. I neglected my writing like I'd neglected my wife, my mother neglected herself, and we both neglected the house.

A siren sounded from somewhere toward the water, releasing three long, true wails before twisting into something more like a wounded cat.

During the evacuation, Fred had stood watch tirelessly over his home, and by virtue of occupying his own porch had served as a kind of sentinel for the block. The rest of us were frequently woken in the night by the sound of his warning shots, but after the first week or two these became soothing rather than frightening, a sign of safety, of order.

The looting had finally ceased to be much of an issue, but I couldn't help feeling vaguely exposed.

I went back inside.

"Zane? Zane, is that you?"

"No, Mom, it's me," I called through the house. "Mom?"

I found my mother sitting on the back porch in the sun, her eyes closed.

"It's me," I said again. "Fred's gone. He says goodbye."

"Goodbye, Fred."

"He says to keep the gas safe."

She squinted up at me. "You can tell Fred that if he has any other opinions about the gas he can tell me personally."

"I think I'm going to see if he left a television."

We'd gotten rid of our TV over a year ago to distance ourselves from the goings-on of people whose actions, to quote my mother, "no longer concern us." I didn't care at the time. I'd never been a news watcher and that's all anything was anymore: news in the form of entertainment or entertainment in the form of news. Who could tell one from the other? Who cared? So I was surprised that this had been my first response to Fred's announcement, a week before, that he'd be leaving.

"What do you think?" I asked.

"I think it's a beautiful day," my mother said, and closed her eyes.

Having cheated herself out of a retirement home in Arizona, it simply couldn't get too hot for my mother. I watched a fat, dizzy bee meander across the deck and rise willfully upward, making for an apple blossom.

"I'm going to try and get some writing done," I said.

I had not been writing.

The book I'd been working on when Seattle evacuated was pure fantasia, a baroque love affair with sound and rhythm and nonsense. But compared to the surrealism around me, it had begun to seem indulgent, and worse, beside the point. I climbed the stairs to my writing room and looked out over lower Ballard, Fremont, and the north side of Queen Anne Hill. What followed had been a period of simply writing down things I saw with no real coherent structure, let alone plot. I'd recorded the big events: the massive exodus, the rise of homesteaders. I'd recorded my responses to the slow collapse around me, the gradual normalization of everything new, the emotional flatlining in the face of Munch-level loneliness, existential dread, and psychic displacement.

I'd then begun to record the weather.

The Space Needle, long since decommissioned, pointlessly hovered in the distance. Closer, gulls circled over the Fremont canal, their bodies sagging below habitual wings. From this view the city remained largely unchanged, pre-apocalyptic. If anything, more serene.

I opened my notebook and wrote, *Hot again.* I scanned the last few pages: all *Hot.* I found a *Hot with showers* three weeks back. The journal was a triumph. Still, I found comfort in the ritual, the being alone, pen in hand. The designated space of it. The view. There was some construction going on a few blocks away—an incongruous level of activity amid the largely pacific streets—and I made a commitment to visit the site as I'd made a commitment to visit it days ago when I'd first noticed it. As I'd made a commitment every day since.

I heard a knock at the front door, then Zane called through the house, having let himself in.

"Ma'am?" he said, always polite. "Mrs. Rose?"

"Hey, Zane," I called down the stairs, "just leave it on the couch, okay? The tomatoes are by the door."

I held my breath to better hear him padding around. He went as far as the dining room looking for my mother but turned back and paused at the couch, then again at the door, where he grunted softly while lifting the box. My mother had been trading vegetables for pot since the winter, when a crop of rutabagas had surprised us in early January. Before my brother moved, she'd kept her drug use more or less hidden for the sake of Olivia, her granddaughter. She'd since grown bolder.

Zane's head appeared at the bottom of the stairs.

"How's your mom?"

Covered with tattoos, his face was nonetheless an honest one, with big blue eyes he put to work mostly, from what I'd seen, in the service of kindness and concern.

"She's fine," I said. "She's a trooper."

"Good." He smiled. "How's the book coming?"

I shrugged. "I need a plot."

"My boss says plots are for gravestones."

"He does, does he? I'll keep that in mind."

"He says art is born of the individual's unique response to his own existence."

"This is some boss you have."

Zane nodded, kind and concerned.

When he left I returned to my desk and watched the construction for a while. Scaffolding had been erected around a house and men were all over it, doing work I couldn't quite make out. Presently a whistle blew and they descended below the green canopy. I stared at my mostly blank page.

Long before leaving, my wife Blake had been worried this might happen. To her, my blank pages signified more than the absence of writing; they signified my mood, my moping and irritability. They signified my level of contribution, finally, to the relationship. I'd come upstairs on several occasions to find her standing at my desk, flipping sadly through my journal, gathering evidence. I hadn't given her children—the least I could do was give her another book.

Of course, she was coming back within the month—at least, she'd said so a year ago. She was coming back to check in, to take me with her. She was coming back to sign divorce papers. Coming back to see what comes next. And when she did, I wanted to have something to show her. But nothing came.

My mother shuffled through the house, and I could hear her clear the coffee table. By the time I got down there she had the bag of weed at her feet and the cigarette machine before her. She was struggling to get a paper in position—a task increasingly difficult for her arthritic, gardener's hands. I sat beside her, marked her stubborn concentration.

"How are you feeling today, Mom?"

"I've been thinking about blood."

"Not because you saw any, I hope."

"Your father used to cut himself on the job. He'd come home at least once a month with some nasty gash, and I'd offer to dress it but he'd shrug me off and say, 'Don't worry about it, Rosie, I clot fast.' He had a high platelet count. He was so damn proud of his clotting. He smoked too much, he drank too much, but he always said he'd die of natural causes."

I put my hand into a pocket of airborne dust frozen by sunlight.

"Anyway, dear, how are *you*?"

"Mom."

She got the paper right, turned to me. "What?"

She always did this.

"Nothing. I think I'm going to go take a look at that construction down on…it must be 59th or 58th Street."

"I think that's a great idea. There are always plenty of ways to get involved in your community."

"Well, right. I just want to know what they're doing. It's hard to see what's happening from my room."

She laughed. "I'll let that observation go without comment."

She turned back to her machine, rolled the paper up to the gum line, and brought it to her face. She scrunched her mouth around to summon saliva, then licked.

When she reached down for more pot I noticed a folded piece of paper—a letter, it looked to me. I picked it up and opened it. The text was strangely askew. It looked like a fax, or the product of an ancient, hand-cranked mimeograph machine. Dry splotches of smeared ink interrupted and obscured some of the words, but it remained largely legible. It was addressed to "The Guild of St. Cooper" and bore the title "On Marbles."

I held the letter up. "What's this?"

"Zane must have dropped it."

My mother took a break to rub her crooked hands and asked whom the letter was from.

"It just says *The Editor*."

The radio crackled again, and we looked at it expectantly.

One day—no one could say exactly when—that radio would roar to life and announce the collapse of the Ross Ice Shelf, a collapse that would cause irreparable damage to the West Antarctic Ice

Sheet, trigger a tsunami across the Pacific Ocean, and temporarily raise sea levels as much as fifteen feet. The radio would then fall silent forever, having served its purpose, and Seattle would cease to exist.

I thought this coolly, having trained myself to summon the details without emotion, without fear. This, finally, was what we'd learned here in our city of the future. It was a being toward death not unlike resignation, though without the knight of faith's heroic slant. Without the transcending irony. It was, rather, the slow enervation of spirit faced by an immovable mover. Sisyphus sitting down.

I looked back at my small, sick mom. She brought another joint to her lips, stuck out her tongue. Everyone wants to die of natural causes, of course. Some are just more impatient than others.

DAY 2

MY YOUNGER BROTHER KENT was a survivor. Actually, he was a mortgage broker who'd taken survivalist training courses on weekends. But he thought the term "survivalist" had negative connotations—was essentially a slur used by those for whom competence and outdoor accountability betrayed emotional shortcomings. "You don't call yourself a writist, do you?" he'd say to me. He'd taken a course in hunting, dressing, and cooking game in inclement weather. He'd learned how to build shelters using materials natively available in three different climates. He'd learned first aid, CPR, basic firearm skills, and how to navigate by the stars. And he was right: we *had* thought he was a little high-strung.

But skepticism must finally confront its own limitations. The facts were plain: he'd made sure our mother's house wouldn't fall apart before its time; he'd stocked the basement with a Mormon supply of water and food; and he'd filled the out-of-use heating oil tank with diesel. By the time he'd taken his family and headed east, no one was smirking at his hobby. Of course, by then there hadn't been anyone left to smirk.

As I broke Fred's house's basement window I thought of what Kent had said to me before stepping up into the truck that would take his family over the Cascades.

"No one is watching, Blake."

I'd found this a strange way to put it, but I'd understood. And maybe stealing a TV wasn't what he'd meant by being resourceful, but I had to say I felt pretty good climbing into that house.

It was dim and still, underground cool, the room tidy though unfinished. A water heater was set against the stairway, and along the exterior walls were shrouded, rectangular forms with metallic legs visible beneath their canvas shawls. I chose one at random and removed the cover, letting it fall to the floor. It was a pinball machine: Star Wars. The one beside it was Addams Family. Unelectrified, the mute machines seemed to amplify the silence of the room, so when I noticed a ball at rest in the start position I reached out and pulled the plunger, letting it spring back into place and make some noise. The metal ball curved up and out of sight behind the tangle of casings and slides and caromed through a series of round obstacles with only dull clinks to mark its passage. It then slid into the central playfield and, after being licked by an inactive paddle, was swallowed by Uncle Fester.

To squeeze the universe into a ball, I thought, looking for the stairs, and to roll it toward some overwhelming question. To say: where in this vacant house lies the boob tube? Where is the TV?

I climbed the stairs.

The small, stuffy house smelled like cigars; most of the curtains were drawn, and the walls looked like the inside of a smoker's lung. The nearest wall was home to a series of slightly discolored rectangles no doubt once hidden behind photos. A glance around the room revealed several other discolorations. Tabletops too bore rings and squares of dust. Everything personal in the room had evaporated, and it made me feel uneasy, like I'd evaporate too if I stayed too long.

I quickly made my way through the house, looking first in an office, then in a guest room. In his kitchen at the back of the house I found the exploded remains of a government radio, shards of plastic littering the floor. Beside the mess was a broom propped against the wall. It seemed like a minor triumph for Fred: not having created the mess, but having left it. I finally found a small TV on the second floor, where it was perched on a dresser in the corner of the master bedroom.

"Oh," I said, "do not ask, what is it!"

I felt even more anxious the moment I touched the set's smudged flat glass, and as I went back downstairs I half-expected Fred to be around each corner, returning for something he forgot, or simply having changed his mind—he'd already changed it once. I pushed the TV slowly through the window and onto the clean-cut grass, exiting the same way I'd come instead of chancing the front door. Once out, I peered up and down the block and then scurried across the empty street like a thief.

Well, not *like*, of course. *As.*

I brought the TV to my writing room and set it down beside my near-blank notebook. Outside, a breeze shook the curled, blighted leaves on the apple tree behind the house and one high branch, taken over by tent caterpillars, drooped with their weight like a swollen fist. I examined my reflection in the TV's dark glass. It wouldn't have been difficult to find news if I'd really wanted it. There were still bars. Public spaces. A paper that still got delivered, though I'd heard its schedule was unpredictable. So why now? I considered this as I plugged the set in and turned it on. Why now.

The first channel was static. The set had no antenna, and for a moment I thought I might have to go back to Fred's to find one, but the third channel came in clear enough. Unsurprisingly, it was news. A heavily painted Chinese woman stood before an animated map of the world.

"Yesterday was the first day on record," she said, "on which no rain was reported to have fallen anywhere on earth."

The image of the globe turned slowly behind her. I turned the channel. Something about Fred's departure had rattled me, had made me feel more alone than the departure of my brother and his family, or even of my wife—though she'd promised to return. I'd clearly counted on Fred in some inchoate but significant way. Fred the sentinel. The angel. Perhaps it was exactly his emotional distance that made his influence real. He'd kept his distance, and I respected that, or envied it. Didn't I, too, try to keep my distance? It was a writer's prerogative. But if writing was the result of a successful gap, then judging by my output I'd failed miserably.

The next program consisted of two men staring straight ahead, having a discussion with one another. They were talking about traffic, or traffic jams, using some unfamiliar mathy vocab. The stairs creaked, and a moment later my mother appeared in the doorway.

"Solutions to the Payne-Whitham model," one of the men said, "are close to those of the Lighthill-Whitham-Richards model when Payne-Whitham is stable."

"Yes," the other screamed, "but traffic is generally observed in disequilibrium!"

After a few minutes of this we were finally shown footage of the traffic event in question, which involved a "phantom traffic jam" that had spontaneously un-jammed, all cars involved somehow spreading out and progressing at speed. It didn't require an understanding of the math to appreciate the beauty, all those hard-packed scraps of metal and glass separating as if repelled by magnetism, as if of a single mind.

The show cut back to the two men shaking their heads in astonishment. On one point both specialists seemed to agree. "I've never seen anything like it," said the calm one.

"Never!" said the other.

My mother left the room.

Flipping through a few more channels, it looked like the rainless day was the big story. The last big story I'd seen before trading our TV for a bicycle and a broken gun was about a lioness who'd escaped the zoo in San Diego, grabbed an infant right out of an unattended stroller, and run south. The beast had made it across the border by the time it was caught, but because of some political friction between Mexico and the U.S., the baby was given asylum and went up for adoption. The lioness, however, was returned to the zoo, where it was publically electrocuted in a televised event called "Cat Zap." The coverage leading up to this event had been exhaustive and unavoidable, and when I began to feel acute pangs of sympathy for the animal, Blake suggested we get rid of the TV.

All the same, I'd snuck out and stolen down to Bad Albert's for the actual electrocution. Men placing bets on various aspects of the process—odds on each second of current, odds on the success itself—crowded the bar, and in this room full of cheering, jeering spectators I'd broken down entirely, weeping as I watched the big cat's eyes roll up and her tongue fall from her mouth.

There was a knock at the door, and a familiar voice called through the house.

"Mrs. Rose?"

It was Zane.

I turned off the TV and went downstairs.

"Did I leave a letter here?" Zane's face was flushed and puffy. Over his shoulder, I could see his bike lying on its side in the walkway, front wheel still spinning.

"You came all the way out here to look for a letter?"

He lived in one of the abandoned buildings downtown—part of some collective I'd heard him talk about with my mother.

Zane ignored my question. "It was just a single page," he said. "No envelope." He held out his hands as if framing a scene. "About this big."

"Eight and a half by eleven?"

"Whatever."

"No," I said. "Haven't seen it."

Zane looked me hard in the face. He seemed skeptical, but it could have been a kind of broad, aimless skepticism he applied to anyone without facial tattoos. What reason would I have for lying?

"Is your mom around?"

"You didn't leave anything here, Zane," I said. "I would have seen it."

"What about—"

"My mother's not feeling well."

Zane turned around and looked across the street. "Fuck," he said. "Who's it from?"

"What?"

"The letter. Who's it from?"

"My boss." Zane's back was still to me, and I stared at his shirt: a T-shirt so filthy its fabric resembled the skin of an animal. The metal tops of disposable lighters had been clamped around the hem like scales.

"Your boss writes you letters?"

Zane didn't respond.

"Is this the same guy who said that bit about art being a reaction to the environment?"

"An individual's unique response to his own existence."

"Right."

"Yeah."

"Huh."

"Look." Zane turned back around. "If you see it, please don't throw it out, okay? I'll be back next week to trade." With that he leapt down the three porch steps and righted his bike. "Also, I didn't come all the way across town," he said defensively. The sun had reached its summit and was beating shadows back east where they began. Zane squinted. "I was just a few blocks away."

After he rode off I sat on the couch where I'd found the letter the night before. The page lay face up, crumbs of pot gathered in its two crisp folds, and I blew it clean before reading.

It was written in an odd, slightly archaic register, and described some children playing marbles, or rather, playing *with* marbles, just sending them careening into one another. It described how these children at first treated every marble equally until they noticed minute differences in the glass balls' behavior, in how they rolled or affected other objects. In how they felt. The children soon began ranking the marbles in an order based on their own observation. The letter then broke off abruptly and spoke of a walk the author had taken with a man named Dale Cooper—a name I was sure I'd heard before, though I couldn't remember where—through a small stand of trees owned by his company, Weyerhaeuser. It went on to describe the beauty of cherry burl.

The letter seemed to me almost didactic in intent, but with its sudden shifts the message was entirely unclear. It was as though I'd stumbled across the encoded transmission of a country at war.

The last letter I could remember handling—aside from the state's formal notice of evacuation—had been from a fan, a zealot who'd found some reflection of himself in a minor character and wrongly assumed my sympathy with some obscure xenophobic posture. I hadn't even finished it. It wasn't the first time a fan had disappointed me with wrongheaded presumptions about my spiritual, philosophical, or mental health. It wasn't the first time I'd wondered whether I was writing the wrong books.

My mother came in with a new bouquet. "Was that Zane?"

"He just stopped by to say hello." I scanned the letter again, stopping at the name Dale Cooper. "Dale Cooper," I said.

"What, dear?"

"Dale Cooper. Ring a bell?"

"Will you cut my hair? It's too hot for this hair."

I looked up to see her placing the flowers in the vase. In peak season, she'd sometimes change the bouquet two, three times a day, either too impatient for natural cycles or trying to squeeze more time from the little she had left. She slid the full vase to the center of the dining-room table, stood back.

"There," she said.

"It's beautiful, Mom."

"I'll get the scissors."

I went back to my letter as she got ready. It was without question more interesting now that Zane had gone out of his way to retrieve it, but I wasn't the target audience. Marbles? Burl?

My mother dragged a stool from the kitchen counter to the back porch. She'd removed her shirt for the haircut, and as she circled the stool, her one remaining breast lay flat against her ribcage as though unrolled, its nipple pointing to the earth. Her naked body no longer embarrassed me. In this familiar wilderness, bodies had become instruments for waiting.

Her hair was too fine, too silky for tangles, but the ritual of brushing it made her happy. She closed her eyes and the sun shone against her eyelids, turning them pink. She smelled like a garden. In the spring, she had taken me to a spot in the yard where her irises grew and instructed me to bury her there. "Iris," she'd said, "the divine messenger!" There were yellow ones and blue ones, even green ones. I couldn't help noticing how close the iris bed was to the vegetable garden, but I'd held my tongue. According to myth, Iris was also responsible for keeping the clouds stocked with water.

"Did you see it didn't rain at all yesterday, anywhere?"

My mother sat entranced, her head tilted upward slightly, her closed eyes smiling.

"On the news," I added.

"Anywhere in the world? That's silly."

I put the brush down and picked up the scissors. Nothing fancy, I was just going to take off length.

"Are you saying it's silly that it didn't rain," I asked, "or are you saying you don't believe the news?"

"I'm saying I knew bringing a TV into the house was a bad idea."

I took a full hand of her hair, and as I brought the scissors to it and began to cut, the full meaning of my mother's death filled me. It entered me as a knife might, suddenly making a space to leave empty. The truth was we were both preparing for it. That television upstairs was my first small, feeble act of preparation, and my mother—resigned but after all still human—knew it.

The lock of hair I cut lay almost weightless in my hand, and I held it out to the side, let it fall to the porch. The breeze had died down, but the silver strands swirled all the same, thinner than my skin. It was an unhappy yet unavoidable irony that here, at the end of the world and almost against my will, my mother and I had become closer than we'd ever been. And now she would die. She would die soon, not even last the summer maybe, and I would be alone in this house with my television, my journal filled with nothing.

I ran my hand across my mother's shoulder, up the back of her neck, and took another lock. I pulled back gently, and her head swayed gently back, her muscles loose, relaxed. The scissors shone terribly in the sun.

DAY 3

ALICE EDELSTEIN STOOD AT my window, the moon bathing one side of her in cool blue light and the flickering candle we'd lit splashing warmth across the other. She absently traced the still-visible outline of my fingers where I'd grabbed her nearly an hour ago. She wasn't mad, just contemplative, and I resisted the urge to reach up from the bed and pull her back down. I'd always had tender feelings for Alice, familial feelings, so I'd shocked myself a year ago when, the first time we made love, our coupling awoke a kind of violence I'd seldom experienced with Blake, or with anyone else for that matter. I'd wanted to dominate her, to consume her, and I'd been surprised by this, and also by her willingness to be dominated, her complicity and submission. Afterward we'd lain together silently for a long while, waiting for the other to acknowledge what had happened, to see if we'd been changed.

"You'll bruise," I said presently.

Alice nodded and opened the window to better hear my neighbor John Fairley playing his saw. The bent notes floated slowly through the black air, and I sat up against the wall to watch her without straining.

We'd since had sex almost everywhere. Empty houses, pitched roofs. Despite her ignorance of the reference, we'd even done it in the road. Since the only person I cared to hide the relationship from was my mother, none of this presented too much of a challenge, and happily the threat of punishment had all but vanished while the thrill of illicit behavior had been slower to disappear. Before Alice I'd never had an affair—a word that by now, while technically true, hardly seemed appropriate. And though it had begun soon after Blake had left the city, I'd never thought of it as revenge. I was plagued by a sense of growing old, but I didn't think it was a youthful frolic. Alice had been only sixteen when Seattle changed, which meant she hadn't really known anything else, at least not in an adult sense of knowing, of longing. My sense was that I needed to own that innocence, to possess it. To fuck it. To rejoice in it and to make it pay.

"Remember when I threw a water balloon at a window you were standing behind and the window shattered?"

Alice frowned. We weren't supposed to talk about the past.

"There were tiny shards of glass in your dress," I said. "You must have been, what, five? You were startled. It was maybe two full minutes before you began to cry."

Alice pointed to the north of Queen Anne. "There's a fire."

I couldn't tell if she was paying attention or not. She turned from the fire to the room, her head lowered as if in prayer. She prayed often, though about what and to whom she wouldn't explain. During these moments she was unreachable. Her small breasts rose and fell slowly.

"I don't even remember why I threw that balloon," I lied.

"Did you hear something?"

"Did I hear something? Well, I *said* something. Did you hear what I said?"

"Something outside. Something in the yard."

I joined Alice at the window. She wrapped her arms around me and I felt the stubble of her shorn pubis against my thigh.

Aside from Fairley's saw, the notes of which were now organizing into a familiar melody, I heard nothing.

"I don't hear anything," I said.

"Wait."

We stood for thirty seconds, sixty. I didn't hear anything but the saw, and was beginning to think she'd invented this noise to distract me from the past. I stroked her black, shoulder-length hair, then quickly grabbed a handful and, feeling playful, pulled. Alice let out a small shriek as I exposed her neck and went in to bite it, kiss it.

But as abruptly as I'd grabbed her I let her go, marched to the door.

"I will investigate!" I said.

I was aroused by the kiss, aroused by the baffling surge of dumb manliness, and as I prepared for the small adventure, my sex dove half swollen from between my legs.

Alice looked at me in surprise, then down at her own nakedness. "I'm staying here."

I quickly descended the stairs, slipped out the front door—my mother's room was beside the back door, and I didn't want to wake her. The night air was cool and dry and the moonlight gave depth to the garden, casting a shadow version beneath it, quiet and still. I crept down the driveway at the side of the house and into the back yard, where I looked up at my window. The candle had gone out and I couldn't see Alice, but I raised my fist into the air as a soldier might, I thought, or a rebel, and just as I did she lit another candle somewhere inside the room and the window came alive, a vibrant hovering screen. And it was as I stood there, naked in the back yard, listening to a now unmistakable and altogether eerie version of "Over the Rainbow" while looking up at my own room, waiting for a glimpse of my teenaged lover, that I suddenly remembered how I knew the name Dale Cooper.

Alice did not come to the window.

Singing Judy Garland under my breath, I waited a moment longer for her to appear before noticing the storage shed's door wagging slowly in the muggy night air. My mother had left it open. It was not a high-security scenario—no lock—but since in addition to my mother's garden tools this shed housed the fuel tank, we went ahead and kept it closed. As I drew near, the sharp smell of diesel replaced that of the damp, earthy coffee grounds my mother mixed into the soil and I heard a scrape, a tiny sound, gone almost before it had happened, and in the moment afterward I replayed it in my head to imagine its source, unsure I'd heard anything at all. I reached for the flashlight we kept just inside the door and stepped slowly into the room, far enough from the tank to be safe but in direct view of whatever might be going on—a cat? God forbid a raccoon. I pointed the flashlight and thumbed for its soft rubber button, but before I could switch it on the room flooded with light from a lantern I had to squint to see. A man was standing beside the fuel tank. He had two large blue plastic jugs with him, into one of which ran a red hose.

"I didn't want this to happen," Fred said.

I had an urge to cover my penis, but I felt doing so would be unmanly. "That's a funny way of putting it," I said.

He pinched the hose and removed it from one jug to put it in the other. The liquid hitting the bottom of the empty tank sounded like someone running a bath.

"What I mean is: I'll be out of here in five minutes. Ten gallons, five minutes."

I found that if I held the flashlight at my side, and angled it just so, I could reasonably cover my groin, or at least obscure it, without drawing attention to the fact. Of course, it probably looked like I had light shooting out of my crotch. "That doesn't sound like two ways of saying the same thing."

"Don't fuck with me, Blake. Just let me finish up and I'll leave quietly. You've got five hundred gallons here—you wouldn't have even noticed."

I sat on my mother's rolling gardening stool. I had no intention of intervening, but it seemed odd to leave him there alone. As the jug began to fill, the splashing sounded less like a bath and more like a piss, and perhaps it was because I'd just had sex that I crossed my legs, beginning to feel like I needed to piss, too.

"We would have just given you the gas."

Fred looked at me with big, dead eyes. "Well, I couldn't risk it. Because I would have had to take it anyway."

We let the full implication of this statement settle into the room and listened to the pitch of the splashes slowly rise with the level of the liquid. On the whole, I felt strangely at ease. There was a stagey quality to Fred's statement that I found comfort in, as though in its inflection lay some subtly crafted escape route, an inversion of the typical trope of evil lurking just beneath the surface. Here the threat was obvious, but wasn't there a hint of safety in Fred's return? Wasn't there a tacit agreement that while we might acknowledge the many paths of disaster, these paths would remain in the subjunctive? We were adults, after all. We were neighbors. I straightened my back and inhaled deeply, confidence regained. It was almost like I wasn't sitting here naked while he stole my mother's gas in the middle of the night.

I realized that the sawing had ceased. John had gone to bed.

"Did you ever watch *Twin Peaks*?" I asked.

"Twin what?"

"It was a TV show made by David Lynch in the '90s. You know David Lynch? It took place in a small logging town in the Cascades."

"Lynch, Lynch…Hey, wasn't he the guy who did *Dune*? I love that movie."

Dune, really? I bit my tongue. Still, our rapport had improved.

"'It is by will alone I set my mind in motion,'" said Fred. "'It is by the Juice of Sapho that thoughts acquire speed, the lips acquire stains, the stains become a warning. It is by will alone I set my mind in motion.'"

"Somehow I wouldn't have guessed you were into sci-fi."

"Into? I don't know about *into*. But I wouldn't deny an attraction to speculative stories. Isn't it a pretty basic human quality to ask, 'What if?' We've been dreaming up alien worlds since we dreamt up Heaven."

He glanced over at me, eyebrow raised. We'd never discussed religion, and I think he realized the potential sensitivity.

"Good point," I said.

He seemed relieved, but it could have just been me.

"Of course," he continued, "I don't believe in Heaven, and I don't believe in alien worlds. Aliens are just a potent metaphor for either the part of mankind we can't control or, if you're a pessimist, the part we should have been able to control if we'd acted sooner."

What side was I on? It seemed clear that Fred had recently migrated from the former to the latter. I thought of the broken radio in his kitchen. And the fact that he'd been turned back somehow, that he was here now rather than somewhere in Idaho, suggested he may have been right to do so.

"So, Fred, what happened out there? If you don't mind my asking."

Fred pulled the tube out of the second jug and coiled it, putting it in a plastic bag and putting the bag in his back pocket.

He screwed a top onto the jug and wiped his hands on a rag lying on top of the tank.

"Carjacked."

"Jesus. So, what, they just siphoned the gas?"

"The gas? Fuck no, they took the whole damn truck."

Fred was now lifting both jugs—five gallons each—and walking toward the door. His large body moved softly, steadily, and I stood to let him pass.

"What's the gas for, then?"

"Old Golf in storage north of here."

He walked up the driveway and I followed, and the moon shone down on us both. What would my mother have done had she been the one to find him? I felt certain nothing terrible would have happened—she'd be angry, and perhaps saddened—but I didn't want to think about it too much. When we reached the end of the driveway I held back, as though crossing the property line would be to cross another line entirely.

"Well," I said, "better luck this time."

Fred grunted and continued up the street.

"Oh, funny thing!" I called after him. "I actually took a TV from your house earlier today."

Fred stopped, turned around.

"That little one upstairs," I said.

"I know," he said.

"Isn't that weird? I guess we're both 'thieves.'" As I raised the air quotes, my penis caught a cool breeze and tingled, shrinking. "Wait—you know?"

He looked up at his house, then over at my mother's. *It is by will alone I set my mind in motion.* He turned and began walking again. "Stay out of my house," he growled.

I tried to picture Fred's big, bent frame crammed inside a Volkswagen Golf. *It is by the Juice of Saphoo that thoughts acquire speed, the lips acquire stains, the stains become a warning.* I pissed, watching Fred until he disappeared, then quickly skirted around to the front door and back upstairs, where Alice had fallen asleep. The candle had burned down and was barely more than a wax puddle on the plate. Its sleepy flicker cast soft, buttery shadows against my lover's back. I decided against waking her. I decided against telling her, for that matter, what I'd just seen. Fred's return would have to be a secret. As would his probably empty threat.

I lay awake with my secrets and watched the sky lighten with dawn. Years before the evacuation, the neighborhood had watched in horror as Fred took a handsaw to the two cherry trees in front of his house. What seemed to begin as a trim turned quickly into an apocalypse as even the biggest branches fell. He claimed there'd been some kind of blight, that the trees would be fine. Even my mother was skeptical. For the next three seasons the trees stood naked, their abbreviated limbs reaching vainly toward the street. He dressed them up as scarecrows one Halloween, and some sympathetic trespasser nailed a sign reading "Help Me" to one of them—a sign Fred left up for over a week as a challenge, an accusation. My mother finally asked Kent to go cut them down already, but my brother refused, a man's land being a man's land. In the fourth season, small but distinct new growth could be seen. Tiny branchlets poked through the rough stubs and began their journey into the open air. Within two years the trees again resembled trees and indeed looked healthier than they had before, their green leaves greener, their sour cherries darker red. I was standing on the front porch one evening with my brother when

Kent nodded across the street and smiled. "See," he'd said. "That's what happens when you leave a man alone."

Dawn was now fully arrived, and in the young light I began to shake. Before long I was sobbing. Quiet at first, tearless, my body shook slowly, softly, as though nudged. But I couldn't stop it, and the sobbing grew. My head pounded, red lines and flashes appeared behind my tightly closed eyes, and I could feel saliva dripping pathetically from my open mouth. My low cries sounded alien to me, inhuman, and I felt estranged, like an unwanted guest. The shaking escalated and with it the sobbing, and it must have woken Alice, because I felt her arm on my bare chest. I focused my attention on the spot where her skin met mine, the warmth there, trying to get it to spread, to radiate out, and as though from a distance I heard a helpless, teenaged voice ask me what was wrong.

DAY 4

THE RHODODENDRONS HAD WON. They coated the entire neighborhood in a glossy green sheen when they weren't in bloom, which of course was mostly, and the houses they once sat tamely before they now towered above or concealed behind a bank of mute, triumphant leaves. My mother had remarked that while they used to be the state's flower, Washington was now the flowers' state. She made light of it, but I knew she thought something was amiss. There had been cases, she'd explained, of certain species growing fifty, sixty feet, but they'd been isolated, and anyway it would have taken much longer for such plants to grow. How then were we all suddenly surrounded?

Heading down 9th Avenue, I passed house after house I had passing familiarity with, but my memories seemed to have been swallowed up during the general implosion. Where do memories go to die? Was it trauma that locked them away, or had disinterest kept them from forming in the first place? Walking by a house I'd been in countless times as a child, I couldn't summon the family name or even the name of the friend who'd brought me inside. I couldn't even picture his face. Perhaps in the vacuum caused by the sudden disappearance of dense civilian life, what remains shifts, reorganizes, compensates for the absence. Anemic infrastructure leading to a blunt, blank metastasis.

I had an urge to break in and look for a left-behind family photo, but my first clear memory, like a guard at the gate, was that they'd actually moved away long ago, the summer between fifth and sixth grade. I tried to picture them packing, their moving truck, anything, but could only see Fred's van, my brother's truck. What was wrong with me? The rhododendrons, I decided, were controlling my mind. Very sneaky.

"I'm on to you!" I called out. "Get out of my head!"

"Fuck you!" someone answered.

I looked toward the voice but saw no one.

Having been described throughout my childhood as a *transitional* neighborhood, Ballard had finally been on the way up when everyone left. Whereas prospective buyers had once been told, "It's a great investment" when what was really meant was, "You'd be brave to buy here," it had more recently attracted enough artists and young people to tip the scales, to become interesting, to attract those people who at once signaled the rebirth and the decline of urban neighborhoods: remodelers. Now big, empty, even unfinished remodels jutted up from the rhododendrons like surfacing, war-torn submarines. Walking by them now, I was reminded of how quickly, after the evacuation, I'd exhausted my interest in enumerating the ironies of late capitalism that had brought us to this point. In the wake of all manner of grave threats or cataclysms, the death of irony had been publicly trumpeted throughout my life. It only truly died when it had become redundant.

The construction turned out to be on 58th Street—I saw it from the corner and held back. The activity surrounding the place was in itself daunting. The days of commiserating over drinks at the local were long behind me, and I rarely left the house anymore but to buy a pack of Zig-Zags or trade tomatoes for canned corned beef. It had probably been six months since I'd spoken directly to someone I didn't already know, and I wasn't convinced I should start. Why create new ties in a place I should be leaving any day? It would send my mother the wrong message, for one.

Three small children, maybe two years old, sat in a triangle in the middle of the street. They were rolling an orange ball back and forth, and it bounced over their legs as often as not, sending one of them scurrying along to retrieve it. I had only recently become able to see children as children rather than as symbols of selfishness and irresponsibility—a success or a defeat, depending on one's perspective—and I watched them for a few minutes, watched them clumsily negotiate the subtleties of independence, until an older kid came up and kicked the ball over a fence. See, Mom?

After having slept most of the day before, my mother had confronted me about Fred.

"My bed is right above the yard," she'd said, "and my windows are always open."

"He didn't mean any harm," I'd responded.

"Well, it's like you said: he's apparently not the man of principle we thought he was."

"I was joking, Mom. That was a joke. Who wouldn't leave?"

"I'm just saying it doesn't make me feel too safe. He knows about the gas, he's now stolen some of it—what's to stop him from telling other people?"

I'd thought about this, especially after his response to the news that I'd taken his TV. But something about my mother's complaint struck me as insincere. She'd never been anxious about this before.

"What do you propose we do? Get a dog?"

"A community looks after itself."

"A community!" I said. "Why didn't I think of that? I'll pick one up next time I go to the market."

She'd said this, of course, without the slightest idea of what communities were available. And here one was, right next door, intact from what I could tell. Active. Cooperative. At least two generations, possibly three.

But what could it offer us?

The house under construction was shrouded in semi-transparent netting hung on the outside of the scaffold, and I could see the outlines of men and women standing along its two stories. The trees on either side had also been shrouded and were held away from the house with ropes staked to the ground in neighboring properties. Whatever was being done, immense care was being taken in doing it.

A whistle blew and people descended from the scaffolding like bugs from beneath skin. They gathered in the front yard and stood before a man, who read something from a book. Most of the group, maybe twenty in all, looked to be my age and were dressed in a way similar to Zane—dark, ragged clothing carefully deployed. I couldn't quite hear what was being read, but the orator's enunciation was broad, dramatic, filled with pauses and barks. It sounded like poetry. People sat in silence for a few moments once the man had finished and then took out bags and boxes and began to eat.

Knowing I wouldn't be disturbing anyone's work, I decided to approach, but before I could take a step I felt a tug at my pants. It was one of the children who'd been playing with the ball, and here he was, standing just behind me, looking up with a quizzical frown.

"Are you a homosessul?" he said.

Wild, near-white hair covered his head and waved about in slow motion. He hadn't yet lost his little teeth.

"I don't think so," I said. "But I'm glad you asked. What's your name?"

The kid made an airplane noise and ran past me to the group, sitting down beside a long, lanky woman gnawing on a turkey leg. The group took little notice of me as I neared, but seemed kind enough, some eyes just skittering across my face during a pause in conversation, others accompanied by a smile or a quick nod. I stood a few paces off, staring up at the house and waiting. I could now make out something of what was going on behind the scrim: they were painting. But it was not the usual house job. Rather than a uniform coat, the siding was covered with bright patches of color. I squinted to make it out and the dark fabric billowed, rippling in the breeze, obscuring my view.

"Take a look," someone said.

It was the lanky woman, her head cocked in the direction of the back yard.

"There's a ladder on the side," she went on. Her mouth shone with grease from the bird.

"He's not a homosessul," her son confirmed, nodding solemnly.

I frowned, feeling outed. "He asked…"

"Turns out his father's gay," the mother said. "So he's been asking around."

"What is this place, anyway?"

"Birth house," she said.

"Whose?"

"Dale Cooper."

The boy ran off to greet someone coming down the street on a bicycle, and we both watched as he tripped in the grass, fell down, picked himself up, licked his hand, and continued running.

"Scrappy little guy," I said.

"You have kids?"

I shook my head. "No. But I do have a mother."

The woman wore dreadlocks pulled back behind her head and gathered like a bird's nest at the nape of her neck. "Well," she said, "I guess that's a start." She began to pack away her lunch, and without looking up stated again that I was welcome to climb up and look at the house. "But we're going back to work in a few minutes, so be quick."

I thanked her and walked down what had once been the driveway. Empty paint cans of various brands, styles, and colors littered the ground, and I stepped in a small puddle of light purple before ascending the loud metal ladder. Behind the veil, even before the color, I noticed the smell. It was intensely toxic, and what little ventilation there was, was insufficient. The house had been painted like the side of a middle school: artists of wildly varying skill levels had drawn animals and trees and large, blotchy objects that were doubtless attempts at something recognizable. A small, flawless elephant cascaded across a blue field of broken chairs that upon closer examination I concluded were likely giraffes. I began to feel lightheaded. I kept walking, determined to make it once around the house before puking or passing out, and came across a likeness of Dale Cooper himself, just as I remembered him from *Twin Peaks*: the black, slicked-back hair, the '50s suit. He was holding out his hand, accepting a key from a Native American, an old man with a grim expression whose wide mouth turned down at the corners, his eyes nearly closed. If it was depicting a scene from the show, it wasn't one I remembered.

Having circled the house, I climbed down and stepped aside, taking several deep breaths while I watched people return to work. Did they simply get used to it? Perhaps they had killed so many brain cells already they didn't notice the difference caused by oxygen deprivation. I looked for the woman I'd spoken to, wanting to ask about the Indian, but spotted her son instead. He was throwing pebbles at a squirrel that ran along the fence in the back yard. The squirrel had a bit of carrot in its mouth and stopped to nibble it, looking down at the boy with what seemed like disappointment. Before I could ask after his mother, I noticed it: there in the middle of the back yard, planted in the ground like it had been there always, was Fred's sculpture.

Startled, it took me a moment to notice it had been put together incorrectly. The flames that had once shot out of its mouth had somehow found their way to the top of the animal's head, giving it an over-proud, foppish look. I walked around the sculpture, looking, I think, for signs of Fred, until the dreadlocked mother joined me and squinted up at the mythical beast.

"I see you've found the cock," she said.

I didn't understand what she meant.

"The cock," she said. "The cock."

"The cock," I repeated.

"It's a symbol of Cooper's dedication to protecting our natural environment."

"You know what's funny? The guy who had this before worked for a gas company." I tried to think what roosters had to do with environmentalism, but I could see I'd insulted the woman, and back-peddled. "Well," I said, "I think it looks like a rooster too."

The woman winced as though protecting herself from a sneeze. "What's wrong with you?" she asked. "Are you okay?"

I was sweating and felt a bit dizzy because of the fumes I'd inhaled, but I didn't think I was too far gone. What was she talking about? I became suddenly anxious. I stepped away from the sculpture. Perhaps it wasn't Fred's after all. Surely there was more than one of these things around. Fred could have made up his story. Fred could have lied. It was a mass-produced lawn ornament sold at Crate & Barrel. It was a mail-order sculpt-by-numbers kit. In any case, it was inappropriate, at the moment, to question the work's provenance, or even its taxonomy. I redirected.

"Do you know a guy named Zane?"

I drew a circle around my face to indicate his ink, and the woman watched as though following a doctor's finger. Hypnotized, who knew what she might reveal? Unfortunately, a car horn sounded before she could answer, and her large brown eyes grew wide.

"Tiger," she called, looking around for her son. "Tiger, come here this instant!"

The boy came bounding across the yard from a hole in the fence, clapping his hands arrhythmically, and together the two walked quickly up the driveway. There was a loud cheer at the front of the house, some whistling and applause. Though curious, I held back for a moment, helping to protect the environment. My encounter with community was not going quite as I'd planned, and these were clearly not my people. A yellow Frisbee soared overhead from one adjacent yard to another. It seemed to move impossibly slowly, I thought, like it should fall instead of fly.

We did some good work, the bird and I, but in the end I had to move on. It's an old story.

By the time I made it to the front yard, people were dispersing from the side of an idling white Lexus. Whoever they'd been cheering for was back in its belly, and the windows, tinted, were rolled up. I walked close enough to see my reflection in the glass and marveled at the clean car, all polish and shine. It picked up some of the color around it, greens and browns glowing in its side panels like a blush. Then the back window silently descended and a face appeared out of the darkness within. It was a woman—at least, it was a girl. I'd never seen a more beautiful face. It hovered a moment, letting me gaze at it. Its eyebrows were fine, almost black, and arched above equally dark eyes, big in their sockets, and glassy. Near-white skin surrounded these features and connected them to the bright red lips of a narrow mouth. I took a deep breath, as though to breathe it in, but it broke my trance by speaking.

"What's your name?" said the face.

"Blake Williams," I said.

Then, from inside the car, came a man's excited voice. "There, you see? I told you it was him!"

The girl nodded and smiled quickly before the window rolled up, and the car pulled away quietly and rolled down the block. By the time it had turned the corner, most folks had returned to work. A few young girls walked about the grounds, securing the scaffolding and piling empty paint cans. I looked for the woman I'd spoken with, but she and Tiger were nowhere in sight. I was about to stop a man with spikes sticking out of his cheeks but felt a hand on my shoulder and turned around. It was Zane. I was in no way surprised.

"Who was that in the car?" I asked.

"*That* was my boss, Russell Jonskin."

"Her name is Russell?"

"Oh, you must mean Aya. Anyway, Russell asked me to tell you he'd like to have dinner with you tomorrow night."

"With me? Why?"

"You wrote *Forecast*, right? *Forecast* is a book that interests Russell."

A feral cat remarkably like the one we'd lost skittered across the street, and Zane craned his neck to follow my gaze. A drug dealer who has strong opinions about art should have interested me, but I couldn't ignore the red flags in this particular case. There was this "birth house," for instance. The cat shot us a glance and then disappeared.

"You guys must be really into *Twin Peaks*," I said.

Zane frowned. "Can I tell him you've accepted?"

"Will Aya be there?"

"Are you fucking with me? This is kind of an honor, Blake." Zane looked off into the distance and sighed. "Yes, she'll probably be there."

"Why not," I said. "Always nice to meet a fan."

Zane walked off toward the painted house. "Great," he said over his shoulder. "They'll be at your place by five."

"Wait, *my* place?"

"Say hi to your mom for me!"

I went home.

The front door was wide open, which was unusual. Last year a raccoon family had moved into the closet in the front room, and after a frightening encounter as the season changed, we realized they must have been coming and going as they pleased through our perpetually gaping and unguarded doors. I leapt up the steps, closed the door behind me, and passed through to the back porch. I was eager to report our neighbors' working conditions, being as they were a reflection of general competence and wherewithal. What kind of protection could we get from a community who didn't even watch out for their own neurological health? Whatever my conclusions on those particular people happened to be, it wouldn't contradict her basic point, per se, but my plan, as usual, was to compensate for my lack of sure footing with quick steps. They're dangerous. They're irresponsible. They're weird. I hit the back porch already blathering, resolved to convince my mother out of forcing me out of the house.

But she wasn't there.

I squatted and squinted to see through the thickening trees, apples obscuring my view to the garden. I called out. I peeked into her bedroom window, then went around back to the shed, which I'd locked the day before. Nothing. I ran upstairs and called down the basement stairwell and waited, listening. I listened hard, trying to hear over my heartbeat. There was no note on the counter, her shopping bag was on its hook, and even her sandals lay upside down in their usual place.

I thought of a cat we'd had when I was a child. One night the cat—so old by then he had trouble walking—simply didn't come home, didn't come when called, and my father had explained over dinner that cats know when they're going to die, and find a place away from their homes to do it. He'd tried to persuade me that this was an honorable thing to do, and it was his honest expectation that I'd be cheered by this information. How could I remain focused on my own private feelings of loss when confronted by the great mystery of natural instinct? I suddenly felt like a fool for never having verified this information, tried to force the thought from my head, and failed. I sat down, stunned. Then there was a loud cough upstairs, and I went up to find my mother smoking a joint and watching TV.

I sat down beside her and took a hit. They were doing a story on a recently uncovered scandal involving the FBI, the black community, and textile manufacturers in Southeast Asia. Apparently, low-riding pants had been popularized by prison moles of a secret government research team whose charter was to prevent the ability to run—an opt-out social engineering mechanism to control minority populations.

"It was the crack of the new millennium," said an outraged Harvard law professor who'd helped uncover the conspiracy.

I exhaled smoke into the TV's gray-blue glow. "Zane's boss is coming for dinner tomorrow night," I said. "Hey, I just saw a cat that looked just like the one we lost. Think it could have had kittens?"

"No," she said. "His boss—you mean the guy who grows my grass?"

"I don't know if he grows it, but yeah, that guy, the man who wrote that letter Zane left the other day."

In the upper right-hand corner of the screen appeared a semi-transparent square that read: GLOBAL DRY DAYS: 4.

"What was that cat's name, anyway? I can't remember."

My mother reached for the joint, took the last hit, then stubbed it out.

"Didn't have one," she said.

DAY 5

RUSSELL JONSKIN AND AYA were about an hour late, and I'd apparently dozed off on the back porch. I woke to a large man staring down at me, his face a broad, sweaty grin composed by fat red lips. As I rubbed my eyes he stood back, spread his arms as though welcoming me to the world, and gave me a full view of his person: a stomach protruded solidly through his open button-down shirt to boast fine white hair, beneath which peeked pink and splotchy skin. He waved excitedly to someone inside the house and motioned for them to join him. Moments later the girl who'd spoken to me from the white car was standing at his side, smiling down at me too.

"I dreamed," I said, "that I was surfing. We were all surfing."

The man nodded vigorously and his smooth jowls shook. "See, Aya? I told you there was optimism in there somewhere." He held out his hand, and as I reached up to shake it he grabbed me and hoisted me to my feet.

"You must be Russell," I said.

"Jonskin, yes. Russell Jonskin. And this is my lover, Aya Karpinska."

Aya nodded almost imperceptibly but did not avoid my eyes. I tried to remember the last time I'd heard someone use the word "lover" without condescension. We all stood in silence for a moment, me still groggy and my guests apparently eager for my complete return to consciousness.

"Your mother let us in," Russell said.

"The salad is almost ready!" she called from inside the house.

"Shit," I said. "I'm the bad son."

"I highly doubt that." Russell motioned to the general area. "Here you are, after all."

I excused myself and went in to see what I could do to help. What a wonderful first impression: a son who snoozes on the porch while his mother prepares food for his guests. Glancing through the living room, I tried to see it as a stranger might—something I hadn't thought to do earlier—but couldn't get beyond the familiar. It did not, at least, look messy. The table was clear. The carpet was clean. The masks were in their places on the walls. Of course, in this environment, cleanliness cut both ways. Perhaps the level of tidiness was unnatural. Would they think we were keeping up appearances? Would they think we were in denial—or worse, anal? The truth was more approximately that we didn't *do* enough to clutter the space. The truth was that my mother and I lived fairly discrete, patterned lives, and perhaps that's all someone would see.

My mother had brought the big wooden bowl down from above the cupboards. It was now heaped with lettuce, dandelion greens, red onions, radishes, green beans, heirloom tomatoes, and fiddleheads, and beside it all sat the coup de grâce: a large package of soft sheep's milk cheese she got from a shepherd passing through the neighborhood the week before. We'd traded a wool blanket for it.

"Why didn't you wake me before letting them in?" I whispered, opening the cheese.

"Blake, dear, I didn't know you were asleep. I was in here putting this together when they knocked."

I noticed an unopened bottle of whiskey on the counter and picked it up. It was a Lagavulin 30.

"I hope you don't mind scotch," Russell said from the porch.

I looked up to see him standing at the door. It was a five-hundred-dollar bottle of scotch, and I tried to hide the fact that I knew this. Russell's chest was thrust forward and his frame took up most of the doorway, but beyond him I could just make out Aya standing at the corner of the deck, looking, it seemed, at the scarecrow I'd made from one end of a freestanding clothesline I'd found in a neighbor's yard. With the loose fabric and hat we'd used, we always thought it looked like a Sasquatch from the corner of the eye.

"I see you've met Earl," I called out to Aya, and then to Russell, "Want it open?"

"Posthaste, good sir. Posthaste."

I unwrapped the stiff soft metal seal and pulled the little cork from the bottle's neck. The sharp, peaty smell rose immediately, and I flared my nostrils to suck it in. It had been a long time, and though scotch had never been my spirit of preference, it was brown, and that's all that really mattered. I looked up and saw my mother watching me, eyebrow raised.

"Having a drink?" she asked.

"It's an occasion."

I took down three small tumblers from the cupboard and brought the bottle outside. Aya was still standing at the corner of the deck, though now she faced in, and a long branch from the apple tree hung a burst of leaves beside her face, a young apple in their center. She was every bit as beautiful as I remembered her—a frail, thin thing, narrow with long limbs. Her long black hair was pulled back from a high forehead, her overlarge eyes well-deep.

I poured three glasses of scotch and handed one to Russell, then walked one over to Aya, who took it with a small nod of her head.

"What should we drink to?" I asked.

Russell stepped forward. "To Seattle," he said.

"To Seattle," I repeated, raising my glass.

"May her dream live on."

I took a long pull from my glass, not taking a lot into my mouth but drawing it in slowly, savoring it, aerating the viscous liquid into an explosion of hot, deep flavors to both assault and sooth. Drinking scotch is being transported to a different world, something familiar yet magical, mysteries in the soil. I didn't remember closing my eyes, but when Russell spoke again I found I had to open them and that I'd missed the first part of his sentence.

"May what be a warning?" I asked.

"Your novel. *Forecast*. Electricity based on denial? Let's hope we're better than that in the end."

I shrugged. My mother brushed by me with the salad bowl.

"Will you get some plates, dear?"

I found the plates piled on the counter, forks and cloth napkins on top. I struggled to grab the stack with my free hand and had to put my drink down finally to pick them up, painfully aware of how aware I was of the glass. How long had it been? I took everything back outside, booze included.

"This looks positively decadent," said Russell.

"Oh, don't be silly," my mother said. "It's just a salad."

"Salad of the gods!" he cried out. "Salad of kings!"

We proceeded to eat amid great groans and inarticulate sounds of approval as the big man shoveled enormous forkfuls of greens into his mouth. He wasn't afraid to use his hands, either. Upon finding a perfect cherry tomato he plucked it from his plate and held it at eye level, pinching it gently, and slowly spun it with his ring finger.

"It's a jewel," he said. "Fuck the rubies."

In his hands the tomato looked even tinier than it was, and indeed I could almost picture it mounted on a silver band. Russell suddenly seemed to become aware that the entire table had stopped eating and was presently staring at his tomato. He quickly flicked it into his mouth and shrank back a bit in his chair.

"Okay, okay," he said quickly. "I can get carried away. But I'm a little nervous. Your son's book had a tremendous impact on me, you see. Aya knows. Didn't it, Aya? Aya never heard the end of it."

"All true," Aya said, and looked at me. She hadn't touched her scotch.

"I suppose you could say it inspired me," Russell said. "As a kind of warning sign."

I was beginning to feel the whiskey, and I felt no need to hide my pleasure at receiving his compliments.

"It's just fantasy," I said, nearly blushing.

Russell leaned across the table and refilled my glass. "Call it what you like, but its playfulness belies a dark, demented heart. And I like that. I mean, emotional transfer? Cars that run on denial? Okay, the metaphor is a little thin, but the message is devious."

My novel, written years before the evacuation, took place in a future Seattle far wilder than the Seattle we actually saw come to pass, and revolved around a technology that turned negative human emotion into usable energy. I raised my glass, deciding to ignore the thin metaphor comment.

Russell continued. "I mean, here you have Seattle—well, the world, really, is the implication—in ruins because we've run out of fossil fuels. Everything comes to a halt. Most things, anyway. We're just barely hanging on as a society. But then we have a second chance! The phoenix rises from the flames, powered by emotional energy! And yet, this emotional energy is actually a product of what? Denial. Lies. So what does that make the phoenix? A sham, at best. At worst, a complete illusion. It seems to me you're calling into question the very notion of rebirth—a belief that has been essential to our *Weltanschauung* since Jesus emerged from his tomb. Where would we be without rebirth? What would our culture have done without this idea that we could recreate ourselves if everything goes south?"

In the silence that followed, my mother stood up and began to gather the plates. "I agree that the book is incredibly pessimistic," she said.

My skin had become warm and dull from the scotch. I pinched myself and watched the red mark on my arm slowly vanish. "It was a love story," I said. "Love is always tragic."

My mother took an armful of dishes into the house, and Russell leaned back, his big, bare belly rising above the table like the back of a cresting whale.

"I once wrote a letter to a friend," Russell said, "and in it I made a joke about killing myself. The joke itself doesn't matter. What matters is that right after it left my pen, I wrote something about how I was joking. I went on writing, but came back to it. Something about the dismissal itself, I realized, made the joke look more like an authentic cry for help. So I began to erase the initial joke, until I realized that if my friend noticed the erasure, he would surely think I was trying to cover up an actual desire to end my life. The only alternative, then, was to throw away the letter and begin again. But as I took out another piece of paper I thought about how much effort I was going through to avoid telling a joke about suicide, and began to wonder, then, if there wasn't something true to the desire after all. Why even joke about it unless it was on my mind?"

"What did you do?" I asked.

Inside, a loud crackle from the radio shot through the house, followed by a low hum that lasted five or six seconds.

"That's not the point." Russell peered inside. It was dusk now, and the hazy light left the house in shadows. "What was that?"

"Well, I have a story too," I said. "I've got a story. I once saw a little girl crying, a little girl, and I laughed to myself because I considered it an expression of innocence. Whatever this child thought was important enough to cry over, I thought, was just, you know, wasn't really important. But then I wondered whether adults only think their problems are more complicated than childhood problems—maybe we mask them behind sophisticated language but it all amounts to nothing more than 'I want that and I can't have it.' Right? So, I thought, maybe it's the child whose sorrow is purer, whose pain is more in line with the universal constants of need and satisfaction."

Russell looked at me for a long time in silence. Slowly, a smile turned up the corners of his mouth, and he took a deep breath, as if he'd just made a tough decision.

"So what did you decide?" he asked.

I slammed my hand down on the table, too hard, and felt a shooting pain run up my forearm. "That either way I was a dick for laughing."

Another crackle, this time louder, and it deepened the following silence. Aya, who'd been close to mute all evening, stood and lifted the large wooden salad bowl. It was now that I realized I was quite drunk. My body hung from me like ripe fruit. I let my arms fall to my sides, let them swing.

"It sounded like an emergency radio," Aya said.

"Yep." I nodded my heavy head. "Yep, yep, yep."

"Wow," Russell said. "I haven't heard one of those in nearly a year."

"I envy you!" my mother called from the kitchen.

"Why envy me? Just get rid of it!"

I sat up. "Oh, no you don't, Mom. Russell, don't give her any ideas. We're not getting rid of our radio. We don't have neighbors close enough to hear theirs, especially now with Fred gone."

"Fred?"

I turned to see the two women navigating around each other in the kitchen. I heard soft laughter and was reminded of the months after my brother's family had left, when it was just me, my mother, and Blake.

"May I ask," Russell said in a low, conspiratorial tone, "if you're working on anything new?"

I shook my head. There was a routine to those days after Kent left that I mistook at the time for stagnation, for an ailment that could be cured by alcohol.

"I'm keeping a diary," I said. "I've been reduced to journaling."

Why hadn't Blake understood that I couldn't simply abandon my mother? It seemed unreal somehow. A hoax. No one could demand such a sacrifice from a spouse. From *anyone*. I glanced back at Russell to find him eyeing the journal I'd left on the porch beside the chair where they'd found me. It was splayed open, face down. It looked like I felt.

"What if I told you I could really use your help with a project that will change history?"

Laughter erupted from the kitchen.

"They seem to be getting along," I said.

"You seem surprised. Who wouldn't get along with your mother?"

Blake loved my mother dearly, and my mother loved her. But I remembered watching them say goodbye, how I'd interpreted my wife's tears as being for me. As though she couldn't show me her true feelings so they were expressed in the safety of my mother's arms. Even then I saw this as an indefensibly selfish interpretation, but I couldn't shake it. Now the memory made me feel dark and hateful.

We watched a crow glide ungracefully overhead, curve around the side of the apple tree, and land with a flap of its wings on Earl's shoulder. Clearly, we'd seen room for anthropomorphism where none existed. I took a deep breath and sat forward, trying to drive the drunk out of me by force.

"Tell me about this project," I said.

"I want you to write about how Dale Cooper helped save Seattle."

"So you want a story?"

"I want a history."

"A fictional history?"

Russell leaned back in his chair and smiled. He might not have admitted to being crazy, but he knew how others saw him. I could already tell he was one of those you-may-laugh-now-but-just-you-wait kind of egomaniacs. I didn't mind. I had a high tolerance for blowhards with good hooch.

"Do you know anything about Chief Sealth?" he asked. "Seattle's namesake?"

"Duwamish chief, mid-nineteenth century?"

I sipped my whiskey. "He was an environmentalist?" I figured I knew as much about him as the next Seattleite.

"Exactly! Exactly. '*How can you buy or sell the sky—the warmth of the land?*' We all learned it in grade school. But what they don't tell you is that his speech, the speech he gave alongside Doc Maynard that smoothed everything out between the natives and us newcomers, was only put in writing thirty years after the supposed fact by one Dr. Henry A. Smith. Notably, the record displays all the hallmarks of Smith's own reasoning, philosophy, and rhetorical flourishes. See what I'm getting at? Chief Sealth was no great environmentalist. Environmentalism was attributed to him as part of a growing romantic ideal regarding the attitudes and beliefs of tribes native to this area. And we learn it in school not because it's true but because we want to believe it. Because in our better moments, it's what *we* believe."

"So," I said, just drunk enough to get a bit belligerent, "you want a story."

"The city is sick, Blake. Look around you. She doesn't know where to go, what to do. Somewhere along the way she got lost, she became confused. It's difficult to imagine now, but one day we will need to rebuild, and in order to rebuild Seattle more perfectly, we will need a more perfect example of the model Seattleite."

"Which, of course! A character from a TV show."

"Just admit you're intrigued, and we can work out the details together."

DAY 6

I SET OFF AROUND midday on my bicycle, and within minutes I was farther from home than I'd been in months. I was headed for the corner of 6th and Spring, where I'd promised I'd give Russell my final answer—still somewhere between "No" and "You've got to be kidding"—and let him show me around his self-described "commune." I paused briefly in the middle of a street where my neighborhood bordered on the more industrial area below it. Three men were dragging taxidermy from a large dark house and stacking it onto a repurposed boat trailer. They brought out two mounted deer heads and a few small furry things I took to be either badgers or woodchucks, and then disappeared inside. A few moments later one of the picture windows shattered, and through it they slowly passed an enormous grandfather clock.

When it was first proposed that Seattle evacuate, the mayor—a man named Harry Wilder—protested he'd stay here until the day he died. He staged a photograph of himself chained to his front steps, his big smile undermining, I thought, the seriousness of his message. And he did stay, in fact. For six weeks he remained in his house on the top of Queen Anne, making a point of biking to an office downtown where his core group of devotees—mostly interns—holed up and tried desperately to maintain some degree of normalcy.

In the end, his wife came down with some vague medical condition that required more attention than the remaining volunteer clinics in town could provide, and with tears in his eyes he addressed the city, and the nation, saying that you could take the man out of Seattle, but he'd be back. He'd made the announcement from his office, and in the background one of those singing fish, on the fritz or running out of batteries, was stuck in a loop, turning toward the camera and singing "Take me to the river" over and over until Wilder angrily motioned for an aide to remove it. The event led to several "Harry's washed up"–type slogans among the diehards, but I'd never blamed him for lying.

Even after years of visible overgrowth and decay, the industrial area south of Ballard seemed significantly less unnatural than the residential blocks around it—there'd never been many people around here to begin with, so it just looked like a weekend. To my right a large, container-like building boasted a big, hand-painted sign that read "Now Hiring," and to my left the neighborhood's power relay station, still nominally in operation, hummed softly.

I took a left on Leary and headed toward the Fremont Bridge. I'd ridden this stretch of road innumerable times as a teenager, bopping back and forth between my house and Gas Works Park, where I'd stood by the half-maintained, cartoonish tubing to do drugs and protest various wars. And to write.

I'd write long, overwrought, underfed essays about power and meaning and war and language, and I'd type them up and pass them around to my friends, thinking I'd surely become the next Foucault.

Though I'd now long outgrown the notion that I had anything to say, I had to admit that Russell's offer had sparked in me nostalgia for that early work—for writing that actually *did* something. I had to admit I was "intrigued." Wasn't this what I was after with my journal-keeping, my would-be witness lit? Ahead of me, in the middle of the street, was an unrecognizable smoldering mound, and I gave it a wide berth. The work I wanted to do would matter to people in a way that fantasy could never approach, that was the antithesis of escape. That brought the reader *closer* to his predicament, to his life. Work that re-engineered the way he saw the world. But that's where the similarity stopped. Russell's interests clearly had no such purity of purpose. He was trying to manipulate, obfuscate, distract. He was trying to fictionalize the world.

As I grew close to Fremont, another bridge stood in the distance against the sky. The Aurora carried Route 99 high across the channel as it widened into Lake Union, and I'd heard bad things about it. Apparently, it had become a kind of gangland, a *Beyond Thunderdome*–like area of advanced illegality within a city of outlaws. I tried to make out the houses I'd heard had been built up there, but could see nothing.

By contrast, the Fremont Bridge, humbled by soft blue paint, appeared slowly, subtly from behind an office building to my right and seemed to welcome me aboard. A group of four men stood to one side of the near end of the drawbridge, but they were huddled together, intent on something happening below. I pedaled along the sidewalk to get a better view, and soon I could make out a man in some kind of face-off with a large dog. They circled each other, the man shouting, and what I thought was a machete caught the sun. But after stopping my bike, I saw that it wasn't metal after all, but a large silver fish. The man had it by the tail, and the dog had its head, and there was no clear advantage.

One of the men snickered, said something I couldn't understand, and I realized that they were Indians. Over a year ago, Muckleshoot had reclaimed the channel as part of the tribe's Usual

& Accustomed Area, and fished there for the now plentiful and still sacred salmon.

"Placing bets?" I asked.

One of the men looked me up and down and nudged one of the others—a tall, thin man in a black leather vest. The two of them took a step forward and folded their arms, the other two seeming to ignore our exchange.

"You want to cross this bridge, newcomer?"

"That was the plan," I said. "Have things changed since the last time I came through here?"

The first man looked down at my feet and whispered something to Leather Vest. There was a pause before I got a response, and I wondered if what I'd said had sounded sarcastic. Or if it had been, in fact.

"You been working up at that Cooper house?"

"The what? You mean that birth house thing? Well, no, I…" I looked down at my shoes and saw they still bore the purple paint I'd stepped in. "I mean, yes?"

Leather Vest scowled. I'd clearly chosen the wrong answer.

"You need to offer something in exchange for using this bridge. You need to trade." Without thinking, I glanced up at the Aurora Bridge, and Leather Vest snorted. "You don't want to use Aurora."

"Ballard's no better," offered the other.

There was a loud, abrupt shout, and I looked back at the tug-of-war to see the man sitting down and the dog trotting away from him, dragging the fish through the long grass. I had nothing to trade. I'd left my wallet at home, had nothing in my pockets, wasn't even wearing sunglasses. I briefly considered trading the bike, but it would take me all afternoon to walk downtown, and then what?

"That ring would do," said Leather Vest.

I held out my fingers and looked at my wedding band. Blake had been surprised when I'd agreed to wear a band, and I'd been surprised by her surprise. The truth was I liked the symbolic trappings of marriage more than I did the institution itself. I imagined her coming back to learn I'd traded my wedding ring to cross a bridge. I smiled and turned my bike around. My face began to sting with heat as I blushed, an anger rising inside me. I took a deep breath and then another as I rode away. The errand was not an essential one. I could easily pass my response along through Zane, or any of those gutter punks for that matter. I didn't have to visit Russell just to demure—all I'd miss out on were the details of his scheme, and his home. And seeing Aya. But being flatly refused access to something I'd learned to take for granted was embarrassing. I got to the end of the bridge and was about to head back the way I'd come when a voice called out for me.

"Nice bike," it said.

The voice had come from a deck four or five feet up that was once part of a dumb bar called the Thirsty Girl and there, in the shade of tree branches that hung over its battered wooden planks, sat a man I knew. His shirt was open and torn at the shoulders. His head was shaved. He poked it from the shade and grinned.

"Echo!" I said. "Christ, it's been forever."

"I don't go by that name anymore," he said, his smile vanishing. "I've grown out of it."

My bike's frame felt hot between my legs. "What do you go by these days?"

Years ago, Echo had been my dealer until he'd spiraled down into a paranoid crystal freak-out and begun to haunt University Avenue with a big blue book called *The Fifth Epochal Revelation*.

"They call me the Source."

"A logical evolution," I said. "I'm assuming the definite article is dropped where appropriate."

The Source grunted.

"So, what have you been doing?" I asked.

He walked out into the sun. Dark, leathery skin ran over his muscles like an oil spill. He had the wiry body of a man as active as he was underfed. He stretched and changed the subject. "Turned back by the Indians, eh?"

"How long has that been going on?"

"A month, maybe two. Who could blame them, though, right?"

I nodded, frowned. Indeed. Who was I to want to go downtown? "Notice that vest one of them wears?"

The Source gave me some wide eyes. It was his turn to nod. "Pretty nice," he said.

"Have you read *Class*, by Paul Fussell? He says you can only use six things made out of black leather without causing class damage to yourself. It's shoes, and belts, and...dog leashes, I think, and—"

"I knew a girl who wore a dog leash," he said. "Carroll was her name. Or Carrie. Probably Carrie. Anyway, she absolutely refused to fuck on the grass, or on any sort of ground. It had to be somewhere elevated, as a matter of principle."

The Source walked around to the stairs and came down to stand beside me. His face looked tired, but his eyes were bright and sharp. He rubbed his chin thoughtfully and looked off toward the canal.

"I wonder what ever happened to Casey."

"Carrie," I said.

"Who?"

"Carroll?"

The Source scoffed and gave me a joking punch in the shoulder. "What the fuck were you headed downtown for anyway?"

The Source was circling around me to look at my bicycle. He knelt down and examined the front tire.

"What would you do," I asked, "if you were given an opportunity to make a difference, but it was a difference you didn't believe in?"

The Source's knees popped as he stood up. He was probably six or seven years older than me, but he looked ancient. No one could say he hadn't pursued something in his life, or taken risks. Though I didn't envy his choices, I had a flash of respect for him just then as I recognized something like courage determining his course.

"I'll tell you, Blake," he said, "that as far as I can tell, this concept—hey, do you want a pull of something strong?"

He took a small flask out of his back pocket and handed it over, smiling. It would have been rude to refuse, so I had a drink. Infused vodka, but I couldn't place the flavor. I nodded my thanks and handed back the flask, which he returned to his pocket without a sip.

"This concept you have," he said, "called 'making a difference' is bullshit. Making a difference to who? To what? To Mars?" He pointed up in the general Marsish vicinity. "Is it something Mr. Mars up there in space is going to see and say, well, finally someone did that, now I can rest easy! Now Mrs. Mars will get off my back! I don't think so. Mr. Mars doesn't give a shit."

I wondered which Mrs. Mars he was talking about. The guilty woman of the forest? I felt strangely lightheaded. "So you're saying," I said, "that I should go with my beliefs."

"I'm saying that what you believe in is irrelevant, so live in the fucking moment!"

I turned to ask him whether that's how he'd describe his own lifestyle, and from the corner of my eye I saw raised arms and swift movement, and my head jerked sideways into bright white light and shooting pain.

The house next door to the one I grew up in had stood unoccupied on and off for much of my early childhood. In my memory the paint was always peeling, the roof always covered in moss, and the monkey puzzle tree with sharp branches hanging over the whole front yard was chronically sick, so that the ground beneath it, littered with knifelike fallen leaves, killed whatever tried to grow there. Brock and Brenda moved in when I was nine.

I'd later understand that they were alcoholics, but at the time I thought they were simply animated. Brenda would shout her Joan Jett songs from the back porch and Brock would see how long he could burn rubber without leaving the driveway, his beat-up Corvette disappearing into big clouds of bittersweet smoke. One morning as I was waiting at the curb for the school bus he called my name, and I turned to find him splayed out on his front steps. He was wearing pajamas and looked disheveled, but he was smiling and seemed honestly happy to see me. His blunt face was sweaty and his blue eyes bloodshot, and he said he'd stayed up all night working on a project.

"What kind of project?" I said.

He stuck out his tongue.

"Tuthit," he said.

"What?"

"Tuthmytum." He pulled his tongue back inside his mouth, swallowed, then said, "Touch my tongue."

I must have made a face, because he sighed and rolled onto his back.

"Forget it. It's probably too radical for you anyway."

"What is it?" I said, falling for his cheap maneuver.

"I ever show you my plants?"

I shook my head.

"Coca plants—my babies. Last night I chewed leaves."

I stared down at him, not knowing what to say. I could hear my bus braking down the block but I couldn't see it yet. I took a step back, tripped on a fallen branch and nearly fell. Brock sat up, as if waking up, as if remembering, suddenly, why he'd called me over, and thrust his tongue back out.

"Tuthmytum!"

I reached forward and swiped it with my finger.

"See? Smooth, right?"

I nodded. It was smooth and slimy, like raw, skinless chicken. I wiped my finger on my pants.

"All my tastebuds fell out," he said. "Isn't that fucked up?"

"I don't know."

"Say it. Say: man, that's fucked up, Brock."

I felt a little scared. "Man, that's fucked up," I said.

Mercifully, the school bus pulled up and I ran to it. As we pulled away, Brock yelled something drowned out in the roar of the big diesel engine, and a kid named Tim asked me who that was. I just shrugged. I knew right away I wouldn't be able to tell anyone about my exchange that morning, that although there'd been nothing truly wrong with it, it would not sound good. I shrugged, turned forward, and sank into the green plastic seat. It wasn't until much later—in Abnormal Psychology—that I'd learned to consider this an awakening of sorts, part of my education about the relationship between what can be done and what can be told.

I replayed this event throughout the afternoon, throughout the evening, as I drifted in and out of consciousness. I'd obviously been drugged, but one of the effects of the drug was that I didn't give a shit, so I lay there, splayed out. Perhaps, I thought, I was sympathizing with Brock. What would I do if someone passed by? Would I call them over? And say what?

Maybe the Source was right. Maybe it was all just storytelling.

I was in the shade of a birch tree, and its small leaves flickered in the breeze, letting dappled light animate the sidewalk and street until the sun disappeared behind Queen Anne Hill. I felt calm, empty, and though I knew I should try to get up, go home—my mother would be worried—I couldn't quite bring myself to move. I'd been given a free pass, it seemed. A ticket to remain motionless, to do nothing. To stay as long as I wanted. And in a way, I felt protected. I listened to the murmur of Indians along the channel and smelled the salt air.

DAY 7

"BLAKE, ARE YOU DEAD? Blake. Blake."

Zane stood over me, shining a flashlight in my face.

"Blake," he said.

I squinted up and closed my eyes. My head throbbed. Gravel dug into my shoulder. My left foot had fallen asleep. I embraced these sensations, found solace in the feeling. In the limbo between stasis and movement a seemingly timeless expanse had opened, which, I felt certain, would swallow me if I let it. It was a space I could remember having tried to expand between hitting snooze and my alarm going off again, a half-conscious predilection for the void.

"Jesus, dude, you had people worried."

I felt a hand on my elbow. Then Zane grabbed my arms and pulled me into a sitting position. I held the position, opened my eyes, and summoned my blankest look. The world is unbelievably cruel! The world stuns me with its heartlessness! I wanted sympathy, but Zane wasn't biting.

"Get up," he said. "Boss wants to see you."

"I should let my mother know I'm okay."

"Handled."

I looked around to confirm my bike was missing. "I've gotta find the Source."

"Don't we all," said Zane. "Come on."

He picked up his own bicycle and straddled it, then dropped his hand to point at the bunny pegs screwed into the rear axle.

"Are you serious?"

I looked over his shoulder at a fire by the water. Dark shapes passed back and forth before it, and I could smell hot grease, cooked meat. It was entirely possible that Echo was part of Zane's posse, that the whole thing had been staged—revenge for having used his pump without asking? A slap on the hand for some unintentional slight? Or perhaps, like Fred, I'd simply committed the sin of possessing something they wanted. I looked into Zane's face for some sign of collusion, but could see only the kid's big, bright eyes and innocent ink.

There was nothing preventing me from just lying back down, or getting up but walking in the other direction, back to Ballard, where my mother would be waiting up, stoned, eating snap peas and watching the news. I scrubbed my face roughly to wake myself, and only then did I notice my ring was gone.

"God damn it!"

I felt around in the darkness, grabbing at the surrounding sidewalk, gravel, grass, but I knew it had been stolen. The world *was* unbelievably cruel! It had taken me weeks to decide between platinum, silver, and gold, to select a diameter and finish, to choose whether the surface would be rounded or flat. It had taken me longer to land on a wedding band than it had for Blake to pick out her dress, and I'd had to defend my indecision against charges that it was a symptom of cold feet, of a reluctance to wear a ring at all. My brother had sat me down and poured me a shot. My mother had given me sad eyes. Blake had required reassurance. But it hadn't been anything like that—it was a matter of my deep faith in symbols.

I stood and, feeling lightheaded, leaned against the tree for support. I brushed my fingers over the egg behind my right ear. It wasn't bleeding but it was tender and big enough to scare me. I stifled a sob.

"You coming?"

My blank face returned, unbidden, but this time I turned it away from Zane. What use is an expression that nobody sees? I shuffled toward him, climbed onto the pegs, and grabbed his shoulders. The shock of having been hurt, having been robbed, the symbol of commitment snatched from my finger, had settled into a self-destructive resignation: not only did I want to take the easier path, but the wrong path presented itself as easier *exactly because it was wrong*.

Zane kicked the bike into motion, and moments later we were turning the corner back toward the bridge. The crew there had changed, but three new men watched us approach, their expressions in plain view, their feelings hidden. As we passed, Zane slowed to say something, to say they should get a good look at my face, that I should be allowed to cross the bridge whenever I wanted.

"If the Editor gets word of you stopping him again," he said, "he's not going to be happy."

I gripped Zane's shoulders more tightly as we turned down Westlake on the south side of the bridge, comforted by a kid I'd only ever condescended to, and we rode the rest of the way in silence.

I hadn't been downtown after dark in over a year. The moon was nearly full but the tall buildings to either side meant we remained mostly in shadow. We rode along beside the decrepit monorail tracks. It felt like entering a stranger's closet and shutting the door behind you while the home's owner wandered through the house. At any moment they'd stand before the door. At any moment we'd be caught.

We passed Pine and Pike, Union and University, and had just crossed Seneca when I remembered what building sat at 5th and Spring. Sure enough, we pulled into the intersection and saw it jutting up out of the street like a shard of glass.

"You're kidding me," I said. "He lives in the library?"

"We all do."

The downtown Seattle Public Library could have been erected by a Saudi prince to remind him of a trip to Alaska. Its irregular glass and lattice frame zagged out of the pavement like a colossal glacier, and consensus was that, in operation, it had been good for everything but finding books. Zane steered us up a ramp and we passed two men smoking by the door to ride right into the building itself. We left the bike outside and passed through one of the library's cavernous atria by the bookshop and a reading room, and at first, in the dim light cast by hidden bulbs, it didn't seem all that different from the last time I'd seen it. The shelves seemed to be in order, though mostly bookless, and the reading desks stood silent and waiting. But as we trudged up the bright yellow, motionless escalator and walked through what had once been the computer room, the changes became more apparent. There were tents. All the desks and tables had been stacked along one wall, and in the clearing an entire village of tents had been assembled. Everyone seemed to be asleep, but even so the hushed space clicked and rustled with bodies turning and teeth grinding, and as we made for another escalator I took pains to avoid the arms and legs strewn in the path like the aftermath of some nerdy all-night number crunch. We climbed another escalator, and then another, and at the top found ourselves in another atrium. It too had been a reading area, and comprised the northwest corner of the building. The north wall itself was a large, jutting chamber that stretched out into the air above Spring Street like an ice cube jumping from a tumbler.

Zane led me south into an area empty except for a bed, a freestanding bookshelf, and two young boys feeding marshmallows to a small armadillo. He told me Russell would be in to see me soon and as he left I caught his wrist. His skin was cold, slightly damp, and I realized what an effort it had been to bike me all the way here. He stopped and looked at my hand on his arm, then up at me with raised eyebrows. "You need anything? Water? Coffee? Coke?"

"I just wanted to thank you for finding me," I said, letting go.

After he left I went to have a look at what the kids were up to. The armadillo, it must be said, seemed rather unenthusiastic, though it didn't refuse the small white snacks. One of the children, a boy with long blond hair, asked me if I wanted to feed it. He held up a marshmallow, dirty and wet from living inside his fist. I smiled and said I'd rather not.

"I'm allergic to armadillos," I said.

The animal had begun to walk slowly away from them, and the other boy—black and nearly bald—pulled it back by the tail and blocked its passage with his skinny legs.

"How many marshmallows have you fed that thing?" I asked.

The black kid reached out and started to pet it. "Nine-banded armadillos are the only other animal besides humans that can get leprosy."

"I see," I said. "Are you saying it's a leper?"

He looked up at me like I was crazy.

The blond one held out another marshmallow. "Roscoe's three-banded," he said.

I walked to the bed, then stood against the glass wall and cupped my hands to see outside. I could see the moon in the sky, a couple lights either out on the water or on Bainbridge Island beyond, but not much else. It seemed even darker than it had on the way here, and I was growing more exhausted by the second.

"They say the darkest hour," sang a voice behind me, "is right before the dawn."

"*Buckets of Rain,*" I said, and turned around.

Russell stood in the doorway, flanked by the boys and wearing what I realized must be his standard attire: a white cotton button-down shirt, unbuttoned, and white drawstring cotton pants. He was barefoot. He patted the kids' heads and nudged them out of the room. The armadillo had ambled over to the bookcase, where a low shelf padded with bright clothes apparently served as its home. Russell took a seat on the bed.

"Have you ever had a religious experience, Blake?"

"That depends," I said, gently touching the egg on my head. "Is God angry with me?"

Russell chuckled. "You're referring to your encounter this afternoon, I suppose. Zane said he found you in quite a state. I was terribly sorry to hear about it. Can I get you anything? Water? Aspirin?"

I shook my head. "I gotta say, you found yourself a great place to squat."

"Squat, did you say?"

"Good one."

Russell picked something off the bedspread and flicked it to the floor. "When the order came, I was going to leave the city like everyone else. I'd packed, I'd set up a place to live—I was going to stay with my brother in Boston—everything. Before I left, I decided to take a walk through the city, a sort of farewell stroll. It was a beautiful day, luminous cumulus clouds hanging in the air like ripe white fruit. I walked through Pike Place and then down and south along the waterfront, and as I was walking back through downtown I felt a drop on my arm, and then another. I assumed I'd passed under an air conditioner or some such, but the droplets increased, and soon enough it was raining lightly, and then more heavily, and moments later it was a downpour. I ducked into a doorway and looked out at the street, and I immediately saw the strangest thing: people across the street seemed to be moving along without so much as a flinch at the rain. No newspapers overhead, no open umbrellas, and as my eyes adjusted I realized that they were not, in fact, being rained on. I looked out and up and saw that indeed it was only raining on my side of the street. But not only was it contained to my side, it was only raining in the middle of the block, just over where I happened to be."

His rhythmic tone seemed to have a sedative effect on me, and I found it more and more difficult to keep my eyes open. Russell, who'd been staring into the distance and playing with his chest hair while speaking, looked up and smiled. "Are you with me?"

"Raining in the middle of the block," I said.

"Precisely. Well, I jumped back onto the sidewalk and hurried along the street—this was on Madison, between 3rd and 4th Avenues, and I was heading east, uphill. But I couldn't seem to escape the rain! I was confused. I turned around and saw that it was no longer raining before the door I'd used for cover. I saw that in fact it was raining *directly over my head and nowhere else*."

"Like in the cartoons."

"Exactly like in the cartoons. Of course, at first I misread the sign—something that doubtless happens all the time. I was thinking, you know, raincloud equals bad. Doom, despair, depression. Received ideas, in other words. I kept walking, feeling like the city was washing its hands of me. Water cascaded over my face and soaked my clothing. But as I paid more attention, my feelings began to change. It was a warm rain, I noticed. It was a soft rain, despite its intensity. And perhaps because I was becoming resigned to it, no longer fighting it, I began to actually feel refreshed. In the heat of the day, it felt nice. People were beginning to stare, and I waved, or shrugged, and the more people stared, the better I felt, and I was walking by this very building, walking north along 4th Avenue, when suddenly I felt the rain slow down and then stop. And when it stopped, instead of feeling relief, I felt sad. Had I been abandoned? But I looked up and saw that it hadn't stopped after all. It had instead veered off the sidewalk, toward the entrance of the library, where it was waiting for me. Waiting for me! I crossed over and entered the revolving doors and stood there, dripping wet. The staff was packing up books and no one paid me any attention, but I came inside and I looked around and I knew it would be my new home."

By the time he stopped speaking it had grown measurably lighter in the room. I looked through the wall of windows and realized that I could now see outside—the interior reflection had melted back into the glass. Dawn was approaching. I felt incredibly tired. My legs seemed unsteady and I must have been weaving a bit, because Russell patted the bed, motioning for me to join him.

"Russell," I began, and my tone must have signaled my reservations, because he held up his hand. I was just tired enough to obey, and walked over and took a seat. Russell put a hand on my shoulder.

"I know you've come here to demure, but I encourage you to look at the bigger picture."

Footsteps made us both look up to see Aya enter the room.

She yawned, rubbed her eyes. "Giving him your spiel?"

Russell stood. "We made some progress. Sadly, the poor man is too tired for the discussion."

"I'm sorry," I said, "I don't mean to be rude, but—"

"Nonsense! You've had a long day, Blake. A long two days! I should have had you taken home straightaway. Aya, will you locate Zane?"

Aya stretched, her shirtsleeves falling back to reveal pure white arms like lines of cocaine.

"I'll take him," she said.

Behind the wheel Aya looked even smaller, more delicate than she normally did. She wore a gauzy, pale yellow dress that deepened the black of her hair, and she smelled yellow too: a tart citrus so fresh it seemed to bring the temperature down a couple of degrees. We drove north on Westlake, Lake Union off to the right, lower than it used to be and filled with the carnage of unclaimed boats.

"He's not crazy, you know," said Aya after a while.

"Russell? Of course not."

"He likes you."

"Well, I like him. I mean, we don't…What do you think he wants from me?"

"He didn't even get *that* far? Christ. He always spends too much time on the preamble. You've got to create tension by

showing what's at stake right away, and then you can move into
the backstory. We're working on his narrative technique."

I glanced over to see how serious she was being.

"I know what he says he wants," I said, "but surely he's fully
capable of—"

"Russell is a lonely man. More than anything, I think he wants
companionship."

We were nearing the Fremont Bridge, and I could already
smell the brackish water. As we grew close I saw that Leather Vest
was back on duty. To my surprise, Aya gave him a polite wave, and
he waved too, grinning like a fool.

"You know that guy?"

"Sure. That's Brian Leathervest."

"You're kidding me."

"Why would I be kidding?"

"Well, yeah."

"He can protect you and your mother, you know."

"Brian?"

"Russell."

"What makes you think we need protection?"

"I just mean no one will bother you if they know you're
working with the Editor."

We turned up 8th Avenue, passed the now silent transfer
station, and climbed our way back into the overgrown residential
abyss.

"Were you and Russell together before the evacuation?"

Aya braked to let two cats cross the street and checked her
rearview mirror after we'd passed them. It brought to mind my
mother's response to sudden stops: an arm springing out to the
side, as though she could catch what my seatbelt could not.

"We've been together for as long as I remember," Aya said.

She pulled up in front of my mother's house. It was now squarely morning. I could hear birds above the hum of the engine.

"We're not actually lovers," she said. "That's a story he tells his guild so they don't think I'm available. Russell is my father."

I scrutinized her face. She was smiling, but I'd seen her smile. This was smaller, almost shy, her chin downturned just the slightest bit. This was mischievous. What could I believe of what she said? She and Russell had fairly resuscitated the cranky spirit of the city around me as though waking the grumbling core of a dormant volcano, and although they seemed to have been candid with me, they were in the business of lies.

Suddenly Aya jabbed her jaw across the front seat and gave me a kiss on the cheek.

"Get some sleep," she said. "See you soon, I hope."

DAY 8

THAT NIGHT I WOKE to find my mother watching TV in my room with the sound almost off. The room flickered with blue and green light, and it played across her face, her eyes glassy and her mouth slightly open as if about to speak. She looked like one of her masks, and for a grotesque moment I imagined her staring down at me from the wall. I dragged myself over and sat with her, staring into the cold fire, trying to catch up with the story. It was about a drowning incident in the Gulf of Mexico. A mass drowning. My mother explained that people in several cities along the Gulf, including Tampa, Mobile, New Orleans, Galveston, and Corpus Christi, had walked out of work, home, school, church, and marched straight to the shore and into the water, drowning themselves.

"News is coming in that it happened in Mexico too," she said.

"Sounds like a death cult."

"If so, they kept their association a complete secret. No one's found any connection."

"Well, the worst way to commit suicide is to tell other people you're going to do it. Have they found a note?"

"A group note?"

"Any note."

"Note that I know of."

In the cool light of the TV, my mother's profile snaked along the dark wall. Her short white hair stuck up like a dandelion gone to seed. "Did you just make a pun?"

My mother reached for the power button. "Do you want me to leave this on?"

The radio was active that day, the continual crackling and sputtering joined by a strange, ghostlike moaning. Twice my mother put a pillow over the speaker and twice I took it off. We'd be able to hear a real announcement through goose down, but it was the principle of the matter, the slippery slope of it. Also, I was irritated with myself, with what I took as a sign of personal weakness, so I was misdirecting. Specifically, I was sitting on the couch, worrying Zane's letter and wondering why I was suddenly wavering about Russell's request. It sounded like an adventure, after all. What did that say about me? What kind of circumstances would lead to an author sabotaging his own integrity—let alone broad social ethics—unless he was getting paid! And what would happen to him if he did? What kind of twisted beast would result? The moaning had reached a crescendo when my mother came in from the back porch, put a single white calla lily in a tall, thin vase, and then walked over and pulled the plug.

"Really, mother?"

"Five minutes, Blake. Just give me five minutes."

"It's five minutes now, sure, but soon it'll be ten, fifteen, an hour. You'll be saying, 'Blake, come on, let's just turn it off for one night.' Then, you know, whoosh!"

Her shoulders sagged. She turned the lily slowly, looking for the right display, and its single undulating lip seemed to wobble like a coin, hiding and then revealing a bright gold spadix.

"Russell unplugged his," she said, "and he seems to be fine."

"Well, Russell also gets followed around by small, highly opinionated rainclouds."

My mother looked up and frowned. "Are you making fun of me?"

I shook my head and was about to explain when the gurgle of a Harley coming down the street turned us toward the window. Moments later a biker passed the house, riding slowly and holding an open book in one hand. He quickly reached over with the other hand and turned the page. He was reading a book while riding a motorcycle. I took this as a sign.

"What if, instead of working *on* Russell's project, I document it? What if I kind of embed myself like a journalist? Watch Russell and his guild from the inside—see how they operate, do interviews, do portraits, unearth scandals. Don't you think it would make for an interesting portrait of post-evac Seattle?"

My mother squinted, pursed her lips, and caressed her white flower. "The calla lily grows as a weed throughout most of the world. Can you imagine turning a corner and, pow! An entire field of them?"

I got up and stood by her at the table. The radio's cord was coiled on the floor like a whip. I was going to use it if she didn't, and she knew it, but I gave her one more chance. "I'll tell you what. Plug that radio back in, and I'll talk to Russell about how quickly we could be alerted when the Ross collapses. I'm sure he can have a lackey warn us, someone who lives nearby. Deal?"

She nodded slowly and reached for the cord. "I just think it's astonishing."

The moaning resumed. We listened to it for a few moments, the clicking making us cringe.

"What's astonishing?"

She nodded at the lily. "Cut one, put it in a vase, and presto: weed no more."

"Well, context."

"Blake?"

"What?"

"Where's your wedding band?"

I thumbed my ring finger and met my mother's eyes. I hadn't told her what had happened because I didn't want to scare her. Instead, I'd told her I'd left the bike downtown because it hadn't fit in the car. I'd told her I'd spent the afternoon sitting by the canal and the evening biking around Seattle. I'd told her I'd had a "lovely day."

"I'm having complicated feelings about Blake," I said. "I think I need some clarity I can't get wearing that ring."

My mother stared at me.

"Okay," I said, "that sounded weird. What I mean is…I don't know what I mean."

She grabbed my hand and held it. Her soft eyes looked into mine. "I think your idea about working with Russell is a good one," she said. "I think you need to be working."

"You do?"

"Blake won't be back for another, what, two weeks? Three weeks? I know you, and you're miserable when you're not working. Forget about the ring for now and see what's going on with Russell. I think he'd be thrilled to know you want to write about him. Thrilled!"

Her enthusiasm warmed me a little. I envisioned following Russell around, pen in hand, fashioning a narrative, the center of which was one man but which told the story of Seattle as a whole.

Of more than Seattle—of a humanitarian crisis. The radio let out a louder-than-usual screech, startling us both.

"I'm going to Alice's," I said.

My mother frowned and headed for the back door. "I hope you're just going to make sure she has her radio plugged in." She went down the stairs to the yard.

The back of my head was still sore, though the swelling had gone down, and because grand ambition has constantly to contend with the minor distractions of a private cause, I began to wonder whether Russell might be able to help me recover my ring. The question was, if I had only a finite amount of unspent capital with the man, how should I spend his interest, his willingness to help? I reached out to stroke the lily as my mother had but stopped short, not wanting to damage it. The delicate flower stared up at me, its mouth open wide, its yellow tongue sticking out.

Alice had adopted a house near Green Lake—a beautiful abandoned Craftsman on the north side—but would often come over the hill to stay where she'd been raised, a cottage that sat on a small rise held intact by a cracked and bulging retainer wall. As a child, even before I knew who lived there, I used to stand on the lawn and repeatedly jump on that wall, trying to break its back. It hadn't made sense to me that something seemingly so close to failing would resist my encouragement.

"Alice!" I called, standing on the porch.

"Blake? I'm in the kitchen."

The living room was empty except for an Eames lounger she'd found two blocks away and asked me to move. In the kitchen, Alice was naked except for sunglasses. She stood at the sink washing carrots. The water sputtered a bit—the pressure had been irregular for months now—and she looked upset. I sat in the Eames as she stacked the clean orange roots in a dish drainer.

"How *are* you?" she asked.

I considered the possibility that she'd heard about my encounter with Echo, but then realized she'd been there the night Fred had returned. It seemed like a long time ago.

"I'm fine," I said. "Fred got what he came for, you know? I'm not worried about it."

"Huh. You seemed worried about it the other morning."

"Well, the event was metonymic."

"Fuck off."

Alice poured a glass of water, then walked out the back door, sat in a beach chair facing away from the house, and lit a cigarette. Alice had the kind of native confidence I envied, but it could present at strange times, emphasizing her youth and making her a little hard to take seriously. I stood in the doorway, looking down at her from behind. Her lithe body looked like a fallen sapling, the smoke from her Old Gold the first hint of fire.

"Do you know the guy they call the Editor?"

Alice brushed a bug off her nipple. "Drug dealer," she said.

"Well, yes. Do you know anything else about him?"

"Big dick."

She could have been serious, for all I knew. She took what she wanted. A crow lighted on the tall white fence with a quick snap of its wings and looked down at us, cawed.

"I wouldn't go that far," I said. "He's just brusque, is all."

Alice blew a stream of smoke. "Did you know crows have neighborhoods like humans? They have districts and leaders in each district and get together for, like, monthly powwows where they bring something from each district to share with the group.

Like, one from Chinatown brings a wonton, and one from, I don't know, the University District brings a nug of weed."

A car drove down a street north of us, then a door slammed, scaring the crow. "You've really fucked Russell?"

"Who's Russell?"

The crow cawed again, the sound of a strangled dog, and flew off.

"Go forth, young crow," said Alice, "and bring tidings to your flock!"

"What do you think the Ballard crow would bring to the powwow?"

Alice was silent for a moment. The skin of her stomach was beading up with sweat, and her tiny blond hairs glistened in the sun. "Boredom?"

"What's gotten into you?"

"Who was that bitch who dropped you off yesterday morning?"

"Bitch? What are you talking about? That's Russell's d— Russell's partner. Russell is the Editor. She dropped me off after a meeting I had with him."

Alice sat up and turned toward me. "Dropped you off? Aren't you forgetting something?"

"I'm probably forgetting innumerable things at any given moment," I said. "Can you cut the rhetoric?"

"Dropped you off *and kissed you.* You left out the kiss, asshole."

"Oh! Yeah, that. It's nothing, Alice, seriously. She's from New York, she kisses. It's just standard over there."

"Huh. Well, last time I checked, we weren't in New York."

A child! I was fucking a child! I was embarrassed for her, but I was also simply embarrassed. Alice turned back around and lit another cigarette, and I rushed to her from behind, smacked the cigarette from her hand, and pulled the back of the lawn chair so it kissed the grass below it.

"Last time I checked," I said, "you had no right to be jealous."

Alice looked into my face with complete acquiescence, her naked body limp. I leaned forward and gave her a quick, sibling peck on the forehead and then lay down on the grass beside her chair. The cigarette had landed a few feet away, and its ribboned smoke made the cloudless sky appear even emptier. We lay like this until the cigarette had burned itself out. I felt dumb for having come—the sex I'd expected was suddenly the last thing I wanted, and now there was awkwardness between us, the same tension that grew whenever I outstayed my welcome. The fact was, we were essentially dissimilar. We connected carnally and not otherwise. She wasn't able, I felt, to properly understand my reasons for being here, and she'd made it quite clear from the beginning that she didn't want to discuss hers. What else was there to discuss? What else could anyone have in common? What we had was circumstantial, convenient, and like anything built on tacit agreement, fragile, which meant that I wanted to fuck with it. I found myself needing to punish Alice for my own insecurity.

"How do you deal," I said, "with the solitude? I mean, I'm not exactly social, but I have my mother. I can't imagine being here on my own."

She let out an exasperated sigh.

"Especially at your age."

Happily, I'd hit a nerve. Alice glared down over the side of her blue plastic lawn chair like the frothy crest of a wave.

"Uh, being away from people is the only way I can keep from slitting my wrists. I'm perfectly fucking happy here. I mean, look around! It's like fucking nirvana!"

I listened for the squeak of plastic as she lay back down, which took some time. I'd expected her to tell me to leave but understood now that she wouldn't give me the satisfaction of a direct command. She wanted me to slink away like a bashful dog, and I would, most likely. I would, soon. But I wanted to end the exchange on a different note to distract me from everything unspoken. Tucked within my statement about needing other people was an admission that I needed Alice. Likewise, her statement—if I could take it at face value—described me as an exception. And though her tone had been sardonic, I sensed the seriousness behind her words. The seriousness and the spite.

In the distance another crow called out, and I imagined it standing in a circle of other crows. Each bird had an object before them: a chopstick, a bud, a candy bar wrapper. Mine had a ring.

"Do you really think that's true?" I said, sitting up. "About the crows?"

Alice picked up an old magazine and draped it over her face. "Does it matter?"

My mother and I read in the living room under the meager wattage of a government-issued energy-saving bulb. I still felt terrible, empty and alone—the way I usually felt after leaving Alice. We'd gone inside to lie down on her parents' bed after a while, and she'd curled up to me, holding me like I'd just saved her from drowning. It was hot, and I wanted to peel her sweaty body from me like a wet rag, but I let her stay, my guilt forbidding me to move, until she relaxed her grip, asleep.

"Do you really think Blake is going to come back?"

My mother looked up, her reading glasses a dragonfly perched on the tip of her nose. "Are you serious? Blake, she loves

you very, very much. She said she'd be here in July, and she'll be
here in July."

I nodded. It didn't matter whether or not it was true. It had
the desired effect. "Yeah?"

"Would I lie to you?"

I shook my head. Of course, all mothers lie to their children,
and I knew this, and she knew that I knew it. But the last few days
had made me feel precarious, and not a little lugubrious, and I was
in need of cheap reassurance.

"How have you been lately?" I asked.

"Me?"

"Yeah. You know, how's the pain?"

My mother took a deep breath. Her small face seemed to float
above her long, deep red dress. "Isn't it funny," she finally said,
"that pain exists inside the body, but the expression we use for it
is 'being in pain.' It's not inappropriate, really. You can be in pain
like you can be in danger: something that's both immanent and
imminent. I hope you never have to deal with chronic pain, Blake.
But so long as Zane's grass keeps growing, I'll cope."

DAY 9

RUSSELL DROVE US UP 65th to Phinney Ridge, his white stomach stuffed behind the wheel of the quick blue convertible Porsche. He accelerated over the cross streets, and Alice, who'd flagged us down outside her parents' house, made girlish sounds as she floated, momentarily, above the tiny back seat while Russell leered at her in the rearview mirror. He'd shown up unannounced that morning, had simply pulled up and honked out front until I came to the door. Two minutes later I'd been convinced to "see something." We crested Phinney, dodged left, and leapt into the air on our way down the other side.

"Are we in a hurry?" I asked.

"Try to be alive," he shouted over the buzz of the car's high revving engine. "You will be dead soon enough!"

This sounded familiar. I tried to remember who'd said it, and watched Green Lake disappear behind the trees as we fell back to its level.

"I'm fine here," said Alice, and the car stopped more quickly than I would have thought possible.

She climbed out and tipped an invisible hat, giving Russell a long smile.

"See you," she said to me, and I nodded.

"That's a fine-looking girl," Russell said as we drove off. "How long have you known her?"

"Since she was a baby."

"Not long, then."

We accelerated onto Aurora and sped south through what used to be Woodland Park, one half of which was a zoo. I looked for any sign of the wild animals that used to be visible from the road, but the trees were too overgrown to see much, and of course they'd all been moved long ago.

"Saroyan!" I said.

Russell winked. "What does Seattle mean to you?"

We dodged a sapling that had pushed up through the asphalt.

"Besides catastrophe?"

"How does Seattle fit into the semiotics of the West?"

I stalled. It was becoming apparent that Russell's whole M.O. was to slam you down in the middle of internal monologues.

"Come on, you've written a novel that takes place here!"

"I wrote about it because this is the place I know best."

"Yes! So tell me what you know about it."

"Are you talking about the passive-aggressiveness? The 'Seattle smile' and all that?"

"There we go. That's a start. There are things we've come to accept. Look, Seattle is an extension of L.A. Seattle is what happens when ambition has kids. But that can go either way."

"I'm not sure I follow."

Russell slowed the car and turned in his seat to face me.

"What this city could be is a wizened calming-down, a coming-to-one's-senses after a period of self-indulgent madness, a reemergence of skepticism following a kind of ontological suspension of disbelief. But the skepticism—and here's the best part—the skepticism wouldn't be total, it wouldn't be commanding or overwhelming. It wouldn't be cynical. At our best, there's an acknowledgment of responsibility underlying our self-image, wouldn't you say?"

He accelerated again, and we sped past a series of decamped crack hotels—the Waldingford Inn, the Dark Plaza Hotel, the Fremont Inn, all blurring together into a foggy memory of bad bachelor parties. *Wouldn't I say?* I wondered. This vision wasn't at all what I'd expected. The Seattle I knew seemed cynical, just not overtly. People had given up hope, they just didn't want to admit it to their neighbors, let alone themselves. So they voted left and honked politely in their hybrid cars. They Seattle smiled. Spikes of gray smoke ahead of us caught my eye, and for the first time I put two and two together.

"We're not crossing the bridge, are we?"

Russell shook his head, his jowls sloshing back and forth. "Certainly not," he said. "No, we're not going to cross. But we're going to look."

"Look at…"

"I want to show you what we're up against."

We approached slowly and stopped beside the final onramp to the bridge. Treetops to either side of the raised road reminded me that although we'd been shunted from the ground, we were still relatively safe.

Russell disagreed.

"Remember that bus accident that happened here?" he asked. "Ten years ago, some rider shoots the bus driver in the head and the whole bus careens over the edge and dives into the roof of a condominium?"

"I heard about it," I said. "Honestly, I was never sure if it had actually happened. I thought it was an urban myth."

"No myth. Zane was on that bus. You should ask him about it sometime. He was on his way to school."

"Holy shit," I said. The air was filled with the sharp, noxious smell of burning rubber. "I can't imagine him ever going to school."

"Well, the Zane you know clearly wouldn't. But it happened, and that crash is written all over his face."

The smoke rising from the bridge shot up in dark jets from three bonfires, midway across, clearly stacked with tires. The houses I'd heard about were no myth, either, but in reality they were no more than shacks, tool sheds, a shantytown in the sky, and I wondered if the same could be said for Zane's bus. I could see perhaps three dozen people, many gathered around tables, two or three perched on the railing, one pissing off the side. They were clearly what my mother would have called "rough around the edges," but they didn't seem all that different from the group of people huffing paint at the birth house: the distressed, filthy clothes and the long, unkempt hair. The preference for toxic fumes. In the distance, Mt. Rainier rose like a blister over the scene.

"Maybe they came here for the view," I said. "So what are we looking at?"

"The uncooperative."

"People who refuse to whitewash the fence."

Russell frowned. "I see you remain far from convinced. I have to say I figured you for the experimental type."

"Well," I said, "I wanted to propose something. I was thinking that instead of—"

Russell held a finger to his lips. "One word," he said. "One more word."

"It's just that, I mean, Dale Cooper is—"

"Look, forget about Dale Cooper for a moment. We'll get back to Dale Cooper. What I'd like to focus on here is Seattle. The future of Seattle, the *reemergence* of Seattle! What kind of form will it take?

Provided over by what spirit? A self-satisfied, arrogant, cynical spirit that's passed through Hollywood like a box office flop and been stripped of ambition—a city that's been beaten and whose primary emotional state is resignation? Do we want a Seattle of spiritual asylum-seekers determined to slouch back out of existence no better than when they slouched in? A pathetic parade of leave-no-tracers marching through history just to clean the streets? Because this doesn't seem to have worked out too well."

"Well," I said, suddenly on the defensive, "I think it's a little unfair to blame Seattleites for the current situation. The scope here is global, right?"

"See, that's the sloucher in you talking, Blake. You're better than that!"

It occurred to me that this was not an argument. Ideas were not being exchanged. They were coming out of Russell's head and they were hanging in the air, ripe fruit trying to tempt, but instead of plucking them I was letting them rot on the vine. I wondered how aware he was of this. I might be dealing with a legitimately crazy person not able to handle a dissenting point of view. Could he be dangerous? Could he have brought me up here to trap me? To throw me to the wolves?

"I think you have some compelling ideas," I said flatly, "and a real vision for this city."

He rolled his eyes.

"Okay," I said, "that didn't sound very convincing."

"It sure as hell did not."

"Here's where I'm at. What I want to do is write about what's going on here. I want to document. I want to describe. I want to push beyond the fantasy. No disrespect, but I'm sick of fantasy. Fantasy is what got us here! Seattle *as it is right now* is worth recording, worth remembering, and you're part of that. What you're doing is part of that."

I was almost certain I'd offended him with the fantasy comment, but I had to indicate how much he was asking of me, show him the distance I'd have to cross for compromise.

The big man sighed, crossed his arms, looked east. Drops of sweat were beginning to stream down the side of his neck and disappear beneath the gauzy material of his shirt, and I realized that I was too hot too. The car was still on and the AC was blasting away, but with the top down most of the cold air escaped, defeated. He turned back. "So, what are you suggesting?"

"I'm suggesting embedded journalism. I'm suggesting you give me access to your operation, to the birth house and to the drugs and to the library and to whatever else is going on, and that I write a book about you. About the Guild of St. Cooper."

Russell's eyes grew thin and his smile seemed to hide a kind of biting. I began to lose hope. He climbed out of the car and walked across the road, where he leaned against the railing and looked off toward the mountain. His clothes hung from his heaping body like sheets of water. His thin hair danced in the breeze. A man imposing, nearly regal, when facing me seemed from behind inexplicably banal, and I tried to summon a level of reverence for him that would warrant the kind of attention I was suggesting. Or at least confidence.

When he turned back his face had lost its rigidity, and I climbed out of the car to meet him, to stand together.

"Even the most superior mind and the most powerful imagination," said Russell, "must found itself on facts, which must be recognized for what they are."

I smiled.

"Do you know who said that?"

I didn't.

"So!" he said with a fat man's chuckle. "I've stumped you."

"What do you say?"

He held out his hand and I grabbed it quickly, not hiding my enthusiasm, and looked over his shoulder at a fight breaking out between two men. No one moved to break it up.

Russell regained my gaze, and tightened his grip. "You write your book," he said, "but you work for me in exchange. You make Cooper come alive."

Not thinking, I nodded. I said okay.

Russell squeezed my hand for another moment before letting it drop, and immediately he was smiling again. He turned around to watch the fight, put his arm around my shoulder.

"We're going to have fun," he said. "You'll see."

One of the men was being pushed perilously close to the edge of the bridge, and though I'd begun to think about how politely to retract my agreement, what I felt was not anxiety or tension or fear of what had come out of my mouth. What I felt, but could not quite reconcile, was relief. I was relieved; I was at ease. The man was now being held halfway over the railing and punched repeatedly in the face. What made the scene extraordinary was that the people around seemed not only unperturbed, they seemed indifferent. At the table nearest the fight, a bald man pulled in poker winnings with long white arms and let out a rippling, high-pitched laugh.

"Should we do something?"

"And you know," said Russell, "I've got considerable time and manpower invested in the Dale Cooper idea already, but hell, if you can think of someone better, I'm more than willing to hear you out."

Having stopped resisting, the beaten man hung limp over the edge, his aggressor gripping his shirt and speaking close to his face.

"Better?"

"Hell, if you want to make someone up entirely, we can talk about that too."

The man was heaved over the edge. His legs flipped up and momentarily hung in the air, then disappeared, and that was that. The remaining man turned and rejoined the group. Russell turned and got back in the car.

"Holy fuck."

"Seriously, Blake, can you come up with someone more interesting than Dale Cooper? I'm open. I'm willing. I'm ready to listen."

That afternoon, I sat at my desk and tried to write down everything I could remember about Dale Cooper. I hadn't seen *Twin Peaks* in probably ten years, though it had made an impression on me. It had been something I'd returned to occasionally, something that scratched an itch. I stared out across Ballard. The television series, like much of Lynch's earlier work, had been paradoxically able to destabilize and to comfort. *Twin Peaks* had made me look at certain houses in my neighborhood differently, had made me skeptical of their quotidian façade, but it had also made me feel like there were at least some other people—people, I had to admit, like Special Agent Dale Cooper—who were there with me, standing outside the mystery and looking in.

Lynch's later work, by contrast, afforded no such companionship.

I looked at my list:

Buddhism
Big jaw
Clean cut, "dapper"
Black suit, formal
Coffee, pie, big appetite, etc.
Belief in the supernatural
Respect for spiritual ways
Intuitiveness
Humility
Fascination/fixation with young women

Number ten stood out, but the general impression was a good one, and I could see how it might have struck Russell—at least, given a rabid flailing about for solutions, which must have been the case. Which was, after all, the case for most of us. Cooper's suitability was nearly irrelevant, anyway—and not only because we'd create a history for him independent of what Lynch had envisioned. More important, there was no way I was going to fuck with the general contours of his profile. A line in the sand, sure, but it felt important to draw one. To push back, if only internally. To struggle against nonchalance in the outrageous face of our whole dark enterprise.

"I saw someone get killed today," I said, out loud, to hear the words.

I felt a little crazy saying this, like I was implicating myself somehow, like I should be keeping it a secret. But the rising emotion quickly subsided and I was left with little more than a feeling akin to nostalgia. It had not been intolerable cruelty, after all. Hadn't it been self-selected? Couldn't the man who'd been pushed just as easily have been the pusher? Couldn't the man returning to his seat have been the one who'd fallen? I went downstairs to find my mother sitting on the couch, reading. She was pale, frail, and nearly swallowed up by her overstuffed furniture. She looked like a newly hatched bird in its nest. A moment after I entered the room she turned the last page of her book and took a deep breath. Then she threw the book into the air.

"Fly away," she said, "and be free!"

DAY 10

I STOOD OUTSIDE THE birth house and waited with the rest of them. There were familiar faces, but the crowd was enormous. Hundreds of people had gathered to see the unveiling, and they wandered around, slow and dazed by the heat, coating the neighboring yards like grazing sheep. The scaffolding had been removed, but the shroud itself still covered the house. It had been pulled up and tied in some sort of knot, a rope at the top running down the side of the house and lying coiled in the driveway. Someone stepped on my toe, looked up at me, apologized. He was small, blond, and very fat, and his ragged ZZ Top t-shirt stretched across his protruding gut.

"When the Foo shits," I said, "wear it."

"You're into Confucius?" he asked excitedly.

I stared.

The small man closed his eyes and stiffened his back. "'The superior man, when resting in safety, does not forget that danger may come. When in a state of security he does not forget the possibility of ruin. When all is orderly, he does not forget that disorder may come. Thus his person is not endangered, and his states and all their clans are preserved.'" He opened his eyes and looked up at me in expectation.

"I thought Confucius was into pith."

He shook his head, scowling. He'd obviously been through this before. "Confucius is deeply misunderstood."

I was about to lie, to say that I did indeed understand Confucius, that I was just joking, when the crowd began to murmur and we both turned to see Russell's white Lexus appear at the corner and slither down the street. As it slowed to a stop, a hush fell over the gathering, and an eerie, worming movement cleared a path from the car door to the house. I was at the halfway point, standing on the sidewalk, and I watched Russell exit the car and turn around, offering his hand to Aya, who climbed out, white as the car, in a long simple gown that made her look like light shining through a keyhole. The pair walked toward the house, and as they passed me Russell winked, mouthing words I couldn't make out. I nodded.

They climbed onto a small raised platform I hadn't seen before, and before a crowd even quieter than it had been moments ago, Russell made a speech.

"Cities rarely have the opportunity," he began, "for rebirth."

He paused to breathe deeply through his nose.

"To be sure, many try. Buildings, entire blocks, can be rebuilt. Downtowns can undergo what they cynically refer to as 'urban renewal,' as though the city were a temporary lease. You can tear down derelict structures, you can repave streets, but no facelift, no new city park can reverse the rot and decay underlying the gradual but inevitable decline. And why is that? Why do you suppose?"

He gave people a moment to consider the question.

"Because a city is not made of bricks and mortar. A city is not a series of streets and telephone poles and sewers and boardwalks and houses and houseflies and lawns and lampposts. Nope. A city, my dear members of the Guild, is people. A city is people, and do you know what that means? That means *this* city," and here he pointed out with both hands, waving them rather quickly back and forth, "is you."

Someone hooted, and a few people hesitantly clapped, uncertain if it was time, if they'd be interrupting, but Russell smiled and nodded.

"Yes," he said. "Yes! Give yourselves a round of applause. Give Seattle a round of applause!"

In the following din of adoration, Russell stood tall and proud on his pedestal, his hair like white fire, and I could see that whether or not he believed every word he was saying, he was profoundly enjoying this.

"Just yesterday…" he began, then waited for the crowd to come to attention. "Just yesterday I was walking with a friend. This friend expressed something it occurred to me that some of you may still feel. 'Surely,' my friend said, 'the ailments plaguing our Emerald City are global in nature.' So why take the blame? Why admit fault for something that everyone else is doing wrong too? Why change?

"The answer is simple, and it's something I think most of you have figured out for yourselves: the city. We do this for the city. The city doesn't care whose fault something is. The rot does not stop rotting, the decay does not cease its destructive course. In fact, the only thing that changes when we do not take responsibility is that we become overwhelmed by these pernicious powers. We become victims rather than redeemers."

Russell paused to survey the crowd. Aya, beside him, looked bored, like they'd just come from another venue where he'd given the same speech—true, for all I knew.

"Is that what we want?" he cried.

The crowd waited.

"I said, is that what we *want?*"

ZZ Top, shaking with energy, shouted, "No!" in a voice cracked by emotion. Taking his lead, the crowd erupted in their own "No," which because of the delay sounded more like disagreement.

"Of course we don't. We're in control of our own destiny. And that means we're in control of the destiny of Seattle."

Russell took a step back, reached down for a glass of water someone had been holding for him, and drank it down in three large gulps, streams of it trickling down both sides of his chin and onto his exposed gut. It seemed like a statement. Leader with his Great Thirst. I wondered whether it was scripted.

"When, as a young man, I first met the spiritual descendent of Chief Sealth," he said, wiping this chin, "when I first met Dale Cooper, I was surprised, astonished to find him looking askance at what I took to be a perfectly healthy city, a robust and alive city peopled with alert, astute, responsible citizens. There we were, recycling fanatics with our vegetable shoes, saving the spotted owl and supporting the service economy—how could he doubt our commitment? How could he question our allegiance?"

Aya now seemed literally to be in pain. Her smile was a thinly veiled grimace, and it was hard to be sure from my angle, but it looked like she was standing slightly bent, slightly crooked.

"But Cooper understood what the people who lived here before us also felt—that the very act of knowing was itself to blame. The false certainty. That once the mystery of our land is lost, once the mystery of our city is lost, once the mystery is sacrificed for the goal of wealth, for the smug and self-satisfied lifestyles to which we've grown accustomed, then we too are lost.

"Which is why, dear members of the Guild, this house is such an essential part of Seattle's imminent rebirth! What could be more mysterious than life itself? What could be more mysterious than the way we come into the world? And that's why I wanted you all to be a part of it, to assemble and lay your hands upon the house and bring it to life with your stories and your imaginations—your minds! To show the world that mysteries still exist, and that Dale Cooper's memory and passion and wonder live on."

He signaled offstage, and I saw the line leading to the top of the house tighten.

"So without further ado, my dears, I give you: the birth house of Special Agent Dale Cooper, Saint of Seattle!"

The cord was pulled taut and loosed a knot, and the shroud fell swiftly, without a snag. The crowd gasped. On top of the abundant and colorful mural, sprawling across the entire thing, were big, black spray-painted letters that read: *NEWCOMERS GO HOME.*

Russell turned around to take it in himself, and he stood there, motionless, silent, with everyone waiting on his official response. "Newcomers" was the slang Native Americans in the area—people who, in general, had their own take on the city's evacuation—used for white people. Aya was at this point actually holding her stomach, seemingly entirely distracted from the goings-on. I'd never seen Russell angry, but I was almost certain of what it would look like: the pinkish skin turned red, the large, loaf-like body turned juggernaut, Santa turned Satan. I was almost excited to see it.

But when he turned back to the crowd his face was serene. He held up a finger, smiled calmly, and said, "What would Cooper do?"

In the moment of silence that followed I could feel people quickly trying to change emotional course, until a low, unconvincing murmur responded with, "Rise above."

ZZ Top was among the grumbling mass, and one look at him confirmed that he was not exactly ready, let alone able, to do the necessary rising. His body trembled with a mixture of excitement and anger and the desire to impose self-restraint. The holes in his shirt were like open sores oozing flesh. I could hear Russell speaking, but my fascination with his acolyte was distracting me and his words seemed far way, so that when the short man turned to look at me I felt I'd been caught somehow, and smiled dumbly, raising my hands in surrender. His expression, however, was not suspicion but curiosity, like he'd just seen me for the first time. People on all sides of me stepped back too, and I looked up, out, into the crowd, to see that everyone was staring at me. Another passageway had opened up, this time between me and the house, and Russell stood at its far end, holding out his arms as though to welcome me into an embrace.

"Blake," he said, "aren't you going to introduce yourself to the Guild?"

Clearly I had missed a critical point.

Nearly entranced, I began to walk down the cleared path, but not before ZZ Top, grinning savagely, grabbed me by the arm.

"Don't forget the possibility of ruin," he said, and then relaxed his grip.

"Gee," I said. "Thanks."

When I got up on the small stage Russell put his arm around my shoulder. Aya was now in such a state that she could not even bear to meet my eyes, and I decided to make it as quick as I could for her, to get her off stage and whatever help she required. Russell explained that I was the author of a book very dear to his heart, and that I'd volunteered to help him tell the story of Dale Cooper for the ages.

"I'm an honor to be here," I said.

Realizing my error, I made a face. I had no idea what I should say, because I had no idea what these people knew. I would have to speak broadly, to refer simply to my enthusiasm and the road ahead, to speak of the future the way I remembered Harry Wilder speaking during the days of evacuation.

"Like Russell has said," I began, "it's going to be up to us to ensure that future generations have someone to inspire them along a virtuous, uh…"

I was beginning to doubt my ability to finish the thought. But just before turning back to Russell for assistance, I stumbled across a line I thought would work.

"The real inspiration on display today," I said, "is behind me right now. It's your hard work and creativity that I hope to use as my own example in the days to come. It's your commitment that made this possible, and if I can only match that commitment in my own work, I know I'll be on the right path. I know by working hard today, we'll make Special Agent Dale Cooper a household name in the Seattle of tomorrow!"

The crowd looked a little afraid, it seemed to me. I wondered if I'd said something wrong, if I'd said too much, but Russell hollered loudly and began to clap, and slowly the crowd joined in, worried expressions morphing into acceptance, even joy, and before long there was such thunderous applause and whistling and shouts that my doubt was firmly overcome. I'd made the speech. I'd rallied. I'd done good.

I waved, shook Russell's hand, waved again. Expecting to shake Aya's hand, or even give her a hug, I was surprised to find that she was no longer on the platform, and I looked across the crowd for her. The applause was subsiding; people were beginning to splinter off and resume conversations they'd been in before the speech. Men were gathering up the fallen shroud; a three-piece band I hadn't noticed before began to play bluegrass, and Tiger was tugging on a man's pant leg, no doubt asking after his sexual orientation.

Scanning the crowd, my eyes passed over a figure standing across the street, standing beneath a large poplar, half hidden by shade, a figure whose entirely inappropriate formal dress caught my attention. It was only an instant—when I looked back he was gone—but it gave me a strange feeling, a chill. Had Russell hired someone to look the part, to play Dale Cooper? Or had some member of the so-called Guild of St. Cooper taken his enthusiasm, his belief in the cause, to an extreme? It could have been something else entirely, I realized—an accident of light. Whatever it was, it threw off my mood, and, like the graffiti, cast a momentary pall over my feeling of success.

"BS," my mother said. "Total horse hockey."

We were watching the news.

"How so?" I asked absently.

I was still high from the unexpected thrill of speaking at the birth house, still weirded out by the figure I'd seen. I was still wondering where Aya had gone, and why. In other words, I was only with my mother in fact. Not truly. And though I wasn't entirely beyond my feelings of guilt, it felt good to have a secret. I tried to focus. The top story tonight—besides the lack of rain, which was now the Big Story in general—was that a farmer had been found in Georgia growing the last known heirloom tomato. My mother wasn't having it.

"Well," she said, "for one, we grow heirloom tomatoes in the garden. So, factually, it's simply false."

She paused to relight the joint she'd been nursing all night.

"But more than that, it's just…it's a silly thing to say. Heirloom varieties are all over the place. They're what get left behind in places that aren't taken over by big farms. An heirloom is just a nonhybrid variety that isn't mass-produced or screwed with by, you know, whoever."

"Mm-hmm." I nodded sleepily. Since I hadn't told my mother about my decision to help Russell in exchange for access to his operation, I couldn't tell her about what had happened that afternoon. At least, I couldn't tell her about my role in it. All she knew was that I'd gone to the unveiling.

"They have to be open-pollinated, too," she said.

"Day ten," I said, pointing at the screen. "No rain for ten days."

"Heirlooms are really the final frontier."

"How long do you think we can go without rain?"

My mother took another long drag.

"By splicing everything together," she said, "we reduce the variety. And by reducing variety, we weaken our defenses to things like disease."

I reached for the joint. "Tomorrow I'm going to shadow Zane on his delivery route."

"Disease and climate."

The heirloom farmer was now being interviewed. He didn't seem to be a farmer, really. He was wearing a business suit, for one. He was holding a yellow tomato the size of a cantaloupe.

"According to the autopsy," he said excitedly, "Abraham Lincoln ate tomatoes like this one the night he died."

The camera zoomed in on the tomato until the entire screen was yellow.

"It's beautiful," said the newscaster.

The hand holding the tomato gave it a light squeeze.

"Spin that puppy for the people back home."

DAY 11

ZANE'S TRUCK IDLED BEHIND him in the street. He'd never shown up in a truck before, or in a vehicle of any kind, and I assumed it was a result of Russell's instruction to take me along on his route. If Zane was upset by my tagging along, his face didn't give anything away. Nothing, that is, except the crash. For the first time, I noticed a Metro bus falling over the edge of his eyebrow toward his temple. It was nearly hidden in the tight mosaic of images on his skin, but now that I knew what to look for I could see it clearly. I wondered what other stories he'd had etched there. A turtle climbed over the edge of his jaw. A small child sat in the bowl of one sunken cheek.

"You're in luck," Zane said flatly. "Bathyspheres are on the route today."

"As in those underwater—"

"Good morning, Zane!"

My mother appeared at my side, and a moment later I was following them through the house and onto the back porch. She asked him about his day, and about his partner—whose existence was a complete surprise to me—and something both sad and wonderful occurred to me: Zane was my mother's friend. In fact, he was her *only* friend.

"Is he still distrustful?" asked my mother.

Zane looked at me briefly and then nodded.

"Well, what did I tell you? When you withhold, people can sense it, and it makes them feel like you've got something to hide. Didn't I tell you?"

Zane looked rather crestfallen. "Yeah," he said.

"Trauma or no trauma, you've just got to let Richard in. Blake knows—don't you, Blake."

"I know?"

"It was the same way with Blake's father, though I was in Richard's place. He had PTSD—totally closed off."

"So how'd you get him to open up?" Zane asked.

"She didn't," I said.

My mother looked at me like I'd ruined the ending. Zane looked defeated. I apologized.

"No, no, he's right, I didn't."

The bluegrass band that had played the day before began to play again. From five blocks away we could hear only the snare drum and a few scattered rising notes of the singer's voice, but the song sounded upbeat.

"I know I've just got to tell him how I'm feeling," Zane said, "but it makes me so angry when he acts like I'm sneaking around behind his back."

My mother stood and gave him a long hug. I watched them embrace and grew a tiny bit jealous. It wasn't just the physical contact; it was the fact that they'd clearly been having this protracted dialogue about Zane's love life without my knowing. They hadn't sought me out, they hadn't included me in any way, and my mother hadn't even thought to tell me they were friends.

"So what's this I hear about you taking my son to a Bathysphere?"

"One of my clients," Zane said. "He's building a home underwater. I mean, it's not entirely underwater yet, but he's building it so it can be, or will be, or *would* be, I mean."

"Would be?" I asked.

"You know, if the tsunami…"

"I wasn't aware the matter was in question."

My mother smiled and patted Zane on the cheek. "You two have a good time."

We headed down 15th Avenue, bumping slowly over the cracked cement in four-wheel drive. Zane hunched over the steering wheel, strangely overcautious. Learning that he was gay had made me see him differently. It made him seem more vulnerable. More likeable.

"Who runs the Ballard Bridge?" I asked.

"Just so you know," he said, "my partner and I aren't, like, completely dysfunctional or anything."

"Everyone's got issues. Russell told me about the bus."

He rolled his eyes. "God, it's like he's proud of it."

"Well, it's pretty wild."

"What it does is support the version of Seattle he likes to convince people about. Big, hypocritical Seattle running itself into the ground."

"That's not the Seattle you remember?"

We crossed Market and the bridge became visible up ahead. To the right, a Brown Bear carwash sprawled helplessly. Zane pointed to the left: Louie's Cuisine of China.

"You know Louie's grandson lives in the restaurant? He hasn't come out since the evacuation. We bring him eggs."

"We?"

"Well, me."

I looked at the low, windowless building as we passed, imagining a skinny boy in a bathrobe pacing around with an Uzi.

"What are eggs?" I asked.

Zane gave me a look.

"What? Sorry I'm not up on my drug lingo."

"I'm not talking about drugs. You think all we do is deal drugs?"

Zane began to say something but stopped himself and braked. At the near side of the bridge stood a large group of Indians. They were standing around a bonfire. It was still early, but already hot, so the fire was obviously serving no purpose other than intimidation. They turned toward us as we drew near. Zane, I noticed, had none of the bravado he'd demonstrated two days earlier on the bike. He pulled up close to them and waved. There was no wave back.

He leaned his head out the window. "Hey, fellas," he said. "Mind letting us through?"

Slowly, slowly, a passage opened up and we crept forward. Zane kept his eyes trained on the far side of the bridge, where another group had gathered and stood around an equally intimidating fire. In the water below the bridge was a cluster of fishing boats, half-sunk, their bows and sterns pointing up at oblique angles like whales frozen mid-breach. As we moved through the second crowd I realized they weren't all Native Americans. In fact, it was evenly split between races. I'd been assuming these were the same people who held the Fremont Bridge, but either I was wrong or they'd been recruiting.

"Sympathizers?"

"Shh."

We headed west along a small road that hugged the canal, passed through an area lined with industrial structures and storage, and drove under the train bridge and by another row of abandoned houses, another area of town that had disappeared into the subtle shifts of color and light produced by disuse, destruction, or both.

"Have you ever heard of the term 'defamiliarization'?"

Zane didn't respond.

"It was coined by a guy named Shklovsky. Basically, it's the artistic practice of reframing familiar things in order to allow people to see them directly, without preconceptions. I wonder sometimes if the evacuation of Seattle was a great work of defamiliarization, but one we were too far gone to appreciate."

"Who says I don't appreciate it?"

"Well, do you take it for granted?"

We were approaching what appeared to be the end of the street, and I could see snatches of Puget Sound ahead of us, and to our left a road called Hooker. Hooker was roughly one hundred feet long, and met with another street heading back the way we came.

"If I was really taking it for granted I wouldn't know it, right?"

"You could have a hunch."

"Sorry," he said. "The term doesn't ring a bell."

Zane stopped without pulling over, leapt out of the truck, and as he pulled milk crates filled with various machine parts from the bed he began explaining the delivery.

"Guy's name is Sergeant George Washington."

I got out. The smell of low tide was intense. "That should be easy to remember."

"He was one of our earliest customers. Already began his work before the evacuation, so the first thing he did was move his whole operation down the road." Zane nodded at the house we stood before, a flat, gray, glassy thing that spilled its stories over the bluff.

"What's he building, exactly?"

Zane handed me a crate. "That's top secret, soldier," he said with a wink.

The floors of the house were barely visible, covered by what looked like plumbing, and we wound single file through a narrow passage kept clear by necessity. Zane called out, "Sarge, Sarge, Sarge" so the man would hear us coming. The tall, narrow windows around the stairwell looked out over the Sound. The tide was way back, the black, debris-strewn bottom sludge exposed like gnarly tooth roots.

"Sarge!"

We descended three flights and went out a door at nearly sea level. The smell down here was even more powerful, and I gagged before being able to focus on what we'd come to see: a series of round steel tanks, ten feet in diameter, lying in a crooked line from the land out into the channel, and a naked, wiry man climbing down from one toward the far end. We put down our crates.

"Oh!" said the man. He began to trudge up through the muck.

Chains linked the tanks together, and the nearest one was tethered to a stone beneath the house. Each tank had one or two small circular windows in its side and an opening at the top, accessible by what looked like a salvaged manhole cover.

"Oh!" said the man again.

When he reached us he wasted no time in rummaging through the contents of the crates we'd brought, grunting approval and once in a while tossing a gasket into the mud. Besides being naked, he was actually quite presentable: he was recently shaven, his hair closely cropped. And despite having been climbing around on his tanks, he seemed oddly clean. Zane caught me inspecting the man and smiled, nodding slightly.

"This is Blake," Zane said. "He wants to know what you're building here."

Sergeant George Washington looked up at me with sharp blue eyes. "Building? Ha. Ha. No. Not building. Receiving, maybe. Hope so."

He went back to the boxes at our feet.

"So you received these Bathyspheres?"

"Information for 'em, sure. Plans."

Zane grinned again. I couldn't tell whether he approved of these answers or he found them embarrassing.

"Where does the information come from?" I asked.

"Oh," he said, "that. Blake, is it?"

I said it was.

"We're receiving information about the world all the time, Blake. From reality, from other people, but do you know where most of it comes from?"

I shrugged.

"Ourselves."

"Ourselves?"

"You read poetry?"

"Some."

"Hold on."

He zipped inside, leaving Zane and me standing there in the sun. Seagulls circled overhead, and one dropped something onto a parking lot on the far side of the channel.

"Ramon Fernandez," said Zane, grinning even wider now.

"Hey," I said, "I know that name."

Zane nodded.

Presently, George Washington emerged from his house with a piece of paper held above his head. He bounced down the rocks and slime, handed me the page, then closed his eyes, stiffened, and began to recite:

She sang beyond the genius of the sea.
The water never formed to mind or voice,
Like a body wholly body, fluttering
Its empty sleeves; and yet its mimic motion
Made constant cry, caused constantly a cry,
That was not ours although we understood,
Inhuman, of the veritable ocean.

He stopped, but kept his eyes sealed shut, savoring the words he'd spoken. I reread the lines until movement out by one of the tanks caught my attention. A woman and a child, both naked, were peeking out at us. They were behind a tank, not in it, but they may as well have been staring out from between iron bars. The woman was young, younger than me, but gaunt, her skin retreating against her bones as if in horror. The child was too young to read, but he mirrored his mother's movements, flinching when she flinched at my stare, darting back before looking again in the tidal pull of curiosity. I looked at Zane and he mouthed the word *family* to me, as though that explained it all. The two disappeared behind the big metal ball, and with a sick feeling it dawned on me that, when the tsunami hit, these people would be inside death traps built from directions a man named George Washington found in a poem.

"That sure is inspiring," said Zane. "Find what you needed?"

Awoken from his contemplation, the sergeant bent down and picked up a small brass elbow pipe. "Yep," he said. "This ought to keep us dry."

We drove back along the water, under the train bridge and past the boat yards, before turning toward downtown. In an effort to keep the engine cool Zane had turned on the heater, so in addition to the already terrible heat of the day, hot air blew against our legs. We passed an overgrown driving range where I'd worked in eighth grade, doing everything from cleaning toilets to fetching beers for the owner. My favorite part of the job had been driving the picker. A range picker is a caged golf cart with a rotating blade that retrieves golf balls from the grass, and it would have been cool enough to drive it around just for what it was, but because the range couldn't cease operation every time the balls needed to be restocked, the picker would be deployed while people were still driving. This meant you got nailed with golf balls—and not just accidentally. Though the official policy was to avoid the picker, most members got a kick out of hearing the pang of a ball against the golf cart's metal mesh, so from the time I'd start out until returning to the dock I'd be pelted with hard white balls. By the end of my shift I'd have a terrible headache, and I'd be jumpy, flinching at objects moving quickly in my periphery. Still, I loved it. It felt like wearing impenetrable armor in a warzone. It felt like being invincible.

I couldn't stop picturing the faces of the woman and child we'd seen with George Washington. The woman's slack expression, the child's timidity, their brutally manifest acquiescence of spirit. It was appalling, and yet their victimhood was strangely unhidden, even overt, as though by standing on the sidelines they meant to be the center of attention. I fought against the feeling that they were complicit in that debased fate. Zane, who'd been quiet for the ride, finally looked over at me and asked what was wrong.

"Delusion is sad enough on its own," I said, "but it's infinitely worse when innocent people are implicated."

We accelerated up a small rise. There were no other cars on the road, but a few people trudged along beside it wearing heavy weather gear.

"Sarge's wife and kid," said Zane, "you're talking about."

"He's taking direction from a poem! Doesn't it bother you?"

"Well, okay, I can see it from your perspective, and yeah, from there it looks pretty bad, I guess. But for one thing, I wouldn't say he's taking direction from a poem. Inspiration, maybe inspiration. But he's a trained engineer. He's not just gluing shit together with bubblegum."

"Huh," I said, unmoved. Crazy is crazy. "He told you this, I suppose."

"Oh, come on. He knows what he's doing."

"Really? So you'd climb right into one of those Bathyspheres when the tsunami starts rolling into town?"

We swerved around a stalled semi that had been left in the middle of the road. The trailer had long since been looted, and its remaining contents were strewn across the road, stainless steel lids glittering like fallen stars.

"Well," Zane was now speaking more seriously, his voice lowered, "that's the other thing. I won't have to. And neither will Sarge and his family."

"Is Russell evacuating them?"

Zane shook his head.

"Are you going to put them out of their misery?"

Zane rolled his eyes.

"Then what?"

"The tsunami is a lie."

There was a black cat clawing its way up Zane's jaw, and I wondered what its story was. Some kind of attack? It didn't look like a house cat, but it wasn't familiar. It wasn't Amund Dietzel's crawling panther.

"Well," I said, "that's a relief."

Zane gave me the same indecipherable grin he'd worn earlier. "Believe whatever you want."

My first impulse was to find the quickest way out of this conversation, but almost as quickly it struck me that this was exactly the sort of thing I should know more about. I should be impassive, should be treating this as though I'm on safari. What do the natives believe? What is the worldview of this peculiar, painted man and his people? Look at his culture's inevitable decay! Look at them press on as though there's hope and create delusional, self-serving narratives to mask the imminent apocalypse! Look at the exotic seagulls!

"I'm sorry," I said. "I didn't mean to be glib. It's just that, obviously, this is news to me. I mean…" I pointed out the window, suggesting the disparity. We were entering Belltown, driving down what had once been a one-way street. "Can you give me any more information?"

"Honestly, I'd probably get yelled at for telling you at all. But since you're best friends with Russell all of a sudden, I'm hoping it's okay. Can you do me a favor and maybe find a way of bringing it up with Russell, or asking him about it? Maybe say you'd heard a rumor or whatever? Maybe in a way that doesn't get me in trouble?"

"Look, Zane, I don't want to…" But I didn't know what I didn't want to do. "My presence must be kind of jarring," I said.

"Don't worry about it. You're all right."

We drove a couple blocks in silence. Zane was genuinely trying to accept me, and I didn't want to belittle or reject his olive branch. I began thinking about my planned meeting with Russell.

Standing before the birth house the day before as the crowd slowly dispersed, he'd actually used the word "brainstorm." As in, brainstorming some innovative solutions. He'd been inspecting the graffiti that had all but sabotaged his big reveal, and had seemed, to my eyes, almost impressed by it.

"Try to think of some iconic things Cooper could have done," he'd said.

Twenty-four hours later, I hadn't thought of anything iconic. My plan was to ask him more questions about our goal. My plan was to get him talking.

We were entering the business district, the empty, cold heart of downtown. Seattle had never successfully made downtown anything more than a stand of swaying towers, a board meeting of glassy-eyed stakeholders with nothing to say. And though by day it had been dense with working stiffs, by night it had looked much like it did now.

"Do you know of anyone in the Guild who wears suits?"

"There's a girl who wears a cat suit about half the time," Zane said. "Trixie? No, Tracy."

"I was thinking something more formal. You know, a businessman kind of guy."

"In the Guild? Doubt it."

We took a left at Spring and began chugging up the hill toward the library.

"Thought I saw someone dressed to the nines yesterday at the birth house."

"Yeah," Zane said, "no."

He hooked into a parking garage and we curled up two flights of empty platforms until arriving at one nearly full of cars. BMWs, Cadillacs, and Porsches lined the walls. A bright orange

Lamborghini sat alone near the stairwell, an exotic orchid. We parked in a long row of trucks.

"Nice Lamborghini," I said.

"No one touches the Lambo."

"That's a shame. It looks like it wants to be touched."

We headed across the street.

The library was full of life: people scaling the metal lattice exoskeleton, cleaning glass with no safety equipment that I could see, and just inside, on the 5th Avenue floor, some sort of aerobics class was being taught. Twenty or thirty men and women in their underwear were gathered before a tall, thin woman with an afro as she barked out instructions to bend, bounce, bend, bounce. She waved to us and we paused to let two boys no older than ten pass by, pulling bright red Radio Flyers filled with canned food. Zane picked up a rectangular blue can, frowned. It was Spam.

"They didn't have their filter on," I said.

Zane scoffed. We were beginning to understand each other.

He led me to a stairwell and told me to go all the way to the top. I shook his hand, thanking him for taking me on his route, and a flash of color caught my eye, an orange summer dress. It was Aya, momentarily visible before disappearing behind a bookshelf. I had an urge to go after her, but Zane stood his ground, held the door.

The stairwell was narrow and the staircase switched back and forth every seventh step because of the building's staggered floors, making the ascent both easier, for all the platform pauses, and seemingly interminable. I began to giggle, looking down to see if I'd made any progress and up to see if I'd neared my goal. I felt like an inverse Alice, who in order to enter another dimension doesn't simply fall but has to work at it. Finally a small door at the top opened up to a lawn. On the lawn was a large, white, open-sided tent. Under the tent was a kind of living room made up of wicker furniture. On one of the wicker chairs sat Russell. He waved me over without looking to see who it was.

I stared out over the Sound and, beyond that, the Olympic Mountains, behind which the sunken sun had left a rosy glow that looked something like a welt. Seagulls swam through the still, muggy sea air, calling to one another with full mouths. The roof was empty except for Russell, me, and a young woman named Dahlia he'd summoned to provide background music. After an uncomfortably slow start, we'd indeed begun to volley ideas back and forth, but it hadn't been going very well. What had Dale Cooper done to make him such an essential figure in the history of Seattle, of the Northwest, of America? To my surprise, Russell had no interest in representing even remotely realistic events. He wanted Cooper to make contact with aliens. He wanted Cooper to invent a technique for breathing underwater. He wanted Cooper to communicate nonverbally with animals. This was not Dale Cooper a historical figure. This was Dale Cooper a superhero. I'd attempted to lead him away from such ideas gently, but the tension between us grew nonetheless. Dahlia had been strumming the guitar for a couple hours, and her languid playing, though not very good, had added a kind of boozy quality to the evening that emboldened me. I'd twice called Russell's ideas "ridiculous." After being at first taken aback—clearly Russell had different expectations of my opinions—he had, it seemed, begun to appreciate my candor.

"I've got one," he said. A sailboat had set off from Bainbridge, and I watched its white sail move, impossibly slow, against the green island. "Cooper gets into a fracas defending the spotted owl. He chains himself to a tree about to be bulldozed, and—"

"Do they bulldoze trees?"

"Or cut down, you know. Fell?"

"I like where you're going, but I think you're overcompensating. Being chained to a tree is a bit too pedestrian. What if he discovers that Weyerhaeuser's CEO has some kind of secret deal with the Yakuza and is involved in female slave trafficking?"

"Hmm. Now who's breaking believability?"

"See, it's outrageous without being absurd," I explained. "Plus, you'd have the beautiful woman angle, too. He could fall in love with one of the slaves."

"The problem is I already have Weyerhaeuser cast in a different light. It's a tree-growing company. Cooper takes nature walks with the CEO. They're good guys."

We hadn't agreed on one single thing so far. Given my position, why wasn't he just charging me with writing something specific? Why involve me in the decision-making process at all? I considered backing off, but at the last moment redoubled my efforts.

"That doesn't mean that something couldn't come between them, later on. People have duplicitous natures—the guy could have the appearance of a tree-hugging hippy and be hiding his dark, slave-raping side from even his closest friends."

The guitar stopped. Dahlia had fallen asleep. Her limp body hung over the instrument like she was cradling a baby.

"I'll think about it."

I considered Russell in the growing darkness, his soft white uniform blurring at the edges. If I didn't blow it, I'd be spending a lot of time with this man in the coming month or so. With the direction Russell had adopted from the start of our conversation, I had no trouble believing that he'd spread a stupid, reckless rumor about the tsunami. Or lack thereof. And in the presence of his unstable charisma and amiable bravado, it was impossible for me to believe he'd acknowledge the danger in doing so. It was this tenuous and naïve relationship between the real, material world and the stories he wanted to tell about it that interested me—that and the near-passive acceptance of this vision among his acolytes. Was it possible that people were, like me, simply going along with him in order to earn his favor? Perhaps no one believed in Cooper. Perhaps people innately understood the slippery path he was leading them down.

"You know," I said, "there are plenty of other details we'll need. Like where Cooper was born, what his childhood was like, who his parents were...that kind of thing. I mean, if this is going into the history books, we'll need to have a complete picture."

Russell waved at me dismissively. "Oh," he said, "I already have quite a lot of that figured out."

"You do?"

"I do."

"Well, you know, that could be helpful. Do you mind sharing it with me?"

"I suppose I could. I didn't know it would be relevant."

"Relevant? If I'm going to suggest believable scenarios, I have to know how he started out. How he got where he was, or is. Youth provides the basic structure for adult values and behavior, right? I mean, you know, that's the idea."

Russell paused to consider this, then quickly stood. "This is exactly why I brought you on board, Blake. This is exactly it. I have Cooper's past written. Or at least significant episodes from it. It's all in the Guild letters. I'm very sorry it didn't occur to me to share those with you, but that's where you should begin. Of course! I'll have them sent home with you."

Dahlia dropped the guitar, waking herself up, and looked at Russell as if she didn't know where she was or how she'd gotten here. The hollow instrument reverberated in the silence, carrying the rough chord of its abuse. I looked back to mark the sailboat's progress, but it had grown too dark—the water stretched out westward, toward the far shore, and disappeared with everything in it. I tried to imagine what it would look like when the tsunami hit. Or rather, just before. The frightening but harmless first rush of water followed by the strong, silent undertow, the water pulling back from the Puget Sound, pulling out into the Pacific as if in retreat. It would be quick, but quiet, the water seeming to drain, to sink, to evaporate, but in fact gathering force, redoubling, coiling like a snake.

Part II

DAY 12

MY MOTHER WAS HOLDING a radio. She was sitting at the dining table, paperwork organized neatly into three small stacks before her, and she was holding the radio with her eyes closed. The cord trailed off the table to the floor, unplugged. It was past ten, and though I was no longer setting an alarm, I felt a little sheepish. Sheepish and irritated. Blake was still asleep, there was nothing "to do," and in the midsummer heat wave, morning was the only truly comfortable time to be in bed. So why should I waste it being awake?

I made a big deal of stretching, then stood before the table.

"I have some things for you to read over," my mother said. Her eyes were still closed. "When your brother gets back, he'll need to read it over too."

I sat down. Through the window behind her, I could see Brock packing his big white pickup. He'd taken his family out of town two weeks ago, then returned to haul out the rest of his stuff.

"Where is he?"

"I don't know. He left early this morning. Scavenging would be my guess."

"Where's Crystal and Olivia?"

Kent's wife spent very little time here. Under the guise of helping her friends move, she'd take her daughter out first thing in the morning and often return after dinner. But I had my suspicions. Surely she didn't have this many friends. A couple days ago I'd asked Olivia—a very serious ten-year-old—where they went all day, and she'd just stared at me. "Out."

"I think she just drives around," I said. "I'm serious. Where could she possibly have left to go?"

My mother opened her eyes and blinked.

"Don't you think it's weird?"

"It's my living will," she said.

I looked down at the orderly papers.

"Shall I walk you through it?" she asked.

Next door, Brock cried out, and I looked to see him dancing around, waving his right hand in the air. He brought it to his mouth.

"Is that the emergency radio?"

My mother nodded. She bent down to pick up the end of the cord and plugged it in. A small red light came on. There was a brief burst of static, then silence. We stared at it, expecting something more.

"Change the station," I said. "I hate this song."

My mother smiled sadly, weakly. "For some reason, it hasn't felt real for me until now."

"Let me see that thing."

She passed the radio to me, but the short cord kept it in the middle of the table. I leaned forward in my seat and held it in the air, turning it over as much as I could. The size of a large brick, it was plastic, practically weightless, and colored a light, industrial brown. The speaker was hidden behind horizontal slats. On the back was a sticker that read:

Property of the United States Federal Emergency Management Agency. It is unlawful to tamper with or unplug this emergency warning system.

"Relief," said my mother. "When everyone began to leave, what I actually felt was relief. I felt lighter and lighter, almost dizzy, as though everyone had been…I don't know, some sort of burden. It's terrible, but that's what I felt."

"Well, you were responsible for their well-being for a long time." She'd worked for Seattle Public Health until her retirement ten years earlier. "They *were* a burden. It's not terrible—it's probably fucking healthy."

When my mother had announced she'd be staying, Kent and I hadn't taken it seriously. We thought it would pass. We thought it was some kind of temporary insanity caused by old age, stubbornness, cancer. I'd been living in New York City and Kent had been planning to bring his family my way, and certain arrangements were already being made. But that was before everyone knew about the radios, about the decision to maintain basic services—she had inside information and knew it wasn't as self-destructive as it sounded. That information was soon made public, but I'd still had half the plane to myself on the flight into SeaTac. By the time Blake joined me, she'd had the whole thing.

"Healthy to feel bad?"

My mother clearly hadn't expected us to move in with her.

"You know what I mean," I said.

Kent poked his head in the front door. "Blake, I need your help."

I looked at my mother.

My brother's pickup was up on the curb, back full of tar roofing shingles. He'd mentioned something about the house needing a new roof, but until now I'd taken it as a rhetorical statement. Yes, the house needed a new roof. The neighborhood needed more diversity. The average temperature of the world needed to drop ten degrees. These things, too, were no doubt on my brother's list.

We climbed onto the back of the truck and started tossing the shingles into a pile on the neglected, overgrown front yard.

"Mom wants us to read her will," I said.

My brother paused, then kept throwing.

"The radio came this morning," I said.

Kent looked up. "What are you, a newsletter?"

"If you'd like to unsubscribe, please send an email to eat my shit."

"What does it say?"

"I don't know. Please take me off the list?"

"The will."

"I haven't read it. I don't think I'm going to."

"Me neither."

"It's probably split down the middle, right?"

"What's split?"

"You know, her estate."

Kent shrugged.

"Do you even know how to roof a house?" I asked.

"Nope."

We finished the job in silence. As Kent's skillset had broadened, so too had his judgments of my character. He'd begun to look at me as a kind of broken tool. There was potential there, so long as he had the patience to fix it. But he wasn't at all convinced that the time required would be worth it. He hadn't said anything like this to me, but he didn't need to. His focused determination was proof enough.

We climbed down and I stood sweating in the sun while Kent parked the truck across the street. He grabbed some tools from the bench seat and, as he passed me, dropped some kind of pamphlet at my feet.

"Will you get that?" he asked.

It was a do-it-yourself manual from Home Despot: *Roofing for Assholes.*

I picked it up and flipped to the end.

It was nearly noon, and Blake was on the back porch in a standing bow-pulling pose. She looked like a tilted martini glass, her head an olive, her bright red face...a pimiento? I'd tried doing yoga with her back at the beginning, but instead of the euphoria it seemed to create in her, in me it just triggered rage.

She looked up, caught me staring at her from inside, and smiled.

"Join me!" she called.

"You won't like me when I'm angry."

Blake hadn't wanted to come to Seattle, but after just a few months here she'd seemed to have a modest awakening. Nowhere was the crude little boil, the clenched fist New York City could turn her into. Somehow, despite the threat and confusion around us, she'd managed to relax. Still, she'd come on the condition that it would only be until we could convince my mother to leave, and since that wasn't going to happen I worried that every day would be our last.

"Where's my mother?" I asked. I'd fallen asleep on the couch, and everyone was gone again.

"Just a second," said Blake. "Let me check my notes."

A lawnmower started up nearby. It wasn't unusual for families to make their property—house, garage, and garden—exceptionally clean before leaving it. I couldn't tell whether it was out of politeness or pride, or whether it was a final act of affection in the love affair they had with the illusion of perpetuity. Moments later a closer, bigger engine roared to life and the lawnmower music was out-sung. It was Brock. I looked through the window to see him walking around his truck, securing the canvas he'd used to cover the bed. Then he took a backpack from his passenger seat and came over.

"Anyone home?" he called, walking down the driveway.

Blake looked at me, frowning.

"Up here," she said.

I walked out to the back deck as Brock climbed the steps, and we met in front of a barely dressed Blake, who tried to hold her tree pose.

"Blake," Brock said, "right?"

"Brock," said Blake.

Brock reached out and wrapped me in a bear hug. "Man!" he said. "May we live in interesting times!"

Over his shoulder, I could see his truck, at idle, visibly shaking. He gave me a tight squeeze before letting me go and holding out the backpack before him.

"Take it," he said. "I can't have it with me over the pass—they got dogs now and they're stopping people, is what I hear."

"Dogs?"

"You know, police dogs. They'd smell it."

I was still holding the pack. I glanced down at it. Brock laughed.

"It ain't gonna bite you, man. It's just weed." He leaned in close and said in a conspiratorial voice, "I thought your mom might be able to use it."

Blake raised an eyebrow, which I tried to ignore. Brock was just being neighborly.

"She's actually not home right now," I said, as if that settled something.

"Damn. Say goodbye to her for me? She's always been my favorite neighbor. No offense. Tell her she's in my prayers. It's a damn shame, her coming down with the big C. They tell me that stuff," he nodded toward the backpack, "really helps with pain and nausea and whatever."

Blake dropped her pose, marched over to her purse, and pulled out a cigarette.

At dinner Olivia sat before an untouched plate of instant saag paneer and Crystal looked on bemusedly as Kent used a steak knife to clean beneath his nails. My brother's wife seemed to find his interest in manual labor curious—not distasteful, exactly, perhaps a little thrilling. But she was a banker's wife and hadn't forgotten. Her blond hair was curled into a bun sitting behind her blue eyes and slightly upturned nose. That same nose gave her daughter a slightly prudish expression, I'd always thought, though it could also have been that her prudishness made me look at her nose that way.

Blake was describing the event of the day: Brock's visit. A gallon-capacity freezer bag full of marijuana sat on the window seat beside the emergency radio, and as Blake spoke we'd all turn to it now and then, as though it were the only evidence of the story's veracity.

"Which was all well and good," she was saying, "until he said, and I quote, 'It's too bad Rose *came down* with cancer.' His words: came down. As if it were a common cold!"

I abandoned the idea of nitpicking over the line, which she'd misremembered.

"He was very nice to have left me his grass, in any case," my mother said.

"So," Kent said, "are you going to smoke it?"

My mother reached behind her and brought the bag to the table, then unzipped it and pulled out a bud five inches long to whistles and gasps. No one at the table had smoked pot in several years, to my knowledge, but we all recognized a kind bud.

"I used to buy pot from him," said Kent. "In middle school."

Kent's wife looked alarmed. "Middle school? As in, eighth grade?"

"Well, sixth grade, really."

"Doesn't surprise me," Blake said. "That man clearly has no scruples."

"That man," I said, "came over and gave us a very thoughtful gift before leaving. That man took his family out of here before coming back *by himself* to clear out the house. I'd say we're talking about a pretty considerate person. Your problems with him are problems of class."

"Christ," Blake said, "here we go with the classism. Really, Blake, it's like poor people would have carte blanche to be creeps if it were up to you. Oh, you're poor? Please, spit on my food!"

The table was quiet. Olivia asked to be excused and went into the living room to play with an elaborate dollhouse Kent had brought home. The entire backside of it was a door and, strangely, staring through the rooms from behind seemed distinctly creepy, while doing so from the front did not, though in fact it amounted to the same thing.

"Classic," said Kent.

I laughed. "Always the conflict avoider."

"Anyway," he said, "I think we can all agree that Brock's a little touched. He didn't leave because of the tsunami, right? He left because of an alien invasion. I mean, by his own admission."

Brock had indeed described the lights to most of us on several occasions, the lights that had shown up, suspiciously, just before the discovery that the Ross Ice Shelf was in critical condition, near collapse. In an unexpected departure from usual sightings, however, he'd said—to anyone who'd listen—that the lights seemed to come from certain trees.

"Is that a class issue, too?" Blake smiled playfully. She was not picking a fight. Today wouldn't be our last day.

"That depends," I said. "Did the aliens leave their home planet of their own accord? Or did the state give them one-way tickets?"

"Planet Giuliani. At least it would be safe to walk the streets."

"Touché."

Blake pushed a spongy cube of cheese around on her plate. "Psychologically, it's interesting to me that someone would find it more palatable to believe in aliens than natural disaster."

"Aliens are out of your control," offered Kent.

"But wouldn't that make it worse?"

I considered this. "They come from trees, right? So part of him is making the link. Aliens are always just a symbol anyway."

Crystal, who'd been silent most of the evening, pushed her plate two inches forward. "I don't think it matters why he took his family out of here. Just that he did it."

My mother, sitting to Crystal's immediate left, reached out and took her hand. My mother felt terrible about her being here— she felt terrible about all of us being here, but especially Crystal. She'd been through a lot. Crystal's father had been abusive, and she'd left home when she was fourteen, getting her GED at sixteen

and putting herself through college. She was somehow both strong
and fragile. When my brother married her, I hadn't been able to
shake the sense that, although we were only two years apart, Kent's
experience growing up must have been fundamentally different
than mine.

Crystal stood.

"If a place itself is insane," she said, "can there be an insane
reason to leave it?" She left the table to join her daughter in the
living room, leaving the rest of us to acknowledge the truth of her
statement. It was pretty heavy-handed but not entirely unfair.

"Anyway," I said.

My mother, still holding the large bud, put it to her nose and
inhaled deeply.

"It's sweet," she said. "I mean, it smells sweet."

"You were right," Kent said, looking at me. "Brock's a *kind*
man."

"That's the pot calling the kettle black."

"It was just a token of his affection," said my mother.

We all looked at Blake. She gritted her teeth, didn't like to be
put on the spot like this, but would usually deliver. "A parting gift
before he blew this joint?"

We heard the door slam, and turned to see that Crystal
had taken Olivia and left through the front door. My brother
stood, apologizing, and went after her. My mother began to say
something but was interrupted by a sharp popping noise followed
by a receding, crackling hiss. I looked at the radio, the harmless
brown box of it, and wondered what we'd let into our home.

"Hey," my mother said, twisting in her seat to see it. "Pipe
down."

DAY 13

KENT WAS ON THE roof with his shingle scraper, and though we'd taught ourselves the technique together just that morning his execution was already expert. He rammed the rod forward and up, and the shingles seemed to fall away easily, cooperatively. Mine suffered from separation anxiety, the nails screaming as they were yanked from the plywood underneath. In the distance a helicopter made broad circles above what may have been downtown Ballard, filming. I looked farther south and counted one, two, three, four others in sight.

"This must be what it's like to live in a ghetto," I said.

"Yeah," said Kent without looking up. "I'm sure it's exactly like this."

I sent the scraper back up underneath a row of shingles and pried. "I used to come up here and lie in the sun once in a while. I had to bring the hose up to scare away crows."

"Mom got attacked a few weeks ago—she tell you?"

"By a crow? No. Like, dive-bombed?"

"Drew blood."

"Jesus, no, she didn't mention it."

I peeked over the front edge of the house to where my mother was standing in the yard, looking down.

"You got attacked by a crow?" I called. "Why didn't you tell me?"

She'd decided that morning to, as she put it, "tame the yard," and had been out front all morning pulling up weeds.

"I told your brother."

"Right."

She looked up at me. "I'm sorry, Blake. I will make a point of telling you next time a crow pecks me in the head."

Fred came out of his house with a pair of clippers and began pruning the rhododendron beside his front porch. A few days ago, men from Weyerhaeuser had been canvassing the neighborhood regarding rhododendron growth and, when permitted, spraying each plant with something they explained would protect it from an invasive species of worm. Since then Fred's rhody had gone through a growth spurt.

"We're going to tame the yard!" I called.

He looked over, expressionless. "You are, are you?"

"Is that sarcasm I hear?" asked my mother.

"Not at all, Rose."

I'd often wondered what our family's reputation had been on the block. The overly permissive parents with kids running wild? The remote, cerebral family who left their property to devalue in pursuit of tragic professions like public policy and social justice? The technicians always experimenting with the newest parenting techniques? It all stuck.

"Well, you'll see," my mother said. "I've got big plans for this property."

Fred nodded. His listless clipping made me suspect he'd come out just to listen in on our conversation.

"Ever been attacked by a crow?" I called.

He rested his clippers on top of the dense bush. "I was attacked by a chicken once."

My brother paused to listen.

"It was guarding a gas station I was supposed to tear down. This was in Kyrgyzstan. They keep chickens as watchdogs over there—crazy, muscular birds that can take out a snake. The family who ran the station was gone, but they'd left this chicken. We were slated to cap the tanks and remove the pumps, so I'm walking the property and the thing comes flying off the top of a stack of tires, right at my head, screaming like some kind of…It scared the shit out of me."

"What happened?" asked Kent.

"My translator whacked it with a shovel and we ate it for lunch."

"No shit."

"Little fucker was tough as nails. Sour, too."

My brother had always respected Fred. He was a single man, never married, and I think Kent saw something brave or righteous in that.

I wedged my scraper into the gutter and eased my way down to the ladder. "Want anything?" I asked Kent.

He gestured at the roof. "Yeah," he said. "Help."

From inside the sound of shingles being pried up seemed deeper, almost painful. I could feel it in my teeth. Blake was reading *USA Today*—the only major paper we could get—and the rate at which she was turning pages suggested she wasn't actually reading. A large tangle of shingles fell past the window, briefly blotting out the blue sky. Blake put the paper down.

"Two," she said.

I yawned. "Two what?"

"There are two articles in the entire paper about what's going on here. And one of them? A style piece called 'Must-Packs For

Your Next Evac.' I'm not kidding. I wish I was kidding, but I'm not."

She showed me the article. The picture showed a suitcase laid out flat and filled with neatly labeled clothes, a photo album, and a first-aid kit. The caption reminded readers that emotional needs were just as important as physical ones. I put my head in Blake's lap and looked up her nose. "Are you saying you wouldn't pack your photo album?"

She looked down and pretended to gather saliva.

"That's *USA Today*." I sat up. "What do you expect?"

"Excellence!"

My phone rang: *Money*, by the Beatles.

Blake got up and found my phone in the pocket of a jacket slung over the back of a chair. "I hate that ring," she said. She tossed it to me and left the room. It was yoga time.

"Nancy," I said, "let me guess."

"You'd never."

Nancy was my agent, and it had been a relatively thankless job so far—the one book she'd been able to place, *Forecast*, hadn't done well, had barely sold, and the one I'd written since had been "too personal." It was on her recommendation that I'd begun the current book—a return to the big, sprawling fantasia of the first.

"Let's see," I said. "They're pulping all remaining copies of *Forecast*, and I'm barred from ever entering Barnes & Noble again."

"Blake."

"I won the *Guardian* award for worst sex scene, and I'm barred from ever entering my wife again?"

"Ew—Blake."

"How's New York?"

"Hot and shitty. Listen."

"Okay."

"The book has sold out, and they're printing another run, a big run. Are you sitting down? A hundred thousand, Blake. The whole Seattle thing has turned your book into a best-fucking-seller. The blogosphere can't get enough."

I looked down at Blake's copy of *USA Today*. The cover showed Kermit the Frog watching Fozzie Bear smoking a joint with the headline "Green With Envy."

"That's funny, because Blake was just saying there wasn't any coverage about it."

"Blake, are you listening to me?"

"Yes, I'm listening. It hasn't hit yet."

"Well, let it hit. Do you want me to shut up?"

"No, keep talking. I need something to go on in the background while I enter a trancelike state."

Nancy started telling me about an interview the *Times* wanted to do, but her voice receded as I entered a trancelike state. My heart began beating faster and I watched my mother enter through the front door and walk past me into the dining room, then into the kitchen, then return to stand in front of me with a glass of water. She cocked her head and asked if I was okay. She asked again.

I nodded. "I'm fine."

"You're what?" Nancy stopped. "What's that supposed to mean?"

"It's Nancy," I said.

Another shadow flitted across the room—more shingles falling. My mother took a long drink of water.

"It's my mother," I said.

"Blake," Nancy said, "stay with me."

"I'm with you."

"You need to get back here."

"I can't," I said. "Not right now."

"You don't think Kent can take care of your mother for a little while without you?"

"No. I mean, sure, but that's not the point."

"The point is that you're on the verge of a serious career breakthrough here. Scrap that: the breakthrough has *already happened*. So now you're needed. You need to stand by your book."

Blake emerged from the bathroom wearing her leotard and brought her yoga mat out to the back porch. I knew she'd be happy—she'd be overjoyed—but I also knew I wouldn't tell her right away. I wanted to hold onto this information, this news. I wouldn't tell anyone, not for a while.

"Blake?"

"I'm here."

"That's the problem. I read something about cell providers pulling out. Is that happening? Are cell phones going to die? I need to be able to get in touch with you."

"Well, they've pledged to keep the data centers running. So it's just the towers that—"

"Blah blah. Listen: think about it. You could come out for, I don't know, a few days. I'm also going to try and get you interviews out there. Tell me you would do an interview in town."

"I'd do an interview in town."

"Gee, thanks. I've gotta go. Pour yourself a drink. Or whatever it is you're drinking these days. Sparkling water?"

"Nancy."

"Yes."

"Thank you."

"I'm hanging up now. Think interview."

"I'm thinking. Hey, tell your brother I said hello."

"Are you kidding? I haven't seen Mitch for weeks. He's deep undercover or some shit."

Click.

I gazed out at Blake, who was in a pose I didn't recognize. There was a dull thump against the picture window, and I went over to examine the glass, thinking a shingle had hit. In the driveway, nearly camouflaged by a pile of dark debris, was a small brown bird, a sparrow of some sort. It twitched, fluttered its wings, stopped moving.

This would change everything for me. This was what I'd wanted, what I'd hoped would happen. It's what I secretly wrote for during dark times when I couldn't write for myself. But instead of feeling good, feeling vindicated, I began to feel anxious. Once they begin to take your book seriously, they begin to take *you* seriously. I knew how it worked. I'd seen it happen over and over again to writers back in New York. One moment they'd be a struggling writer and the next, after some break or other, poof, they're an "expert" on something vaguely related to their book, forced to hold forth on topics they have no business in. A book about hippies? Op-eds and essays in the *Times* about the new antiwar movement. Primary character a chef? Let's hear you weigh in on *Fresh Air* about the popularization of molecular gastronomy, or write a column for *Rolling Stone* about touring the drive-thrus of Iceland. Now I would be an expert. An expert on decline, collapse. On the future! The more I thought about it, the more anxious I became. Being forced to opine about the general social, political, or cultural goings-on made me want to puke. I knew nothing. I had nothing to offer; I was psychologically insulated from reality, and the only thing I could even remotely claim to know was myself. It was staggering to me that people had time for anything else, that they could read the right books and watch the right documentaries and be in the right place at the right time and that they could actually discuss these things with authority and aplomb. People whose primary vocation was making things up! People who specialized in the particularization of universals, asked to generalize on particulars! This was a nightmare. Was there a way around it? Was there nothing I could do? Could I just do nothing?

"Thanks for all your work out there," said Kent.

Startled, I turned around to see my brother standing in the doorway. He was drenched in sweat, filthy, and his right hand was bleeding.

"Sorry," I said. "I was on the phone with Nancy."

"Did she have any roofing tips?"

"Just checking in."

"Am I going to get any more help from you today?"

"Absolutely. I'll get you a Band-Aid."

DAY 14

I woke up with the alarm, having been inspired by my conversation with Nancy to set one. I wanted to get up, to write in the morning like I used to, like I was out of the habit of doing. Especially if I'd be resisting interviews, I reasoned, I needed a great follow-up to *Forecast*. Something for the fans. Similar but different. A book that didn't seem to turn away from my "voice" but that felt like an evolution, a maturation. Fortunately, I'd begun just such a book before the evacuation, and though I'd put it down since returning to Seattle, I had the sense that it wouldn't be too difficult to pick up where I'd left off. The radio was set to a classic rock station but it was just the DJ talking. She kept saying she was going to take me through the hour, then playing a clip of car horns. Blake waved one arm around in the air as if struggling to close a curtain. It dropped back into bed once I pulled the plug.

"Sleep in for both of us," I said.

In the kitchen, Crystal was pouring herself a glass of water and Olivia sat at the counter eating apple slices with crumbled blue cheese.

"Your cheese is moldy," I said, rubbing my eyes.

"It's supposed to be moldy," she said.

"They just say that so you'll eat it."

"Mom!"

"He's just joking with you," said Crystal. "That's the way Uncle Blake connects with people."

"Your mother is right," I said. "Let this be a lesson to you, Olivia: never joke about cheese."

Crystal rinsed her glass and set it to dry. "Are you almost ready, sweetie?"

Olivia nodded, stuck an entire apple wedge into her mouth, and slipped down from the stool. She held her hand over her mouth, then, after seeing her mother wasn't looking, opened it to show me.

"Mmm," I said. "I love moldy see-food."

Olivia giggled.

I opened the coffee grinder to pour in some beans. There were grounds caked below the blade, and I banged it against the counter to set them free.

Crystal grabbed her purse from the counter. "Well, we're off. See you tonight."

I poured the dislodged coffee grounds onto a paper towel. We'd run out of filters, as had the store. There would be no more filters. "Seriously," I said, managing my grounds, "where the hell do you go every day?"

Crystal cocked her head as if making a decision. There was beauty in her. She reached for Olivia's hand, and together they walked out onto the back porch and down the steps.

I ground some more coffee, poured it onto the paper towel with the old grounds, and then carefully put the towel into the coffeemaker, folding the corners down so they wouldn't interfere with the water. I thought about where I'd been in my book before putting it down. The story was about a public relations war between two self-help seminar gurus, narrated by a double agent, a mole within one of the seminars sent to discover whether a carefully guarded technology called Existencelastic Macrobial Foreshortening truly resulted in "transpositional epiphany," as the brochure said it would. If I remembered correctly, the mole had been driving up the gravel path to the retreat's offices when he thought he saw, running through the woods, someone who looked exactly like himself. He'd stopped his car, opened the door, and stepped out. The figure in the woods, too, had stopped and turned around. And suddenly the perspective had shifted, leaving the reader in the mind of the person running—a version of the mole who'd experienced the Foreshortening process, had gone AWOL, and was now being chased by agents from the very guru who'd sent him: an egomaniacal hirsute barber named Shya Scanlon.

I poured myself a cup of coffee and sipped at liquid too hot to have taste.

"I mean," I said aloud, "where the fuck do you go from *there*?"

I suddenly felt apathetic. Nonetheless, I was committed to finishing the book. Or, at least, to continuing. To "going on."

There was a knock at the door, and I hurried over before the noise could wake up Blake. It was Happy Edelstein.

"Hey, Hap," I said. "Today's the day, isn't it. Wow. You know, Brock just took off—"

"Have you seen Alice?"

"I got up like ten minutes ago."

"Last night, maybe? She disappeared. We think she ran away."

Happy's face was pale and his eyes were bloodshot; his hair, normally so carefully combed, was a greasy mess. He was a thin man, cave-chested and gaunt, but he looked almost intimidating just then.

"Shit, Hap. I haven't."

"We've been packing, you know. Today was the day, early. Last night she said she was coming down here to say goodbye."

He teetered on one foot, looking over my shoulder into the living room.

"Happy, seriously, I haven't seen her. Do you want to look around? We wouldn't take in a, what, seventeen-year-old girl?"

Happy squinted at me, sizing me up. "Sixteen," he said.

"See—she'll turn up, won't she? I just can't imagine…Hey, let me go ask Kent. Okay?"

Happy just stared.

I climbed the stairs, thinking maybe I should be running. Walking might make a suspicious man more suspicious, but running might cause more alarm than necessary—I truly did assume she'd turn up—so I compromised by taking two stairs at a time. Alice would come back, I thought. No doubt she was secreting herself away with some boyfriend, saying her goodbyes.

Kent lay nearly sideways in the king-size bed he'd been sharing with his wife and daughter. He looked up at me as I entered the room.

"I haven't seen her," he said.

"You heard?"

He nodded to the window, which was open.

"Well, shit."

Kent rolled over. "There's nothing even remotely so resourceful as a teenage girl."

"Great," I said. "That's what I'll tell Happy."

"What's going on?" my mother called from across the hall.

"Alice. Have you seen her?"

"Oh dear," she said. Moments later she was following me back downstairs, where she went straight to the front door and tried to console Hap. "It's just what they do," she said, and thumbed in my direction. "Believe me, this one ran off every chance he could get. But then he'd get hungry."

I nodded, spreading my arms as if to say, *See? Here I am, at my mother's house!*

"She'll come home."

Happy turned slowly, faced the day, took a deep breath. He walked down the three steps to street level and without another word made for Fred's. What else could he do? I had to assume that variations of this scene were playing out all over the city—teenagers tempted to see an evacuated city as a giant parent-free playground. My mother was right, after all. I would have done the same. It was scary to think about Olivia disappearing, though she was far too young to adopt any but her parents' perspective on such major events. Still, it was somehow comforting to be reminded that other perspectives were possible. Not just possible: manifest.

In the front yard, my mother had cleared out a lot of the weeds and had laid down stones to mark partitions. A few of them formed a semicircle below a holly tree she'd been threatening to cut down for years. The tree was beautiful but had grown to interfere with the power line running the house. It now wore a blue *X* of painter's tape.

"What's that for?" I asked.

"Sythia."

That evening Blake and I took a walk. It was still hot, but a breeze had picked up and was moving cool, salty air in from the Sound. We passed the Edelstein house and saw them sitting on a standing porch swing, looking solemn. I waved and said we'd keep an eye out. Alice's mother, Josie, brought her hands up to her face. Happy gave me a dirty look before turning to comfort her.

"Nice one," Blake said under her breath.

"Well, shit."

Two squirrels ran across the street and swirled up the trunk of a fat oak. We watched them chase each other insanely, chirping like birds.

"They're probably pretty stoked about the evacuation," I said.

"I doubt it. No more free handouts. Why haven't I met those people?"

"The Edelsteins? I don't know. Actually, I do know. Well, I don't know, maybe I know."

"Wow."

"Well, there was this thing."

"Oh my God, don't tell me you—"

"No, Jesus! The story is, I'd just heard from Nancy about selling *Forecast* and I was visiting my mom—remember? I was coming back from the store with a bottle of wine, and Alice was looking at me through the window and I waved, and then I saw an un-burst water balloon in the yard, and I picked it up and chucked it at her. You know, it was just a playful thing. But the window broke. It was an old single-paned piece of glass, and it shattered. Josie came to the window—this was in the afternoon, and Happy wasn't home—and…"

"What? And what?"

"I can't believe you thought I slept with Josie."

"I was just giving you shit."

"No, you weren't."

"Tell the story, Blake."

"So Josie comes to the window and asks me what happened and I kind of stammer it out, and then run up the lawn and get to the front door, and she meets me there and she opens the door and we look over at Alice, who's still shocked. She's not hurt, and we both burst into laughter. I think it was just out of relief, you know, but the minute we begin to laugh Alice snaps out of it and starts to cry.

"I'm apologizing, and somehow I tell her about the book, and Josie's just floored, like she's never met an author, and she disappears into the kitchen and comes back with this bottle of champagne, and we basically proceed to get drunk. We drank her champagne and opened the wine I bought. We didn't even clean up the glass.

"So Happy comes home and there's his wife, drunk on the couch with a, well, not a stranger exactly, but there was broken glass all over the floor..."

We walked for a little bit in silence. Blake was obviously irritated, and the more I thought about it, the more I worried that it had actually been some kind of trespass.

"I can't believe you didn't tell me about this," Blake said at last.

"Tell you what, though? I mean, nothing happened!"

"What do you mean nothing happened? You broke a window, nearly hurting a young girl, then got drunk with her mother."

We stopped at a corner to let a moving truck pass. A young boy waved at us through the window, then flipped us off.

"Well," I said, "nothing untoward."

"But it could have. It was a charged moment. It was the kind of moment that can easily lead to something happening."

"So you admit nothing happened!"

"I would have told you about it. Actually, I wouldn't have thrown the balloon, nor would I have gotten drunk in some strange man's house, alone. But if I did, I would have told you about it."

"Well, I did tell you about it, technically."

"Just now?"

"Yeah, you know, isn't that proof that I wasn't hiding anything?"

"I'm not saying you're hiding something."

"What *are* you saying, then?"

"I don't know, Blake. That you're careless?"

"I'm careless now."

"You put yourself in a potentially dangerous situation, and you didn't even notice how potentially dangerous it was! I'd say that's careless."

"So now we're assuming that it was potentially dangerous. Was I, like, moments away from fucking her? Please, tell me."

"Who knows? Who knows what would have happened if Happy hadn't come home."

There was no way to win this argument. I picked up a rock from the front yard of an abandoned house and threw it through a window. Blake stopped and looked at me, stunned. What was I trying to say? I didn't know, exactly, but it felt good.

"Hey!"

We turned to see a man step out onto his front porch across the street. He was wearing a bright pink jumpsuit and holding a baseball bat. There was a figure behind him, too, but I couldn't make it out. Spouse? Another man with a bat? He stared at us questioningly, trying to look tough and almost succeeding, probably the way I would have had someone thrown a rock through Brock's window.

"Let's keep walking," said Blake calmly. "Please."

"Sorry," I called to the man.

The day had ended without me noticing, but with Blake walking three steps ahead I became acutely aware of the darkness. The city had shut down power to two-thirds of the streetlights—an effort at conservation that, in light of the spike in crime, had been met with fierce opposition from both neighborhood watch groups and national public health associations like WIC. I knew we were in greater danger statistically, but it was only walking under the odd streetlight that I felt exposed. I noticed we were taking a route that didn't take us by the Edelsteins. Was Blake doing this intentionally? I hoped so. I liked to think she wanted to avoid the site of our disagreement. It was a small act of grace that gave me hope. Blake had once pointed out a story to me on some blog about a married couple who, every year on their anniversary, swallowed their wedding rings. Fishing the bands out of their shit the next day, they claimed, was a symbolic act. Blake had found it utterly disgusting, but I'd secretly been touched. Of course, I hadn't told her my true feelings and had made a big show of my agreement. But clearly I hadn't learned.

When we arrived at the house I tried to get a look at the Edelsteins' front porch but couldn't see it. In my mind, they were both still sitting there, on the bench swing, waiting for Alice. I felt terrible for having made Josie cry, and I felt terrible for having spent that afternoon with her, drunk. And for the first time, I realized Alice wouldn't be coming home.

DAY 15

DETERMINED TO KNOW WHAT the fuck they were doing, I'd been waiting for Crystal and Olivia in my mother's old Escort for almost an hour—enough time to reverse my decision, reverse it again. Hearing about the success of my book triggered something in me, somehow, and made me feel unimpeachable. But I felt a bit creepy sitting there, frankly, and because I didn't even understand my own motives the creep factor stuck. By the time they came out and got into their car, I'd decided to go through with it half because I didn't want to run into anyone on my way back inside and have to explain myself. They pulled onto the street and fifteen minutes later I was following them up the north side of Queen Anne Hill.

My brother had lived on Queen Anne, had fallen in with the philanthropist, wine-tasting crowd. Nibblers, he'd call them. He used to complain about working downtown only to come home to a view of his office.

"It's like being a plumber," he said to me once, "and having windows that face a sewage treatment plant."

"You're comparing Seattle to a sewer, you realize."

"*Au contraire*," he said. "I'm comparing it to a plant."

During the ride out of Ballard I tried to think of something to say to Crystal should I be caught and confronted. My first thought was to say she'd left Olivia's windbreaker, a thought which got me several blocks before I realized that for this to have even the faintest hint of truth I would have had to make some attempt to get her attention on the drive instead of keeping a safe distance behind. That, and I'd have to have the windbreaker. I then briefly flirted with honesty, but "to see where you go" was obviously dodging the question.

Queen Anne was an aristocratic enclave initially served by trollies that were hauled up by a descending weight on tracks beneath a street on the south, downtown side of the hill. I used to break into the tunnel through a manhole to do drugs, and I'd always thought the whole thing was ripe for metaphor: A rich neighborhood with inhabitants who required an underground system to reach it. Judging by the absence of even the slightest sign of life, reaching it was clearly no longer a priority for anyone except Crystal.

When she turned down the street they used to live on, I pulled over.

"Wow," I said. "Okay."

Sure enough, they pulled into the driveway of their old house.

After they disappeared inside, I crossed to the opposite side of the street and made my way down the block, scampering through overgrown yards from house to house. I figured my best bet would be to set up camp in a house across from theirs, and fortunately one of these had been under construction. Long white strips of plastic sheeting hung from a half-demolished wall, and I snuck through it into what had once been a kitchen. Looking for stairs to the second floor, I took a hall toward the back of the house and into what looked like a library. Books were strewn about and the fireplace even seemed to have been recently used. I took a poker and poked through the ashes: more books. A partially burned spine revealed the volume to be an Encyclopedia Britannica,

Eleventh Edition, EVA to FRA. I tried to think of what would have been in it. Evangelism, of course. Evolution. France. There was a standing chalkboard against one wall, and on it was written the word "Day" and then, in a spot that bore the chalky smudges of multiple erasures, the number 15.

"Fifteen days," said someone behind me.

I turned quickly, slipped on a magazine, and fell into a pile of paperbacks.

"Fuck," I said from the ground. "Sorry, I was just…"

The man who'd spoken was in late middle age, slight, and unshaven, his brown beard laced with silver hair. He was wearing an oxford shirt and crumpled tie. He was not threatening.

"No worries at all." He smiled at me and took a step backward. "I'm Bertolt. Call me Bert."

I got up and stood uneasily by an empty bookshelf. "Hello, Bert," I said. "Blake."

"Sorry to have startled you."

"Sorry for the intrusion."

"Nonsense! I'm happy for the company."

I looked around, trying to avert my eyes from the fireplace. I felt it might be an embarrassing thing to acknowledge the burning of books.

"I'm not squatting," Bert assured me.

"Okay."

"This is actually my house. I'm a history professor at Seattle Pacific University. This is my house, and fifteen is the number of days since my family left. Seattle Pacific University has been relocated to I don't know where. All the students: gone. You know what I think? I think they would have left independent of the evacuation. They would have left because that's simply what people do. They seek freedom. They move forward. *Away* from history. How, I ask you, can one be a teacher with no students? They don't mention that in the handbook."

I nodded. "I'm sorry to hear about your family."

"Who?"

"Your family?"

"Let me tell you a story."

"Actually," I said, "I've got to go meet someone, so…"

Bert considered this, running his fingers through his beard and slightly swaying as though keeping time.

"How about if I just give you the gist," he said finally.

"An overview?"

"A moral."

"Deal."

"Okay, let's see. It's probably something like: illumination can lead to blindness."

I squinted my eyes and cocked my chin, pretending to capture the full weight of his words.

"Well," he said, "it's more impressive if you go through all the particulars."

I nodded, then hurried down the hall and out through the plastic in the kitchen. I crossed over to the house next door to Crystal's, and looked back to see Bertolt peering through the window at me, staring out from the damaged container of his life. He waved.

Exoskeleton, I thought.

He hadn't tried to stop me, or call out for me, or in any way interfere with my sudden departure, and though I was glad he hadn't, it also seemed to amplify the sadness of his situation. The bald resignation of it. From my spot in the neighbor's yard I had the same view Kent had grown to hate: downtown Seattle standing up smartly to the left, and on the right, the placid Puget Sound patrolled by a lone police boat puttering slowly past the once-busy piers. The windows of Kent's house facing me were to the foyer, the dining room, the kitchen, and the family room, and at first I didn't see any movement.

I thought about Bertolt's small, lonely wave. I'd once been to see a performance of Bertolt Brecht's *Threepenny Opera*, and in it actors marched across the stage between scenes with large signs indicating the play's themes and plot points. Brecht had insisted on producing "epic" rather than "dramatic" theater. He wanted to highlight the artifice. He wanted to fight the suspension of disbelief. Standing there behind a hedge, I imagined Crystal popping up into a window, holding a card. What would it have said?

When she did appear, she was holding a plate. She'd apparently been in the kitchen the whole time, hidden between two windows, and she walked from the kitchen into the dining room, put the plate on the table, and called Olivia, who came to the table and sat with her back to me. Crystal walked back to the kitchen and I cautiously moved to stand directly under the window.

"Do you want some milk, Olly?"

"Yes, please."

"Another pancake?"

"No, thank you."

They didn't speak much, giving away nothing of their reason for visiting the house, and after eating they went out front. I slunk toward the back of the house, thinking I'd just hide until they left, but they didn't leave. They brought out a bucket and some soap and pulled a hose out to the car. I stayed another two hours. After washing the car, they spent some time on the back porch, then went into the family room, where, from what I could tell, they played a board game. I finally left on account of the heat and my own hunger, and it wasn't until I pulled up in front of my mother's house again that I understood what they were doing.

My mother was in the front yard, and stood to greet me.

"Where've you been?" she said.

"Just driving around. Have you seen Kent?"

"He's giving me gas."

"Mom."

"He's around back."

I looked at the work she'd done. The yard was almost entirely clear of weeds, and she'd moved some dirt into a small berm by the fence. "This is exciting."

"There was a man here asking about you this morning."

"What did he want?"

My mother frowned, shook her head. "Unclear. Information? He just asked where you were. He complimented my garden."

"What was his name?"

"Oh, rats. I was afraid you'd ask that. Blake, sweetie, I didn't ask. I'm sorry, but he threw me off somehow and I didn't think of it until he'd left."

"Well, what did he look like?"

"He was handsome, smartly dressed. Suit and tie, black."

"God damn it," I said.

"Not the man. The suit and tie were black. He was actually quite fair-skinned. He looked like a Mormon."

I left my mother and headed down the driveway. She called after me, apologizing again for having not asked the man's name. Blake was standing in a window as I passed, mouthing the words,

"Where have you been?" I held up a finger and went out back, where I found Kent pouring the contents of a ten-gallon gas can into the unused oil reservoir that stood in a small shed at the southeast corner of the house.

"I know this looks dangerous," he said, "and that's because it is, kind of."

"Do you know what your family has been doing every day?"

Kent stopped pouring and put the gas can down. "They've been going to my house."

"And, uh, okay, so you know."

I was in fact surprised that he knew. It didn't seem to line up with the kind of pragmatism he championed. Then again, he might not approve.

"I suggested it," he said.

Then again, he might have suggested it.

"Don't you think it's unhealthy?"

"I don't know, Blake. What's the appropriate response to this situation?"

"Point taken. But you know, it's just—"

"We're leaving, Blake."

Along the fence beside the oil tank were vine roses my father had salvaged from a job site years ago and planted for my mother's birthday. One had shot off the top of the fence and was reaching out, up, bending under its own weight, away from the house. I couldn't look Kent in the eyes, so I turned and headed back the way I'd come.

"Blake," he called after me. "Don't say anything to Mom."

The phone rang four times before Nancy picked up. I'd walked down to the corner for privacy and was sitting on the front steps of a house I hadn't been to since childhood. A drunk driver had once jumped the curb and slammed into the living room in the middle of the night, and though the house had long since been repaired, evidence of the crash lingered in the form of a large, car-stopping cement pole topped by a spray of rusting rebar. I'd thought the project was unfinished until I realized that the whole world was.

"Sorry," she said. "I was on another call."

"Nancy, here's the deal. I haven't told my family about the book. I don't want them freaking out and losing focus, because there's a lot to do here, and they need to stay focused, okay?"

The only reason I had to lie to Nancy was the simple fact that I didn't quite understand the real reason I was keeping the news from everyone. It was certainly not something an agent would understand.

"Do what you need to do, Blake. Hey, I'm glad you called because—"

"Wait, I'm not done. The reason I tell you this is because I want my family to be left alone. I don't want you sending people to my house. I'll do interviews, okay? But I want advance notice, and they'll be conducted elsewhere."

"Blake, Blake, first of all, fuck you. I'm over here making things happen for you, and you're what, complaining about your privacy? Please. Second of all, what on earth are you talking about?"

"I'm talking about a reporter coming here, to *my mother's house*, and asking her about me."

"Well, I don't know anything about that."

"Have you been talking to anyone?"

"Yes, in fact I—"

"See, well, when you do, be sure to tell them not to—"

"Blake, when did this happen?"

"The reporter?"

"Yes, when."

"Today, maybe an hour or two ago."

"Well, then it couldn't have been me."

"But you said—"

"Remember when I said I was on the phone when you called?"

"…"

"That was King 5 news, an NBC affiliate. And yes, we were talking about you, and yes, they want to do an interview, but I hadn't spoken to them until just then, and they're the first people I've spoken with…and you're welcome."

I could hear street sounds in the background, and imagined her walking down 27th near her office. I knew that street well. I pictured the well-mannered, boutique lunch spot called *Service* she'd taken me to a few times. *Service.* I pictured the stupid club across the street that, though closed by day, was the site of a stereotypical assortment of comings and goings that Nancy loved to describe: women in tortured furs stepping out of Hummer limos and shielding their eyes from the sun as they were chaperoned through the heavy, iron doors.

"How's the club?" I asked.

"Cut the shit, Blake. What's going on with you?"

"I'm sorry. My brother is leaving. Kent and his family are going to leave us—they're going to leave my dying, cancerous fucking mother."

"Shit, I'm sorry. That sucks."

This was not Nancy's department. She waited patiently for me to change the subject.

"Well, what's the deal with NBC?" I asked.

"It's for Monday."

"What's today?"

"Wednesday."

"I can do it."

"It's at the studio. No one will be stalking your family."

"I'd like to make some feeble joke here to let you know I'm trying not to take myself too seriously, but I can't think of anything because I'm taking myself too seriously."

"Don't sweat it, kid. I'll take a rain check."

I began walking back home, and from the corner I could see Happy and Josie talking to my mother. They saw me, waved, and headed up the street. When I reached the house my mother was holding a flier. It was a picture of Alice, a phone number, and the words: *Please Call Us. We Love You.* My mother seemed shaken.

I took the page from her hands and gently wrapped my arms around her. I could feel the unevenness of her chest against my body, her breathing and her warmth. I tried to hold her tightly but without squeezing. Her soft, silver hair smelled like the earth she'd been working with, and I inhaled deeply, held it in, held my breath.

DAY 16

AFTER READING OVER THE book I'd begun before everything fell to shit, I felt like abandoning the project. The fantastical plot and airy themes that before felt somehow noble in their abstraction now felt merely escapist. I was worried that the only literature it made sense to pursue was that of witness, and I knew exactly nothing about witness literature. I could think of a couple books. *Night*, of course, by Wiesel. But I hadn't read that since high school. And *The Gulag Archipelago*, by whoever, which I simply hadn't read.

"Mom," I called. "Mom?"

"I'm on the back porch."

I went to find her standing arms akimbo, looking out over the yard. It would plainly be an even bigger challenge than the front, with its baroque tangle of weeds and overgrown implants. I could tell she was intimidated.

"Would *Uncle Tom's Cabin* be considered witness literature?"

My mother turned to me and frowned.

"Please don't stop talking to me," I said.

"I seem to remember putting you through school."

"I think I'm going to write something different. Journalism maybe, but also autobiographical. Just personal observations and reflections, you know? Something that's true for a change."

I looked over her shoulder at the swirling mass of green beneath us. I knew a complex set of natural laws governed the behavior of all these plants, an organizing principle, but it was lost on me.

"I think I might want to be more *involved*," I said, "or something."

"You can do anything you set your mind to."

"Seriously, Mom? Bromides? I'm opening up here. Got anything more concrete?"

"Blake, I'm sorry. I'm just focused on this yard right now. I'm trying to visualize success."

"What does success look like?"

"Less."

A big orange cat leapt onto the back fence and surveyed the yard with us. I'd seen this cat around for the last week or so—clearly it had been left behind. Its tail flicked around for balance.

"Blake?"

"Mother."

"What's One Eyed Jacks?"

"Are. What *are*. There are two of them in the deck. I think hearts and spades."

"That's the other thing that man wanted to know. He asked if you ever went to One Eyed Jacks."

"One Eyed Jacks," I said. "That's from *Twin Peaks*."

"The television show?"

"Someone is fucking with me."

The cat had disappeared from its perch. I found it creeping through the yard, half hidden by the overgrown fauna. I pointed, and together we watched as it slithered along. I'd read somewhere that the most dangerous predators on the planet in terms of their success rate were common house cats. This one, however, was less fortunate; moments later a squirrel ran up a dogwood in Brock's yard. The cat followed as far as the tree, but then abandoned the project and began licking the base of its tail.

Kent passed the pasta. We still hadn't spoken much, but I'd passed beyond most of my anger and had begun to think about what this would mean for Blake and me. She was talking about her time scuba diving at the Great Barrier Reef—a subject that, despite the tacit theme of environmental degradation, always put her in a better mood. One could not, apparently, be down there surrounded by such a gorgeous, self-sustaining ecosystem and not maintain some hope about the fate of life on Earth.

"I'd be satisfied," said my mother, "with sustaining life in Seattle for a little while."

Blake shrugged. "We could learn something from coral, is all I'm saying."

"Doesn't coral reproduce asexually?" Kent asked. "Because that would be a deal-breaker for me."

"They can reproduce both sexually and asexually," Blake said.

"Oh, okay, then. I'm in."

I leaned back in my chair and smiled broadly. I would miss my brother terribly, I realized. I also realized I was staying. And I wasn't just staying for a while. I wasn't just staying longer. I was going to stay until the end. I felt a sob rise in my chest and had to close my eyes to keep from crying. Strangely, the feeling was not just sadness at the prospect of seeing my brother leave or of watching my mother die. It was not just fear at facing the likelihood of a tsunami. It was also relief.

"Blake's in another place," Kent said.

I opened my eyes. Everyone was staring at me.

"Everything all right, honey?"

"When I was probably sixteen," I said, "just about when I figured out I was the center of the universe, I used to close my eyes in bed and listen to Mom and Dad talk. I didn't think of it as eavesdropping at the time—I don't even think I listened much to what was being said—but it was astonishing to me how life simply carried on in my absence. Mom, you'd be talking about your work, or taxes, or the news, or whatever. You know, just unremarkable, quotidian whatever—the more banal the better, actually, because I'd lie there and listen and think, there's no way people would intentionally make this stuff up to fool me into thinking the world was real."

My mother was wearing a look in her eye I knew to be one of sly approval. It was a look she wore when some peculiar slant of perception tickled her.

"I'm so glad you decided to believe we exist," she said.

I leaned forward. "Yes, me too."

Kent began to bring the dishes into the kitchen, my mother disappeared into her bedroom at the back of the house, and Blake came around the table to sit beside me. She could see I'd had a moment of some kind, and was being tender. She quietly took my hand and ran her fingers along the inside of my arm, gently, softly, so that it gave me gooseflesh.

"Are you all right?" she asked, once we were alone.

"I'm sorry about yesterday."

Blake sighed. "Me too. So what's up?"

"It's just the book. I don't know. I look around me and... I've just spent so much time blocking everything out that I look around me and everything is barely recognizable."

Blake pushed her face close to mine and opened her eyes wide. "Everything?"

I nodded toward my brother, who was standing in front of the sink, running water drowning us out.

"I look at Kent: all of a sudden Mr. Fix-it. What can I do? I'm dead weight around here, and it's kind of painfully obvious."

"Wow," Blake said. "Two clichés in the same sentence!"

I pushed her away, and she giggled.

"Oh, come on, I'm sorry, I was kidding! Look, you're being a little dramatic, don't you think? You're here, and that's what matters. You're here."

Blake picked up a piece of carrot from the table and slipped it absentmindedly into her mouth.

"You're right," I said. "We're here."

I stood. It will be terrible, I was thinking, when I have to remind her of this conversation and use her words against her.

"I'm going upstairs for a second," I said. "There's a line I need to get down on paper before I forget."

"See? There we go."

I walked upstairs and paused at the top, listening to Blake tell Kent that I was feeling useless. Kent made some remark I couldn't quite hear, and Blake laughed. I went through my room and out the door to the roof. My mother had put the door there with the idea that a roof deck would follow it, but it would now forever open to the flat black tar of the addition. I crawled around to the side and up to the peak. The roof tiles crumbled slightly under me, sending a trickle of sticky grains down to the driveway below. The sun was disappearing behind the Olympics and the dying light caught along the brutal spikes of the monkey puzzle tree. A light breeze spun the pinwheel fixed to a house on the block behind ours. I watched for crows.

"Hey, up there—psst."

I looked down toward the voice, one I nearly didn't recognize, to see a small figure standing right at the edge of light cast from the living-room window. It was Alice. She was partially hidden by the overgrown vines along the fence separating our driveway from Brock's, peeking up and into the house as someone's movement flicked a shadow across her face.

"Your parents are worried," I said.

"Can I come up there with you?"

I pointed to the ladder—still up against the side of the house. "You're welcome to try," I said, "but you'll have to cross in front of that window, and if you're seen I can't promise my mother won't march you right to your folks' house. Or even Kent."

She waited for a moment and then moved swiftly up the ladder. On the roof, she crab-walked over and sat beside me. She was wearing cutoffs and an overlarge orange T-shirt with the word "Californication" on it in silver, puffy letters.

We sat for a while in silence while the sun set. "How would you describe that sunset?" I asked finally.

"I was just thinking that," Alice said. "Maybe, fleshy? Or no, a wound?"

"The sun set like an open wound."

"Yeah, see?"

"Well, I'm not sure that covers the range of colors we've got up there. Don't you think we should somehow indicate the spectrum?"

"Meh," she said. "Do one thing, and do it well."

"I like that."

To the south, vast darkening patches were eclipsing neighborhoods until now speckled with light.

"When I was probably about your age, I used to look out my window," I said, tapping the roof, "and wonder what was going on behind each spot of light. It was incredible to me that so many people were living their lives, doing whatever they were doing."

"Huh. I guess it's true what my dad's always saying."

"What's that?"

"Kids grow up faster these days."

"Ouch."

"Hey, isn't that your mom?"

I looked down to where Alice was pointing, and sure enough, my mother was carefully walking through the back yard. She looked over her shoulder, but only at the porch below us. I held my finger to my lips and we watched in silence as she pulled a cigarette out of her pocket and lit it. Seeing my mother sneak a smoke was fun, in a childish way, and Alice was stifling laughter. It was silly, I thought, that my mother would find it necessary to hide her behavior from us, her family. The thought that she'd expect us to get mad saddened me. This was *her* house, after all. We were all just guests. It wasn't like she was doing drugs.

Then it dawned on me.

"I don't think that's a cigarette," I whispered.

Alice looked at me with delight, and a laugh rose up inside her that she wasn't able to contain. It was a squeal, a bird call, really—a strange, nearly inhuman sound that, in the silence of the falling darkness, hung in the air like a warning shot. My mother looked up and I ducked, pulling Alice down with me, and we lay on our backs on the roof. The stars were coming out, spraying the sky with flecks of white paint. There were more of them, I noticed, now that the city had cut its level of light pollution, and I was reminded of my first days in New York, where it had always seemed to be night without sky.

Below us, I could hear my mother crunching back through the tall, dry weeds toward the house.

"Shoo!" she said. "Shoo, shoo!"

I peeked over the edge of the roof and saw her staggering around, arms raised and waving, trying to protect herself.

Part III

Part III

DAY 17

THE LARGE PALE WOMAN sitting beside me scrolled through an app affording her an endless supply of aphorisms for the train ride home. I looked without moving my head, straining to see what wisdom she'd been given. For the sake of authenticity, the lines appeared on a scroll, a weathered papyrus curled at the top and bottom. She read each one quickly, then, with a flick of her thumb, hurled it into the digital abyss.

The first one I could see clearly was from Dante. "The experience of this sweet life," it said.

Flick.

The next was from Woody Allen. "Seventy percent of success in life is showing up."

Flick.

The top quarter of the screen was a rotating banner, a flashy number tempting the woman to download a video game prominently featuring swords.

The next one was from Anonimous. "Life is too short to be sensible."

Anonimous?

The train shifted on the track and everyone swayed like anemones in a gentle undertow. I stood two stops later at Delancey, and the woman I'd been sitting beside glared up at me accusatorily. The features of her fat face seemed to have been pushed back into her head like the buttons in an overstuffed couch.

"They misspelled anonymous," I said, and left the J train into the damp, heavy air one story below the street. People swarmed around me without touching, as though intuitively synchronized—something I had yet to master—and I stopped, started, making my way to the stairs in erratic bursts. At the top I took in the sharp smell of trash and called Mitch Earl, the only person I knew in New York. Mitch was a private investigator and knew everything.

"Blake," he said, "make it quick."

"Was there some ancient Greek person named Anonimous with an I? Like a king or something?"

"A king with one eye?"

"The letter I. In the name. A sage? There's a quote I saw in this app, attributed to Anonimous with an I."

"Hey!" he screamed into the phone. "Hey, get the fuck over here! Blake, buddy, sorry, I'll call you back."

Click.

Traffic streamed toward the Williamsburg Bridge, and I walked against it for a couple of blocks to my apartment—an armpit above the backside of a Chinese restaurant famous for its tacky décor and expensive private rooms. The basement kitchen doors yawned grotesquely at me as I passed, exposing enormous bowls of raw, glistening meat. I walked up four flights to my apartment, opened my door, opened my fridge, opened a beer, opened my laptop, and stood in my kitchen as night fell, staring at the glowing screen.

I was in a productive phase.

Honking brought me to the window around 11 p.m. On the street below, two yellow cabs were trying to angle through the same single-lane space between a group of people and a delivery truck. Men in white were bringing boxes from the truck down the steps into the sweaty crotch of my building, and the men in the cabs were leaning out their windows, yelling in a foreign language. It was a wonderful scene—the type of culture clash I'd moved to this city for, just the type of smashed plate I'd hoped would shake me, wake me from my post-collegiate slump. I climbed onto the fire escape.

The group had begun responding to the honking with shouts for the drivers to stop, to shut the fuck up, to fucking go fuck themselves, until one of the men, clearly drunk, stood before the cars and began to piss in the street. The two cabbies got out of their cabs and chased the still-pissing man around the stalled traffic, screaming that they were going to call the cops, until the man's friends came to stand by him, arms crossed and cocky. The drivers shared a brief exchange and returned to their cars, then one by one backed down the street and drove off in different directions.

One of the men noticed me watching. He was wearing sunglasses and a yellow dress shirt with the collar popped.

"You get a good show?" he called up.

I waved.

"Fuck you!" he screamed.

I went back inside. I was in no condition to keep writing. I lay on the bed of my dark apartment, listening to Delancey, to the pulse, the ebb and flow of the city's tidal traffic. That's how it felt to me, like a tide. The city swelled with people a few times a day: in the morning, somewhere during midday, and then again in the evening. Different people, true, but they all worked in concert to create a feeling of high, rushing water moving through fixed architectures of iron and stone. My phone rang, and I let it. It would be my brother, my ex-girlfriend, or my mother. Were any of them worth getting up for? Maybe my brother. But he was least likely. It could also have been Mitch, I supposed. He'd invited me to a poker game that night, just around the corner, but I didn't have the energy. He always invited me out, tried to drag me from my natural state of isolation to places I would never have otherwise seen—one night an old speakeasy, another an illegal boxing match. Almost every event was inconvenient, sketchy, and vaguely embarrassing, and his goal seemed to be simply to let me take it in, to share with me the thrill of access. It was a city built around the granting and refusing of access, and I kept reminding myself that the entire point of coming to New York had been exactly that, to see what I could get into.

I reached down and felt around for my clothes.

The crowd I'd seen outside was gone. The delivery truck was gone, too, leaving Orchard an empty vein. I walked north, across Delancey and into the center of the neighborhood. It had been my mother after all. Her message was brief but she sounded grim—she'd either spoken to my father or gotten back a bad test result. Either way, I didn't want to hear it yet. I passed a bar Mitch called Motor Shitty, one of the first places he'd taken me. It was the kind of bar that gives mixed signals about how seriously it should be taken, and I thought Mitch enjoyed that ambiguity. He had a unique ability to sincerely shrug off the strange. I thought of the first time we met, how he'd simply shown up at my door, unannounced, with a six pack. He'd been asked by his father, who'd been asked by *my* father, to welcome me to the city. He'd explained this briefly, as though it happened all the time, and pushed past me to the kitchen.

"I haven't spoken to my father in over a year," I'd said. "I didn't even know he knew I was here."

I learned more over the course of the evening, slowly, as though Mitch were meting out a rare and precious resource that had to last us. Our fathers had met years ago in South America—my father working for a dubious plutocrat that Mitch's father, a private investigator like Mitch, was there to tail. They'd become unlikely allies, then friends, though Mitch said they hadn't seen each other in person since. This didn't sound like friendship to me, though it did shed light on my father's interpretation of distance. Perhaps it was because I felt so differently that I felt close to Mitch. He held some secret, I sensed, some connection to my father that I might never have.

On the corner of Ludlow and Rivington there were so many people in the street that a man riding a bicycle slowed to a stop and simply grabbed someone's shoulder to keep from falling over. Two tall, glossy black women seemed to be having an argument, but as I got closer to them I realized they were just excited.

"He looked good," one said, "but he didn't look *too* good."

"That's why he looked so good!" said the other.

They stepped over a girl sitting with her back against a trashcan in a puddle of vomit. Beside her stood a man talking on the phone and shaking his head.

"This is totally different," he said.

I went up Ludlow toward Houston.

I was very nearly finished being continually dumbstruck by New York, but I was nowhere near over the tempo, the pace that both accelerated my pulse and somehow enervated my spirit, turning me into a slack, buzzing thing. I texted Mitch to let him know I was near, and he said to tell the bartender I was there to see Goldie.

A bar back with the sentence "This is water" tattooed on his left forearm led me down a narrow staircase echoing with loud voices and laughter, and at the bottom we passed through an equally narrow hallway. It was hot and humid. Beer and booze boxes had been stacked against one wall, so we had to turn sideways to reach the door at the far side. The room was small with a low ceiling. Mitch sat with three other men around a mirrored table with empty beer bottles strewn underneath and a large pile of cocaine on top. They were playing Texas Hold 'Em but put down their cards as I came in. Mitch generally kept a conservative look appropriate for blending in anywhere, but the other men wore black jeans with crisply rolled cuffs and white t-shirts. Their faces were puffed up and splotchy, their eyes bloodshot. They'd been drinking hard and farting all night in this stuffy underground lair, and the smell was close, earthy and sweet.

"What's this?" one of them said—a bald, fair-skinned man with large, purple birthmarks covering his face. He bent forward and sucked a big line up his nose.

"My friend Blake," said Mitch, waving me into the room. "He's a writer."

The bar back tapped me on the shoulder and then disappeared back down the hallway. I smiled, hoping they wouldn't expect much of me. Moments later a toilet flushed and a door opened, and out walked a dwarf. He had dark hair, bushy eyebrows, and bright green eyes he used at me sharply.

"Goldie," he said, and held out his hand. "Mitch gives you the nod." He walked to the table, stood on a chair, and did a line. "Maybe you can help me settle something. Jake here is trying to convince me that memory is the same as experience, because it excites the same parts of the brain."

Jake's eyes widened. "They did studies."

"But I say that's bullshit," the dwarf continued, "because let me ask you something."

"Okay," I said.

"Can you have a memory of a memory?"

The man to Mitch's left raised his hand in a lazy wave. "I'm Ronnie."

I nodded. I tried to remember something, anything.

"Do you mean a memory of having a memory, or a memory of the memory itself?"

Goldie thought about this. "I like you," he said. "So what I'm thinking is, if you can't have a memory of it, it's not an experience. Which means it's, whatever, something else. A whole different type thing. I don't give a shit what's going on in the brain."

"What's going on in my brain," said the birthmarked man, "is pussy."

"Nice, Flynn," said the dwarf. "Here we are trying to have an intelligent conversation."

Flynn turned to me with a suddenly grave look. "All I have to say is, watch *La Jetée*. Tragedy is the only thing that separates memory and reality. Want a line?"

I considered his offer, and his face. There was something familiar about this man, I thought. Likely I'd seen him around the neighborhood. The marks on his face seemed to be some fungal bloom, and they called out to be read as one looks for shapes in a cloud. The other three men regarded me with blank expressions, but I couldn't read Mitch. He didn't seem judgmental, but he also didn't seem high.

"Blake is meeting my sister Nancy tomorrow," he said.

"Going to score yourself a big book deal, eh?" Goldie had picked his hand back up and was eyeing the flop. From my position I could see he had a low spade flush.

"Just an informational interview," I said. "Still, I'd better not. I'll probably be hung over as it is."

"Speaking of, wanna earn your keep?"

I supposed I probably did.

"Since you're standing, I mean. Go up, get a round of tequila from the bar. On the house. Jerry'll give you a tray."

On my way back upstairs I realized I should probably leave. The bar was almost empty, people dressed in black standing in small clusters like crows, and the bartender left one to join me as I leaned against the bar. He raised his eyebrows.

"Jerry?" I asked.

"What do they need?"

"Tequila," I said, and drew a circle on the bar.

He nodded and turned his back. The music throbbed loud and slow, making the whole place feel underwater, the people swaying tidal, their conversations drowned out. The subjects were doubtless the same subjects people were discussing in bars all over the city, all over the world. It didn't matter. It was an experience both highly specific and absolutely general. I wondered how I could work it into my book. It suddenly seemed like the ideal book would recreate all such moments, and in this way become entirely autobiographical while remaining a fantasy.

A woman walked toward me from a booth on the far wall, and I stood aside somewhat clumsily. Instead of ordering, though, she faced me at the bar, put on a thinking face, and leaned in close.

"My husband," she said, "said I could kiss anyone in this bar."

She was an inch taller than me, with short, slicked-back hair and a short black dress. I looked over her shoulder at the man she'd left, alone now in a circular booth. He raised his glass and tilted his head, and mouthed something that could have been either "Be my guest" or "Eat my pants."

"Lucky you," I said.

DAY **18**

I STARED GROGGILY AT what I'd written before meeting Mitch and Goldie's crew. Rocket the gay talking dog had just described a plot by a fast-food entrepreneur to grind stray pets into chili. I called in sick and went to the corner for coffee, feeling a little fragile and panicky. It was only 10 a.m. and already ninety degrees. An ice truck stood outside the coffee shop, and two stocky Mexican men were carrying large blocks of ice down to the basement. One of them passed me as I stood in line, cool air radiating off him.

"The ice man loadeth," I said.

"Accuse me," he said.

I stood aside.

Everyone seemed on edge.

I took my coffee across the street, found a spot in the shade, and kept watching the ice. Storing ice was a nearly surreal departure from daily life, I decided, something as foreign and antediluvian as plowing a field with oxen or sailing a square-rigged tall ship, and because of that it was satisfying to see. It was scrappy. Pragmatic. My phone rang.

"Hi, Mom."

"Hello, sweetie. Is this a good time?"

"I'm about to meet that agent I told you about."

"Oh good! Tell me how that goes. I'm just calling to check in. Been thinking about you, thinking about what an amazing adventure you're on."

"Yeah, it's something."

"Something? It's wonderful, Blake. I'm jealous! We all are."

I flashed to my encounter at the bar last night, the strange woman's tongue in my mouth.

"Who's we?"

"Well, your brother."

"He's not jealous," I said. "He thinks it's absurd."

My mother went silent for a moment. "You know, your father always wanted to live in New York City."

"Really? He never told me that."

"Oh, yes, always. It was on his list. The problem of course was that he wasn't interested in making the necessary lifestyle changes."

I'd kept one eye on the man in the booth, and he hadn't seemed at all pleased by his wife's choice. It had all seemed fairly dangerous. If I hadn't had Mitch downstairs, I probably wouldn't have done it.

"Mom," I said, "come on, I don't want to hear it."

"Well, the point is, you're doing this incredible thing, and we're all rooting for you. I'm rooting for you."

So now I was a high school softball team. "Thanks, Mom. Hey, I gotta go, okay? I have to catch a train."

"The subway! I love it. Okay, honey. Call me this weekend, will you? I want to catch you up."

"I will."

"Promise?"

"Promise."

"Oh, and stay safe tomorrow. Hottest day on record!"

After my mother had hung up, I scrolled through my contacts until my father's name came up. I didn't have him under "Dad."

The phone rang, and rang, and rang, and went to voicemail.

"You've reached me," it said, "in a manner of speaking."

One of the workers dropped a block and it shattered on the sidewalk, bright shards skittering into the street like white mice. I went down into the subway.

Nancy Klein, née Earl, was a senior literary agent at the Roger Klein Agency, which operated out of a loft in the Flatiron District. That was about all I knew. I surfaced at Madison Square Park and looked for a while at the north-pointing wedge of the building that gave the area its name. Like the ice, the existence of literary agents seemed to me a kind of quaint anachronism. A human monocle. So I wasn't prepared whatsoever for the young firebrand who ordered me up past the doorman and then ordered me to sit down at her desk.

The office was empty. Book conference. Nancy sat with her back to the window, leaving me to squint against the glare, which I feared gave my face an attitude of incredulity, which ironically I was—incredulous, and hiding it well, save for the squint. She was thin, small shouldered, with bright red hair. I didn't see the family resemblance.

"What about you?" I asked.

"What about me what? Want some coffee?"

"The conference, I mean…Yes, thank you."

"There's a machine by the front desk. Help yourself."

I walked back the way I'd just come in, past floor-to-ceiling bookshelves. There was even a rolling ladder, and I climbed onto the first rung.

"It won't roll if you're standing on it," Nancy said. "I just had other work to do. Besides, they're a drag."

The coffee had clearly been sitting all day and smelled burnt. I added two packets of sugar and a creamer and stirred with my finger for lack of a spoon. Drinking more coffee was probably a terrible idea, since I was nervous enough already, but it would give me something to do besides fiddle. I came back to her desk and sat.

"I'm fine," Nancy said, "but thanks for offering."

"Shit, I'm sorry. Would you like—"

"I'm pulling your chain. Your solipsism is cute, really. So Mitch tells me you're a writer. Why do you write?"

"I'm working on a kind of fabulist novel about—"

"Not what, *why.*"

She was toying with me, but she seemed serious, too, and of all the questions I'd prepared answers for, this hadn't been one of them. Who sits around wondering this? My pause was too long.

"And don't tell me it's because you *have to*. I don't buy that crap. Authors like to pretend there's some deep, urgent need that amazingly points them to the computer and forces their fingers around. Please tell me you're not one of them. Please tell me—"

"I started writing to impress girls," I blurted out. "Well, one girl in particular."

This was bad. I watched Nancy's face contort into a sneer, but then quickly relax, the smile becoming genuine. She nodded. "There we go. Thank God. Now we're getting somewhere."

"I don't know why I write," I said, trying not to lose the momentum. "It's not to impress girls anymore, at least not exclusively. People, maybe. To communicate. Um…"

"Fiction, you said? Bit of advice: fiction's dead. You're just starting, right? Switch gears. Memoir. Any incest in the family? Drug abuse? Alien abduction? Or popular nonfiction. Pick an ordinary object and show how it's connected to everything else. *Salt* sold. *Cod* sold. The surprising history of milk. The importance of belt loops in the evolution of modern warfare. Whatever. But not fiction. Why make something up when there's so much great, you-can't-make-this-shit-up material around you already?"

It seemed to me that I myself had been thinking something along these lines the night before in a way I couldn't quite articulate. But it also seemed irrelevant, an argument about as likely to change my behavior as the awareness of global warming had.

"No aliens, I'm afraid."

"Not that you remember, anyway. Don't sell your family short. There's probably some juicy pathos lurking right below the surface. All the best shit gets sublimated. I'm not offending you, am I?"

"No, I know what you mean. It's just that I'm in the middle of this thing, and I'm pretty sure I want to see where it takes me."

Nancy gave me an exasperated look. It seemed like something she'd practiced. "Another writer trope I loathe. The idea a book is 'taking its author' somewhere. C'mon, you know? Own it. Take responsibility."

Writing isn't about taking responsibility, I thought, it's about avoiding it. What I said was, "Yeah."

I sipped my coffee, now lukewarm and nearly undrinkable. The sunlight slammed into the side of my face in the air-conditioned room. Across the street was a nightclub, and through the window I could see a large man holding open the door for three women teetering out on heels. There was doubtless more than one memoir between the three of them. Hidden pathos is one thing. How far would I be willing to dig? And couldn't that energy be better spent creating a new world with instructive pathos of its own?

"Anyway," said Nancy, "send it to me when you're done."

We shook hands. I said I would. She seemed to think there was a wealth of independent presses putting out just about everything being written, which sounded both promising and discouraging.

I wasn't ready for that conversation anyway, so I tried not to think about it.

I flagged down a cab out front, and the moment I got in the door across from me opened and a pan-faced woman leaned in and asked if I was going downtown. I said I was, but before I could voice an opinion about sharing the cab my phone rang and I answered it without thinking. Sure enough, when my brother's low voice burst through the line I immediately regretted not letting it go to voicemail.

"You've got to talk to Mom," he said.

"I talked to her this morning."

"Well, not enough."

A long, bare white leg stretched in front of me, followed quickly by a long, angular body and finally a head, long, bleached blond hair spilling from it like water from a pail.

"What do you mean?"

Another woman began to enter the cab, and her elbow knocked the phone from my hands. I retrieved it from the floor and quickly stepped out. The first woman craned her neck out of the cab, frowning. I motioned to the phone, and she closed the door. Cars had begun to pile up behind the cab, and the street suddenly filled with impatient honks.

"Sorry," I said, walking up the street. "What's going on?"

"She had a bad test."

"I knew it! Fuck. Why didn't she say anything?"

"She said you sounded busy."

"Unbelievable."

"Well, that's Mom."

"Yeah."

"It looks really bad."

"Lumpectomy?"

"They put mastectomy on the table."

"*What?*"

"I told you. Bad."

"I don't fucking believe this. Why didn't she say something?"

This was bullshit and my brother probably knew it—I'd been avoiding any real conversation with her for weeks, not the other way around. I walked out of a shadow, and feeling the sun on my face I squinted up into it, closed my eyes.

"Just call her, okay?"

"Of course," I said.

"Well."

"Well, what? It's hard to know what's happening from here."

"I'll let that statement go without comment. What are you doing, anyway? Are you not at work?"

My hand dropped to my side. I was being judged, and it felt appropriate. I experienced a rush of something like envy. Here I'd been talking about art and meanwhile my brother was back home, protective, judgmental, righteous. My mother dying, or something like it. I began walking. I could hear Kent calling my name through the phone I'd failed to hang up—it felt, in my hand, like a stone.

DAY 19

MITCH KNOCKED ON MY door at 9 p.m., and fifteen minutes later we were driving toward the Lincoln Tunnel. I wasn't sure how this had happened, but as had become a pattern with Mitch, I went along with it. He was silent, and I thought he might be annoyed about the night before. But he may simply have been focused. I didn't ask. I enjoyed the silence. After hearing from Kent I'd barhopped from the Flatiron to the Meatpacking District. The whiskey wore off and I'd lain in my bed with the heat and the noise from the street and I'd felt the guilt growing inside of me, settling in, roaring in my ears the way white noise grows louder and louder until it disappears and you with it. I'd lain like that through the night and then called in sick again and lain like that through the day, and when Mitch had shown up I'd dragged myself downstairs and out onto the curb and climbed into his waiting car. The distraction was nice. The silence was nice. Being in a car heading into the dusk was nice. We were on our way to a nice little town in New Jersey called West Milford, and on the far side of the Lincoln Tunnel, with the city behind us, Mitch seemed to relax.

Traffic opened up; we began passing through suburbs and other low-lying development, and the darkness around us became amplified but unthreatening. I glanced over, trying to judge his expression. Mitch was prematurely graying, but his face was boyish, with a rosiness to his cheeks that shone through his smooth, naturally tan skin. He had an enormous nose that somehow made you trust him, but quick, alert brown eyes that sparkled with mischief.

"How are you doing?" he asked finally. Between highways, the road wended through a depressed, incidental area home to auto body shops and ministorage. It looked like a junk drawer.

"I'm depressed."

Beside a big pile of bedsprings stood a shirtless Asian man watching us pass. He brought a brown paper bag up to his face.

"Did you hear about the shrimp?" said Mitch.

"I'm not sure."

"You'd know, believe me. Turns out shrimp all over the Indian Ocean are dying. In the billions. They've been turning up dead on the surface of the water, and scientists have been investigating, you know, and they've been stumped for months. Like the bees. Remember the bees?"

"What was it, colony failure."

"Colony Collapse Disorder. Still happening. Anyway, they did some tests and they figured out these shrimp were packed full of Prozac. Tons of it was being pumped into the sea, defective pills being produced in factories all along the Indian coast, and these shrimp have been ingesting it and rising to the surface."

We crossed a river and began passing a field to our left. To the right, on a smaller road running parallel to our own, a diner plated in polished chrome advertised Eggs All Day.

"So they overdosed?"

"That's what they thought at first. But it turned out that, all pumped full of Prozac, they were actually leaving the darker, colder areas of the water and seeking light."

"You're fucking kidding me."

"Thing is, it's warmer closer to the surface, and it doesn't have the microorganisms they eat. So there they are, swimming up to the light out of, what, happiness? A sudden burst of self-confidence?"

"*Joie de vivre.*"

"Exactly. But in the process, they're basically committing suicide."

"Great. Now I'm even more depressed."

"Well, think of the shrimp, my friend." A semi blew by us, laying on the horn, and Mitch's next words were obscured. "Sometimes," it sounded like he was saying, "in order to stay alive, you've gotta resist the urge to alter your past." But it could have been "path."

We were silent for a while. I was imagining clouds of shrimp ascending through the cold, dark water toward some kind of utopia, a promised land of light and warmth and transcendence. Mitch's police radio chirped and he leaned forward, turning a knob to silence it. I stared at the nearly featureless black box. Mitch was the kind of inherently competent person who, like my father, made one feel generally useful while at the same time reinforcing a kind of learned helplessness. My father always had a task for everyone, and the result was you'd wait for his order. If an order wasn't forthcoming, you'd stare dumbly at your hands, wondering what they were for.

"Will your father be there tonight?" I asked. Mitch worked with his father, was slowly inheriting the family business.

"Nah," he said. "He's been working the case, but we're really just there to take a couple pictures tonight. Simple stakeout. Before we map out the mark's usual route we might tag team it, but there's no indication that he'll be doing anything more adventurous tonight than hitting a high note."

"He's celebrating?"

"Karaoke."

"He's celebrating karaoke?"

"He invented it, didn't I tell you? C'mon. We're going to a karaoke bar. Actually, we're going to an Elk's Club with a karaoke machine."

The suburbs had become exurbs, our connecting route became another highway, and we began climbing foothills. The car slowly rose and fell, a lullaby motion that gave me the distinct impression that instead of moving toward our destination we were more truly receding from something, that the city, long lost from our rearview mirrors, was nonetheless our journey's true subject.

As a child I'd been panicky, anxious, with terrible nightmares that caused me to fear not just sleep but my bedroom itself. Either in deference to my mother or unable to stand it himself, or both, my father had started putting me in a backpack and bringing me on long motorcycle rides through the winding roads along the waterfront. I looked forward to these rides, but mostly I loved being taken away from the source of my fear—so much so that I'd fall asleep, only to wake again in the morning, in my bed, as though the ride had been a dream. What struck me about it now, driving into the wilderness with Mitch, was that although I could remember certain sights, sounds, and smells from those rides— the chrome fenders and orange tank, the hum of the engine and the sweet toxicity of exhaust—in no memory could I dredge up an image of my father's face. It was just me, the bike, and a flat expanse of leather back. Could it really be said that we'd *shared* those experiences? Or did we exist merely in parallel, two people, in their own ways, pushing back the night to reveal our own desperate infinities?

Mitch's car, a Honda Accord, was far from the Triumph of these memories, but it was a comfort, and he clearly took great care of it—it was impeccably clean and, aside from the CB, all stock.

I gave the dashboard an admiring pat.

"It's the go-to car for P.I.s these days," he said. "You just can't use those big American cars anymore. They stand out, draw attention. Plus they can be mistaken for squad cars. Not really what we're going for."

"Your father drive an Accord?"

Mitch guffawed. "Dad drives a Cadillac," he said.

"But doesn't that—"

"He figures he's earned it. Part of him knows it's stupid, but there are some things I just don't push with the old man, you know? I think he's waving the white flag."

"Yeah," I said.

"But that's the least of it, really. Then there's the Internet. Files used to have to pass through, you know, x number of hands before reaching their destination. Each hand was an opportunity, in my dad's day, to grease gears, ask and return favors, affect outcomes… Now it's one button and everything's pulled up, sorted, organized, and compared. Where's the chase? My dad doesn't even know how to read his email. He has me print it out."

"So he's unable to keep up? Or is it just that he doesn't like it."

"Neither. He thinks the truth is just too easy to come by now. There's no angle in it."

We entered a long stretch with no streetlights. We were one of very few vehicles on the road, and on the dashboard glowed little white lights, a constellation of relevant facts. We slowed as a pair of shining eyes low to the road stared at us, then darted into the woods. Mitch crept forward until we passed the crossing point, looking out, I imagined, for any other members of the family. I struggled to remember a sympathetic anecdote to relate about my own father, or the Internet, or the truth, but could only think of a time my father had brought me and my brother to a public pool. I couldn't have been more than ten.

"So we're at this pool," I said, "playing with neighborhood kids, and there's a rumor going around that someone's put eels in the water, and that they're actually swimming up people's butts."

Mitch gave me a quick glance.

"You know, just kids saying kid shit. I had no idea what an eel even was at that point. Anyway, so it's fun at first, but it begins to get more frantic, the younger kids crying and leaving the pool, whatever, and I kind of don't believe it until I think I see a small black squiggly thing floating around right beside me, right? So I kind of spin and thrash around, and then I can't see it anymore, and Kent—"

"Your brother?"

"Yeah, Kent opens his eyes up real wide and looks horrified, and says he saw it crawl into my bathing suit."

"Fuck."

"Exactly. So I just about lose it, scramble out of the pool on the verge of tears and find my dad sitting there reading, and I'm all blubbery and basically freaking out, and I begin to pull down my bathing suit to find the thing, and he asks what's going on and then sort of grabs me by the shoulders and says, 'Blake, did you physically see it go in?' And I have to admit that, well, no, I didn't. And so he says, 'Then don't take off your suit.' And this has stuck with me I think because it was this moment where I basically submerged myself in his authority, let it douse my own doubt and fear and assumptions, which were of course in retrospect stupid but at the time seemed very real."

"He woke you up."

"Exactly. It wasn't so much what was the truth, but that I could accept this version of it."

Mitch let that sit for a while and so did I. After a couple minutes I changed the subject.

"So who's the guy we're staking out?"

"An interesting case, actually." Mitch immediately grew more animated. "He's a gambler, but he's a *successful* gambler, or was. He made a lot of money, made a lot of investments. And now he's filing for bankruptcy."

We passed a sign for West Milford. We were getting close.

"So what's the angle?" I glanced over at him, wondering if he'd acknowledge the term I'd used.

"The angle is that someone he owes money to thinks he's actually still cash rich. Their lawyers have hired us to gather evidence of unusual or excessive expenditure."

"Huh," I said.

Mitch seemed to sense my disappointment. "But the guy has some colorful hobbies," he said. "For one, he's a peeping Tom. We've actually followed him around his own neighborhood, where he's got a little route he takes once or twice a week, half a dozen houses he hits just as people are headed to bed."

"No shit. So you're watching someone watch people," I said.

"Another peccadillo is his habit of impersonating a federal officer. He's been picked up for that a couple times over the last decade or so."

"He dresses up like a cop?"

"Federal. FBI."

"Oh, right, of course. So…"

"He wears a black suit and flashes around a badge, which is really just a piece of paper for the Bureau. He's talked his way onto crime scenes, into people's houses. He's even testified in court as an expert witness."

"That's wild. So what does he do? I mean, what's he after?"

"Honestly, he doesn't seem to take advantage of it. Or, you know, no more than what it is."

"Amazing," I said. "What'd you say this guy's name is?"

"I didn't. It would be unethical for me to give you the guy's name. Now, if you happen to pick it up while we're at the Elk's Club, that's not my business."

This seemed overly formal, given the fact that Mitch was taking me along and telling me all about the case, but I understood the need to control information. He was an expert, and sometimes expertise is an act of withholding. We passed another sign for West Milford, and up ahead I began to see the soft glow of artificial light against the dark summer sky. A small plane flew overhead, seeming to descend.

"So what are we looking for, exactly?"

"Well, we have our case more or less buttoned up—that's why my father chose to sit this one out—but what we're missing is that last really definitive…I don't know. The court is a drama, and it's always nice to have something truly memorable for the jury. Something that defines the whole case. Let's just say it would be great if he drove up in a Ferrari."

"How long have you been watching him?"

"Nineteen days."

There was no fancy car in front of the West Milford Elk's Club. There was a gravel lot, mostly empty, with weeds tufting around a pole doing double duty for power lines and a dull yellow light. The building itself was almost unmarked, its single story depressed below a flat roof, and a small window beside the door held a collection of trophies. It was a place children would avoid, teenagers would ignore, and adults would "find themselves in." Mitch brought me around to the trunk, where he pulled out two trucker hats and a bright orange hunting vest.

"Believe me," he said. "You'll want to fit in. Oh, and one more thing. Turn off your cell phone. They know me in here, but we're trying to keep a low profile, and regardless of who calls you, you'll talk like an out-of-towner."

I did as he asked, and in we went.

The room was sparsely furnished, somewhere between a bar and a basement rec room. Most of the twenty-odd people inside sat around a square bar in the center of the room, and most of them were smoking. I followed Mitch to the bar. The bartender was the only woman present, and she was at least ten years younger than the people on the other side of the counter. She smiled at Mitch and began drawing a pint of Yuengling.

"Two?"

"Please," Mitch said. "How's tricks, Shelley?"

Shelley wore a pink T-shirt with the words "You Got Served" across the chest. She was girlish, with loose, wavy blond hair and an expressive face that scrunched up as her eyes rolled. "How do you think, Mitch? Who's your friend?"

"This is Blake, a buddy of mine from way back."

Shelley reached across the counter to shake my hand. "Welcome to the Club."

We took our beers to a small table some feet from the bar. Mitch scanned the room. He nodded to a couple of men, smiled, then held up his glass.

"Here's to old friends," he said.

"Which one is he?"

"Not here yet."

An hour and a half and three pints later, I was having a good time. The jukebox was playing songs everyone knew, and I'd struck up a game of pool with a man named Harry who'd been a figure skater before becoming an arc welder. I'd told him about the book I was writing—or failing to write—and he'd eagerly launched into story after story about his days on ice. His big belly belied his athletic past, but his tales of competitive skating were lively enough to keep me from focusing on the table, and I was getting creamed.

"But I knew in my gut," Harry was saying, "that the attitude of my free leg wasn't going to cut it for the flying layback I was trying to land."

I was trying to picture this man in a glittering, skin-tight leotard.

I nodded, shot, missed.

I was littles.

"Did you land it?" I asked.

"Oh, I landed it all right. But I was so busy thinking about my attitude that I forgot about my spine."

"That doesn't sound good."

Harry sunk his final stripe and left himself a nice angle on the eight ball, but just as Harry was lining up his final shot Mitch came and whispered in my ear, "He's here."

The bar was directly between where we were standing and the door, so I could see only some bright red and orange plaid moving between tables, the man's head hidden behind the raised liquor shelf. There was a jovial murmur audible even above the jukebox, which was now playing "Baker Street." The song's saxophone soared and, combined with the smoky, low-lit room, lent an almost mystical quality to the man's entrance. Half drunk, I was pleasantly pulled from the scene, gently coaxed into a state of bemusement as though hypnotized just enough to appreciate my own lack of willpower. It was, after all, not really my life I was living here. It wasn't even the life of the person who'd brought me here. I was a parasite twice removed, a ghost haunting a ghost, and the buzz I felt was not just from the booze but from my near-total absence of connection. Freedom without the existentially attendant responsibility. I'd never be back here. I'd never see any of these people again, and they'd forget me the minute I left.

"Blake, man, you missed it."

Harry had sunk the eight. I congratulated him on the win, moving to excuse myself from the table, but he looked disappointed and shook his head.

"There's no way I can keep that shot. I have to pull the ball and shoot again. A man can't win a game when his opponent's not looking, friend."

"Really," I said, "come on. I know you made it fair and square."

"Shelley!" he called. "Two shots."

"No, listen," I said, but Harry was already on his way to the bar, and he quickly returned with a shot of whiskey held out before him, another near his lips. He nodded encouragingly, and not wanting to disappoint the man further, I took the glass from his hand and took the gold liquid into my mouth.

"Thanks," I said, my throat constricting.

"Don't thank me," he said. "That one's on Dale."

"Who?"

"Blake!"

Mitch was standing by his table, seeming tense. I still couldn't see beyond the bar, but there was a loud cheering and clinking of glasses, and then the bright plaid shirt began moving back toward the door.

Mitch flicked his head. *We need to leave*, was the message.

I apologized to Harry, who, though sorry to see me go, thanked me for the game.

"People around here," he said, "just don't understand the kind of sacrifices real art requires."

Mitch and I met at the door. He seemed sober and alert. But after the air-conditioned bar, the heat outside was almost unbearable and gave me a woozy feeling I tried to hide.

Mitch looked at his watch. It was midnight.

"What are you up to," he said under his breath.

I followed his gaze across the lot, where the man in plaid was standing with his back to us at his car door. It was a plain American sedan, the kind Mitch avoided these days. The man was average height, thin, and his hair was black, slicked back. He opened the door, and as he turned to climb in his face shone under the single light standing over the lot. It was Dale Cooper.

DAY 20

WE TRAILED THE CAR through town, then east along a winding arterial that splintered off on either side into tree-lined neighborhood streets. I was shaken, drunk, and deflecting Mitch's curious looks by leaning my head against the cool glass. I wasn't ready to speak. It felt like I'd had a sudden encounter with someone from my past, but I couldn't summon which past he'd been part of. Someone I'd known from college? A teacher from high school? A friend of my parents? Maybe I'd simply seen him on the news. I'd seen a report about him, about his crimes.

We turned right on Airport Road and Mitch grew excited. He asked me to pull a cell phone out of the glove compartment, and moments later he was speaking to his father.

"I don't know where he's headed," Mitch said. "But yes, of course I'm prepared to go."

We stopped at the entrance to the small airport—a landscaped clearing with two metal buildings that seemed more likely to hold packages than waiting passengers. Mitch turned on his CB and began scanning.

"All static," he said into the phone. "I know, I know. I'm going to."

Mitch held the phone to his chest and told me he was going in.

"Going in where?" I asked.

"To the airport. If he...shit."

Mitch was looking over my shoulder, and I turned to see a small white plane gathering speed on the runway. It was headed in our direction, and soon rose slowly into the sweaty night sky. Mitch jumped out of the car and jogged toward the closer building, then around the corner.

The radio chirped.

I didn't feel like running to catch up, but I didn't want to sit in the car, either. I took the keys from the ignition and wandered in the direction Mitch had disappeared. Walking reminded me how much I'd had to drink, and I tried to keep a straight line as my heavy body swayed back and forth like water sloshing inside a jug. The more I thought about that moment of recognition, the more the feeling changed inside me. It felt much different than a memory. It was as though I'd looked toward the shape of a man but seen a hole in the world. Less like a memory than a premonition.

I peeked around the corner. The field was empty and the buildings seemed closed. Mitch was nowhere in sight. A statue stood between the two structures and the airfield, a tall Native American man holding his hand up in something between a friendly wave and a stern warning. There was no breeze, no birds, no airport personnel. It seemed impossible that an airplane had departed only moments before. Just as I was taking in the eerie emptiness, however, movement alongside a dark, silent van beside a loading dock caught my eye, and a bright white chicken toddled out onto the grass. Its contented, perky clucking was a comfort somehow, as though chickens wouldn't exist in a strange, unreliable world.

I edged closer to it, inching toward the Indian. Perhaps it was a pet. Or maybe a watchdog of sorts, here to scare away rodents. It didn't seem frightened of me, either way. I was able to get within two feet of it. I crouched. I reached out my hand.

"What are you doing?"

I swiveled on my feet, too quickly, and spilled over onto the cool grass. The chicken startled and ran back to the van.

Mitch jogged up to me.

"Come on," he said, "we're heading north."

He helped me up and we walked quickly back to the car.

"That plane is going to Niagara Falls."

"How'd you figure that out?"

"I bribed the controller."

I looked around.

"You found someone?"

"The controller."

We got in, buckled up, and I handed Mitch the keys. He was surprised, as though it had been unnecessary to take them.

"It seemed odd to leave them in," I said.

"Are you okay?"

I nodded, and as we pulled away from the airport I looked back to catch one last look at the glowing white bird.

When we hit the highway, Mitch gave me the option of being dropped off, of staying at a motel or waiting for a bus back to the city. I refused. Though I'd decided to keep silent about Dale Cooper, I needed to see him again. I wanted to have that feeling again, that feeling of familiarity, of affinity. It was fading from me fast, and as I tried to keep hold of it, tried to examine it, it seemed less like something lived through and more like something dreamt. The car pointed north, to Buffalo, and I, as though in pursuit of this apparition, with the gentle movement of the car conspiring with the beer, began to nod off.

"I've been thinking about your question," Mitch said.

I responded groggily with something that sounded like *car* or *gone*.

"There's no king named Anonimous with an 'I'—I looked into it. But the problem here isn't the misspelling."

"No?"

"The problem is that anyone can just make something up, and poof, it's right there next to Shakespeare."

I woke up on a daybed in a small living room filled with light. Mitch, who I seemed to remember having fallen asleep in the recliner across from me, was gone. In his place was a neatly folded towel. The room itself was tidy but cluttered, filled mostly with books and antique laboratory paraphernalia. A large microscope sat on the floor, its tray home now to a moldy Petri dish. Jam jars with large bugs suspended in a viscous fluid lined the shelf directly behind my head. A chart, hung from a tripod in one corner, was titled *The Periodicity of the Elements*.

On the opposite wall hung a painting depicting a pastoral scene with a large farmhouse in the background, and in the foreground three Belted Galloways and an autumnal oak tree with an empty rope swing. Smoke curled out of the farmhouse chimney, and a large brown stippled squid flew through it in the sky above the house. I leaned in, trying to confirm that the squid was not an original feature of the painting, but I was interrupted by the sound of banging pots.

"Leave me alone," said a man's voice. "I'm making my own coffee like some sort of homeless person."

A woman's face emerged from the doorway to the kitchen. It was large and oval, of indeterminate age, with bright brown eyes that seemed to inspect me with a hint of polite condescension.

"It stirs," she said, not to me.

"Ask if it drinks coffee," said the man.

"Well?" she said, and smiled.

"It loves coffee," I confirmed.

These were Megan and Chad, friends of Mitch whom he'd spoken of after we'd pulled off the highway, the change of speed having woken me. She was, if I recalled, some kind of computer programmer with socialist tendencies, and he was a painter. Or vice versa? Megan disappeared again and more banging ensued.

I stripped the sheets off the bed and replaced the pillows it apparently wore by day. In the kitchen, the two were literally arguing about the price of tea in China.

"It's totally reasonable, dummy," Megan was saying. "If all currency were edible, it could only devalue to a point."

Chad grunted, and presently there was a high-pitched squeal, after which Megan came running out of the kitchen, twisted her dishtowel into a whip, and edged back in. This was clearly the kind of fundamentally happy couple whose bickering was essentially an off-gassing of hearts overburdened by love. I looked out the window. We were on a lake. I couldn't remember the name, or maybe I hadn't been told. Someone far off on the south bank was zipping around on a Jet Ski.

"Be careful, it's strong."

Chad held out an espresso-sized cup toward me. Chad was in his mid-forties, maybe older. His face was alert, but his skin was blotchy, a drinker's face.

"Thanks," I said.

He spun around and quickly navigated through the difficult room to a computer desk in the corner, where he sat, booted up, and loudly slurped his espresso. He was a large, solid man, but the way he moved was agile, athletic, as though he were somewhere deep within his own body, operating it by remote. He eyed me, and the room seemed to expand with silence.

"Quick," he said finally. "Say something funny."

I tried to cobble together something about the old table of elements—I happened to know it contained no noble gasses—but before I could vocalize anything he reached over, touched his mouse, and the room flooded with the warm, avuncular sounds of NPR.

We listened and drank our coffee. A guest on All Things Considered was explaining that more divorces have their origin in Home Depot than in any other single space.

"What department?" the host wanted to know.

"We're still mining the data."

I asked Chad where Mitch was.

"He was on the phone with his dad, arguing it sounded like, and then he took off heading north."

"Doesn't sound good."

"They're always arguing. They basically hate each other."

"Really? Wow. I didn't get that at all."

"Well, he doesn't volunteer it." Chad seemed irritated. "Anyway, if you're getting along with your parents, you're not doing something right."

"So, conflict is king."

"Conflict, discord, disruption, disunity, and probably most important: competition."

"I'm in competition with my mother?"

"For the very air you breathe. Children basically want to kill their parents."

Megan entered the room and stood with a large bowl, stirring. She shook her head.

"Don't let him fuck with you," she said.

"I don't mind," I said. "It's interesting, because my mother's actually dying of cancer right now and I've been putting off returning her call."

I hadn't planned on saying it, but now that it was out I was happy I had. I let the statement stand, looked out at the lake, and imagined Megan glaring at her husband, him shrugging back at her as if to say, *How could I have known?* It gave me the upper hand.

"So if you're right," I said, "then maybe I'm just trying to distance myself from the unhealthy part of my family, my gene pool. Maybe it's pure animal instinct."

The person I'd seen zipping around across the lake earlier was gone, and the water was a glassy, cloudless sky. The radio cut out, buffering, and in the silence we heard the crunch of gravel in the driveway. Mitch had returned. He banged through the door to the kitchen and came to stand beside Megan. I heard him wait for something to happen.

"What did I miss?" he asked.

"Nothing," I said, turning. "We were just joking around."

"I knew it!" Chad said, and dove underneath his desk to reboot the router.

Mitch moved on.

"I've found him," he said. "He's staying at the Hilton. Tonight we watch him gamble."

DAY 21

WE CROSSED INTO CANADA close to midnight. That afternoon Chad and Megan had left for Brazil, where Megan was going to do a series of watercolors on the *favelas* in Sao Paulo. Mitch and I had been left to "fend for ourselves." For Mitch that meant sitting at the computer and trying to dredge up more information to explain Cooper's sudden move. For me it meant not calling my mother, watching *La Jetée* three and a half times, taking naps in the sunny window seat, and staring at the tiny waves that lapped ceaselessly against the close rocky shore.

While Mitch explained to the border guard that we'd been visiting friends in Buffalo and had not brought our passports, I kept thinking about the short film. In it a man must travel into the past and then the future in an attempt to save the world. Haunted by a vague childhood memory of seeing someone killed in an airport, the man eventually discovers that it is he who is to be killed, and that he has been remembering his own death. Not only was the story strange and beautiful, the film was not made of moving images. It was a series of stills. Why had the director chosen still imagery to tell a story about time? And why did it seem like the perfect choice?

The guard finally waved us through, but not without a warning. "You're okay coming in," he said, "but you might have more trouble getting back home."

We accepted the risk.

The highway curved gently into the darkness, and in the distance to our right the hotels and casinos of Niagara Falls glowed purple and red. I had not been to the famous waterfall before and was surprised to hear what it had become.

"It's like a miniature Vegas," Mitch said. "Except the water feature is real."

"So it's no longer the honeymoon hotspot of yore?"

"Oh, I'm sure it's still full of honeymooners, it's just that tastes have changed. The Falls aren't enough anymore. You see them from your hotel room while ordering a room service T-bone after losing your wedding cash at craps. I don't think anyone's under the illusion that this is a romantic destination. It now serves a practical function. It's a distraction."

The place we came to couldn't quite be described as a town. A red-light district, maybe. A three-block radius of brightly lit gift shops, hotels, and chain restaurants. We parked across the street from a place called Nightmares.

"Last time I was here," Mitch said, nodding to the haunted house, "someone had to be carried out of there on a gurney."

"Look." I pointed to a grassy, undeveloped plot of land beside us. It was filled with fireflies. They slowly rose and fell, their light nearly invisible under the dazzling displays around us. It almost seemed as though they were trying to compete. Or protest. We kept moving. The streets were oddly vacant, which together with the bright signs left me feeling exposed. Mitch must have felt it too, because he led us off the street and through a lattice of parking lots that terminated at our first stop: Casino Niagara. We were let in a side entrance by a man dressed in a red jacket and pants who smelled like alcohol. He tried to smile as we passed but only managed to lift his wiry eyebrows. The casino floor was a level below us, red-carpeted stairs striped by smudgy brass banisters leading down to rows of shiny machines, and we stood for a while as Mitch scanned the room. The din of coins, jingles, and bells filled my ears, the individual sounds canceling one another out so that the result was not an amplification of noise but a muted quality, as though we were underwater, or wearing earplugs. People roamed from machine to machine in slow motion, their expressions slack and glazed, and as we descended into the scene I was reminded of a line from *La Jetée* that had struck me as truthful without being entirely clear: *Time builds itself painlessly around them.*

"He's playing blackjack," said Mitch, pointing.

Cooper was no longer dressed in the red plaid of a backwater woodsman. He was wearing a tuxedo. His pale complexion glowed and his slick hair glistened, and I had the distinct sense that this was somehow closer to how I'd known him, or how I knew him, or how he was supposed to be. He was standing on the far side of the table as we approached, and Mitch led us around and out of view to stand beside the Honey Pot, a slot machine featuring dancing bears. The machine was occupied by an old woman on a respirator, and she looked up at us nervously, respirated, and then continued on with her big red button.

"So what do we do now?" I asked.

"We wait."

Though Cooper looked natural in this setting, he also seemed oddly detached. While others cheered for big wins or offered condolences for big losses at the table, he was not invested in the group. He placed his chips easily, nonchalant. He took his losses in stride—though none seemed to be large—and his wins with a slight nod to the dealer, then a tip. It was as though betting were a smooth muscle movement, something like breathing at rest and not the wind sprint it was for everyone else. He took out a small compact to check his tie.

"Did you read that article?" I said. "I forget where it was. Something about how people learn addiction as one of the earliest experiences of their lives?"

"Shhh."

"*Harper's?*"

"Seriously."

Apparently, mothers taught a kind of learned helplessness to their children through the subconscious withholding of breast milk. Sometimes you cry and get it, sometimes you cry and don't—exactly the unpredictable reinforcement pattern at the root of a gambling addiction.

Mitch stopped a waitress and asked her for a glass of water, giving her a five-dollar bill for her trouble. A thin man with bifocals stopped beside us and watched the old woman pressing her button, then moved on when he realized there was nothing to see.

Why then, I wondered, were there not more gambling addicts in the world? Perhaps this trait expressed itself differently depending on circumstance. After all, gambling is highly regulated and has a serious stigma attached to it in most circles. Gambling could take more innocuous forms in such cases—like ill-informed consumer behavior, say. Or unprotected sex.

By now I was thinking about my mother. I'd never known anyone who'd had a mastectomy. A woman I'd known in college had found a lump once, but it had turned out to be a benign cyst. Her name was Kari. Or Carey. I remembered sitting with her and some friends in a common area of my dorm the day she'd had her biopsy. She'd seemed to be in shock: staring into the near distance, quiet and unresponsive to the flurry of forced activity around her. A football player named Doug kept offering her a candy bar and ended up in an argument with the hall monitor, Stacey, who claimed that candy was a carcinogen. "What were you *thinking*?" she'd said again and again. Eventually Kari or Carey ate the candy just to shut them up.

Mitch leaned in close and told me he was going to run to the bathroom, that he'd be back in two minutes, and to keep out of sight. I redoubled my efforts to focus on the matter at hand. Cooper was standing before a sizable stack of chips, but he seemed to be playing an even game, so it was impossible to say whether he'd begun with more or started with less. To my surprise, I'd begun to normalize his presence. The feeling I'd had initially was long gone— itself a memory I couldn't quite summon—and had been replaced by a sense that Cooper and I had something in common. In fact, it was becoming apparent to me that I was not watching a stranger at all. What that made him was difficult for me to say, but I tried to give this new experience room to emerge more completely. For time, I supposed, to build painlessly around me.

I felt a tug at my shirt, and looked down to see the slot woman gasping up at me with wide eyes. I followed a crooked, pointing finger to the screen before her, where three golden bears were lined up across the center, and as it dawned on me that she'd won a jackpot, the clatter and whoop of her machine rose above the cacophony around it and began to draw passersby. The old woman looked stricken, and I thought for a terrible moment that she was going to have a heart attack. People were now gathering and cheering, and I leapt behind a nearby column hoping to avoid the spectacle, and Cooper's attention. I looked toward the men's room door, but Mitch was nowhere in sight. The radius of well-wishers expanded, engulfing me even ten feet from the woman's machine, and I poked my head around the column, thinking the crowd would provide cover. There, however, staring straight at me from the far side of the blackjack table was a distinctly peeved-looking Cooper, and as I watched, held by his gaze, he gathered his chips and moved quickly across the room.

I had no time to make a good decision, so I followed. As I shot through aisles of slot machines, I determined that Mitch would call me upon returning to find me, and his subject, gone. But by then the rationale was nearly irrelevant. I was in pursuit. I knocked against the same waitress who'd brought Mitch water and she nearly spilled her tray.

"*Arschloch,*" she said.

"*Gesundheit,*" I said back.

I followed Cooper to a door marked Hotel Staff Only and through it into a short hallway, the walls of which were cluttered with posted rules, safety posters, bulletin boards, and a large gray timecard machine. People brushed by me, unconcerned, and though Cooper was nowhere in sight I saw a swinging door swing beside a Missing Persons poster of a young girl named Beth. I ran to catch it.

The adjoining room was a cafeteria, empty but for two men on ladders hanging a banner above the main doors. Only half the lights were lit, and they shone in rows across the ceiling, reflecting in big black picture windows that, I imagined, looked out across the Falls. One of the men turned to me after adjusting his end of the sign.

"Can I help you?" he asked.

The banner read: *Welcome, Weyerhaeuser Investment Summit!*

"Did a man come in here? Tuxedo, slick hair, arms full of poker chips?"

The first man looked over at the other, who, without turning around, spoke slowly.

"This area of the hotel is reserved," he said, "for a private party."

I stood there for a moment, not knowing what to do. Mitch must surely have returned by now, and there'd be no shame in heading back to the casino floor to explain what had happened. Who could blame me for losing Cooper? But a greater part of me felt compelled to see this through, to locate the man before reporting back. To have an idea, at least, where he'd gone.

Large round tables adorned with green tablecloths and triangular paper trees filled the cafeteria.

"Is this the Weyerhaeuser from Seattle? *Weyerhaeuser* Weyerhaeuser?"

"Hey, what did I say?" the second man said, turning around.

He hung his banner corner from a hook and began to climb down the ladder. I took a step back, only a few feet now from the swinging door behind me, close enough to hear the staff hurrying about their errands in the hall.

"Look, just a yes or no is all I'm asking. If he didn't come in here, great. He's not part of the event either, so maybe you told him to leave too. Did he go out through the front door?"

Why wasn't Mitch calling, I wondered. The man began walking toward me from across the room. He had curly red hair, and it strobed slowly as he moved beneath the lights. I took out my cell to see if I'd missed a call, but its screen was dark—I'd turned it off the night before. I pressed the power button and the screen lit up, but it would take a minute to boot and find a signal. I didn't have a minute. The man came closer, and I stepped back again, until I could feel the cool metal door against my shoulders. I noticed the first man, still on the ladder, was speaking quietly into a small radio, and I heard it click on and off as he sent and received. Surely calling Security. But then why the aggressive posturing? Was I about to be physically removed from the room? I decided to save him the trouble and pushed back against the door—if he wanted me to leave, fine, but there was no cause for altercation—but the door did not open. I looked back through the head-high window to the hallway beyond, the hallway I'd just come in from, and found it dark. There was no activity, there was no staff, and the red-haired man was closing in.

My phone let out a single, clear note to indicate a voicemail, and I stepped quickly behind a round table while dialing Mitch. When I looked back up the man was standing two tables away, the first man coming quickly to join him. Together, they moved toward me, splitting apart, and by the time Mitch answered they'd gotten to either side of my table and the first man reached forward and slapped the cell phone out of my hand. It skittered across the floor and, still on, weakly broadcast Mitch's voice.

"Blake! Blake, what's going on. Blake?"

"Help!" I called. "Look for the Wey—"

The redhead grabbed me and wrapped a big hand around my mouth. I struggled against his grip, pulling at his arm and kicking backward, but he held fast, engulfing me, and lifted me off the ground in a bear hug tight enough to push the air from my lungs. As quickly as he squeezed, though, he released, just enough to let me gasp, his hold now more like a swaddle.

My body went limp. The man smelled like women's perfume, a sweet, bright smell that tingled my nose, and as he held me, the other man looked up at me and shook his head. I farted. Someone emerged from the shadows along the side of the room, mere feet from where I'd stood. He was still partially obscured by darkness, but I could see his silhouette against the illuminated wall behind him. It was Cooper, not a hair out of place.

"Did you know," he said, "that New York City has a goose overpopulation problem? It's true. And as they pose a threat to airlines operating out of the Kennedy, LaGuardia, and Newark airports—not to mention the smaller airfields in the area catering to private and other non-commercial aircraft—the Department of Agriculture has taken it upon itself to cull the population using a variety of tactics meant to make their preferred habitats inhospitable."

Cooper's voice was calm, dispassionate, but not cold. It was instead curious, alive with a sincerity that betrayed the seriousness of his interest in this anecdote, as though he were working something out for himself, and, though he was speaking to me, I was incidental to the process.

"These tactics include oiling the eggs, planting tall grasses, scaring the birds away with trained dogs, and a variety of other measures. But do you know what the primary tactic is? Don't answer. The primary tactic is deception."

With this, Cooper stepped forward, allowing me to see him clearly. For the first time since the Elk's Club parking lot I felt a rush of recognition, an untethered emotional response that flooded my body in waves. It was more powerful than déjà vu, more urgent, as though I hadn't had this experience before, but *should have*. As though the universe were somehow correcting itself, or at least correcting my position in it. Cooper's tuxedo was tight and immaculate, painted on, and he signaled to the redhead, who let me down slowly, then released me. As my feet touched the floor I staggered, then felt hands on my shoulders. I tried to nod.

"Deception," I said.

"Your friend Mitch is a good man."

I felt my bones settle, saddled again with weight.

"He's a good man, but he's on the wrong path. To be fair, I've given him no reason to think otherwise—in fact, his pursuit of me has helped establish the credibility of my cover—but I simply failed to predict that you'd get involved, so for this, I apologize."

At first, I was focused on the cover story. Which part was the cover? Could it be that the very same sham-FBI shenanigans and money troubles Mitch was documenting were only an illusion Cooper was using to…to what? But then I realized that another part of his speech was far more troubling.

"Wait a minute," I said. "You *know* me?"

I began to feel a tingling on the back of my neck. My face felt hot. I took a deep breath to calm myself but myself would not listen. Cooper motioned to the two men and they took their leave through the main entrance, the Weyerhaeuser banner still hanging askew above it.

We were alone now, and he drew closer and perched on the edge of a large round table. He asked me to sit.

"Blake," he said, "you set this all in motion."

"I did?"

I was holding onto nothing now. My fingers left the tabletop.

"You were the reason I went undercover in the first place. It was you who discovered what Weyerhaeuser was up to with our extraterrestrial visitors, and you whose first experience with transpositional epiphany led us to the discovery of Existencelastic Macrobial Foreshortening."

As Cooper said these words I felt a tightness in my chest. I put my head down on the table, and its coolness on my forehead relieved me, for a moment, of the lightheadedness I felt. But it was a momentary distraction from an imminent impact. I was soon nearly swooning under the force of Cooper's words as they sought purchase on something inside me that knew them to be true.

"Stay with me, Blake. Are you with me? I need you to take a deep breath."

I tried to answer, but my sight began to go splotchy. I felt Cooper standing over me, his hand on my back.

"Blake," he said, "Blake, you need to listen to me."

His voice was in my ear, saying something I couldn't understand as my consciousness began to follow my sight, to grow patchy and blank, and after some lapping, wavelike movement, to recede, to pull back deeper and deeper into a long, gradual, tidal undertow toward some sodden, sudden vanishing point in a picture-still sea of nothing coming.

Part IV

DAY 22

It was summer, I was free, and I was stoned. Blake and I stood, not in front of the work itself, but before the plaque that explained how it should be seen. It reminded me of how our relationship had been—we'd been a couple for two years before I'd gone off to college—forever talking about "what we meant" and spending increasingly less time simply being in love. It struck me that perhaps all high school relationships were instances of a collaborative project delineating the archetypes around which we'd model the real relationships to come. I tried to think of a good way to share this observation with Blake as she stood back, looking hard at the lithograph, her dark hair curling in front of her face like a shy child's.

"Orange," she said, quoting the plaque, "is red brought nearer to humanity by yellow."

I joined her in considering the piece. Like a lot of Kandinsky's work from this period, it looked like a disassembled clock. That or road kill, a too-curious bird flattened by a semi.

"Do you think that means he's associating yellow with humanity," I said, and then, flexing Chem 101, "or that yellow is just a reagent necessary for the transformation?"

Blake sighed—a habit she'd picked up since we last saw each other. I didn't press it. I knew she harbored the slightly embarrassing grudge held by those who've been left behind. Besides, the nine months I'd been gone had been on the dry side, and I was hoping she'd suspend her grievances for some afternoon fucking.

After we'd exhausted the Seattle Art Museum, or at least exhausted ourselves, Blake and I wandered out into the spotty midday sun and ambled down 1st Avenue. I'd heard some things. Blake had been unhappy. Blake had had a breakdown. Blake had joined a cult. I did not bring these things up, wanting to let her find the right time to explain, but she'd caught me stealing concerned glances, as if a look could shatter the fragile lattice of a personality she'd built back up from scratch, and I knew that she knew that I knew. Frankly, however, she seemed anything but fragile, so I wasn't sure what to believe.

We took a right on Spring and schlepped west up the slope. It was a weekday, and everywhere men and women bustled about in business casual. Blake's simple white summer dress bore elaborate white stitching, so that its shiny thread shone here and there in patterns as she walked and she looked not just out of place but ghostly, a specter haunting the mirror world around us.

On 5th we crossed toward a construction zone. High walls of blue particleboard surrounded the block-sized property, and although nothing could be seen above them, head-level diamond holes had been cut every ten feet. We stood at different diamonds and looked down into the open pit. They were still working on the foundation, and out of the earth surfaced significant concrete squares, home to rebar rods jutting up like fountains of water alchemically transformed mid-spray. Men in hard hats and orange vests swarmed around large yellow earthmovers and called across the lot, waving their arms, or else stood, shovels in the ground, and smoked.

"I don't remember what was here," I lied.

"Not surprising. You probably went there a grand total of never."

"A store for funny hats?"

"That's not even clever."

"A gay bathhouse?"

"Close."

"I give up."

"It was the library."

"You're kidding me," I said. "They're getting rid of the library? I thought we were all at least going to pretend that books still mattered."

"Oh, we're still pretending, all right. They're building a new one in its place. Some fancy thing. The architect is someone."

Near the port-a-potties in the northeast corner of the lot, on the roof of what could only be described as a shack, stood a small sapling with large, wet-looking leaves. It was in a pot.

Blake stood on tiptoe, her hands brought up beneath her chin, her head tipped back. Something about this image reminded me that it was Blake who first convinced me to believe in something. Or rather, to question the irony and chronic sarcasm that had once characterized my every waking minute. It wasn't that she'd been dull or in any way unable to partake in the serial one-upmanship that throughout high school had become the default mode of interaction between me and most of our friends. If anything, she'd been dangerously spot-on in sussing out someone's emotional soft spots and directing pithy, squirm-inducing barbs their way. No one would have called her anything but quick-witted. And perhaps that explained it. Perhaps irony had come too easily for her, and thus sincerity had been the greater challenge, one she'd encouraged only sometimes in others but had increasingly demanded of me. She'd once told me that if life were a test, I'd wait until the end and cram.

"I know what else I'd like to cram in the end," I'd said.

She caught me staring another stare of concern.

"What?" said Blake.

"Nothing."

"How's your mom?"

If there was any high left in me, it was now entirely borne away on the wings of serious shit. I wasn't sure how she'd heard, but I wasn't surprised she knew. My brother could have told someone, a friend or an old girlfriend—he'd always dated up, age-wise—now close to Blake. Or, for all I knew, Blake was still in touch with my mother, who tended to adopt my exes as though she owed them something. As though in acknowledgment of my unfair treatment.

"The biopsy hasn't come back yet," I said.

My mother had discovered a lump.

"But how *is* she?"

I thought about this. How was my mother? I hadn't planned on coming home for the summer. I'd planned to spend some time in New York City—somewhere I'd never been—and possibly visit some family in Long Island, relatives on my father's side I'd only met once at a family reunion when I was twelve. I'd hung around campus for three weeks after finals trying to build up momentum, but my mother had found a lump and I'd come home and now here I was. I'd flown in yesterday and here I was. What was so complicated about that?

"She's fine," I said. "You know my mom."

"I know she's one of the most generous people I've ever met, if that's what you mean."

I got the distinct impression that sex was out of the question.

"Do you think," Blake said, "she would have told you if she didn't need your help?"

I looked back through the diamond. I didn't like the tone Blake was taking with me. It was accusatory, but worse, it seemed a little sad. Her fears about me had been confirmed. She was disappointed. Worst of all was the fact that, from the moment I'd heard about the lump, I'd absolutely *known* it was cancer. It was a feeling I could neither explain nor express— like everyone else, I'd told her, told her to her face, that it was probably just a cyst, that it was probably harmless. But I knew otherwise.

"What do you think that tree is for?" I called through the little window.

I looked for Blake's nose poking through her diamond, but it didn't come.

"It's like a spirit animal," I said. "Like some kind of ancient druidic defense against bad luck. Wasn't it the Druids who gave us Christmas trees?"

I was trying to think of a pun involving port-a-potties and the word "protection" when I felt Blake's hands on my shoulders. I turned around and she was standing behind me, her back to traffic, looking up at me with watering eyes. I had once wanted to write the book of love with this person, and now there seemed to be a library-sized chasm between us. How could I tell her there was no hope? How could I explain that the best thing to do was simply move from one moment to the next, doing as little damage as possible?

Blake put her arms around my waist and leaned in, pulling herself into my body and tucking her head beneath my chin.

"Go be with your mother," she said. "It's really nice to see you, and we should hang out again soon, but go be with your mom. Just be with her."

———

On the bus home, the woman sitting beside me was reading *Bartlett's Familiar Quotations*. She flipped through randomly, then stabbed her finger down onto the paper with a hollow pock. The first was from Elie Wiesel. It said, "I was the accuser, God the accused." The next one was from Ronald Reagan: "Facts are stupid things." Another seat opened up and I moved.

Seeing the excavation site had rattled me a little. They'd torn out the city's heart, and without the blood of books pumping through its veins, it was only a matter of time before we'd shrivel and sink into the Sound. What if, like so many redevelopment projects, it took far longer than expected, or simply stalled in a budgetary limbo? The image of that gruesome hole would stay with me for days.

The bus ran along Lake Union, crossed the canal, and snaked through Fremont, a place once cheekily self-described as "the center of the world" and now coming to resemble it more than the hippies and artists who'd nicknamed it would have liked. Five or six years ago, I'd been walking home along this route from an antiwar rally at Gas Works Park. It had been cold, unusually cold for Seattle, and I'd used my last dollar to buy a large coffee from 7-11. Toward the end of my walk, feeling it was not radiating enough warmth through the paper cup, I'd poured it over my hands. This decision did not, in retrospect, make any sense. Had I actually made it? The thing about knowing my mom's test would come back positive was not only the knowledge itself, the mystery of its origin and the terrible weight of keeping the secret. It was also that I experienced no associated feeling of loss. I knew this was a product of denial, but that didn't prevent me from feeling guilty. Or from trying to escape. The fact was, Blake had sent me back to exactly where I didn't want to be. Of course, facts are stupid things, as I now knew. But still.

The bus let me off two blocks from home, and I hadn't taken more than four steps before a neighbor pulled up and offered me a ride. Her name was Josie, a literal beauty queen—her husband kept her crown on the mantel, much to Josie's embarrassment—who'd been mercifully flirtatious throughout high school, when just about all other adults had been toxic. In back was her daughter, Alice, reading a book with an elephant on the cover.

"Hello, Alice," I said, turning around in my seat. "How old are you now?"

The girl looked out the window.

"How old are you, sweetie? Blake asked you a question." Josie winked at me. "I don't think she remembers."

Alice rolled her eyes. Josie pulled over. For a moment I thought it was because of her daughter's response, but we were simply at their house.

She got out, helped her daughter down, and pulled a couple bags from the trunk. Then she stood outside the passenger-side window and bent over, smiling quizzically. Alice giggled, seeing me still in the car. What was I doing in their car, just sitting there? I got out, thanked Josie for the ride, and headed down the block.

Josie called to me, and I turned to see her head poking out the door. Her daughter was already inside.

"You're here for the summer, right? Stop by sometime!"

I waved. I wondered what a woman like Josie saw in her husband, Happy. Happy was a stiff, distant man. Not handsome. Not rich. Not happy.

My brother's old Datsun was parked in front of the house and my mother's Escort was in the driveway. The overgrown front yard made it difficult to walk up the path to the front door, which for this reason had fallen into disuse, but as I walked around to the side I noticed a cardboard box the size of a small refrigerator standing on the porch. My mother and brother were sitting on the back porch, smoking. I chose to avoid making the obvious observation about this.

"What's with the box on the front porch?" I asked.

My mother tried to blow a smoke ring. "It's for your father."

"Any word from him?"

My father was doing a job for some Russian czar up in Alaska, where all flights had been temporarily cancelled due to an eruption of Mt. Redoubt. He was trying to get home. He would be home as soon as possible.

"He said we should expect a big package."

My brother went inside and returned with a bag of chips. He'd put on some weight since I'd gone to college, but it suited him. He was taller than me, and with the added padding he had the kind of gravity big men have. I tried to picture him with Blake—she'd always liked his directness.

As if reading my mind, he asked about my day. "How's OB doing?"

Other Blake.

My mother swatted at him, and he spilled a few chips onto the deck. He crushed them and swept them between the boards with his shoe. I shrugged.

"What does redoubt mean, anyway?" I asked. "Isn't it like to call into question? Like an aspersion?"

My mother coughed. "Blake, seriously. First of all, an aspersion isn't to call into question, it's slander. You're thinking of dispute."

"I don't think so."

"I know so."

I went into the house. "I'm going to open that package," I said.

I grabbed a knife from the kitchen and brought it to the front porch, where I went to work cutting through the tape across the topmost seam. Down one side of the box were staples, however, so even after opening the top I had to tear the thing apart carefully to avoid getting poked. My brother came and stood at the doorway, munching chips.

"So," I said, "you haven't seen Blake recently, huh?"

Kent grinned.

"I knew it!"

I was about to give him shit for this, but at that moment the stapled side of the box came loose and packing peanuts spilled out onto the porch. Inside the box, something bright and metallic and unrecognizable glinted through the foam. I scooped out more peanuts and pulled away another side of the box and what emerged was some kind of sculpture. Thin plates of metal, possibly tin, were assembled in the shape of an animal, possibly avian. It was steely blue, with green and yellow accents, and presently a red, lightning-like piece fell at my feet. Apparently, the thing had been damaged en route.

"Thoughts?" I said.

"It looks like a bird," said Kent. "Chicken, maybe?"

My mother came to stand beside Kent; she peered out at the unidentified object. Beside my brother, she looked even smaller than she was, and her thin, pale face seemed to shimmer and float in the darkness of the house.

"It's a fort," she said, following up on my earlier mistake. "A kind of fortress."

"A chicken fortress."

"Kent," I said. "Do you have any more weed?"

DAY 23

I WOKE LATE TO find my mother standing before a table covered in bouquets. Her hair, usually in a bun on the back of her head, was down now, and it seemed to me that more gray had come in, thin stripes of it running through the straight brown stuff coating her shoulders and neck. She turned to me with a big shitty grin.

"Aren't they beautiful?" she said.

But the smile wasn't insincere, not really. It was just wound up in something bigger than her gifts. Several cards were tented at the bases of their respective vases, and I picked one up. It was from "South Central WIC" and read, "Our thoughts are wish you in this difficult time." I showed her the card.

"Wishful thinking," she said.

I continued to the kitchen. "I'm surprised so many people know."

It was not that my mother was a private person. She was amiable and frank. But she hated to be a nuisance—something at odds, I'd always thought, with her '60s activist past. I poured myself a cup of cold coffee and stuck it in the microwave. The doorbell rang and she went off to accept another bouquet, leaving me with the vaguely funereal display. The situation was serious, but this seemed premature. She hadn't even been diagnosed. And when she received that diagnosis—my instincts on this had not changed—wouldn't the second round of flowers lack impact? Or were stuffed animals next? My mother brought in the new bouquet and placed it with the others. These were white, with soft, drooping stems and downturned blooms. They resembled heads in prayer, I thought, or mourning, though the card explained that they meant hope.

"How are you doing today," I said, not a question exactly. My coffee beeped and I pulled out the steaming cup.

"I've been thinking about poetry," she replied. "I've been rereading Carl Sandburg these last few days."

She closed her eyes and stood a little straighter.

"'When you come back we may sit by five hollyhocks,'" she said. "'We might listen to boys fighting for marbles. The grasshopper will look good to us.'" She peeked out at me. "What do you make of that?"

I yawned. "It's pretty early."

"I think that's an essential part of poetry. The not knowing."

The room smelled terribly of flowers. I thought this might be a good time to tell my mother I was thinking about planning on dropping out of college. Perhaps the poetic spirit would let her look past the obvious weakness of my response to the vulnerability of dorm life, something my roommate had once compared to a "fish tank without the glass."

"I've actually been writing a little, lately," I said.

"You've always had an artistic temperament."

My mother moved her face around over the flowers, and before I could broach the college topic Kent came bounding up the back stairs. He'd been out all night and looked both disheveled and invigorated, his movements alert, jerky, exact. He passed me on his way to the fridge and grabbed a beer. With a quick twist he palmed the cap and flipped it into the trash. My mother didn't seem to notice this, or if she noticed she didn't seem to mind, and I marveled at the way he had her trained: my brother, only seventeen, had the run of the house.

"Fuck," he said. "Crazy night."

"Where were you?" I asked.

"Have you seen the news? Last night there were thirteen separate sightings. That's more than the last two weeks combined."

He was referring to the UFO sightings that had become Seattle's cause célèbre since the beginning of June. First reported by two firemen on a routine inspection in Wallingford—they called it in, thinking they were seeing illegal flares of some kind— the Seattle Lights, as they'd been dubbed, had since been showing up all over the greater Seattle area with no apparent pattern or cause. Some described them as slowly falling flakes, something like radioactive snow. Others claimed they moved in tight circles, or zagged at head level between buildings and trees. No one had yet caught anything on tape, which gave the skeptics ammunition for all kinds of armchair explanations.

"Seems like you might have seen a thing or two yourself last night," I said.

Kent took a long pull from his beer. "Some guy from the UW said it was probably a mass hallucination caused by anxiety about the future of the world. Like, everything's going to shit, so here's proof that we're not alone."

"Great, so just when we need a reality check, we're having a collective escape fantasy."

"He said it was hopeful."

"You know what I *did* hear this morning," said my mother. She was rearranging the bouquets, putting a vase of tall lilies in back. "There is a kind of tiny saltwater fish that was found to turn in the same direction all at once, everywhere in the world. One school of them will be in the Indian Ocean, say, and another in the South Pacific, and they'll all be dodging around in unison."

I looked at my brother, who smiled. "You can't even tell what's real anymore."

"See, but that's the beauty," said my mother. "That means you have control."

I grew quiet.

Kent belched.

The phone rang.

"How long have the lights been going on?" I asked.

"Twenty-three days," my brother said.

The sculpture wasn't very heavy, but it was delicate and awkward, and carrying it around to the back yard was a chore Kent and I could manage only slowly, afraid of contributing to its incipient collapse. My brother kept shaking his head and rolling his eyes, a wordless reiteration of his conclusion early on that I shouldn't have torn the box open out front. The fact that we couldn't have known what was inside didn't seem to mitigate his opinion that I was to blame. But it didn't matter. I enjoyed his jokey frustration, just as I enjoyed, at least in retrospect, Blake's disappointment. These were safe, familiar things. These were things I could live with. We found a spot relatively clear of weeds and set the bird down. There was the question of a stand, but Kent suggested we pour a small concrete slab to mount it in. He kicked the ground with his foot, testing the density of the soil.

"I think we're good," he said.

"So you and Blake are pals now?"

"I don't know. Maybe."

Over the course of my freshman year it had begun to dawn on me that I might not be well-suited for college. All around me people had been positively blossoming in the relative cushiony, slack-jawed freedom that is college life, while my attempts to mimic their enthusiasm were so forced that classmates actually commented on my peculiar state. They could sense I was not truly enjoying myself but simply ingesting large dosages of drugs and alcohol and, once sufficiently high, overcompensating with a kind of reckless, spastic exuberance it was clear to anyone present I would regret, retreating into an even more obviously superficial pantomime of behaviors I took to be natural.

My brother and I worked in silence digging a small, square hole. He'd borrowed some quick-dry cement from Fred, and it sat in the growing heat, a light, weightless dust hovering above the open top. Once the hole was ready, Kent read the instructions on the side of the bag and went inside to fill a bucket of water. It struck me that, without him, I would never think to use cement. Intellectually, I recognized that it was doubtless a simple task, and the bag indeed bore clear instructions for its use. But there was something remarkable about my brother's seemingly native expectation that such instructions would be perfectly suitable, would fill the gap between inexperience and effort. I had no such faith.

When he returned, the khaki mop bucket brimming but not spilling, I stood aside.

"Do you think Mom sheltered us too much?" I asked.

Kent put the bucket down and handed me a trowel.

"I mean, do you ever feel like you're not equipped to deal with…" On the verge of saying it out loud, I realized how vulnerable finishing the sentence would make me sound.

"Blake, are you going to help or just stand there?"

"I wonder if Dad will even like this."

"I wonder if he'll even see it."

"True."

Kent carefully poured cement directly into the hole, trying to keep the dust level low, and then motioned for me to ready my tool. I knelt and stirred the clotting dust as Kent slowly poured in water. Dirt from the hole's sides got tucked into the solution, but it didn't seem to matter much, and we quickly filled it with a grainy fluid that reminded me of a thick gray milkshake. Next we set the sculpture's feet into the cement and propped the thing up with a scrap of wood. We stood back and admired our work. It was growing hot, and sweat stood out on Kent's forehead, which he wiped by bringing up the front of his t-shirt. It now bore a wet, upside-down version of his face.

"We hang out sometimes, I guess."

"Okay, that's perfectly fine."

"Mostly we talk about Tidemark, but lately also about her…" Now it was my brother's turn to trail off, and I suspected he too knew how his sentence was supposed to end.

"Her what?"

"No one, never mind."

"So it's a person, huh? Her boyfriend? Does she have a boyfriend? Come on, I'm going to find out soon anyway. We're meeting up tomorrow. She said she had something to tell me."

Given the circumstances, I didn't feel like my lie was a breach of trust.

"I'll let her tell you about him, then."

"Huh."

Kent reached out and gently shook the sculpture. In the sun, the metal glinted sharply where not covered in paint, and I squinted to avoid a silver sliver of sun.

"So, Tidemark is this cult she's in."

Kent waved his hands around his head to shoo away a wasp.

"Let me guess," I said, "it's not a cult."

"Well, it's not."

"Does it have a charismatic leader?"

"Yes."

"Does it have a set of behavior modification principles referred to as a 'technology'?"

"Um."

"Does it encourage its members to get other people to join?"

"Fuck off, Blake."

"Oh my god, you haven't joined too, have you?"

"No comment."

"You have! Shit, Kent, are you fucking kidding me? You're seventeen!"

"I didn't join, okay? I went to a kind of introductory workshop thing."

I shook my head in a way I hoped read grave disappointment. The wasp came back and Kent waved his hands again before giving up and heading around to the deck stairs. I followed slowly. Was I angry with Blake? Maybe. Ultimately, I was sure it was harmless, but as something I didn't understand it made me wary. When I got up to the deck, Kent was sitting in our mother's chair and sucking on the end of a small glass pipe. He held the smoke in, held the pipe out, and exhaled.

"They're not dating, exactly," he said. "He's way older. And he's in the FBI."

DAY 24

JOSIE HADN'T GONE TO college. She'd married Happy, her high school boyfriend, after learning she was pregnant—this during the beauty contest whose outcome was trumpeted by the crown still on display—only to miscarry in her second trimester and fall into a long, near-fatal depression. Though her prize carried with it a partial scholarship to Western Washington University, an overlooked contingency required the "half-ride" to be ridden within two years, which she missed, sending her back into a tailspin not weeks after she'd finally emerged from her depression long enough to get her application paperwork together and submit.

We sat on her front porch, and I listened to her story over coffee and homemade biscotti while waiting for Blake to pick me up. It was a little uncomfortable, both because of the story and because I was distracted, looking down the street for Blake's car, and could feel Josie's acute sensitivity to these glances. I wanted to apologize for them, to tell her not to interpret them to mean I wasn't fully invested in the conversation—except that's exactly what they meant.

"Well," I said, "you didn't miss much."

Josie rolled her eyes. "Oh, come on, you must have liked *something* about your first year."

She bribed me with another biscotti, and I bit.

"There was one class," I acknowledged. "It was about self-deception."

A pickup truck drove slowly down the street. It was painted red and yellow and had some kind of bird logo painted on the passenger-side door.

"It was about the different ways you can deceive yourself. We read Freud and a guy named Habermas, some other guys…"

"So what is it?"

"Self-deception? It's basically the ability to hold two opposing beliefs at the same time. For some reason this was always represented by the letter P. As in, P and not-P."

I could tell Josie was trying to think of an example, so I gave her one.

"Say you're an alcoholic, I mean you're really addicted, and you know this, or part of you knows it. But at the same time, you tell yourself you're in control."

"Okay."

"But it gets more interesting on a bigger scale, maybe. Like global warming. There's all this evidence to support it, and it's basically a fact, right? But there are tons of people out there who come up with all these crazy reasons why it's not true. I mean, they know it's true, part of them, but they'll also believe anything that contradicts it."

Josie seemed ruminative.

"It's about being driven, for whatever reason, away from unpleasant truths. Like if there's some kind of personal responsibility at stake. Or a moral imperative you're trying to escape."

We were quiet for a time. I wanted to finish my coffee, but a thin film of cream had developed on the cooling liquid's surface. I heard the hollow knock of wood on wood, and through the screen door I could see Alice sitting beside a simple puzzle, its oversized wooden pieces scattered on the floor.

Another car came down the street. Josie stood and began to gather up the dishes. Her fingernails, I noticed, were bitten down to the quick.

"You're right," she said. "I'm not missing much."

On the way to Queen Anne, Blake explained the change of plans. We'd decided to go to Discovery Park, where during high school we'd analyze ourselves on walks as circuitous and interminable as our conversations. But since Kent had apparently confessed to spilling the beans, she'd decided to address the matter directly.

"I just want you to see for yourself that he's not a creep," she said.

"An FBI agent hanging around an eighteen-year-old girl? How could that possibly be creepy?"

Blake accelerated through a yellow light.

"Listen, Dale is important to me, okay? Be nice."

What kind of a name is Dale, I wondered. It sounded Southern, small, like the name of a cattle rustler. Or a cowhand. Dale Evans. Dale Earnhardt. Chip n' Dale. I wasn't jealous, really. Though I'd been hoping for sex two days ago, my feelings for Blake were roughly platonic—she could be fucking the mayor for all I cared. But that didn't mean I wasn't judgmental. I didn't like the idea of her with an older man the same way I wouldn't like the idea of her with Kent. It was aesthetic more than anything.

We circled up the hill and crossed a small bridge spanning a ravine on the north side, then parked on a slight incline. Blake's '70s Chevy's doors were heavy, and we had to work to keep them open as we climbed out. I followed her up the block and down a street, and when it became apparent that we hadn't parked anywhere near Dale's house, I voiced my dissent.

"Driveway full?"

"Dale is a cautious man."

We walked on. It was not a neighborhood I'd spent much time in, and I gazed wonderingly at the large, stately brick houses nestled behind formidable oak trees lining the street. Their gnarled roots propped up slabs of sidewalk so that we had to step up occasionally, though we were not climbing. It seemed reasonable to ask whether his caution was due to their difference in age or to his work in some way, but I didn't ask. Either way, it put me on edge. Blake turned down a driveway to a small communal area in the center of the block, a large lawn flanked by pea patches, and we cut across, slipping through a fence and down to the basement door of a modest white house. She opened the door without knocking, and we entered.

The rec room was done in masculine hardwood and forest green. In the center was a pool table with deep red felt, home to a thin layer of dust; the balls had been racked at one end, and at the other a cue ball sat in the saturated red field like the tip of a bone. We climbed up a tight stairwell that cut back twice in the span of one floor and emptied out into a bright white kitchen. Everything was immaculate here, and gave the impression of long disuse despite the lack of dust. A muted voice could be heard from another room, and as I followed Blake down a hallway toward the front of the house it grew louder, until I could recognize it as the stern singsong delivery of radio news.

We paused at the doorway to the living room. Across from us stood a man leaning over a large table—the only piece of furniture out of place—with his left arm raised, index finger extended. *Just a minute.*

"You've brought Blake along," the man announced. His voice was even and almost clipped, but entirely without menace. "He's one hundred and fifty-five, maybe one hundred and sixty pounds, with a pronate gait, and favors his right side."

Blake, who was standing before me, looked back up at me, eyes wide. The newscaster was speaking about the Seattle Lights, and in the minutes we waited for Dale, I learned that more had been seen, that hotels were booked as believers the world over poured into the city. A barista, interviewed about increased business, said, "At least we know the aliens' intentions are good. I just hope they don't want a cut of the proceeds."

Dale turned around, a big grin on his open face, and walked directly to me with his hand held out. He was dressed in a simple black suit, white shirt, and a red-white-and-blue, diagonally striped tie. His slicked hair was combed back in an almost '50s style. He had soft brown eyes, a strong chin, and a tall, narrow face bearing no blemish or wrinkle whatsoever. He looked much younger than his age, though he was certainly twice ours. We shook.

"I had a dream last night," he told me, "and I'm hoping you can help me understand it." I looked past him to the table he'd been standing over, and without following my gaze he said, "Pendulum clocks."

"What?" I said.

"I fix pendulum clocks. It's a hobby that helps me relax. Blake, a man needs a hobby to help him relax."

I looked at Blake, and she swatted me gently on the arm.

"Would you two like any coffee?"

Blake said she would, I declined, and as he went to get Blake's cup I walked over to the table home to Dale's hobby. The clock's casing was nowhere in sight, but the guts were splayed out on a white tablecloth, all the cogs separated and organized into a line, slender metal arms arranged beneath them, and a large spiral band of some kind off to the side. Dale came back with a cup for Blake and one for himself, and they sat together on a pale yellow sofa that flanked one side of the room.

"So what's wrong with it?" I asked.

"The grasshopper escapement. It's a tricky one, not often used. Most escapements are very simple, but this kind must actually push the gear back in order for it to move forward. There are several moving pieces, and each one has to play its part perfectly for the clock to keep time."

I looked up from the table and noticed that there were yellow ribbons surrounding the front of the house. This place was condemned.

"So what was your dream?" asked Blake.

There were drab landscape paintings hung on the wall, and on the small end table close to me framed family portraits of people not Dale. Dale regarded me with his same maddeningly open expression and put down his cup.

"You're uneasy," he said to me.

"What *is* this place?"

I was thinking it was time to go, and my question sounded surly. Blake made a face.

"This place is a model home. Almost forty years ago, Weyerhaeuser tried to break into the business of manufactured homes. They owned the land, they owned the wood, and it seemed reasonable to simply build the houses too—something the industry refers to as vertical integration."

I frowned.

"It didn't work, perhaps due to mismanagement, but at any rate they kept the property—there are several houses like this throughout the city—and it was almost forgotten until recently. Now the houses are set to be demolished, though what Weyerhaeuser plans to do with the property is a closely guarded secret."

Dale's voice, though not unpleasant, was nearly robotic. It was even and formal and informational, without a hint of judgment. Either he had no opinion about the house or the fact that he was in it, I reasoned, or he was so guarded that his secrets must have been enormous.

"So you're essentially squatting," I said.

Blake choked on her coffee and went into a coughing fit; Dale reached across and took the cup that was jiggling at the end of her arm, and rubbed her back, saying, "Breathe, breathe." Once she'd recovered, Dale turned back to me and slapped his hands against his knees. "Blake," he said, "that's *exactly* what I'm doing. You call it like you see it, and I like that."

"But doesn't the FBI put you up? I mean—"

"Part of the investigation. All part of the investigation."

It felt as though he wanted me to ask, *What investigation?* So I didn't. I was uneasy, as Dale had put it, and wasn't at all sure I wanted to know any more than I already did. I felt indirectly exposed by him somehow.

The newscaster was now talking about a drought affecting large swaths of country throughout the Mid- and Southwest states, and she mispronounced dust bowl, "dust bowel."

"Dust bowl," she said after a pause.

Dale retrieved his coffee cup, and after taking a sip said, "Have you ever noticed, either of you, that once a radio host misspeaks, it's very likely that they'll make more mistakes before the end of their report?"

"I've totally noticed that!" Blake said.

"Have you ever thought about why that is?"

"They're too focused on not messing up."

Dale snapped his fingers and pointed at me with a grave look. "That's precisely what's happening. That's precisely it. Well, but it's not exactly that they're trying not to mess up—they're simply trying to speak clearly. They're focusing on the language, the language of the text before them."

"What should they be focusing on?" asked Blake.

"That's the question, isn't it. Unfortunately, there's no single answer. Each person must determine his natural point of focus. For some, it may be a small tingle at the base of the spine. It could be a physical object in the room, a totem perhaps, or even something ordinary, such as, in the case of a radio host, the red blinking light signifying that she's on air. Only when the body feels liberated of the mind's tyranny of attention can it operate smoothly. The Eastern mystics have understood this for ages, but in our day of rabid intellect, it's a lesson easily forgotten, or simply never learned."

A car drove down the street, and Dale paused, holding his finger again in the air until it had passed. I had the impression he could have told us the vehicle's make, model, year, and type of tire, but I realized this only meant that his act—it was obviously an act—had been successful, and I pushed the thought from my mind.

"Now," he continued, "let's try to apply that logic on a larger scale. What if our intention was not to read a printout over the air, but to compose a song? Or to make a big decision? Or to solve a mystery? In this case, a red light wouldn't do. We'd need something more fully immersive, something entirely unrelated, or only tangentially related, to our goal. And it would, by necessity, be something demanding a longer amount of time, a greater degree of our mental facility."

He looked back and forth between Blake and me. P and not-P, I was thinking. P and not-P.

"Your clocks!" Blake announced.

"You're in top form today, Blake," Dale said. He leaned over and playfully pinched her nose, giving it a wiggle. It occurred to me in that instant that there was no sexual dimension to their relationship at all.

"So you try to solve mysteries," I asked, "by fixing clocks?"

"Precisely."

"Does the FBI know about your tactics?"

"The Bureau understands that my approach is one guided in part by intuition, inspiration, and a fine-tuning of my relationship to the spirit world, if that's what you're asking. And there happen to be aspects of this case that indicate these characteristics may be of considerable use."

Dale gave no hint as to whether he'd been put off by my question. His delivery was so matter-of-fact, so sincere, that he seemed perhaps even a little naïve.

"Which brings us to my dream."

Blake sat up straight. "Oh, yes, tell us your dream."

"In my dream, I am visited by a being made entirely of light. It comes into my room, hovers over my bed, and tells me, 'To find the solution you seek, you must employ a novel idea.' A novel idea. I must say this has me stumped. It's both obvious—of course I need a novel idea—and completely broad. I have to say, my dreams are usually more helpful than this."

Blake was completely enthralled, and had begun to enumerate different synonyms for the word novel. "It means different, right?

But doesn't it mean, like, strange? Strange means foreign, so maybe it's an idea that comes from somewhere else. Somewhere alien, even! An alien idea. Maybe this is connected to the Seattle Lights!"

"That's extremely interesting, Blake. I love the way your mind works."

I was irritated by Blake's enthusiasm. "A novel is also a book," I said flatly. "Maybe you're just supposed to write a book about it. Whatever 'it' is."

Blake began to say something in protest, but Dale stopped her. "There are no bad ideas here."

Apologizing, Blake stood and sternly motioned for me to join her, and after explaining to Dale that we had to be somewhere we didn't have to be—me shaking Dale's hand and agreeing we'd see him again—she began to drag me toward the basement stairs. This was all fine with me. This was how she'd been spending her time? It seemed to lend credence to the idea that she'd suffered some kind of break. She looked up to this odd man without any sign that she perceived his oddity. Instead she responded like an eager student to his seemingly rhetorical questions, and took seriously what I might have, were it not for taking her lead, laughed off. Was it a continuation, a manifestation of her war on irony? Had she taken herself a bit too seriously? There would be no discussion about all this today, I knew. After embarrassing her before Cooper, I'd be lucky to get a ride home. And yet, as I followed Blake's march back across the communal lawn, I had to admit that, truly, there was something infectious about the man's apparently artless sincerity. Despite my uneasy feeling about Dale Cooper, I'd just passed a not inconsiderable amount of time during which my mother's cancer was the furthest thing from my mind.

DAY 25

SOMEONE KNOCKED ON THE front door and my mother, eyes closed, whispered, "Would you?"

After a quiet morning, we'd moved to the back porch, where she was sitting in the sun, not moving. I was reading the paper. The Seattle Lights, it turned out, were not Seattle's alone— sightings along the Himalayas, in Japan, in Borneo, and in the UK had also been reported, though there was even less agreement in these areas about their nature, behavior, or even appearance, and because the very rural regions in which they'd been seen lacked a modern communications infrastructure, many sightings were all but dismissed from the official account. It seemed to me that as the phenomenon grew, its credibility diminished, as though people had simply gotten caught up in the fun. Perhaps it was a harmless distraction after all.

"I think Kent was right," I said, standing.

My mother *mhmm*'d—of course she had no idea what I was talking about—and said she was expecting something from her lawyer.

The dining-room table was overrun by flowers, though they'd finally stopped coming, and as I passed them my nose tingled with their undifferentiated richness. I held my nose as I opened the door, trying to stave off a sneeze. It was Happy. He was with Alice, who remained partially hidden behind his legs. He was crying.

Or rather, he had been crying. But now, as he saw me look at his flushed, wet face, he began to cry again.

"I'm sorry to ask," he said, "but I wonder if you could look after Alice."

"Happy, what's going on? I mean, of course. For how long? Is everything okay?"

"Just for the afternoon. It's Josie. She's in the hospital. She hurt herself and I have to…"

He pulled his daughter from behind him and prodded her toward me, and as he did she began to cry, and as she cried he began to cry harder. He took two deep breaths and turned back down the steps. His car was idling in the street, its door open, and he climbed in. Then, with a wave of his hand, he was gone.

Now sobbing uncontrollably, Alice tried to follow her dad, to get free of my hands, and I had to struggle to get her inside.

"Don't worry, Alice," I said. "Your dad will be back really soon. Everything's going to be okay."

My mother came charging through the house. "What happened?"

"It's Josie. She's in the hospital." I made a face I hoped would communicate something and let go of the little girl's arms as my mother reached down and picked her up.

"Shhhh," she said, "Sh-sh-sh-sh-sh. It's okay, sweetie. It's okay."

My mother carried her into the living room, bouncing her gently and swaying. Alice seemed big in my mother's arms, too big, and her squirming made them look like some kind of two-headed beast trying to hold itself together even as it tore itself apart.

"Can I get her anything," I said, "do you think?"

"Unless you have her mother in your pocket, I doubt it. We just have to give her some time—don't we, Alice? Just a little bit of time!"

She'd *hurt herself.* This was clearly no fall, no sprained limb. I tried to summon my morning with Alice's mother, but in competition with what had come later, with Dale Cooper and his clocks and his dream, the memory was in full retreat. I was well aware that one's first response, upon learning of something like this, was to accept, escape, or assign blame, depending on one's personality type. My mother bounced around, and on her shoulder perched Alice's face, red and disfigured like a third-degree burn.

"Shhhh," she said. "Shhhh."

When another knock came, I figured it had to be Happy, come back after realizing that to leave his daughter with a dying woman and her wastoid son was a bad idea. I opened the door half-thankful, half-ready to defend my mother against any judgment of her parenting skills. It took me a moment to place the man before me.

"Hey, Blake," said Echo. "I thought I recognized this house."

Echo was a drug dealer who occupied an orbit in my social galaxy far enough from the center to be safe, but close enough not to spin away entirely; someone I knew well enough to feel awkward about just buying drugs from, but who I'd never invite anywhere unless he had some.

"What are you doing here? I mean, you know, what's going on?" I stepped onto the porch and closed the door behind me. Echo had aged in the year since I'd seen him: his face was long unshaved, with greasy whiskers sprouting out of his chin and in patches on his cheeks. His eyes were tired.

"Jesus," he said. "Someone needs a nap or something."

"It's a neighbor's kid. Her mom tried to commit suicide, I think."

"A neighbor's kid, huh?" he said, as though that were the significant part of the story.

We stood together for a moment, Alice's muffled wail seeming more distant than it actually was. Echo wore a green short-sleeve polo shirt with a company logo on the breast pocket: *Emerald City Errands*.

"Oh, you must be here for my mom."

"I've got a package for someone named…" He removed a manila envelope from a messenger bag at his side and read the label. "Rose Williams?"

"That's her," I said, reaching for the package.

Echo pulled it slightly away, a dealer's reflex, then handed it over reluctantly. "She's supposed to sign."

"Well," I said, "she's got her hands full right now."

A woman walked by, reading while walking her dog, and after she passed Echo leaned in, raising his eyebrows. "Hey, you need anything?"

"Like, a package delivered?"

"Fuck off. Seriously, I got buds, acid, blow, whatever."

"So this is, what, a cover?"

"Gas," he said, and nodded back at his company car, a little Honda pulled halfway in the drive. "I go all over the place, man, and they don't even check the mileage."

I was actually impressed, and failed to hide it.

"You should go for a drive with me."

"We have a houseguest." As I said this, the crying suddenly ceased. Anyway, it would be shitty for me to leave my mother alone with Alice, and if I were to leave, it certainly wouldn't be with Echo. His beeper went off, and he brought it up to eye level as though looking through a tiny pair of binoculars.

"Hey, I gotta go," he said. "Last chance."

I smiled and shook my head, then opened the door as he sprang back down the steps. Inside, my mother was sitting on the couch with Alice in her lap, reading from a picture book. She looked up at me, and the calmness, the clarity of her face surprised me.

"Are you going out?" she asked.

In a minute there is time for decisions and revisions which a minute will reverse. The two-headed beast had come to an arrangement, I realized, and it was giving me permission to take my leave.

"I'll be back soon."

"Okay, sweetie. Is that for me?"

I put her package down on the couch beside Alice, who looked up at me in irritation—I was interrupting the story. I backed slowly out of the room. My mother would be fine, of course. Alice would be fine. Truly, it would be condescending to think otherwise. What did I know about taking care of children? Echo had just begun to pull away from the house, but stopped when he saw me, and reached over to push open the passenger-side door. Minutes later we were driving south on Aurora through the zoo.

Traffic on the road had slowed to a stop-and-start, had left us nearly idling between the lush green overhangs of Woodland Park. I had not asked where we were going and was not really concerned. We drove for a time beside a convertible driven by a dark-skinned woman with long arms, and I tried not to stare.

"What the fuck," said Echo.

We swerved to the side so he could look up ahead, but a small rise prevented us from seeing the traffic jam's cause, and with the park to either side we couldn't change our route for the next quarter mile. I reached for the stereo, but Echo told me not to bother.

"All static," he said. "It's the only shitty part about this job. I keep telling them to fix it, but they tell me it's not high on their list of priorities."

"I could see that."

"Yeah? I think morale should always be high on a company's priority list."

"I could see that, too."

"What's up with you, Blake? You seem dyspeptic." Echo grinned.

"I wouldn't know," I said.

"Gloomy."

"You remember my girlfriend Blake?"

"Or pessimistic."

"She's in some weird relationship with an older guy. It's not sexual, I don't think, but he's got some kind of control over her. I can't figure out what to do. Or if I should do anything."

"Irritable."

We approached a pedestrian bridge, and on it a young boy holding a blue balloon was standing with his father. The father looked down at us, smiling and speaking to his son, who ignored both the traffic and his dad. The kid let go of the balloon and watched as it rose higher and higher until, just as it was about to disappear over the treetops, it snagged on a dead oak branch and darted back and forth like a fat pet. In a short burst of forward movement, we crept under the bridge and came to another complete stop. This one lasted two, three minutes. Five. Engines began turning off.

"This is un-fucking-believable," said Echo.

"Must be an accident."

"Well, duh."

"At least we're out of the sun."

Echo looked at me and considered.

"See, I'm not pessimistic."

Echo turned off the car. He reached across my lap, flipped open the glove compartment, and removed a tin box. The top sported a piece of duct tape bearing the words FIRST AID. We were in the far right lane, and beside us an older woman in a beat-up Dart gripped the steering wheel as though still moving.

"If that's for the accident," I said, "I'm sure they have everything they need."

"Yeah, but *I* don't have everything *I* need."

Inside the box was all manner of drugs. There were two rolled-up sandwich bags full of white pills, a few tiny Ziploc bags of weed, and he rifled around until he found a flat square of paper. He undid a folded side, sprinkled a small mound of white powder on the back of his hand, and snorted it, then held the square in my direction. I reached for it but he pulled it out of reach, saying, "Give me your hand." I held it out, palm down.

After we'd done a couple bumps of coke, he pulled a joint out of his box, placed the tin back in the glove compartment, and climbed out of the car. I joined him, standing on a small tuft of grass that rose from the sidewalk and terminated in the cool, damp stone arch. Traffic still had not moved at all, and sirens could be heard clearly, though it was unclear from what direction. Under the stone bridge, sounds echoed back and forth, always changing, as though we were slowly spinning. The coke had made my front teeth go numb, and I lightly tapped them as my thoughts accelerated. We could easily get caught, I was thinking. There would be nowhere to go, I was thinking. Yeah, I was thinking, but how could the cops even get in here? Ha, I thought.

The pot mellowed me out, but it didn't return me to normal. I was on a track parallel to sobriety—an alternate reality where everything was both more sinister and more fun. The underside of the bridge echoed with whispers, and the idling cars choked out beautiful plumes of exhaust that undulated in the sun beyond the edge of the bridge's shadow.

"Have you ever wondered why a house feels empty sometimes and not other times?"

Echo took a hit from the joint and passed it to me. "Because sometimes there are people in it, and sometimes there aren't."

"I was in this house yesterday. There were three of us there, and there was furniture and, you know, everything a house has. But it felt totally empty. It just, like, emitted a feeling of emptiness. It's difficult to describe, but you can be in a completely empty house, meaning nobody's home, it's just you—you don't even have to live there—and the house doesn't feel empty. Or, you know nobody's there, I'm not talking about feeling like someone's watching, or some kind of haunting, but a real sense of presence, or maybe, no, maybe it's just the absence of a feeling of absence. That's more of what it's like. So why is that?"

I suddenly felt entirely alone. It was the drugs, of course, but a shiver ran through my body so forceful it almost made me drop the joint. Echo was not a companion, I saw clearly, and this was not a little ride. It was a betrayal. Nearly everywhere I could think of was more important than being here, so why had I come? I came because I was trying to sabotage my chances of being a good person. I stepped into the sun and could see the blue balloon still caught in the high branches, nearly invisible against the sky above.

"When I was growing up," Echo said, "I used to love it when no one was home. That was the only time I could relax. I won't go into it really because it's kind of depressing and also stereotypical and boring, but let's just say that my dad was a fucking dick and my mom was a moron. Is. Anyway, I'd come home from school, say, and open the door really slow, as slowly as I could, like by opening it slowly I could just freeze time and look around and then make a decision about what I wanted to do, whether I wanted to stay or leave. My dad would always be out, still at work. But my mom had some weird schedule and sometimes she'd be there and sometimes she wouldn't. So I'd poke my head in and look for her keys or her purse or something, or I'd listen to whether the TV was on, but I think more than anything it was just a feeling, like, yep, the house is empty. Or, nope, someone's home. Maybe it was something I'd hear, really. But that's not how it seemed to me at the time. At the time, there was some kind of intuition, something so subtle I wasn't even aware of it, and what I'd feel, standing there at the door, was either a sickening sense of dread—someone's home—or a lightness, an overwhelming feeling of possibility and freedom—no one's home."

I brushed my hand across the moist stone of the bridge and Echo gave me a nudge, pointed. A white sedan was driving toward us on the sidewalk. It was coming slowly, but neither of us had noticed it before, which made it seem sudden, fast, and we froze. It stopped five feet from us, and a man with cropped hair, reflective sunglasses, and a mustache climbed out. Echo hid the joint behind his back and smiled stupidly, but the man stood before him and without a word pointed down to where he was holding it. Echo brought it around before him as though in a trance. The man took it, brought it to his lips, and took three quick puffs. Then he handed it back, returned to his car, and passed by, driving toward the source of stalled traffic.

"Yeah," I said, "that's not really what I meant."

DAY 26

KENT AND I SAT on the couch, my mother in her antique rocker, rocking. The house was so thick with afternoon stillness it felt like a Jell-O mold—each of us perched in our respective chairs like a constellation of canned fruit frozen in soft green space. I said so.

"Yeah. I can see how it might seem that way to a stoned person." Kent turned to me slowly. He'd been reading *The Weekly*, and he pointed to an ad in the personals. "Read that."

> *Looking For The Lights?* You: a believer wanting proof.
> Me: an ex-Marine with experience in guerilla warfare. The
> Seattle Lights are coming from the woods. Let me show you.
> "Make Contact" for details.

"What are you doing looking in the personals?"

Kent grabbed the paper back and glared at me.

On the radio was a story about a local man who, when flushing his toilet, got some backsplash into his mouth and, startled, sprang backward gagging, then slipped on the wet floor, fell against the toilet, and broke his neck. His girlfriend witnessed the entire thing from the bedroom, and in the interview could only say that he'd always been extremely graceful.

"I'm not stoned," I said. "I'm buzzed."

Kent stood. "So, wait, the guy poops with the bathroom door open?"

"Something about that story stinks," said my mother.

I nodded. "You've said a mouthful."

We were nervous. Mother's results would be in soon. Soon as in hours, minutes. Soon as in now. All day I'd been wanting to bring it up, to ask my mother how she was feeling, but it seemed like an impossible question. Then the envelope appeared. Reappeared, rather. It was a plain white thing, a big shingle with my mother's name scrawled across the front. It had come by messenger, so it had no addresses, neither to nor from, and without a word she'd put it, unopened, on the table beside the bouquets, and it sat there, quiet and with a curious gravity. My brother and I had stood before it, transfixed, more than once. I was finally high enough to break the spell.

"What's with the envelope, Mom?"

Her hair was pulled back into a tight bun, and because it was so fine the shape of her skull was revealed. She looked at me kindly, firmly.

"You know, Blake, and Kent, both of you boys, you know of course that whatever happens, you'll be taken care of. I promise you'll both be taken care of."

"Mom," Kent said, "don't say that."

"No, I need to know that you understand. Tell me you understand."

My mother's face had lost the softness it had worn before, and her eyes were dark now, impassioned, almost scary. Kent's bottom lip began to quiver.

"I understand," he said.

"Yes," I said. "Me too."

"Because you two are the most important thing in the world to me. You know that, right?"

"Mom, come on."

"Don't *Mom come on* me, Blake. I'm serious."

"I know."

"Do you?"

"Yes."

We sat in silence again, and it wasn't until minutes later that I realized she hadn't answered my question. Of course I knew how much she loved me and Kent—she frequently reminded us. So why did I feel embarrassed, somehow ashamed, by her bluntness now? Kent was sitting with his head low, staring at his hands, and I couldn't get a read on him. The stillness had returned, but I could no longer call it thick. We were not couched in some comfortable goo, we did not seem connected by anything at all—it was absence, not presence, that described the space between us.

The gravel in the driveway announced a visitor, and we listened to the footsteps go back to the porch staircase and up the stairs. Blake appeared at the glass door. She waved, smiled, came inside.

"Am I disturbing you guys?" she said.

My mother got up to give her a hug. "No, dear, come right in. It's good to see you!"

Kent went outside to smoke, and my mother went to the kitchen to decant a bottle of white wine. It was her new thing—leaving white wine out after opening it, letting it warm. "The tyranny of ice!" she'd exclaim. Blake came and sat with me. The afternoon sun had crept from the windowsill to the couch's high plush back, and from there it would cascade down to the seat and run us off.

"What's going on?" she asked me quietly. "Should I come back?"

It seemed like she probably should. I tried to picture my mother being told she had cancer. Blake was not in that picture.

"Dale wants to talk to you," she said.

"Blake."

"He thinks you may be on to something with your inter-pretation of the word 'novel.'"

"Blake, listen."

"I know it's weird, but he takes his dreams very seriously."

"Blake, I think you should—"

The phone rang.

Still standing in the kitchen, my mother drank the full glass of wine she'd poured for herself, then another she'd poured for Blake, and stepped forward to answer it. Blake stood and began to move toward the door, but stopped short when my mother held up her hand. Blake looked at me. The options were to stay and witness the havoc caused by the call or to leave before she got the message, therefore adding humiliation to the mix. She sat back down. My mother spoke very little, saying her soft yeses and nos, nodding. The color had left her face and her hand was on her hip, her left leg bent at the knee, her feet bare. This summer, I thought, would be a summer of little trips. Little trips to the hospital for treatment. Little trips to the lab. Little trips to the pharmacy and to counseling. Little trips to the bathroom to vomit. Little trips to bed. And if she beat the cancer? There would be a reprieve from these trips—a temporary reprieve, and then they would resume. And who would take her? Who would hold her hand and hold her hair and who would save the receipts? The sun began to bathe Blake and me with light, heat, and I thought of my father in the cold recesses of Alaska, waiting out the interminable storm.

I leaned in close to Blake, and she put her arm around my shoulder. "Okay," I said. "I'm in."

My mother put the phone down and slowly walked to the table, picked up the white envelope, and began to tear. As she tore she began to weep. She wept and tore and grew angry, tearing more violently, tearing pieces into smaller pieces, and Blake began to get up but I held her there, pinned her to the couch, in the sun, so that my mother could have more time to tear and to weep.

Kent came back inside, went straight over and took her in his arms. They stood there for a moment, my mother still gripping white scraps in both hands, wrapped in my brother's arms, my brother whispering "Shh, shh, shh" and gently rocking side to side. I joined them, putting my arms around them both. Blake's face was wet from silent crying, and she stared at our small union as it tipped to one side and then the other, my brother's weight shifting us all.

"I'm so sorry, Mom," I said.

She shook her head.

"We'll take care of you," I said.

"No, no." She shrugged us off and stood facing us. "No, it's okay."

"What do you mean?"

"It's benign."

My brother acted first. He whooped loudly and grabbed her around the waist, then lifted her into the air and spun. My mother screamed and started laughing, beseeching him to put her down. Blake came and stood with me, and we smiled as Kent refused her request, spinning and spinning, shouting until my mother's screams turned back into tears. He returned her to the floor, and because she looked unsteady I pulled out a chair so she could sit.

"This calls for a toast," I said.

I poured four small glasses of wine and handed them around. I felt detached from the news. It wasn't that I didn't believe it, but I still believed its opposite, too, and these two opposing thoughts were in different corners of my mind, refusing to budge. It was as though I was witnessing good fortune through a lens of personal defeat. But what had been my defeat? So I smiled, smiled authentically, certain that my body language wasn't giving me away. This was truly wonderful news, after all.

We raised our glasses.

"To…" Kent began.

To what?

To the absence of cancer?

"To freedom," said Blake at last.

"Yes." My mother smiled and nodded. "To freedom."

We drank, and as we drank I began to see that the toast applied to all of us. I watched Blake nudge my mother and laugh. The sunlight now fully flooded the house, drenching the table and torn paper like spilled orange juice, and I marveled at how Blake always had the perfect thing to say at the perfect time. My mother broke from us to open another bottle of wine, and I joined her in the kitchen. She is going to live, I thought, trying desperately to believe it. My mother is going to live.

"To *life*," I said.

"Yes, sweetie. Can you hand me the corkscrew?"

"So what are you going to do?"

"Do?"

"Yeah, you know."

"Well, go back to work, for one. But not today!"

Bottle open, she pushed past me to the dining room, filled the glasses, and began cleaning up the paper she'd torn.

High clouds glowed orange in the sunset sky. My mother was in bed, Kent passed out, and I was sitting on the back porch steps with Blake, nursing the last beer in the house. Night sounds were beginning to fill the air, birds and crickets and small scurrying creatures, and a breeze tapped together the long, spiky branches of the monkey puzzle tree, tapping like fingernails on a tabletop, like the sound of waiting.

"I bet half of what you hear at night," I said, "is just what you'd hear in the day if the day wasn't so loud."

We were sitting close, though it wasn't cold, and the skin of Blake's bare shoulder brushed against my arm as she leaned forward to flick an ant off her toe.

"Can you believe that bus thing?"

A strange new sound came alive, louder than the rest. Not a bird—it was some kind of instrument, a flute maybe. Or some kind of recorder? It was a haunting, hollow sound, and while it wasn't playing melodically, it was obviously intentional, a kind of meandering note that twisted and bent as though drunk.

Blake turned to me. I could feel her stare on the side of my face. "You know about the bus thing, right?"

"I guess not," I said, "because I just said 'what bus thing' in my head."

"Some guy shot a bus driver? And the bus drove off the Aurora Bridge and landed on an apartment building?"

"Jesus. When was this?"

"Yesterday afternoon."

Clearly this had been the cause of the traffic I'd been stuck in with Echo. I thought of the man who'd smoked Echo's weed. An undercover cop? I finished the beer and gently tossed the bottle into the driveway.

"Do you intentionally avoid the news or something?" Blake asked. "This was the only thing that's been able to push the Seattle Lights off the front page in days."

"You remember my neighbors Josie and Happy? I think I've told you about them. Little girl named Alice?"

"You were over there when I picked you up."

"Yeah, well, Josie tried to commit suicide yesterday, I think."

"You think?"

"Well, she 'hurt herself,'" I said, using air quotes.

"That's kind of not the same thing, is it?"

"Did you see my air quotes?"

"Who are you getting this from?"

"Her husband. He brought their daughter here, and we watched her while he went to the hospital."

"Yesterday?"

"Something about how he said it. 'Josie hurt herself.' I don't know. But so I was preoccupied."

"It just careened off the side of the bridge, apparently. No one else died, which I basically can't believe."

"What the heck *is* that, do you think?"

"I don't know. One of those slide whistle things?"

"Yeah, I bet you're right."

We listened for a while, but the playing stopped and there was laughter, then the laughter died off and the night sounds returned. Or, rather, they became noticeable again. Then again, I thought, some of them could very well have paused; birds, for instance, scared by the slide whistle. Cats, curious.

Blake leaned over and kissed me.

DAY 27

BLAKE AND I STOOD in the pea patch behind Cooper's house. A family of rabbits munched on red leaf lettuce nearby; the mother eyed us warily as her babies huddled over their lunch buffet. A woman who'd been kneeling in a neighboring flowerbed stood and, seeing the rabbits, angrily scared them away, stomping her feet.

"Little fuckers," she said.

"Aren't rabbits good for gardens?"

The woman looked at me like I was stupid, which probably wasn't far from the truth. She took off her gardening gloves, pulled out a pack of Marlboros, lit one.

"No," Blake whispered, "I'm not sleeping with him."

Since our kiss, my curiosity about Dale had deepened, and I'd begun to second-guess my earlier conclusion that their relationship was sexless. Perhaps I'd just decided that for my own piece of mind—something that had been easier to come by when I'd given up hope on us myself.

"But."

"But nothing."

It was obvious Blake was hiding something, but I figured I could work on her slowly. I had the entire summer, suddenly, to do what I wanted. "Okay."

We went in through the basement door and up the steps, and I found myself looking forward to seeing this man, who, despite his relationship with Blake, seemed harmless enough—he was an overgrown eight-year-old, with all his childish enthusiasms and sincere fascination with the world.

Dale greeted us with coffee, pointed to a map he'd laid out on the table that had held his clock.

"*That*, my friends, is what we're up against."

The map was of a wooded area south of Seattle.

"There's a Tidemark Forum retreat out there this weekend," Blake said. "And Dale wants us to go."

"Us?"

Cooper stood beside me and pointed to an area he'd circled, the letter W scrawled in the center. "Weyerhaeuser," he said.

"That's that," I said, "you know, that tree-growing company."

"More precisely," Cooper said. "Tree gene-manipulating company."

Blake was sitting on the couch, thumbing through a magazine, and she looked up just as I looked over. "Just hear him out."

"I'm not *not* hearing him out," I said, irritated. "I'm waiting to hear what there is to hear!"

"You're frustrated," Cooper said, "and I don't blame you one bit. Let's start with Tidemark."

It was true; I *was* frustrated. But not with him, or this. I was frustrated by Blake's assumption that I was impatient. Was she upset that I'd asked her about sleeping with Cooper? I thought this had been a pretty reasonable thing to ask. It was possible she felt our kiss had been a mistake, but if so, why hadn't she said so? I tried to make eye contact with her again, but she was ignoring me.

"Okay," I said.

"Tidemark is just a cover. Tidemark is a way to get close to Weyerhaeuser. You see," and here he pointed back at the W,

"Tidemark is the only organization that owns land anywhere near here. Weyerhaeuser began buying it all up at well above market value—our first red flag—but Graves refused to sell. He didn't need the money, and the forest there holds special spiritual significance for him."

"Graves…"

"Bobby Graves," said Blake, "is the founder of Tidemark."

Cooper continued, his eyes narrowing after a long nasal inhale. "To Graves, the trees there represent an alphabet, and by walking through the woods one can spell out one's own destiny."

For a moment he seemed lost in thought. It was clear from his tone that Cooper had respect for this Graves person.

"Blake said you thought I could help," I said.

"Right! Yes, your idea for writing a novel."

"Well, that's not—"

"Blake tells me you've been writing. Is this true?"

"Well, you know, I've just been…Yes. Why not."

"That's what I like to see: own it! Graves happens to be a big supporter of the arts, so what I'd like you to do is go in there, notebook in hand, and explain that you're writing a novel about a person going through a program like Tidemark, someone who's experimenting, for instance, with the technology they use."

The house was silent for a moment, save for the soft crackle and snap of glossy paper. Cooper was dressed in the same suit he'd worn before, or perhaps he had more than one identical suit. I admired its crispness.

"You want me to take notes," I said.

"It's what I want notes *on*, though. That's the kicker."

"Weyerhaeuser."

Cooper snapped his fingers. "Attaboy. Of course, it's my duty to tell you that your role as an FBI informant is strictly voluntary—I hope I haven't led you to believe otherwise. There is also the matter of pay, which will be taxable, and some other paperwork that we'll go over should you decide to volunteer your energy. But before we get into all that, please, tell me, are you interested at all in helping?"

I put my coffee cup on the map's key, already rippled and stained with several brown rings. "Can you tell me any more about the case? Kinda hard to know whether I'd want to help without knowing what's going on."

"Ah, well, there's the rub. You see, until I get a verbal agreement from you, I'm afraid I can't disclose any more details than I already have."

Blake had put down her magazine and was now watching our conversation intently.

"Did you go through this?" I asked.

She nodded.

Cooper grinned, as though marveling at this gem of a paradox. One thing that was clear to me was that if I wanted to know more about his relationship with Blake—if I wanted to come between them—I was going to have to play along with this little mission. I was going to have to involve myself.

"When is this retreat?" I asked.

Cooper was standing over his map, but turned quickly, not a hair out of place. "Tomorrow."

On the drive to Discovery Park, Dale gabbed away nonstop, commenting on the drivability of compact cars, the city's decision to raise rather than bury power lines, the improbably steep northern slope of Queen Anne, footbridges in general, the danger and beauty of trees planted on the median, the smells of low tide and of crustaceans in particular, and, before I stopped paying attention, a Mister Freezee truck that reminded him of a large fissure that had been discovered in something called the Ross Ice Shelf in Antarctica.

"Mark my words," he said jovially, "that's going to come around and nip us in the tuchus."

After a crash course in Tidemark Forum's trademark technology, called Existencelastic Macrobial Foreshortening—something that, even having been explained to me, made utterly no sense—Dale announced that in addition to explaining more about the case, he'd like to "get to know me better," and suggested a walk. Blake had volunteered Discovery, and though I didn't like the idea of a place I still felt was *ours* being used in this iffy, platonic way, I went along with it. Now here I was, being chauffeured around with this blabbering tour guide. I sat in the back seat's pooling sun feeling heavy-limbed, somnambulant. Literally along for the ride.

We parked on Emerson and walked along a footpath that splintered after a few yards, one walkway heading west along the park's border, another straight ahead into a large open field, a third hooking northeast toward some half-abandoned barracks. Still lolling along, I didn't even notice at first that Blake had gone right where we'd gone left, and I must have looked bewildered, because Cooper spoke to me as though I were a child.

"Don't worry, Blake. She'll meet back up with us soon, okay?"

I nodded and inhaled sharply, waking up.

"C'mon," he said.

We walked down toward the cliff overlooking the water. The park ended in a bluff, a drop-off at the bottom of which ran train tracks where bums and punks would gather. Puget Sound was calm today, and a tanker pushed ponderously toward the Strait of Juan de Fuca, headed out to sea. Gulls circled above it—some, I knew, would ride it across the Pacific, only half-aware that it wasn't land.

"Blake thinks very highly of you," Cooper said.

Now that we were alone, I noticed that in addition to being youthful and enthusiastic, his voice was also almost snide, condescending in a good-natured, unintentional way. Which made it worse.

"I want you to know that the Bureau appreciates what you're doing. Your *country* appreciates it."

I nodded solemnly. Who would have thought I'd ever do anything the government approved of, let alone appreciated? It wasn't more than a few years ago that I'd been protesting the war, dealing drugs a little, doing drugs a lot, and hoping the Northwest would secede from the Union and form something called Cascadia.

We walked farther, down to the crumbling edge of the bluff where metal beams had been hammered into the cliff to hold a railing of railroad ties. It was so overbuilt that I'd often wondered, coming here, if the cliff wouldn't collapse under the weight of exactly what protected people from falling off of it. The Sound glistened in the sun, and we watched a regatta tacking around buoys outside a marina just south of the park.

"So what will I be doing, exactly?"

Cooper gently grabbed my arm, turning me to face him. "We have reason to believe that Weyerhaeuser's chief executives are involved in human trafficking."

"You mean…what do you mean?"

"We've been seeing some peculiar activity. This is an organization that makes extensive use of overseas shipping, especially between here and Japan, and some containers have been circumventing Customs, heading straight from the shipping terminal to the Weyerhaeuser Research compound near Eatonville—that spot I showed you on the map. Additionally, special vans have been seen making trips from Research to parts of Seattle, to residential homes. We've done our homework. These are not authorized deliveries of any kind, nor can these trips be explained by an officially sanctioned, permitted program, research or otherwise. In a nutshell, Blake, it's a mystery. We're actually working closely with the Japanese government because they've been seeing the same behavior in another land management company on their side. Now, the trafficking element is just a suspicion so far—we haven't gathered any conclusive evidence— but the operation conforms to no other pattern we know, so we can't rule it out."

Just as he was finishing this sentence, a Golden Retriever bounded up, and without hesitation Cooper crouched down and began to pet the animal, calling it a good dog and scratching behind its ears.

"I want you to know that the Bureau would never put you in harm's way. You'll be watched at a distance, and besides, you won't be going anywhere alone, or even off the property wholly owned by Tidemark. And you know what? If you don't see anything, or notice anything out of the ordinary, no problem. Your compensation is not dependent on results in any way."

Saying this, he stood up and the dog rushed back to its owner, a man in a red plaid shirt who waved and kept walking.

"Wow," said Dale. "It is just an absolutely *beautiful* day. This is the kind of day you want to relive right after it's over."

I looked around for Blake as Dale kept talking.

"Did you know that here in Seattle lives the man credited with defining the term 'déjà vu'?"

She wasn't anywhere I could see, and as I scanned the park I realized that the man whose dog had come over was nowhere in sight either. In fact, Cooper and I seemed to be the only people here.

"Vernon Neppe is his name. His definition of déjà vu is 'any subjectively inappropriate impression of familiarity of the present experience with an undefined past.' I've often considered that phrase: inappropriate familiarity. Let me ask you something, Blake."

I was relieved to see Blake appear finally beside one of the barracks and wave. She was wearing the same white summer dress she'd worn when we'd met downtown a few days ago, and it made her stand out from the lush green around her like a hole in the world.

"Shoot," I said.

"How would you describe yourself? Actually, let's narrow that down. What do you think one of your most essential traits is? What is that characteristic you believe sets you apart?"

Blake began to walk toward us, a shard of light shining down the small hill, and along with a renewed confidence I felt defensive. Dale Cooper, I thought, surely wanted me to name one of those self-important qualities young men love to believe of themselves: smart, perhaps, or insightful, even deep. And though I wouldn't necessarily argue with these descriptions, I didn't want to give him the satisfaction. And that was probably why, thinking of how far I was prepared to go to prove something—I wasn't even sure what—to an ex-girlfriend, I chose something else, a kind of low-hanging fruit I'd never really considered to be impressive. It was something I didn't expect, and so I thought he wouldn't expect it either.

"I'm determined," I said.

Cooper looked into the distance and nodded gravely. "The truest wisdom is a resolute determination, said Napoleon. Yes, determination. A mature choice, Blake, a mature choice. I'm very impressed."

"Well," I said, now a little embarrassed, "you just do what you have to."

"Exactly. You do what needs to be done, and there's humility in that, which is actually one of the most unsung but essential qualities of an agent, if you don't mind my saying."

Blake was now close enough to hear what he'd said, and joined in with a cheery, "What did I tell you?"

I searched her face for some hint that there was more to the exchange than what I understood but could find none. There was only Blake's easy smile, her dark hair blown by a salty breeze across her flushed, delicate skin. There was only her hand reaching out for mine, the warmth of her touch. I knew the meaning of these things. I could name it. I held her hand and turned my face to the bluff.

DAY 28

I SLEPT FITFULLY, WAKING up hourly with the sense that something was wrong, that I wasn't where I should be, that I'd overslept. I worried about the mission in a general sense, and worried too about whether going along with the plan would be "good" for Blake in some deep but unarticulated sense—wouldn't it be better for me to express my misgivings about her relationship with Dale? Shouldn't I try to force Blake, or at least encourage her, to admit the peculiarity, the vague perversity, of her liaison with this creepy older dude? More specifically, I was anxious about the writing. I'd been asked to provide notes about what I saw and encouraged not to let Cooper's assessment hinder or alter in any way my own. But I was already overthinking it. As I dragged myself downstairs, my exhausted mind circled repeatedly, stupidly, around the same thoughts they'd been circling all night.

This was an opportunity, after all. Mine would be the official report, or the foundation for it, the raw material. "Write what you see" was my only instruction, but Cooper's only evidence of what I'd seen would be what I'd written. In truth I'd have free rein to write anything I wanted. I could discover evidence of foul play in even the most banal encounter, or find no evidence of anything at all. I could find something entirely different—I could send Cooper on a wild goose chase! Nothing that wouldn't stand up to plausible deniability, of course, but I couldn't deny the mischievous impulse to tinker. I'd feel no compunction sending the FBI after Bobby what's-his-name. The world could do with a few fewer cult leaders. Wasn't a cult just a more subtle and insidious form of human trafficking? Self-elected, willful enslavement to a cause that didn't serve those who enacted it? Who lost the ability to judge themselves, let alone their leader, with any degree of objectivity.

Kent had left for some overnight camping trip, and I thought the house was empty until my mother appeared from the bathroom, carrying a mask.

"Morning," I said. "What's that?"

She lifted the thing to her face and peered out through its narrow eye slits. The mask was made of stained wood and was roughly cut—chiseled, it looked like—with gouges in the cheeks and lines in the forehead and a little howling, round mouth.

"I found it at Goodwill," she said, and held it up to the wall across from the bathroom door. "It spoke to me."

I shuffled past her into the kitchen. "I hope not literally."

"There's something about masks, don't you think?"

"What is it about that one in particular? It seems…I don't know, I want to say *elemental.*"

"This is the mask of my new life. This is my new face."

"Are you okay, Mom?"

She finally found the right spot between two windows in the dining room and began to hammer in the tack. Once the mask was up she grabbed her purse and headed toward the back door.

"Have to run, sweetie. Still catching up on what I missed while I had cancer."

After she left I stood before the mask. Its expression wasn't anything familiar, was instead a kind of ur-expression, a summation of all possibilities a moment before the facial muscles conspired into something sympathetic.

When Blake arrived I was sitting on the couch listening to Dylan's *Hard Rain*, feeling misty and nostalgic. She saw my watery eyes and she looked concerned, sat down beside me. Hot, flat light pressed everything down' outside, the still day looked fake, and as Blake put her arm around me Dylan challenged his blue-eyed son, his darling young one, to face the ugly world.

"I'm sorry," I said. "I'm just exhausted."

"Where's your mom?"

"Look at the mask she brought home."

Blake walked up to it and frowned, nodded. I couldn't tell whether she was missing what I'd seen, or whether it was easier for her to accept. She peeled me off the sofa and we locked up the house. I could see Alice up the street in her front yard, which meant Josie was home, but as we drove by I didn't see her in the darkness beyond the yawning front door, and before long we were heading south on I-5, Mount Rainier jutting up in the distance like a whitehead. A few years ago, my mother had taken my brother and me to a place partway up the mountain called Paradise where you could park and hike a little in the snow, and I remembered being told to stop running because the air was thin. It was the first time I'd ever considered air being anything but air.

The truth was, I *did* know what it was. My confusion, having turned quickly into acceptance and relief, had finally, having nowhere else to go, settled into a stagnant pool of self-hatred.

"I was convinced my mom's test would come back positive," I said. "Did I tell you that?"

"Hey, but it didn't!" Blake rolled up the windows and began to fiddle with the AC.

"Well, right, but I was *positive*. Isn't that weird? Like, kind of fucked up?"

"You were preparing yourself for the worst. I'm pretty sure that's normal."

"No, no. I've prepared myself for the worst before. Remember that time we found those keys?"

"You're kidding, right? That's totally different! This is *your mom dying*."

"I'm not talking about the seriousness of the thing you're preparing for. I'm just talking about it reaching its superlative state of badness—whatever that is, you can mentally prepare for it, and it feels like...it still feels like it's in the future. If you're preparing, it's in the future. It hasn't happened, and because it hasn't happened, you can be, like, okay if, if—actually, that's just it. It's still an if. An if can't be an is. You prepare, but there's time between you and whatever, the guy finding us in that closet. With this it was different. It didn't feel like anything was in the future. It was that she had cancer, and we just hadn't been told by the doctors yet."

Blake hit the dashboard, trying to get the AC to come on, but it was broken so she rolled the windows back down.

"Blake, I'm really sorry you're feeling bad, but you're freaking out about this for no reason. You went through something that you couldn't have prepared for, that there's no precedent for that makes any sense as a precedent. Okay? Maybe I'm not explaining it very well, but you just can't compare anything to your mom maybe dying. Unless I guess your dad has died. Or your mom has almost died before. That hasn't happened, has it? Has Rose ever almost died?"

I shook my head.

"Blake?"

"Oh, sorry, no."

"See, that's what I'm saying."

"Yeah, but I just—"

"Blake! Your mom is okay. You were scared, but it's okay. She's alive. She's going to live."

We were slowly passing a motorcycle carrying two people, and the passenger was a girl with a miniskirt hiked up around her waist. She was wearing a thong, so her butt cheeks were exposed and the vibrations of the road made them ripple.

"Besides," Blake said, "you sound like a retard: if, isn't, is, if, isn't, is."

The girl on the bike turned toward me, caught me looking at her ass, and flipped me off. I waved.

"So you've never been to this camp?" I asked.

"Retreat, and no. I've just been to classes. The retreat is expensive."

"Have you met this Graves guy?"

"Seen him."

We were silent for a while. The stretch of highway between Seattle and Tacoma was flanked by small rises home to trees that gave the impression of a forest, though I knew that behind them lay hidden the predictable exurbs of Tukwila, Des Moines, Federal Way—neighborhoods no doubt built with farmed wood from Weyerhaeuser, it occurred to me. It really was an enormous company, something I'd always considered a "Seattle company" in the way I considered Boeing a Seattle company, and Starbucks a Seattle company, and Microsoft a Seattle company, though it was less visible, somehow, lurking behind the scenes. Why risk it all with some kind of slave trade? It didn't really make sense, but a thing doesn't have to make sense to exist.

"I'm still not clear how you and Dale met."

"We met at…"

I scanned the traffic in front of us to see what was distracting her, but cars were sparse, and everything seemed to be moving smoothly.

"At where?"

"I'm trying to remember."

"Wasn't very long ago, right?"

"Yeah, no. I mean, a few months?"

"Was it during one of those workshops?"

"Workshops?"

"Tidemark."

"Hmm."

"You don't call them workshops?"

"I'm thinking."

Signs for Tacoma began to appear, but we turned off I-5 and took 18 toward 167. I tried to give Blake time, but I wasn't quite sure why she needed it. It was a simple question. Was she trying to think of a good lie? Had she expected me not to ask?

"Hey," she said, pointing to a vehicle on the side of the road up ahead, smoke billowing from underneath the hood. "Isn't that Kent's truck?"

"Shit, don't stop."

"Don't stop? What are you talking about?"

"Did you tell him where we were going? I'm pretty sure this is not a conversation we want to have."

Blake nodded, braked, and swerved into the side lane, then tapped the brakes again as the car's wheels met the gravel shoulder. A ghost of khaki dust overtook us when we finally came to a stop.

"Jesus," I said, but Blake had already leapt from the car and was jogging back to my brother, who didn't hide his surprise.

When I reached the truck, they were already arguing.

"What do you mean you're okay?" Blake said.

"I mean, you know, I'll figure it out. You don't have to—"

"Where are you camping, anyway?"

"I'm…it's like over by…"

Kent was up to something, but because we had our own secret I didn't want to press it.

"Beautiful spot," Blake said. "What the fuck are you *really* doing?"

Kent's shoulders slumped. It was interesting to see him cave under the pressure of big-sister scolding. A Miata meeped as it went by and all three of us turned to flip it off, and it was that moment of camaraderie, I think, that did it. Kent closed his hood.

"I'm going to Tidemark," he said.

The drive started out tense and ended up silent. Kent was clearly embarrassed at having been caught sneaking off to join a cult; Blake and I didn't want to explain our situation and therefore didn't want to press Kent about his. He said only that he'd been invited during the introduction seminar he'd gone to and had been planning on coming for weeks. Blake's half-truth was that she'd wanted me to see what all the fuss was about. I explained to Kent that I was sorry he felt like he'd had to lie, but one look from him served as correction for this fatuous claim. With a judgmental, snarky brother like me, he clearly did. We focused on the road.

The Tidemark property snuggled up to the west slope of Rainier at the end of a long, unmarked dirt drive that passed alongside a forest in various stages of growth—some patches newly clear cut, others planted with saplings, still others covered in what I took to be juvenile trees, their needles a startling bright green, fairly glowing. An old man on a tractor waved us into a parking space, and we stood by the car for a bit, taking in the retreat's collection of off-white yurts. They radiated outward from a single-story log-frame meetinghouse, all within a forest of tall pine that cast dappled sun down in moving, lifelike splotches as though the camp was just then in the process of appearing. Blake read from a pamphlet explaining that the first scheduled event would be a welcome and introduction by Graves, after which an early dinner would be served and the students would have time to mingle.

"Students?" I said.

We found our names on a board by the parking lot—we were all assigned to different yurts—and wandered off to claim our beds. The drive had made me sleepy, and as I walked through the grounds in the sharp piney smell of the woods, I watched with a kind of dull satisfaction as people roamed the grounds chummily in small groups or convened at the open flaps of their yurts. Everywhere was the happy chatter of reunion, and it reminded me of how I'd stay awake as a child during my parents' parties, listening through the floor to the unintelligible adult conversations. Now, as then, I didn't know what was being said, and I didn't *want* to know; it seemed to me that it was exactly the not knowing that was important. It was comforting to know that people were saying things, leading lives that were in no way dependent on me. The barely distinguishable names, the calls across the camp, the bubbles of laughter rising to the top—all this made me more and more tired as I finally found my yurt, climbed the three steps to its open door flap, and entered the cool, canvas-smelling interior.

Four metal beds made a square inside the curved walls. Three of these beds were still empty, and on the fourth lay a large man with his back to the room. I heard a soft, muffled sobbing. I took a bed by the door.

I dreamed of sitting with Dale Cooper in the living room of his house on Queen Anne. Old pendulum clocks lined the walls, and their simultaneous ticking strobed so loudly it severed each second from the last. Cooper held a large, shiny green leaf, which he raised to his mouth and bit. As he chewed, his mouth began to fill, puffing out his cheeks as though he were blowing a horn. Although the clocks were ticking in unison, each one told a different time. I could hear Blake laughing in another room, and as I stood to look for her, Cooper grabbed my arm and opened his mouth. His tongue was lousy with maggots, and he reached inside and began to claw them out until nothing was left but a thin, pink sliver of flesh that receded back into his throat. I leaned in, looking more closely, and he opened his mouth wider until my head nearly fit inside. Suddenly I was inside his mouth, a fleshy cavern that arced over my head. I looked out past his teeth at the room beyond, where Blake walked toward me and peered into the opening. She was no longer laughing. I tried to call out to her but could not. The mouth closed.

"Blake."

"Mmm-hmm."

"Blake, wake up." Kent nudged my shoulder.

"Mmmm. I'm up."

"You're not up. Are you coming to hear Graves? His thing is in five minutes."

I raised my head and squinted. Kent was in the door, framed in bright light, and I looked around the yurt to let my eyes adjust. The sobbing man had left, and the other two beds were now home to bags. I sat up, sweating and foggy-headed from the nap.

"Where's Blake?" I said.

"Haven't seen her since we got here."

We walked in silence to the meetinghouse. The building held two hundred people, all of whom sat on folding metal chairs facing a stage, and because the sun was flooding one side of the room everyone held their hands up to shield their eyes as though in salute. Blake was nowhere in sight. Kent pulled me down to sit with him at the back of the un-sunny side. He shifted in his seat and fiddled with the seams of his t-shirt—something he did when he was nervous—and he kept craning his neck to get a better view. I realized I should probably talk to our mother about this. Surely it wouldn't be okay that her younger son was getting caught up in a cult. I was about to ask him how he'd paid for the retreat when everyone stood up with a deafening round of applause, cheering and whistling: Bobby Graves had taken the stage.

The monolithic man wore all white: loose white pants and a billowy white shirt unbuttoned to the middle of his chest, which boasted big tufts of white hair. The hair on his head was white, too, and had been pulled back into a limp ponytail. I pictured him in a green room, sitting in his underwear before a mirror, his white outfit laid out on the chair to one side, the suit he wore to the performance hanging on the door. There was a distinct theater about it, as though he'd studied a guru manual. Why white? Why the ponytail? Maybe conforming to stereotype put people at ease, opened them up to manipulation in a way they wouldn't be if they had to "read" his appearance. A small microphone curled across his cheek like a sneer. After a moment he held up his hands in what seemed to be a cross between "That's enough" and "Ta-da," and though the clapping struggled against death, it finally settled down.

"Thank you," he said in a voice made for radio. "Thank you."

As he spoke, he began to drift slowly from one side of the stage to the other.

"I want to speak with you tonight about how you got here. Look at the people sitting next to you. Look to the right, look to the left. That's right, that's right—say hello, why not? Take in your immediate situation. We're doing this for two reasons, the first being: you're sitting beside people you have something in common with. Anyone want to guess what that is? It's easy, come on, there we go, yes! Excuse me? Exactly: we're all here."

His massive body moved like an iceberg, and it provided a hypnotic accompaniment to his speaking, which, deep and forceful, was also slow, ponderous, rhythmic. His body was his voice incarnate.

"Now, I know that sounds pretty obvious, doesn't it? And, well, it is. It's obvious. But that's what makes it even more tragic that people just don't let themselves be aware of it. That's right. We ignore it. We take it for granted. We forget it. We deny it. But there it is, and let me tell you, it's powerful. A powerful thing. To a great extent, what we're going to be learning how to achieve over the next couple of days can be summed up in this way: we're going to be learning how to realize where we are. Sounds easy, right? Ha ha ha! Easy as pie! But more goes into it than you think, because, well, where are we? We're *here*, yes, here in this room. But we're also part of a story. That's right. What's the story? Well, the story of your life. And where does your life take place, besides space? Anyone want to—yes! Who said that? Thank you! Yes, in time. We're *here* in time. So we're here in time, and we're here in space, and that's one of the things we have in common with one another, everyone together right now in this room.

"So what's the other? What's the other? The other is that not one of you chose to come here today. Now, I'm going to say that again and give it a moment to sink in, because it's going to need to sink in, because you're not going to want to believe it, and you might not believe it even after it sinks in, but we'll be working on that. So let me say again that aside from being here in space and being here in time, the other thing you have in common with one another is that *not one of you chose to come here today.*"

Here he stopped, like he said he would, and looked around the room, grinning like he'd just told the best joke imaginable. I looked at Kent, and he was smiling right along with Graves, and he turned to me for a moment and winked, as if he, or as if they all, were just now letting me in on this amazing joke the man on stage had told.

"Looking out at you all, I can see who's been here before, because the folks who've been here before are smiling with me, and those who haven't, well, you'll need a little time, and that's okay. But so let's look at that a little closer, yes? Because what can that possibly mean? What can it mean to have come here without having chosen to come here? You're saying, 'Well, nobody forced me.' And I hope that's true—was anyone here forced? Ha ha ha! No? Good, good. No, and that's an important distinction, you know, that just because you haven't chosen something, doesn't mean it's against your will. Right? Not against your will. But where does that leave you? Let's see. Let's see where that leaves us. It's like a mystery. It's exciting, isn't it? I'm excited! Are you excited to solve the mystery? I hope so. Okay, let's think back to how you got here, okay? This will be different for each of you, so please do this privately. In your own head! Think back, in your head, and look at the circumstances that led to you coming here. To you, quote, 'deciding to be here.' Unquote. I think you'll see how, for each of you, that decision was really made for you in some way, in a lot of ways, and it's really going to be your project for the weekend to learn how that happened, why it happened. Now it's not all bad, right? You're here, and you're in a good place! I don't mean to say that these things that guided you here were bad or unhealthy or in some way out to get you. They wouldn't have led you here, right? If they were out to get you. But what if the circumstances had been different? Think of all the people whose circumstances don't lead them here, but somewhere unhappy or unhealthy. Addiction? Violence? Loneliness? Despair? So it's important to try and figure out, see, how to take back some control over these things. And that's what we're here for, really, that's why it's a good thing we have the chance to share some space and, what else? Right, some time, too. How are we going to do that? Well, that's for tomorrow's workshops, but it's going to involve the generation of myth. And as a peek into the future I'll say that it's going to be about using analepses—an-a-lep-ses—to recreate your own mythos. Are you with me? No? You'll get there, I promise. And through that process, through the use of that technology, we'll be defining your stakes, and defining your mission, but you know what? You know what, tonight it's not about any of that. Not yet! Tonight you're in for a treat, because look around you! Tonight it's about eating some good food, meeting some new friends, and taking in this magical setting. This setting outside, the forest, the trees, these are going to be active participants in your process, and I want each and every one of you to spend some time with them this evening. Don't forget where you are, don't forget when you are, and you'll never forget who you are, and with that I'll say welcome, and thank you, and we're so glad you ended up here. Welcome to the next phase of your life. The beginning, really. The beginning of a life you can really, truly call *your own*. Welcome, welcome, welcome!"

There was a moment of silence—stunned silence, I thought— before the crowd erupted into a round of applause dwarfing the first in both volume and length, and I decided to slip back out the door and wait for it to end. I looked for the edge of the compound, where the true forest began. Two gray squirrels chased each other around the trunk of a nearby tree. A woodpecker could be heard rattling away. It was truly a beautiful place, I had to admit, and despite what I'd have to endure over the next two days, despite the bafflingly long-winded, infuriatingly vague, embarrassingly condescending tarot-card platitudes I'd just sat through, I knew I wouldn't mind walks in those woods.

"Blake?"

I turned at the sound of Blake's voice and was surprised to find her with Bobby Graves. She looked like a child beside this mountain of a man, and stepped aside as he reached out his big sweaty paw to shake my hand.

"I've been looking forward to meeting you since your agent called. I want to assure you that you'll receive absolutely no interference from me. Snoop around! Take your notes! It's an honor to be able to provide the canvas for a fellow artist to do his work."

Here he stopped and beamed at me.

"My agent?"

"Dale, is it? This was a week ago."

I looked at Blake, who avoided my eyes. "Right," I said. "I'm glad he called. I'll just be observing, you know, but…"

"Of course, I hope you'll take the opportunity to do the courses."

I nodded.

People began leaving the building, and soon Graves was surrounded by devotees. He grinned as if to say, hey, it comes with the territory of being a cult leader, and spun off into the eddies of urgent need.

Once we were alone, Blake said she was certain Graves had his dates wrong. Yes, Cooper called to reserve a bed and to make sure I'd be given the freedom to roam, and perhaps it may have even been before I agreed—not because he knew I'd agree, but because he had to get my name in, should I choose—but it was certainly not a week ago. We hadn't even met a week ago!

Which was my point exactly.

Kent emerged from a nearby group of people, his expression a confession that he'd overheard our exchange. He stood for a moment without speaking, and in that moment we all turned our backs on the group of acolytes and gazed west through the trees, into the slowly setting sun.

"So," he whispered, "do you guys want to go see the lights?"

DAY 29

THAT EVENING WE'D GATHERED around a fire pit and suffered through interminable testimonies of epiphany and personal transformation from those who'd attended the retreat before, and it hadn't been until well into the night that we felt able to slip away unnoticed. Except we *were* noticed—joined, in fact, by a dozen other people who, as we crept through the woods just outside of camp, overtook us and fell into the growing single-file line snaking through the woods. We hadn't been given much information about the excursion, but I'd thought it would be a good excuse to poke around on the property's edge—if caught by Tidemark, or even Weyerhaeuser, we could come off like clueless stoners.

As we snuck through the pines, our faces caught intermittent moonbeams, glowed momentarily, and then disappeared like fat fireflies. My brother's, shown now and then in profile ahead of me, wore a concentration I almost envied, his brow knit and jaw set, and I was amused by my own relief at learning that instead of getting caught up in a cult, he was just out chasing aliens. Who could blame someone for being tempted to find out for himself what all the media attention was about? Never mind the absence of credible firsthand witnesses—all that was obscured by the froth of anticipation, the greedy, compulsive push for a scoop. The way we were left to our own interpretations laid bare the prime directive of our hearts— were we cynical, optimistic? Were we scared? Intolerant? Apathetic?

This last was clearly not the case, and the line of us hummed with expectation. Twice I tried to get Kent's attention, to ask if he knew anything about our destination or what he'd been promised, but he only shushed me and told me to keep moving.

It was thirty minutes outside of camp when we finally saw a light in the distance, and a tall, lanky man who'd taken the lead held up his hand as he came to a stop. He pulled out his own flashlight, then turned it on and off in short bursts. The light ahead went off, then back on, then off again and stayed that way. We moved toward the now-dark spot slowly, carefully, and could soon make out a figure standing before the unearthed root ball of a massive fallen tree. He was an older man with close-cropped hair and a headlamp. He'd been the first person we encountered earlier that day, the man who'd waved us into our parking space.

"I'm George Washington," he said, "and I'll be your guide."

There was a snicker from someone in our group, and he looked angrily into the dark.

"Something funny you want to share?" he asked. "No? Good. I put an ad in the paper because I think people have the right to know what's going on. But if you don't have respect for the mission, you can turn right on around and skedaddle."

Skedaddle? Was this a test? The group remained silent if not respectful, and when he was satisfied with our acquiescence he went on to explain that we'd be marching on for roughly a mile until we came to a place, and that the place we would come to was owned by Weyerhaeuser, and that Weyerhaeuser guarded it with extreme prejudice.

"You could be shot," he said plainly.

This caused a stir, and after some argument and complaint—frankly reasonable, I thought—about not having been told this from the beginning, half the group peeled off and started heading back. Blake held my hand and looked at me strangely, curiously, but did not pull, did not turn away.

I leaned in and whispered, "Do you think this has anything to do with the trafficking?"

Kent remained standing right up front beside Washington. Was I being irresponsible by letting this continue? Absolutely. But I thought I should gauge the danger for myself before insisting we leave. Surely the man was being histrionic. Whatever lit thing he'd found—A grow lab? A landing strip? Dressed Christmas trees?—it couldn't be important enough to kill for.

I marveled at my own composure as we continued walking. It wasn't disbelief, really. Not entirely. Even if he was entirely full of shit, there was plenty of reason to be wary of George Washington. But somehow my interaction with Dale Cooper had inured me to the anxiety I might normally be feeling. He seemed to be an inoculation against the strange, despite his own deep strangeness. I felt not numb or complacent but disembodied. My toes began to tingle.

When we finally arrived at the site, there was nothing there— only forest in all directions, as there had been for thirty minutes of difficult travel. I was tired, my calves hurt, and I'd run into something sharp with my face. So when George Washington began to speak again, his hushed, anxious tone grated. I sighed sharply, and almost instantly he grabbed my arm, just tight enough to lead me to his side, where he explained to the small group that I'd volunteered to go first. It was entirely unclear where there was to "go," but when he pointed toward a particularly dense stand of trees I walked slowly but unafraid. There did not seem to be anything odd about the trees—I could see between them, where

moonlight fell just as it fell around me, painting the needle-strewn
ground with a thin, pale coat. I stopped a couple feet away and
turned back. Washington waved me on. I took one step, then
another, as though sneaking up to scare someone, but it wasn't
until I was inches away that I saw anything unusual.

At first I thought it was a trick of the night, an optical illusion
caused by darkness, the moon, my own exhaustion. But when it
happened again it was seismic. A kind of wave rippled through
the entire stand. It felt like the moment an earthquake strikes, and
for a moment, as my mind tried to make sense of what I'd seen, I
was swaying. It was as though the floor of the woods was vertical,
or as though there wasn't any distance between it and the trees
themselves. It didn't make any sense. I leaned forward.

"Touch it with your hand," whispered Washington.

Touch *it*? What was *it*? But I reached out, putting my hand
between two trees, and my fingers touched something. It was cold,
or cool, and soft; it was something I wasn't prepared for, and I
yanked my hand back and made a noise. The ripple returned,
spreading out from where my hand had been, and because I'd
seen it once I could now *see it*, rather than focusing on my own
response. The rest of the group reacted as I had the first time,
gasping in disbelief and fright, but I was transfixed. It felt like
a vertical surface of water. Fluid, but not chaotic. Composed—a
network of infinitesimally small points strung by spider webs. It
stuck to my fingers as I pulled back my hand, and I rubbed them
together to see that they weren't wet, or worse.

George told me to keep going. "Go slowly," he said. "It won't
hurt you."

Extending my arm, I could feel the cool softness and now
slight pressure around my fingers, like denser air. I pressed, kept

pressing, and watched in shock as my fingers began to vanish. I pulled my hand back slightly, watched my skin reappear as I did, then pushed it back in. It was a mirage, I realized, only there was something there, a sheet of light, though dark, like a projected image. I plunged my arm in, and when nothing happened to me, I looked back at Kent, who grinned, at Blake, who looked stricken, and at George, who gave me a nod of encouragement. I closed my eyes and put my head through, holding my breath. I could feel the cool border run down my face and around my neck. My head was fully submersed, and I could not breathe, could not open my eyes. What I felt wasn't fear, but the anxiety of placing an enormous bet. The imminent commitment of it. The sacrifice of control.

Finally, it was Blake who grabbed my hand and startled me into opening my eyes, gasping.

What I saw was a forest, though another kind of forest. Gone were the pines, replaced by gnarled, pedaled trees, enormous but somehow squat, like overgrown bush. And there were lights. At first, focused on the nearest tree, I saw a dozen, perhaps two dozen lights, tiny, illuminated pinpricks moving slowly around the tree's large, shiny leaves—much like the leaf, I realized, from my dream. The forest extended well into the distance, and there were lights around each tree, two dozen lights multiplied by hundreds, thousands of trees, slowly moving, swaying in a lazy chaos, swirling like dust in a ray of black sun.

I let myself be pulled back out and turned to face Blake; she looked at me with eyes wide and mouth agape and she continued to squeeze my hand, pulling me into her, pulling me back from the veil. Washington explained that we could all pass through, that we didn't need to file in between the same trees, but the group paid no attention—they were waiting for a description.

What was in there, they wanted to know. What did I see?

I opened my mouth to speak, but I quickly realized that a mere description was so insufficient as to be misleading. I didn't see lights swirling around trees inside of a force field of illusion—I saw the basic assumptions of my life exploding, the world changing irrevocably, commitment to fact falling away and an irrepressible freedom taking its place. And though the experience had overwhelmed, postponed my emotional response, now that I looked back into the woods I'd been walking through toward some unknown destination, toward this very spot, trudging along with petty grievances after a man I presumed to be wasting my time, I was overcome by a kind of innocent gleefulness, an expansive, joyful optimism that rang through me like an alarm, waking me up, shaking me out of a near-morbid indolence. I reached out to Blake and wrapped my arms around her, and though I felt her body stiffen, I delighted in this strange instant of her unknowing. Soon enough she would see what I'd seen, and we'd be reunited on the far side of her skepticism and fear.

Kent looked at me, and Blake looked at me, and Washington was looking at me, smiling because he knew, and I looked at the darkened, expectant faces of the small group. What had I seen?

"I saw," I said, "the leaping greenly spirits of trees."

I stood aside and swept my left arm into the invisible darkness, beckoning the group. Kent stepped forward, along with another man, thin and fidgety, and they pushed their hands through the illusion to feel it on their skin, then walked in. A woman followed, and another, sisters, followed by an old woman with bright pink hair. Left were Blake and George Washington, and he nodded for Blake and me to enter. I held out my hand, and after Blake took it we walked slowly through with the old man right behind.

As I watched the transformation of emotions on Blake's face, my ears filled with sounds of amazement from the others. They ooohed and aaahed as if at a fireworks display, but quickly went silent as the profound reality of the vision settled in. Blake's eyes swelled with tears and she said the word *beautiful* before catching a sob in her throat and swallowing, preferring not to speak.

Together, we walked forward into the trees, one row in, two rows, and above our heads the lights slowly circled the leaves. People were spreading out, lost in their own worlds, seeing the same thing yet experiencing their own private apocalypses of scale, and just as I realized that I was more keen on witnessing their experiences than experiencing it for myself, just as I'd begun to condemn myself for being unable, even in the face of such magic, to face my own annihilation, Kent tapped me on the shoulder and asked what the big bush was in our front yard at home.

"The what?"

"In Ballard. The bush."

"You mean the rhododendron?"

"Yes! That's it. That's what these are."

I looked up. They were four, five times the size of any rhododendron I'd ever seen. But yes: the shiny, waxy leaves were the same, and the twisted apple-tree trunk.

"Is anything going to be the same?" I asked.

"Yes."

Blake, suddenly between us, grabbed my hand and squeezed it. "Look."

A little farther ahead, the pink-haired woman slowly spun, her arms outstretched and her head back. Three of the lights had descended from the trees and were curling around her arms and head in a kind of ecstatic dance, a spontaneous communication of mutual curiosity. The woman began to laugh, and coo, and say, "I can feel them!" over and over. The sisters stepped forward, hesitantly raising their arms, not spinning, but walking out and looking up and making small waving motions with their hands, beckoning. Soon they too were surrounded by lights. One of them held her hand before her face, watching as the tiny lights spiraled around her arm, her mouth wide in awe.

"Okay, everyone," George Washington said, "I think we should start heading back."

No one listened. The twitchy man joined the others with the lights, raising his arms straight up as though preparing for a dive.

"Seriously, people—remember what I said about the place being guarded. I've seen guards on the perimeter before…"

He began to walk toward the strange ritual unfolding, but stopped short as the lights around the pink-haired woman suddenly rose—all but one. They rose up and hovered motionless as the one remaining light began to descend. It was difficult to tell whether she saw this or not, her face obscured by her hair, her eyes half closed, but her body kept spinning and her arms kept waving, and when, in a punctuating flip, she threw her head back to face the sky, the light shot down into her open mouth and she stopped suddenly, her arms dropping to her sides and her shoulders slumping.

There was a brief silence, and then one of the sisters shrieked and I turned to see that all but one light had risen above her too. She looked at us, motionless, her face contorted with terror.

"Run!" George called to her. "Run!"

Her sister grabbed her hand and pulled and together they started toward us, but they hadn't taken three steps before lights entered them too, entered their mouths, and like the first woman they froze in position, their expressions blank, their eyes unfocused, unseeing.

All at once Kent, Blake, and I turned to run, but where the end of this secret grove had been now lay lighted trees as far as we could see. Had we gotten turned around? I spun, but the lights surrounded us completely. I was growing dizzy, faint, as though I'd been toppled by a big wave and eclipsed by current, when I saw Kent, calm, point.

Blake and I followed, and though I didn't look back, I could tell by the silence that the lights had not released their victims. Kent dodged beneath a low branch, and lights began to follow him as if pulled by eddies in the air. They were getting closer, and Kent was weaving, looking above him and panicking, slowing down, when suddenly a head appeared between two close-standing trees to the left of us, and with it an arm, and the arm reached out and grabbed Kent and yanked him sideways. Kent disappeared and the head returned and I could see now that it was Cooper.

"Quick," he said calmly.

He pulled Blake and me in past him to either side. Kent was there, his face and body slack but alert, conscious, and after looking into Blake's eyes to make sure she was okay, I noticed Cooper was half in, half out of the forest edge. He was calling, trying to get someone else through, until he turned abruptly and looked back at us.

"Are you okay?"

I nodded.

George Washington emerged from the forest ten feet away and immediately fell to his knees and pounded the ground with his fists.

When I looked back at Cooper, the invisible curtain had changed. Instead of projecting an illusion of continued forest, it was now reflecting us. There I was: Kent to one side of me and Blake to the other; there was George Washington on his knees, pointing both into and out of the hidden forest, and there was Dale Cooper, a two-headed body, stretched and distorted by the reflection down his back. And as I began to realize with a crushing certainty that this reflection was somehow a kind of seeing, of perception, a light crossed the mirrored boundary, just inches behind and above Dale's head. Blake let out a cry and I uselessly called his name, but it was too late. The light dropped directly down into the top of his head, and his arms dropped and he froze, staring blankly at us as the others had.

Blake leaned forward and Kent held her back, and then the three of us turned and ran. We ran away from the forest, into the dark trees toward camp, and I looked back to see if we were being chased but all I saw was us, running in the other direction, my face shining back toward me, a pale disc floating up from the black forest floor. I remembered what Graves had said about how we'd arrived here, and what I'd considered dumb at the time came to me now with the force of inevitability and I tried to remember, to look back. I tried to piece together how I'd come, how I'd reached this exact spot, and the more I tried to picture it, to remember it, the more it receded from view, pulling farther and farther away like the sea before a great wave.

Part V

DAY 30

AT THE BUSINESS END of a too-long summer month without rain, the ubiquitous metastasized rhodies had begun to visibly wither, their once slick, plump leaves now wan, their crooked, overextended boughs sagging and slack, and the Lights, fearful for their food supply, were agitated. They swarmed the overworked white vans filled with the zombied arborists who watered and pruned the ailing flora—some had even been found trying to penetrate the protective suits worn by people who'd volunteered to stay put. Weyerhaeuser, speaking on behalf of the visitors, explained that these latter were the unsanctioned actions of errant or otherwise rogue Lights, but of course no one really believed this.

Would it have mattered if we had? Would it have mattered to those of us who'd already been Lit, who'd already served the Lights once, twice, and lived? Or to those who'd been Lit but not yet called to serve—and of these, would it have mattered more to those who waited with eagerness to serve, or to those who waited with dread, just hoping their survival was part of the plan? These groups comprised most of the people still in Seattle, and none of them wore suits. The rest of us, here to work triage or simply pay witness, had already decided to put others before ourselves—an act that had at its root the sort of deep resignation that relieved vague, ambient threats of the Lights' power to incapacitate.

I'd recently crossed the threshold between taking the situation for granted and *knowing* I was taking it for granted, and in addition to inspiring a return to some level of fascination with Weyerhaeuser, the Lights, and "the state we're in," the knowledge had made me nostalgic: for my brother, for Blake, for more innocent times. This nostalgia stood in marked contrast to the kind of blunt exasperation shared by most people not in the throes of ecstasy or fear, and it was strangely awkward, embarrassing. It was bourgeois emotion, superfluous and unearned, and because I'd kept it to myself it had grown stronger.

Home alone, I watched a pair of arborists fuss over the rhododendron across the street in what used to be Fred's front yard. Around them spiraled a dozen Lights on different orbits, though one splintered off now and then to run an errand. I was waiting for two things: Zane, who'd be coming by with some Klonopin, and Alice, who'd just be coming by. The television was off, the air conditioner was off, and the Weyerhaeuser radio murmured on its lowest volume from beneath a pillow in the kitchen. Last night a parade had passed down the street, nearly a hundred near-naked men and women drumming and dancing and celebrating their recent decision to "let the light in," a refrain sung to the tune of Foreigner's *I Want to Know What Love Is*. They'd left makeshift confetti strewn around—torn-up scraps of paper that made the block look even more deserted than it was—and one of the arborists was picking a few pieces of it out of the lower branches of his tree. He held one up and a Light zoomed in to hover before it as though trying to divine its origin. Was the scrap being read? Smelled? Photographed? Or was it being processed in some way entirely unfamiliar? In all the years since the Lights had moved into this city—into all places with a similar climate—we'd learned not one practical thing about how they lived, or even whether they *were* alive, technically. I stepped away from the window. My head throbbed. Where was Zane?

There were two reasons I wanted the delivery before Alice showed up: mostly to avoid her judgmental stare and the associated feeling, however brief, of guilt or something like it; but also, I had the sense that Zane had a thing for Alice, and I didn't want to encourage them. Alice was easily swayed by confidence, and I knew she was already drawn to his dark past, his strange connections. His facial tattoos. They were much closer in age, after all. Really, it was stupid of me to be fucking her. I thought about how, although my mother was skeptical of my relationship with Alice, she never once raised the issue. She kept her opinions about it to herself.

And then I thought: Shit, I started thinking about my mother right after I was thinking about fucking.

Basically, I needed to leave Seattle. Why did I stay? At first I'd had a role to play. After having been witness on that terrible night at Tidemark to the strange dangers of our alien visitors, I'd turned my firsthand account into a kind of cottage industry, selling the story locally, then nationally, then publishing my "expert" perspective as the Lights went from deniable rumor to unwanted guest, to anxious equal, and finally to master. I went on the morning news. I went on the evening news. I went on Oprah. And, for a time, Dale Cooper had secretly supplied me with the inside scoop. He'd been the one to investigate the growing symbiosis between the Lights and Weyerhaeuser, the first to notice that those who'd been Lit, after having awoken from their initial coma, would lead practically normal lives until they were "called," and the first to observe that the calling was without discernable pattern—that they were simply *changing* things. Tinkering. I dutifully relayed all this to the media, speaking directly into the camera, wearing the face of a man who understood the gravity of the situation but who'd risen above, who'd empowered himself with information.

Around the house, however, empowerment was nowhere in evidence. Clothes were strewn around and dirty dishes piled on almost every surface. Books, open and closed, lay around the easy chair, accented by crumpled pieces of paper. A disassembled lamp stood beside the dining-room table, its tattered cord wrapped around its neck, its shade, slightly torn, perched above the bulb like a crooked top hat. The place was a catastrophe. But there was something else, too—something deeper and less identifiable. Something a few hours spent picking up wouldn't erase. The doorbell rang.

Zane had been Lit a few years ago but he hadn't been called to service yet, at least not that he remembered. Either way, he didn't wear protection, and despite knowing this, despite having seen him hundreds of times without it, I still suffered a small surprise upon opening the door.

"Hey," I said, "get in here."

He grinned.

Inside, he apologized for being late though we'd never agreed on a time, then hooked his thumb back the way he'd come.

"Yeah, they showed up an hour ago."

He grunted. "Knives locked up?"

Zane asked everyone to lock up anything that could be used as a weapon when he was around. Occasionally, people called to serve ended up injuring, even killing, friends and loved ones who happened to be in the wrong place at the wrong time. There was some debate over whether these victims were the object of the service or simply got in the way, but it wasn't something Zane wanted to risk.

"Yeah," I lied.

He stood at the window for a moment and watched the action across the street. "Hear they found more fallen rhodies?" Zane was a gossip, but he was sincerely invested in the future of the city, and I often thought of him as a kind of town crier. He was referring to a recent spate of defaced and destroyed rhododendrons. I nodded.

"Fuck, man, this is big. They leave some initials in the stump, too. DC. No one knows what it's about, but it has Weyerhaeuser freaked. And the Lights, of course."

DC was of course a reference to Dale Cooper—at least, this was the running theory. I was surprised Zane would feign ignorance. Did he not trust me? Perhaps he actually pitied me for having once been so close to the man-cum-myth, the figure many now revered as the only person capable of standing up to the Lights. Having been so close and then unceremoniously cut off. Cooper had suddenly vanished only two years into the new world.

Zane sat on the couch and began digging through his bag. My k-pins were right there on top, and he seemed to be intentionally overlooking them—no doubt making me sweat in that time-honored tradition dealers have, the subtle resentment they're unable to hide completely from their clientele. For this was our relationship: I was a client, and a good one at that.

"Well, whatever's going on," I said, "they won't get away with it for long."

Zane looked up, shrugged. It could go either way, he was saying.

"Oh, come on. You really think they have a chance? Why would it be any different than last time?"

Felling rhododendrons had been one of the first responses to the discovery that the Lights relied on them, but it hadn't lasted.

Soon Lights stood watch over every single tree, sent armies of zombied men after anyone who came close. It was a nasty scene. It had been a signal. We sleep. We sheep.

Zane only shrugged, and it occurred to me that he might not be a sympathizer after all. With his attitude of peaceful resignation, I'd always assumed he was a member of the so-called Illuminated, but perhaps there was some layer of grief beneath the calm exterior, or some well-subdued struggle, or anger, or rage. I scanned his smooth, inked skin for twitches, muscle spasms, anything that might betray the energy of internal conflict. I saw nothing. Who the fuck was I kidding? A drop of sweat ran down the side of my face and I flicked my eyes down to his bag.

"Yeah," he said, "I remember. But this time it's different."

His hand, I could see, was gripping the pills, but he kept his arm wedged inside the backpack and looked at me expectantly.

"What?"

"You got the schedule?"

"Oh! Fuck, I'm sorry."

I leapt up and ran into the back room. One of the programs my mother supervised was a fleet of outreach medi-vans that cruised the city, delivering first aid, counseling, STD tests, and the rest. Identical to the Weyerhaeuser vans for the sake of anonymity, they were also patternless in their routes to avoid overcrowding. Patternless, but there was a schedule, created weekly by management, depending in part on areas of need and in part on what the previous week's experience had been. There was simply not enough care to go around, and as this was also the case, apparently, for prescription drugs, we had an arrangement.

I brought a copy back out to Zane, who gave it a cursory glance before stuffing it into his bag. Whoever had the schedule could conceivably receive more timely, consistent care, but it seemed to me that if the same people showed up at the vans everywhere, the medics would become suspicious. So what did he use it for? Who cared.

He was counting out the k-pins when we heard someone climb the back stairs. Startled and guilty, I spun around with my hands, holding nothing, behind my back, and Zane stood suddenly, toppling his bag and spilling its contents on the floor before the couch. He sat again as quickly, scrambling to stuff it all back in, and I headed toward the back door, ready to deflect Alice's attention. But it wasn't her. A suited form appeared on the porch and, still outside, began to unzip its suit and reach for the door. I knew before she'd opened that it was my mother.

"Hello, dear," she said and, seeing Zane, nodded.

She closed the door behind her, pulled off her mask, and turned her suit down around her waist, leaving it to flap behind her like coattails.

"You're home early," I said, hoping I didn't sound disappointed.

"I decided to take the evening off. It's humid, I'm tired, and it's…Jesus, Blake, it's hot in here. Why don't you have the… and the radio! Blake, honey, please don't muffle the radio. If you got caught up in some service action here I'd never forgive myself."

As she scolded me she took a bottle of white wine from the refrigerator and unscrewed the top. Zane came up behind me and clumsily, I thought, shoved a bottle of pills into my hand, its telltale rattle unmistakable. My mother pretended not to notice.

"Would your friend like a glass of wine?"

"Zane," said Zane, smiling obsequiously. "And no, thank you. I must be on my way."

"Zane, yes, I'm sorry. I knew that, didn't I."

"You *must be on your way?*" I said.

"Yeah, I don't know where that came from. Anyway, gotta go. See you later. And nice to see you again, Mrs. Williams."

He left out the back door, and my mother watched him disappear down the side steps from the back porch. She liked him, I could tell, though she barely knew him. Adventurous and progressive as she was, my mother enjoyed being treated with deference.

"I think you make him nervous," I said.

"Maybe he just caught a glimpse of his reflection."

"Those tattoos are episodes from his life."

My mother finished her wine and poured herself another glass, and I felt a glaze of sweat slick the palm holding the pills. Passing her on the way to the bathroom, I noticed that her face was tired, the skin sagging around her eyes and mouth, and her color wasn't good. She'd been working too much.

"Imagine," she said, "a whole society…"

"I'm listening!" I said, closing the door.

"Imagine a whole society in which everyone wore their stories on their faces. You'd know where you stood at a glance."

I shook out a Klonopin and popped it in my mouth, salivating as the pill touched my tongue. In the mirror, my face looked tired too, though I hadn't been working. It looked tired and stressed and my eyes were bloodshot, bleary, like I'd just woken up or was about to fall asleep.

"Unless the images weren't true," I called.

The radio got louder and the air conditioner came to life. The house was now swimming in sound. Even through the closed bathroom door I could feel waves of information washing over me, through me, vibrating my bones. It was a minor annoyance—I was committed to keeping the experience this side of neurosis—but it did make me wonder if perhaps I was alone in feeling so overwhelmed. Did others simply handle it better, or was I more sensitive? I'd learned at some point about people so sensitive to chemicals that they simply couldn't live anywhere normal. The entire landscape of gas stations and grocery stores and polyester clothes was like a field of landmines ready to blow them into enervated balls of elbows and knees. There must be an analog for information. I splashed water on my face and shuffled back into the kitchen.

An Imminent Action Warning was being announced, and my mother stood by the radio, leaning on the counter with a frown of concentration. Her fine, short white hair stood everywhere at attention, turning her head into a dandelion at seed. I came up beside her and blew on it.

"Quit it."

The IAWs were the reason we'd been issued the radios—they helped us avoid accidental run-ins with the hive-minded people in service. The Lights had found a way to indicate to Weyerhaeuser the area to be affected by such service—it was rumored to be an enormous map of the city, which could be illuminated block by block—but could not or would not explain what the imminent action was to be. Some actions altered an entire block, perhaps even leveling it, while others made small adjustments like stripping a house of copper wire. In one case I'd read about, three zombied women had entered a store and opened a single window in the storeroom.

Presently it was announced that the IAW was to affect a short length of shoreline at Myrtle Edwards Park.

"Thank God," my mother said, and took her bottle to the dining table.

As details were given about the number of people involved and the estimated duration of the service, my mother nursed her wine. This would, I knew, begin the evening's routine, each of us with our poisons, slowly nodding toward an hour when we could safely and quietly put the day behind us, and with increasingly heavy limbs I walked to the window by the back door and stood beside the row of hanging protective masks, gazing expressionless from their hooks. Once the announcement had been made, the radio went back to normal news, or at least what passed for normal these days: a kind of lily had been engineered to last over three months after being cut. It would be a boon, said an expert, for the grief industry.

DAY 31

My MOTHER HAD LEFT by the time Alice arrived, though it was still early in the morning. I wondered where Alice could be coming from. I was in bed. I'd taken another Klonopin before sleep and the world was still swimming in and out of focus, my heartbeat loud in my head. A hummingbird was coming and going from something just out of sight, and I watched it through the window by my bed, watched it hover and dodge and dart, its body sagging from its neck. I vaguely recalled sitting the night before in a stupor at the small table I used for writing, staring at the pad, willing words that might revive my aborted attempt to write a novel. Determined to break out of journalism, I'd shuttered myself up with my mother and the idea of writing a simple, sweet love story with an urgent faith in destiny. What I'd written instead was a scene about a young man who tongues a stranger in a noisy New York bar while her husband watches from a dark booth. The novel was already a triumph.

After announcing herself at the back door, Alice began moving through the house. I heard her in the kitchen, the dining room, the living room. She was mercifully silent on the topic of my living situation, and I was thankful for it. When she began to climb the stairs I leapt up to close my notebook, embarrassed by its mostly empty pages. I was naked, looking for clean underwear, when she entered my room, and she walked right over and took my flaccid penis in her hand.

"Sorry I didn't make it yesterday," she said.

Her hair was pulled back into a ponytail, which gave her taut face an alertness that seemed almost innocent.

"You're fired," I said.

"Yeah? Well, your eyes are out of focus."

Admitting defeat, I crossed the room after spotting a pair of boxers by the door. Disappointment from someone half your age has a special sort of intensity, but it's also easier to dismiss. Boxers on, I made for the small bottle of pills by the bed, opened it, and popped one, swallowing dry. I grinned at Alice, but she wasn't looking at me and hadn't seen my performance; she was instead reading a piece of paper.

"Hey!" Leaping over a mess of dirty laundry, I grabbed it from her hands. "What did I tell you!"

"It's not your damn book," she said. "Fuck, Blake."

I turned my back to her and inspected the page. Indeed, it wasn't one of mine. It was a letter of some sort, addressed to *The Guild of St. Cooper*. The paper had been folded and refolded several times and had worn thin, two small tears beginning at its outer edges and running toward each other in the center fold.

Resistance is afoot, it began, and it went on to describe two small children playing with marbles. Because of their protective suits, they could not properly grip the glass balls. It then likened this scenario to the ability of people, living in the shadow of the Lights, to affect change in their environment. The suits were both actual and symbolic barricades to the will of the people, the note opined, and it ended with a vision of people once again able to walk free, naked to the world. I recognized the airy, free-associative nature of the thinking immediately, and as I skipped to the bottom of the page, confirmed my suspicion by finding the signature *DC*.

"Where did you get this?" I asked.

Alice's face sagged. I reached out toward her in apology but she flinched.

"Alice," I said, "come on. Have I ever hit you?"

"You're being weird."

This was probably true.

"I'm sorry. It's just…it's the book. I'm blocked, and it's really frustrating. I don't know what the fuck I'm doing, is basically what it is. Come here, I'm sorry. I didn't mean to scare you."

She slowly stepped forward, and I too stepped forward, and we embraced in the golden tea-steeped room. What I'd come to love about Alice was the way she danced along the edge of child, lover, and mother—someone unafraid to counsel me, yet fragile enough to need guidance. Her hair smelled like fruit. She felt small. I was not looking forward to seeing her called into service. Once in a while, as we lay together in the dark after making love, I'd stare hard into her skin, seeing if I could find the Light within her, looking for some glow, like a flashlight held up to a palm.

"So really," I said, "where?"

"It was just folded up in the corner of the living room."

"Show me."

Downstairs, she pointed exactly where Zane had been with his bag. Alice sat on the couch and gazed out the window, and I stood where she'd found the note and read it over again, thinking of what Zane had said about the trees. Could Dale Cooper still be alive? Could he be leading an underground revolt? I tried to think of the last time I'd seen him—surely on one of the occasions he'd scooped me for a story on the Lights. I fell into a kind of reverie, thinking about the period just after my first encounter with the Lights in the Weyerhaeuser woods.

Still humming with the existential implications and rattled by the attack, Blake and my brother and I had driven back to Seattle in silence, unsure of what to do. We didn't know what to say to one another, let alone anyone else, so we'd kept the event hidden for two days, half-assuming that someone else would release the information, half-expecting to read about it in the paper, see it on television, hear it on the radio. We huddled in my mother's house and avoided her, unsure what was expected of us, what we expected of ourselves. But nothing came.

And on the third day, Blake left, saying she was going home, saying her parents would be worried.

And on the fourth day, she was on the news.

And on the fifth day, I began to write about what had happened.

After I sold the story to the *Seattle Weekly*, it was picked up by *Time*, which asked for an expanded version, and it wasn't long before I became the go-to correspondent for all things Lights-related. Which is when Cooper got back in touch, and on the condition of anonymity became my source. He was the first to explain that, after entering you, the Lights lay dormant until awoken and called upon for some sort of coordinated movement— the first of innumerable insights he gave me over the next two years until, after being outed by Weyerhaeuser as a person of interest, he disappeared, and with him my supposed expertise.

There was no outcry, no debate; there was no mention of his disappearance at all. Still, I expected to be contacted by his office at the FBI. Surely, I thought, they knew of and condoned his actions. What of the paperwork I'd filled out? I'd never received the payment he'd promised, but that could easily have been caught up in red tape in the confusion following our mission. The fact is,

I was never contacted at all, and it seemed to me he'd been ignored entirely by those responsible for his safety. He'd been written out of the story.

I considered Alice, staring out the window with the relaxed posture of someone fully at home in a crisis. I envied her ignorance of a world before the invasion, and while I didn't quite understand her reasons for staying, I would never, I'd long since decided, challenge them.

"Have you heard of this before?" I asked, holding up the page. "The Guild of Saint Cooper?"

"I don't even know what guild means."

"What about the initials DC?"

"Washington."

I cut the conversation short.

Much of the morning was spent trying to fuck and finding myself unable to perform. Although this had been happening with embarrassing regularity, today there was a perfectly good explanation, and I cleaved to it desperately. Had Zane, I wondered, left the letter on purpose for me to find? Was there truly an underground movement afoot? And the most important question: was Cooper still alive? I was far from knowing whether to believe it, but I could not deny that I wanted to.

I also wanted to talk to Blake.

It had been years since she'd vanished into the deep recesses of Weyerhaeuser's publicity machine, and we hadn't spoken in all that time. Our common history had by necessity become obscured so that I'd no longer have to think of it when I saw her face on television, read her name in the paper, heard her voice on the radio. Yet for all that, she was far more of a force in my life now than she'd been when we'd been in love, though much of the influence was invisible, or rather carried out by others, unconscious actors manipulating the landscape and the people around me in ways both subtle and overt while Blake arranged an official narrative of these events. I could only imagine that she'd come to the same conclusions others had if she were told of the initials carved in the fallen rhododendrons. She may have even seen this letter, or another like it. And if she'd not yet been involved in an attempt to find Dale, to shut down his operation, surely she would be soon.

"Blake," said Alice. She was standing at the bedroom window, looking out across lower Ballard. "Earth calling Blake. Come in, Blake."

"Mmm?" I looked at her.

"Blake, do you think they'll ever leave?"

"Will who leave?"

"The Lights."

I looked at her naked body in the window and felt nothing.

"What do you think would be the best way," I said, "to get through to the Chief Publicity Officer of Weyerhaeuser?"

Alice scrunched up her face. It dawned on her who I meant. "OB?" she said.

"Don't call her that. But, yeah. Blake."

Alice promptly turned her back, facing out, and she stood very still. Then she marched quickly through the room, picking up her underwear, picking up her shorts, picking up her T-shirt, her socks, her bag, and with her arms full marching out the door and down the stairs.

"Alice," I called out. "What are you doing?"

I sprang from the bed and went down to find her pulling clothing on forcefully, jabbing one pale, skinny leg into her pants and then another. Still naked, I stood back and covered myself.

"Alice, I'm sorry. I'm just thinking this DC thing through."

"Fuck you, Blake."

"Please, okay. I'll drop it, I just…"

Her breasts danced as she pulled a sock on, hopping on one foot, knee raised. She looked down to my crotch, her face darkened, and she stopped struggling with her clothes, opened the door and disappeared. I ran to close it but saw that there were no Lights in the immediate area, and because I was surprised by the day's small breeze on my skin—something I'd not felt in ages—I stood and watched her finish getting dressed.

"Please don't go," I said.

"You're the most self-involved person I've ever known. Do you even realize that? You probably don't, do you. You probably have no idea how self-involved you are."

"See now, that's a trap. Come on, Alice. I need you."

"What you need is to grow up and get a fucking life."

She glowered at me, but suddenly her face changed from anger to something else, and with a slow shake of her head she started walking away. I ran out to the sidewalk and stared at her in disbelief. It was somehow amazing to me that she was leaving, and it occurred to me that, quite possibly, she would not return. The sun shone down on my naked body, and though the day was hot I felt cool, or free. No walls, no plastic suit, nothing between me and the world.

"Alice, come back! What do you want me to do?"

She kept walking, and after a moment called back, "I don't know, Blake. Why don't you ask your mother?"

I watched her go until the sound of a car on 65th Street reminded me how exposed I was. I lifted my face up to the sun as Alice's words echoed in my head, allowed myself to close my eyes for a count of five. One, if there was anyone on earth who might have a chance of convincing Blake to leave Cooper alone, at least until I had the opportunity to find him myself, it would be me. Two, I had to try. Three, though she could not have known where her advice would take me, Alice was right. Four, my mother could help me get through to Blake. Five, I opened my eyes and a wave of anxiety shot through my body, flushing me back up the front steps and into the house.

DAY 32

MY MOTHER WAS ALARMED by my story, which I explained in as much detail as I could. She'd always known Dale Cooper had been my source, known I'd thought him dead, knew my ambivalence about the initials in the trees, so she wasn't surprised that my curiosity had been piqued by the letter. But my intention to pursue it concerned her.

It was not yet fully day, and the kitchen was filled with a blurry grayness broken only by cones of light from lamps above the counter. It was a quiet hour, and when my mother closed the silverware drawer it sounded like a slam. She stirred her coffee.

"Don't misunderstand me—I applaud your interest in helping."

"Well," I said, "I wouldn't call it helping, really."

"Oh? What would you call it?"

"I don't know, Mom. I just wouldn't want Dale to be…I mean, a resistance movement that's…"

I had not yet, I realized, articulated my interest, even to myself. Surely I wasn't thinking of joining the movement, if there were one to join. Surely I didn't think there was a chance of getting rid of the Lights. No number of fallen trees would be enough to starve them. Then what? Did I simply want to know for myself whether he was indeed behind it?

"I just wish you'd have more interest in helping on a practical level instead of chasing abstractions."

"Dale Cooper isn't an abstraction, Mom."

"Is someone having disappeared years ago, whose only presence consists of his initials, concrete?"

Perhaps, I thought, I just wanted to see Blake.

I missed Blake, but did I want to see her?

No, I decided, I did not *want* to see her. I had to.

"Are you saying ideas are unimportant?"

My mother suddenly grew grave. "Blake, how would you feel if I asked Kent to come back to Seattle for a little while? I think it could be good for you."

"Kent? Come on, Mom. I'm okay, seriously. I just want to have a few words with Blake."

There was a long pause during which my mother's expression went from worry to resignation. "Well, she's a difficult woman to get to, as you can imagine."

"But."

"But I could probably get you close."

We drove downtown, slowing at each checkpoint to press our IDs against the glass. Though most zombied people could drive if they'd been doing it for long enough, something as simple as showing an ID was beyond their reach—the theory being that the behavior was too new or unusual to exist in the deep memory areas Lights controlled—so the checkpoints served as an early warning sign for service activity. My mother explained they were in the process of breaking each existing area in half, doubling the checkpoints. It would give them more finely tuned coordinates for responding, but it would also be a pain in the ass.

It had been a while since I'd left Ballard, and I was surprised at how much had changed in most areas. Buildings had been demolished, their pieces either neatly stacked or missing, their foundations broken and removed from the earth. Large holes resulted, but there had been no effort made to fill them in, and these areas were grossly pitted as by some meteor shower. And yet, for all this, there had still been almost no activity downtown.

We passed a woman pulling branches off a sapling by the side of the road. Her dress was torn, and her movements looked mechanical, but we couldn't see her face, so there was no way to tell whether she was Lit or just insane. My mother called it in anyway, giving the woman's location. Someone would show up within fifteen minutes and try to deliver first aid if it was needed.

"How much do you see of that," I said. "I mean, maybe she's not Lit, but how often do you see some kind of service that only involves one person?"

"It's not usually the case, but it's frequent enough."

"Doesn't it seem weird?"

My mother glanced quickly at me, then back at the road. She'd always been a nervous driver, and no amount of time on the road could cure that. "As opposed to the things going on that don't seem weird?"

"Oh, come on. You know what I mean."

"Honestly, Blake, I don't."

We crossed down, closer to the water and away from my mother's office. Elliott Bay spread out before us, high and still and smooth, and I thought of the ferries that once crossed it, carrying people to and from Bainbridge and other commutable distances now largely unlit by night. Public transportation had been one of the first government services to go as people started avoiding crowds. After the trees had been revealed, the Lights had little reason to hide—not that they'd been very good at it to begin with—and though they weren't aggressive, once exposed they began entering people here and there, almost inquisitively, as though they too were ignorant of what could result. Then two dozen Lights encircled and entered a group of immigrants gathered outside the Federal Building on their way to renew their visas, and though they weren't called up for service right away, it was enough to cause mass hysteria. People left, people looted, people locked themselves in their homes.

We passed an empty parking garage that had been partly disassembled. One side, still standing, bore stacks of concrete curbs and rebar. The sign out front said EARLY BIRD SPECIAL.

"Where are we going?"

"To a site. Remember last night? You heard the broadcast, I think."

"The park?"

"Yes. They just want me to sign off. There are a few souls still active."

It was strange to me that the City had adopted the term *soul* to describe a person carrying out his service, and stranger to hear it coming from my mother—an atheist for as long as I could remember. It was strange, but it fit.

A perimeter had been established a few blocks from the site, and a man wearing the City's stark green protective suit saw my mother and waved us through. I had not seen a real service in progress, aside from tree maintenance crews, in many months, perhaps over a year, and even then I hadn't seen the late stages, when most casualties were reported. We parked in a long narrow parking lot facing the water, zipped up our hoods, and my mother leaned over to check my seams.

The site was just beyond a large, once-manicured berm a hundred yards down the footpath into the park, and a coworker walked with us while providing details of the service and those involved.

"They dismantled six park benches," he said, his voice muffled by his mask, "and took down a couple dozen young maples. But that's not what—"

"How many souls?"

"Thirty-seven. Some have stopped, and they're okay. Abrasions."

We approached the berm, where three City men stood off to one side in conversation. One nodded at us, and the other two stopped talking, turned.

"But," said my mother.

"But the big part of this, and we didn't see it coming at first, is the hole."

My mother stopped and shook her head. "Oh, Christ," she said. "You're talking about diggers."

"It's pretty gruesome. I'd like to get a green light to inter-vene."

We walked on.

"Mom," I said.

I could see now where the ground gave way to a large hole, maybe twenty feet across. At first it appeared to be empty, but it was deeper than I expected, and as we got closer I began to see small brown bursts of dirt flying out of it, and to hear a soft scratching sound. My mother walked forward with the man but I held back, suddenly afraid to look down into the pit. Around me dirt was strewn over the ground in mounds of various sizes, with larger piles on the far side. The hole wasn't round, I noticed, but square, with walls nearly perpendicular to the surface. It was as though a foundation were being dug.

A suited man appeared from the way we'd come and met with my mother as she stood at the hole's edge, looking down. He wasn't wearing any protective gear, but he was animated, loose,

and waved to the three City men still huddled by the shore. My
mother gestured down into the hole and began speaking to him in
a hushed voice. He held up his hands as if in protest, as if to say it
was out of his control. She pointed down again, sternly; I could see
that her body had grown stiff with authority. She poked her finger
one last time and the man looked down. The smile drained from
his face, and he pressed his lips together in certitude or resignation,
or both. Beyond them a pair of gulls hovered above the water,
borne on a breeze I couldn't feel. I was shocked by how quickly
I'd gotten out of my depth. How had I thought I could simply
immerse myself once more in the goings-on of the Lights, of the
city, of Weyerhaeuser? The fact was, I'd never really had to do my
own research. My articles had always been no more than acts of
translation—I'd created narrative tension around facts and details
fed to me by others to be broadcast by others. I'd been nothing
more than a conduit. My mother began walking toward me but
veered with the path back to the parking lot.

"Clay should be able to put you in touch with Blake," she said.
"I'll be in the car."

I watched her walk away, half wanting to follow, and the
unsuited man came to stand at my side.

"Your mother is a shrewd woman. She should have gone into
business."

What was that supposed to mean?

"She's a public servant at heart," I said.

"Clay Baynes," he said, taking a step forward and holding out
a hand. "I believe you're looking for the woman I work for."

Clay was twitching slightly, something that could have been a
kind of low-level Tourette's or just too much caffeine.

"Yes," I said. "I want to talk to Blake."

He smiled, stiff-lipped.

"I could pass along a message," he said.

"I need to see her personally."

"She's a busy woman. Why don't you just let me pass something along. It's a big favor as is, trust me."

"I'm an old friend," I said. "If you just—"

"I know who you are, Blake. And like I said."

"Look, I could just go down to Weyerhaeuser and—"

"You wouldn't get anywhere near her."

The three City men started laughing, and though I knew it couldn't be at my expense, the timing made Clay bolder.

"Do you want to write it down? I've got some paper in the car." His smile was a smirk.

I pulled the Guild letter from my pocket and unfolded it before him, holding it up.

"I've got all the paper I need right here," I said. "And I think Blake might want to hear me out."

His smile vanished. He held up a finger and fished for his phone. Since the cell towers had fallen into disrepair, satellite phones were all that was left and they looked silly, big and bulky, like antiques. Clay finally got his free from his pocket only after he'd turned its contents inside out. A pen, two business cards, and a few white pills fell to the ground as he walked back to the hole for privacy.

It occurred to me that I might have not only ruined the likelihood of seeing Blake, I might be in serious trouble. Weyerhaeuser was above the law, and if they thought I was a threat, that I was somehow involved or had information about an organization responsible for the destruction of the Lights' food source, there was absolutely nothing I'd be able to do to escape mistreatment. There was only

one way I could think of to unfuck myself: tell Clay where I got
the letter. Claim that this had been my intention. Zane didn't mean
that much to me, after all. Aside from his delivering my drugs, we
weren't close. That left a purely ethical dimension to the issue I was
fairly sure I could navigate—wouldn't it be difficult for my mother
if I were locked up? Wouldn't it therefore be hard on all the people
she helped? To keep her in the clear, it would make sense to sacrifice
a drug dealer. I wondered whether they'd expect me to become part
of a sting operation. I wouldn't be able to track him, per se, but his
schedule was regular so it wouldn't be that difficult: we'd simply have
to wait until the following week.

Clay finished his phone call and, after another look down into
the hole, walked back my way. My muscles tightened. My mother
would disapprove of the entire thing.

Clay shook his head. "Well," he said, "congratulations, I
guess."

"Listen," I said.

"A car will come around tomorrow evening at six and pick
you up."

"A car?"

He bent down to gather what had fallen out of his pocket, and
a burst of dirt flew out of the hole behind him.

"What about them?" I said. "Aren't they going to be pulled
out of there?"

"Not a good idea to mess with people in service. You can mix
up their brains and they'll never regain consciousness."

"But that other guy said—"

"That other guy doesn't call the shots. Your mom does. And she
struck a deal." Clay stood up. "I'd put that away if I were you," he
said of the letter, still unfolded, in my hand. "You don't want *them*

to see it." He nodded over my shoulder, and I turned to see a dozen Lights moving toward us from up the path, deeper in the park.

I quickly tucked away the paper and scanned for other Lights.

"Six o'clock," Clay repeated, and he started heading back. I waved to my mother, though she didn't appear to be looking in my direction, then noticed that Clay had overlooked one of the business cards. I picked it up and on impulse jogged to the edge of the hole.

My mother once told me that the most difficult part of her job was catering to people who hurt themselves while serving because they didn't actually want to stop. It was like caring for addicts, she'd said. Whatever access the Lights had to the nervous system, it either didn't include pain receptivity or else they chose to ignore it. Either way, people had no sense that their bodies were damaged. Even in the throes of death, she'd said, they were clawing toward some ineffable goal.

The square hole was roughly ten feet deep, and the men and women in it were in various states of debilitation. Some of them seemed to struggle against their own physical exhaustion, their arms reaching forward slowly toward the dirt, which they merely brushed before the weight of their own hands was too much. Others, strangely haywire, writhed in place. But at least three of the souls were still hard at work, digging down and out with hands coated in wet black soil. Their hands were strange somehow, their fingers blunt, and with the thick, ubiquitous mud it took a few moments before I understood what had been making the others squirm.

Averting my eyes, I flipped over Clay's small card. The name on it was Mitch Earl, Private Investigator.

DAY 33

ON THE DRIVE DOWNTOWN I noticed we were being followed. It was a plain gray sedan, not new but spotless. I couldn't make out the plates except to note that they weren't from Washington. It had tailed us from Ballard to Interbay before I brought it up, but the driver dismissed it with a grunt I took to mean it was probably an added level of security assigned by Weyerhaeuser itself. I knew I should be at my best with Blake, but I'd slept fitfully, filled with anxiety about the meeting. What should I say to her? Should I try to appeal to a younger version of herself? Should I beg? Was I hoping for some kind of reunion? Friendship? Was I just going there to see her? My exhaustion left me scatterbrained.

Before we turned down 2nd Avenue into Belltown we passed a deer and fawn by the side of the road. They were eating from low-hanging branches and didn't even look at us, though the car was no more than four feet away. The vehicle smelled slightly of clove cigarettes. What kind of person worked for Weyerhaeuser? Were they all already employees, or had the company actively recruited during the exodus? Blake had not been an employee, obviously. I tried to focus. People don't change, I assured myself, just their circumstances. Blake would be Blake.

We parked before the high wooden walls surrounding the block once slated for the new public library. I'd heard Weyerhaeuser had taken over this property, and assumed it had built something. But no structure could be seen above the ten-foot blue particleboard. The holes I'd once looked through with Blake had been covered. The driver took me to a door at the top of a three-step ramp, pushed a buzzer, and looked up, nodding into a surveillance camera overhead while I watched our tail park a block away. I waved.

When the door buzzed, the driver pushed against it, and as he did so he turned slightly to me and said something that sounded like "Get ready."

"Get ready?" I said, and then we were inside.

I was not ready.

There was not nothing behind the particleboard walls after all. There was something, and the something was enormous. It was glass and steel and strange and it rose above us like a broken shard, like an iceberg. Like nothing I'd ever seen before. Lights were moving into and out of it; they zoomed past the driver and me as we stood there—me looking up with my jaw fully and officially dropped, him patiently waiting. After I'd taken a few deep breaths I was able to answer to my satisfaction the basic ontological question, and armed with this conviction I overcame at least one layer of my disbelief.

"It's a building," I said.

The driver raised his eyebrows. "Good," he said. "That's good. Would you like to go inside of it?"

I took one last look up and behind me, over the wooden wall toward the street. From here I could see the slight shimmer of the mirage—the same kind that had hidden the secret forest years ago—and just as I was recovering from the first shock, another came crashing in like a wave: these could be everywhere. I thought of the partially deconstructed buildings throughout the industrial neighborhoods to the north. I thought of the hole I'd seen the day before. I nodded to the man, and he walked toward a glass door that opened as he reached it. I followed him inside.

There was very little furniture; the rooms themselves were large, like atria, though nothing was growing, and though the walls' angles were unusual, the material was glass and concrete and steel and not some substance from another world. We traveled up through the open spaces on escalators bisecting the building, shooting through it at odd angles and avoiding some floors altogether. In a room with a ceiling that sloped down to a glassy point near the floor, the driver left me to sit at a white desk displaying the usual office accoutrements: a computer, a phone, a pad of paper. It also held some less usual items: a small glowing globe that hovered over a square blue stand, a ribbon that sparkled with streaming digits, and something that looked like a shriveled human ear. I heard the footsteps of several people come and go in neighboring rooms, but I didn't see anyone else, nor did I see the Lights I'd noticed from the outside, which had seemed innumerable and everywhere at the time. I was unused to wearing a suit inside, and though it was not hot in the room, it was noticeably stuffy. I briefly pulled the mask away from my face and neck, rearranging myself inside.

"You don't have to wear that in here."

Blake waved off three or four Lights at shoulder level, which disappeared down the hall as she entered the room. It was impossible to ignore the disappearance of the easy, open gait she used to have, a kind of broad, roaming liquidity that had made it hard to guess her next move. She sliced forward now with precision and, having met my eyes at first, now completely avoided them until she'd taken a seat on the far side of the desk.

Besides being a robot, she looked as beautiful as ever. She hadn't aged so much as refined. Part of me was terrified of this new Blake, but another part wanted to jump up and laugh and try to provoke some acknowledgement from her that everything was strange, delightfully strange. I looked hard into her eyes: nothing.

"May I see it?"

I knew what she meant, but I stared blankly in disbelief.

"The letter," she said.

"Blake."

"Please."

I laid it on the desk between us, and that's when I noticed the reflection of a Light in the glass wall behind her. Blake noticed, too, or rather she noticed the Light itself, and she froze, very briefly, almost imperceptibly, and then subtly nodded and put her hand over the hovering globe. The globe opened, the Light quickly flew by me and into it, and the globe closed. Blake looked up at me as if this were an entirely normal procedure: *Of course the Light goes in the globe—it's a Light globe.*

She picked up the letter and scanned it, holding it close, examining the margins and folds. I'd prepared my response to what I thought would be her first question—Where did you get this?—but she didn't ask. Instead, she asked if she could have it.

"Have it, as in I leave it here?"

"Yes."

"No."

"Then can I copy it?"

"Make a copy? Sure."

Blake took the shriveled ear, placed it on the page, and I watched as it sprang to life. It unfolded and then inched quickly over the entire page. Once it was finished, Blake fed it a blank piece of paper torn from her notepad. The ear grew larger as if ingesting the pulp of the page. The next stage of the process was slower, and Blake picked up the silent, empty slack of the room when she saw me staring at the weird, fleshy thing reproducing my letter.

"There's some new technology around," she said.

"Blake," I said, "what the fuck."

"I understand you've been living with your mother. How is she?"

"Determined."

For the first time, Blake smiled. "Yes, that's true."

"And busy trying to clean up messes made by your little friends here."

The ear had now recreated roughly a third of the page—but it wasn't merely a copy, it was *exactly* a copy. Not only was it duplicating the words on the page, it was doubling the page itself, the texture, the folds and rough edges. The color.

"Do you know," Blake said, "that the Lights are growing suspicious of the lack of rain? They suspect that we, that humans, are intentionally withholding it."

"I assume you've told them we can't control the weather."

"They claim we've changed the weather before."

Blake's hair was pulled back into a severe bun, and with her chin lifted in an attitude of investigation, her neck, already long, seemed like a boast. It was insane to me just then that I knew that neck, that I'd nuzzled up to it, caressed it with warm, love-stained lips.

"Why are you telling me this?"

"Why did you come here, Blake?"

"I came to..." I leaned in and lowered my voice. "I came because I figured you'd already know about the Guild—"

"Yes."

"I also figured that you'd be engaged in locating Cooper, or at least in verifying his existence and involvement."

That smile again.

"So I've come here to ask you to let it be."

"Let it be."

"Assuming there's an it at all."

When Blake sat back I realized she'd been leaning in too. Had this merely been an automatic response, or had she too wanted to mute the exchange? Over Blake's shoulder I could see a group of people marching down 4th Avenue. They were chanting, or seemed to be—I could see their mouths moving but heard nothing. They were a ragged crew, with no suits, and they moved slowly but seemed energetic, hands raised, some dancing.

"Please," I said.

The ear finished its duplication and shriveled back into its former dried apricot form. Blake picked up the page and held it in the light. She smelled it—the first sign I'd had since sitting down that there was something inside her I still recognized—and frowned.

"I understand you've stopped writing," she said.

"Well, that's not entirely true. I've turned to fiction. I'm writing a love story."

"That's a shame. You were such a strong journalist."

"Oh, please. Everything I wrote was handed to me on a—"

"That was then."

"It's good to see you," I lied.

"Bullshit."

Sign number two.

"I miss you."

"Blake, is there anything else you can tell me about this letter?"

"Not really. But, you know, like I said."

"I wouldn't worry about that."

She was already standing before I realized the meeting was over. She came around the desk and offered me her hand. I reached out with plastic fingers and she took them graciously, shook them warmly, looked into my eyes.

Shooting down through the lighted chambers of the building, if that's what it was, I began to process our conversation, if that's what it had been, and to wonder what I'd accomplished, if indeed I'd accomplished anything at all. The sun had fallen behind the buildings across the street, and I felt a large and growing loss. I'd lost Blake. I'd lost her forever. Despite not having seen her in years, this came as a surprise. A shock. There must have been a mistake. There'd been a miscommunication between us, something lost in translation or simply unsaid— something hidden, even.

The driver lead me back outside to the roar of a crowd I'd seen from Blake's office. And as we walked back to the wooden wall surrounding the building their chant became clear.

"Light us up," they called. "Set us free."

We slipped out and directly into the crowd. Many were amputees, some in wheelchairs. Others appeared to be physically whole but were profoundly filthy or otherwise obscured by facial hair, by strange helmets and masks, by the shopping carts and other wheeled objects they pushed. Some were naked. No one was wearing any protection.

They moved loudly but slowly, and some stopped altogether when we emerged from the door in the wall. A tall, angular man in short pants with bright pink feathers in his hair looked directly at me and said, "Free yourself from darkness."

The car was surrounded, a wheelchair blocking the passenger door, and as I considered whether to ask a double amputee to move, someone called my name. I looked down the block into the oncoming march.

"I know who you're looking for!" a man yelled.

It was the person who'd been following us. He was standing half in, half out of his car, and the people were thinning around him, just the stragglers and barely mobile. I looked back to my driver.

"Free yourself from darkness," he said. "See if I care."

"I'll be right back."

I pushed toward the gray sedan, trying to avoid touching too many people. I was nervous that my suit would be punctured, or even intentionally torn. I ricocheted between the ailing men and women like a pinball struggling back up the board, their plea ringing in my ears. The man held out his hand long before I could reach it, as though he were holding it out to a person swimming, a person drowning, and by the time I gripped it I felt this might have been true in a way.

"Hello," he said. "I'm Mitch Earl."

"Private investigator," I said.

"You're quick."

"Well, literate."

"I'm assuming you were stonewalled up there." He nodded past me, back at the library lot.

"You can see it?" I turned back, squinting.

"Let's just say I'm familiar with the layout. You wanna get outta here?"

For the first time I noticed his accent. It came out in certain words, a looseness. I looked down at the license plate: New York.

"You know about Cooper?"

Mitch winked, and his youthful, rosy cheeks bunched upward. "A little. I was actually hoping you could fill in some gaps for me. Want to go for a drive?"

The crowd grew louder, more excited, as three or four Lights moved slowly over the tops of people's heads. They were out of reach, but that didn't stop people from heaving their broken bodies into the air in an effort to cross their path with a bare hand, a bare head. And that was when I realized that Mitch Earl wasn't wearing any protection—something I must have seen but not noted in the confusion of so many unprotected men and women. Despite knowing that those who were Lit weren't a threat unless in service, I couldn't help feeling a little skeptical. I moved slowly back from the car, trying to think of an excuse to refuse his invitation, and bumped into a woman with wild eyes who held a soggy rag in her mouth. I stepped to the side to let her pass, and, turning, tripped over a seated man I hadn't seen. A moment later I was out.

DAY **34**

I CAME TO IN the dark. And then it wasn't darkness at all, but a blindfold. I had a headache radiating from where I'd been hit, and the cool, smooth cotton on my eyelids gave me something to focus on, something soothing, almost. I could feel that my suit had been removed. I was seated, my feet bound and my hands tied behind my back. I did not panic. I did not struggle. I became slowly aware of the temperature and of the smell and sounds in the room, and my awareness of these things swept outward deliberately, carefully, settling on one sensation and becoming familiar with it before moving on. Was I in shock? Was I in denial? The blow I'd suffered had hollowed me out, and while the fight seemed to have been drained out of me, so too had the fear. I felt a calmness that stretched each second, reminding me of the moments that, as a child, I'd enjoyed between my mother waking me up the first and second times for school. After she'd left my room I'd lie there, on the brink of sleep, half-convinced that I could continue in that suspended state forever—a sensation that was among the most wonderful I'd ever felt—so long as I kept the balance between waking and blissful oblivion. The moment I fell back into sleep, my mother would have cause to return and wake me a second and final time. And if I became too fully alert, time would move as it usually did: too quickly. But until either of those states took hold I was free, free from the stuff of life and, most important, free from myself. Perhaps it was because of this fond memory and my woozy mind that I was able to sustain a kind of flaccid resignation as I groped about with all senses but sight.

There was a bright green, tangy smell, a scent somewhere between growth and decay that was sweet to inhale but syrupy, heavy and damp, and felt like a chore to breathe. I attributed this to being in a basement, to being underground, and it was oddly familiar, this aroma, but for some reason it made me feel vaguely embarrassed, as I might about smelling bad myself, or noticing someone else's odor and feeling sorry for them. I drew the slow air further into my lungs, until I noticed a sharp trace of alcohol behind the floral mask. Now my sense of it switched. It was not the earthy smell causing my embarrassment, but the booze, or their combination. And just as I'd reached this awareness, I also realized that it wasn't that I'd experienced this scent before—I'd written it. Behind my mask, I envisioned the scene: a boy reaching out and touching the naked, slimy tongue of his neighbor, breathing in the rich stench of tobacco and whiskey and half-masticated leaves. It had been the first story I'd written, my first taste of doing something other than reportage. I'd not shown it to anyone, and to be confronted by it now, or by a trace of it, a mirror, was unexpected. But I couldn't say it was unpleasant. There was a hope in it, an optimism that, like the freedom gleaned from my morning ritual, lifted me into a strangely euphoric state.

It was in this state that I noticed the radio. On it was one of the four or five usual voices: a deep, calm but swift voice full of rubber and dirt. There was the slightest bit of static around the edges of certain words, which led me to believe that it might be a weak signal, that we might be slightly out of range. There was some Lights activity on Martin Luther King Jr. Boulevard in South

Seattle; people were advised to stay clear of the area between Myrtle and Othello until further notice. There was a mandatory watering of all rhododendrons on private property. There was a report made about the parade I'd witnessed downtown, just a simple statistical account—162 persons involved, two-thirds of whom were male—followed by a reminder that mere encounter with a Light was insufficient cause for Illumination. That the Light had to *want* to enter. Then another voice came on the air. It was female, and spoke sternly but not without a certain sympathy. It took me a moment to realize it was Blake.

"It has been decided," she said, "that an expedition will be formed to assess the possibility of creating a temporary relief from the current drought—both local and elsewhere. The solution will entail the amputation and overseas transfer of a glacier. While many glaciers are under consideration, after preliminary studies, the Ross Ice Shelf—roughly the size of France—is currently the primary candidate."

I thought of what Blake had told me at our meeting, that the Lights suspected us of having caused the drought that was threatening their food supply. I thought then of my mother, listening to the report at home, or perhaps just letting it drone on in the background. It seemed incredible to me that she'd sacrificed any aspect of her mission to help me reach Blake, especially after challenging the validity of my goal.

Blake continued on, outlining a research schedule, and explained that we couldn't be sure exactly when the decision would be made, nor how long after that the glacier would be amputated. She kept using that word, *amputated*, and I wondered if it was a technical term, or a direct translation of something said by the Lights, or whether Blake, as a product of her interaction with the invasive species, had somehow become abstracted, askew, so that she was still recognizable to herself but appeared off-kilter to the rest of us.

My head pounded. I'd been unable to maintain that blissful middle ground, had slipped too far forward into a wakeful state, and the smell, once so rich with allusion and depth, was now just flatly dank, stale, impenetrable. I twisted my arms gently, testing the ropes that bound them, and this small resistance had the effect of making me more aware of my exposure, my vulnerability. My skin broke out in gooseflesh, and I became unusually aware of those parts of it not covered by clothes.

The pressure in the room changed—airflow, an open door—and I heard footsteps coming as though down a hall. There was a crisp, close echo, which folded fast upon itself, making it impossible to tell how many people had entered—certainly more than one—but they stopped all at once, not far from me but out of reach.

I struggled despite myself. "My suit," I said finally.

"Your suit has been removed for your safety."

The voice was distorted, a low, digital growl, disconnected beeps lined up into quickly shifting notes. Nonetheless, I felt certain I could hear the PI's voice behind it.

"That doesn't make sense," I said.

There was a low, inscrutable murmur.

"Are you the person called Dale Cooper?"

I'd heard the question clearly but it took me by surprise, so alien was the concept, and in the silence after it had been asked I tried in vain to retrieve it in my mind, and failed.

"Is Dale Cooper your name?" the voice said.

"What the hell do you mean?"

"Answer the question."

Why would Mitch be asking me this? Was it a performance for someone else listening in? I tried to feel my skin, to determine whether I was wearing a sensor—perhaps I'd been hooked to a polygraph—but if anything was taped to me I'd already normalized the pressure. The voice spoke again.

"Is Dale Cooper a real person?"

For the first time in years I thought about meeting Dale Cooper. The impression he'd given me had been far from normal, with his clocks and talk of personal focus. What had he said? That concentrating on something outside the present circumstance could bring clarity that direct attention never would. I tried to reach back out to the sounds, the smells of the room I'd used only moments before to attain a kind of transcendental euphoria, but my mind was scattered, my attention shifting too quickly, pushed and pulled by the small movements of my interrogators, by my clothing against my skin, by the silence I realized only presently indicated the radio had been turned off. Small things, I knew, were being asked of me, but I could not bring myself to the precipice of speech. I felt as though I were skittering across smooth water like a flat stone, and even as my forward motion slowed, the rate at which I hit the surface increased and gave me the thrill of speed, the intensity of action. Here I was, responsible for verifying the existence of Dale Cooper, and under the pressure of this simple directive losing the ability to account for my own.

"Do you know where Dale Cooper is?"

"No," I said at last. "No!"

To say that I *said* this, however, is misleading. I don't remember the word coming out of my mouth. I don't remember my lips moving, my tongue on my pallet, my nose vibrating with sound. What I remember is the feeling of confession. And after my confession, of being lifted, chair and all, into the air.

After being taken outside and untied from the chair, I'd been pulled rather forcefully into the back of a van, where I was free to roll around, bumping against what I assumed were the feet and shins of men seated to either side. As the van drove I tried to divine our location from the pattern of turns and stops and long, straight shots, but time after time a turn would come where it couldn't in my mind, or we'd get up to speed on a stretch of road that should have been short and slow. This went on for a time until it occurred to me that intuiting our route was impossible unless I knew where we'd begun. I must have been given a drug to relax me, I realized at last, for though part of me felt certain that I was at best headed for continued—and harsher—questioning, and at worst disposal, another part of me felt equally as certain that I was going to be safe. Happily, the latter part was in the position of informing the former, and I occupied myself for a while with listening in, hearing the soothing, knowing predictions work to mollify the stream of panicky outbursts and complaints. I was exterior to them both, disembodied inside my skin. Before long, however, I grew tired of this exchange and decided to poke around.

Behind me was a long corridor that terminated in a heavy-looking metal door, the kind I imagined finding on a ship or a submarine. The corridor was rounded in its top and bottom corners, and together with the gunmetal color, this confirmed my sense that I was underwater. There was a slow creaking and a series of taps coming from all around me, and though they didn't seem overly threatening, they did inspire me to walk down the corridor. As I inched toward the door I looked more closely at the walls.

They'd resembled metal at first, but their texture seemed too flat somehow, as though more lead-like than lead. I reached out with my index finger and, without the application of much pressure at all, it sank, upon contact, into the gray surface. I pulled back, alarmed, only to find that my fingerprint had been left in the warm, damp substance.

Just as I retrieved my hand I began to hear voices, or perhaps just a single voice, coming from behind the door. It was unintelligible from where I stood, mere murmuring, but as I drew closer I could make out words. *Cry* was the first word I felt certain I'd heard correctly. Then *see*, or *sea*. I moved closer and heard something like *aces*, then *tragic*, then as I drew closer still I could make out phrases—strange, incantatory phrases I struggled to make sense of. Was it "Drunken choral water called"? Was it "The meaning of lungings of the otter and the wind"? Was it "The single artificial word she sang"?

Only with my ear to the door, my ear slowly sinking into the door's dull flesh, did I realize, finally, that it was poetry. And so, without trying to understand, I finally heard it most clearly:

> Oh! Blessed rage for order, pale Ramon,
> The maker's rage to order words of the sea,
> Words of the fragrant portals, dimly-starred,
> And of ourselves and of our origins,
> In ghostlier demarcations, keener sounds.

And in the deep silence after the recitation my body relaxed, and because I'd been holding myself from leaning too hard on the soft door, I fell against it, and because the door itself was something shy of solid, I passed through.

Inside the small, rounded room was a bare wooden table at which three naked people sat. Two women, one young and the other old—daughter and mother, I decided—were facing me. They were not shy, but they looked at me with a sorrow that while resigned had not settled so far into their selves that a glimmer of hope for me could not be felt. I traced it across the girl's brow before it disappeared back into the meekness of her eyes. The figure facing them was male, and though his bony back was covered with age spots, it was strong in its ropy thinness, like a sapling that had grown old but not up. It wasn't until the man turned around in his chair that I recognized him as George Washington.

"Ah, good," he said. "You'll be safe here."

I opened my mouth to speak, but instead of sound bright light poured out, flooding the room with a whiteness so sharp I had to close my eyes. And with my eyes closed my body lurched to one side. I felt hands at my arms and legs and heard the opening of a sliding door. I was placed down on a hot, gravelly surface, and something that felt like a small, balled-up blanket was dropped on my side.

"Count to fifty before removing your blindfold."

I rolled onto my back, felt the sun on my face, and tried to nod my assent. The door slammed and the van drove off, leaving me with only the sounds of birds and the distant hum of a lawnmower. I began to count, but I could get only to ten, fifteen, before my attention would wander from the task. The bonds that linked these numbers had grown weak, it seemed, and I'd be left groping for whatever number came next to mind rather than next in line, before, with a start, beginning again, flush with anxiety that I'd arrive at my target too soon and see something I shouldn't.

Why had I been let go? How could Mitch have been satisfied by my answers—or my singular answer. Hadn't I dodged the first two? Perhaps my incredulity had been answer enough. I tried to remember being held, the experience of it, the sense perceptions, but failed. It was impossible for me to feel anything other than the sun's heat on my face. The hard, dry surface at my back. My head began to pound. Eighteen, nineteen, twenty. The blindfold no longer provided any relief.

I'D SPENT MUCH OF the following twenty-four hours shut up in my room, sleeping and trying to determine both what had happened to me and who, if anyone, I could tell about it. My mother was obviously not an option. Who else was there? My brother, if I could even get through to him, would simply instruct me to leave town. Not only that, he'd insist my mother leave too—who could say, he'd say, whether my abductors would be content with just the one abduction? They hadn't learned much, after all. Perhaps they'd be back. Perhaps they'd just taken me to scare me and would now wait and watch, assuming I'd lead them right to Dale Cooper. Perhaps the whole family was at risk. The irony was that I'd been very nearly prepared to tell Mitch Earl all of what I knew. Why had he thought it necessary to scare it out of me? The possibility remained that it hadn't been him, of course, or that he was operating under orders. Could Weyerhaeuser have been responsible? It didn't seem likely that Blake would think it necessary. But surely there were people who could override Blake's opinion. The Lights themselves, for instance.

The other question that remained was whether or not I'd been Lit, but I couldn't figure out how to answer it. What would being Lit feel like? I imagined my clothes fitting just slightly tighter, my body having made room for another life. I pictured my skin faintly glowing with an aura that irritated the air like heat radiating off the road. I thought of all the smooth muscle movement within my body: the heart, the lungs, the skin secreting oil; I thought of my empty intestines, because I was hungry, a dumb caterpillar of processed food—surely there was no shortage of places to hide inside a man, places I'd never considered. Would I even recognize the visitor as unrecognizable? Perhaps the presence of a Light inside me would masquerade as something utterly familiar, like nausea, or sadness, or gas.

I got dressed and descended the stairs slowly, carefully, not wanting to disturb the headache I could feel sleeping in a lacuna of the bone above my eyes. It reminded me of my brother's claim, as a child, that if he concentrated he could move an itch he couldn't reach to a place he could. From the middle of his back to his stomach. Or if he was feeling lazy, from his leg to his arm. He could even, he swore, move it around the surface of his skin until it disappeared, like an ice cube. Had he been honest with me? I couldn't remember whether or not I'd believed him at the time, but it had become an anecdote I'd use occasionally, whenever the subject of the body/mind dichotomy was raised—usually in small rooms full of smoke and sweaty young men. In truth I would have loved to see Kent. Where had he brought his family? I couldn't remember. As I came to the bottom of the stairs, I realized I could barely even picture his face.

The sun burned monstrously outside, and I dreaded its flattening hotness as I looked at my suit hanging by the door. They'd thrown it down at me after taking me from the van, careless of my condition or else sure of it. My mother had left the radio on; it was reporting a story about a man found tampering with a particle accelerator in France. The man was from the future. He'd been sent here to fix a glitch. I pulled the plug.

———

Alice answered the door, squinting up at me with a grimace. Her naked body was a lake I could fall into, and I hovered on its edge, trying to get my balance. She sighed loudly and stood aside, then walked past me to the kitchen as I pulled off my mask.

"You can't stay," she said, opening a bottle of water.

"I need to talk."

Sunlight shot through the window to my right, and in the silence I watched the lit dust slow. After glowering at me for a moment, Alice walked back out back to where she'd been sunbathing. I stopped in the kitchen to get a glass of water, and in the cabinet found a knife block wrapped in tape behind Christmas-themed coffee cups.

"Zane's been here," I said through the screen door.

"Is that what you need to talk to me about? Christ, Blake."

"No," I said. "I'm sorry. I just noticed the knives."

"The knives? Listen, dude, are you *trying* to be creepy or what? Do me a favor and stop standing there in the doorway looking at me."

She was propped up now on one elbow, shielding her eyes with her other hand like she was looking far out to sea, like she was looking right through me.

"Well?"

"Sorry," I said again, and stepped out of the house. The only other chair was across the yard, so I sat down where I was and leaned up against the house. Alice lay back and closed her eyes.

"Can you tell me," I asked, "about when you got Lit?"

"Will you promise to leave?"

"I promise."

She sighed and then fell silent. A minute passed, then another. Had she fallen asleep? The wind picked up, changed direction, and the tall pine in a neighboring yard dropped a dry, dead branch.

"I haven't thought about it in a long time," she finally said.

"You were young, right?"

"It was really early, yeah. The evacuation was still going on. I was going from place to place, you know. Mostly abandoned houses. Looking for food, a nice bed. It was easy in the early days. Everything was left, really nice stuff. Like everyone had just gone to church. Anyway, I was in a huge house over by the water. I'd found it at night, so I hadn't seen it all, really, just eaten some soup, opened a bottle of wine, and crawled into bed. But I wasn't sleeping well, and I woke up and they were in the room, maybe a dozen of them. At first I thought it was a dream, and I just looked at them, half asleep. I even remember thinking, right before kind of waking up and realizing, you know, I remember thinking they were kind of cute, they were happy little guys."

Her voice had softened. She was once again that adventurous child acting out, drinking wine, sleeping in big beds, but she was also that little girl realizing she was about to be entered by an alien force, and she tensed, nearly writhing with hatred and fear as she described it.

"It was rape," she said. "They rape you is really what it is. You're held down, not by physical force but by the fear of being touched, like being surrounded by an electric fence. The one that entered me came forward slowly over the top of the bed, straight at my face, and when it was two or three feet away shot at me, stopped one last time, and then disappeared around the side of my head. There's a space I can't remember, but afterward I jumped out of bed and ran through the house. What I hadn't seen before was that an entire side of the house was missing—that there had been construction going on, and the plastic had fallen and one whole fucking side of the house was open. It was the most alone I'd ever felt, and I sat there looking out over the water until morning. I must have been stunned, because I have this memory of the sun coming up over the horizon, but this is facing west, right? There's no way I would have seen the actual sunrise."

She lay still, then, though her breathing had escalated, and I waited, wanting to give her some time. A piece of white paper swirled into the air just beyond the fence and hovered for a moment before disappearing out of sight.

"What did it feel like?" I finally asked.

"Feel like? I just told you."

"No, I mean, did you feel any different? You didn't see it enter you, it sounds like. How did you know it was inside?"

"Are you fucking kidding me? What do you mean I didn't see it enter me?" Alice sat upright with such force that her wooden chair shook.

"I just mean you didn't see it actually pass through your skin."

She seemed shocked.

"Look," I said, "I'm not doubting what happened, I just—"

"It sure as fuck sounds like you are, Blake."

"I'm just asking you about the sensation."

"The sensation? It felt awesome! It felt great! It was like an orgasm!"

She stood up and roughly nudged me aside with her knees, then stomped into the house.

"Alice," I said, "I might have been Lit."

The stomping stopped.

"I didn't see it happen, though, so I'm trying to figure out how else you can tell."

Silence.

Footsteps.

"You're serious, aren't you?"

I turned around. Her face had changed. Sympathy made her look older, and in the flat shade of the dark hall her silhouette against the far window seemed bent, as though she were carrying something just out of sight. I nodded.

She knelt down then, embraced me. My suit crinkled and slipped against her sweaty arms, and even through the suit I could smell the sweetly cooking smoke of her suntanned skin.

"Come inside," she said quietly.

She brought me into the living room and pulled on some clothes she'd left in a pile on the bathroom floor. I thought about Zane coming here, about how they must have stories to share, to exchange but also to create together. I'd never been able to create a story with Alice, too busy creating my own to let her in, to let her navigate. Yet here she was, finally, at the helm.

The light had changed; it crept now across the floor and up the wall, where it caught fire in a horrid cut-crystal polyhedron hanging in a small window and brought to mind the "emblazoned zones and fiery poles" of the poem I'd heard in my dream. What had George Washington meant, I wondered, by being safe? And where had I been?

"Fear," said Alice, entering the room. Her light clothes hung from her tiny frame like tissue paper.

"I'm sorry?"

"You realize the fear is gone."

I looked down at my suit, my barrier.

"Not at first, really," she explained. "At first it's like you've been pushed off a cliff and you're waiting to hit the ground."

"What's weird is—"

"But then it sets in, and you realize that everything you've been running from has already happened."

"What's weird is that I don't feel anything."

"The decision has been made, and though you'll be called for service at some point, it's beyond your control. At first you're worried about what you might do, but after a while you realize that you feel free, freer than you've ever felt."

"I don't know what I feel."

"You realize that freedom is freedom from fear."

I considered this. It made freedom sound like something passive, and anyway, why were we suddenly talking about freedom when all I'd asked about were feelings? A moment ago she'd been seething with hatred and yet here she was, trying to communicate the finer points of faith from the far side of transcendence. Alice looked at me with what seemed to be an expression of challenge, even suspicion.

"You'd agree if you'd been Lit," she said.

DAY **36**

AFTER MY CONVERSATION WITH Alice I'd come to realize that I'd *felt* more or less the same my entire life. I'd felt the same growing up. I'd felt the same in high school. The same in college. I'd even felt the same after we discovered the Lights. The world had changed, but had I felt any different? As a person? Not that I remembered. Of course, who's to say that what one remembers feeling isn't just a projection of what one feels at the time of remembering? A person might, in a nostalgic mood, find humorous a statement he experienced originally as cutting. He might, feeling doubtful, find embarrassing an observation he'd made with a swell of pride. I gazed out across Ballard from my room. I'd been unable to forget what Blake had said about my journalism, decided to write a piece about my abduction, and so—after reading what little I'd gotten down, hating every word—had set aside my novel and begun summoning my memory of that strange event. I'd forgotten to turn off the radio downstairs, and its murmur spun moodily through the house. I wanted to pull the plug, but something kept me seated, stuck in my southward stare, and I hovered there on the verge of action, quite aware of my body though alien to it.

I woke at dusk, having fallen asleep at my desk, to find my mother standing in the doorway at the top of the stairs, bathed in the orange light of evening and wearing her suit pulled down over her shoulders as though she'd come inside, come upstairs, and then simply lost track of time. It was the first I'd seen of her since my abduction, and for the same reasons I'd been avoiding her the last twenty-four hours I kept my head close to the desk, hoping my awkward position would prevent her from reading me. But she wasn't reading anything. Her body looked bent in, her face slack and expressionless. I asked if she was okay.

"Just another rough day."

I turned back to the window to take in her view. A seagull, disoriented maybe, was flying westward a few blocks away, and a few smaller birds flew up to harass it.

"It's a beautiful night," I said.

"Sure. Join me for a glass of wine?"

I followed her downstairs and through the darkening living room to the kitchen, where she decanted a magnum of bad wine into a green glass flower vase. I remembered she'd bought that vase before all this at a nearby boutique glass art shop, and something about the complete frivolity of such a purchase made me happy.

After pouring two glasses, she told me of some discouraging signs that Weyerhaeuser and the Lights were growing more unwilling to compromise, growing more erratic and unpredictable. Apparently they'd disappeared from two jointly managed clinics without warning, then refused to make an official comment about their actions. She refilled her glass.

"It was almost like a denial of their presence there to begin with," she concluded.

Animated by the wine, she went on to talk about some of her coworkers, and as she described the refusal of Ginny Wang to wear gloves when passing out first-aid kits, and how Joe Vargas had shown up to work two weeks ago with a mouse lemur, the source of which he refused to divulge, and as she laughed at her assistant, Joy Lightfoot, whose unflappable attitude was both a subject of ridicule and absolutely, life-savingly necessary, I realized how long it had been since I'd had a normal conversation. My mother paused for a moment, looking for a way to capture the true significance of her assistant, and without her voice the radio's drone began to fill the room with news.

"It's like," she said, "it's almost like…"

The story was about a certain species of ice worm that, through Arctic thaw, had been reintroduced into northern oceanic ecosystems, making its way into the stomachs of gunnels and pricklebacks and then eating them alive from the inside. "This may well alter the entire food chain," a soft-spoken ichthyologist said gravely.

My mother marched over and, for the first time I could remember, yanked the radio's cord from the wall.

"It's like we can't continue unless we're lying to ourselves."

I tried not to seem surprised. "What's a prickleback?"

"Blake," my mother said, "I'm not going to ask where you were the other night, but I want you to know that I'm sorry for what I said."

"What did you say?"

"I'm just happy to see you inspired, sweetie. If Dale Cooper inspires you, I'm one hundred percent supportive."

I wasn't sure I would have used that word, but I supposed it was a fair description in a very general sense. Inspiration as the spark of will, of action.

My mother looked at me, expecting more. I didn't blame her. I expected more of me, too. I stalled by taking a long sip of wine, refilling my glass. The sunlight had slanted, and looking out the eastern windows was treacherous. I squinted at a chip of light charging through the room.

DAY 37

BACK AT ALICE'S HOUSE, I stood at the door with my back to
the wind. Whereas the last time I'd come to see her had been a
conscionable act of self-preservation, today's mission was harder
to define and could easily come across as unnecessary, a favor
easily refused if she wasn't in the mood. Still, I raised my hand,
balled my fist, knocked. Though I hadn't wanted it to, my mother's
affirmation had had its desired effect; I was determined to follow
my instincts. Or rather, I was determined to escape them—
depending, I supposed, on whether my self was something to be
overcome or instead something to reveal, release.

Hearing nothing inside, I tried the door and was surprised to
find it locked. It had not been locked since her parents moved out.
I didn't even know she had a key. I leaned out over the railing of
the small porch to peer in the living-room window, looked about
at the smooth, bare floor and, beyond it, the kitchen bar counter
half hidden in shade. The hall was darker still, save for the small
blaze of backdoor window through which I could see a swatch
of green. A flicker caught my eye, something quick and dark
darting through the small bright square. I crept along the side of
the house. The grass was tall and dry and crackled as I passed, but
with the breeze as cover I got to the fence without making much
noise. The fence around the back yard was just over six feet, and
the door, though unlockable, was home to rusty hinges and a loud,

difficult latch. I knew I wouldn't be able to enter surreptitiously, so I waited, listening. If Alice was hiding from me, would she really be in a mood to help? And if it was someone else, a lurking stranger, I was in no position to defend the property, let alone myself. But it was a kind of abandon that had brought me this far, and as I still felt myself in its grip, I began to plot my next move when I heard whispers.

There were two voices, and the exchange was rapid, heated. One was male, the other female, and though the wind obscured most of the words, those I made out—"still" and "he" and "out" and "go"—began to form a picture of what was going on.

"Alice," I called. "I know you're back there. Is Zane with you?"

The whispers stopped then started again, only lower and more violent, a vicious hissing. I eyed the latch. Where could they go, after all? I listened for changes in the tenor of their spat and fingered the mechanism. It was looser than I'd expected; in fact, it slipped up willfully.

"Zane?" I called. "I just want to talk."

"Just a second," said Alice, a tremor in her voice.

Just a second? That seemed odd. If they'd been fucking, fine. I had a hard time believing Zane was shy about his body, and Alice's was no mystery. I gently tugged the door and it opened a few inches—not enough to slip through, but enough to embolden me.

I gave them a count of three and then announced my entry.

Immediately there was a scrambling sound, and I pulled hard. The door moved another two inches but got stuck on the grass, so I grabbed higher and pried it open like a wedge to push myself through.

I entered the yard just in time to see Zane dropping over the fence on the far side of the lot. Alice looked terrified—an emotion

I'd never seen on her face—and I held up my hands in some kind of protest before turning around and throwing myself against the fence door. It gave way, the upper hinge ripping out of the post, and I spilled out into the driveway and ran to the front. Zane was speeding around the corner, heading south.

"I just want to talk!" I yelled, and ran after him.

Running in a protective suit is not advised. The breathing vents, while quite sufficient for normal air intake, become overtaxed. The wicking property of the liner fails. Visibility is poor. Still I ran. I ran around the corner and down the block. He was younger than me, and lithe, but I was gaining on him nonetheless, heaving and wheezing as I went. We ran two blocks, three, four, and though the gap between us was closing, I knew I didn't have much left in me. Finally he zagged right down 58th Street. By now I was only ten yards back, and when he stopped to pick up a bicycle from the yard I closed the distance and grabbed his seat, spilling him to the ground. I collapsed on top of him.

Zane seemed almost to welcome the end of the chase; he offered no resistance, and together we lay like exhausted lovers. I wanted more than anything to pull off the hood of my suit, but instead I gulped down what air it let through, and hoped it wouldn't take me more time to recover than it did Zane. As we lay there gasping I studied his face, and for the first time I read his tattoos not as signs of defiance or bravery but of cowardice. He hid behind those images like a mask, showing people his past so they wouldn't see his future.

"Zane," I began. "I need—"

"I'm sorry," he said. He seemed truly afraid. "It wasn't my idea, I swear."

Not his idea to sleep with Alice? This didn't surprise me.

"I don't care whose idea it was," I said. "Anyway, that's not what this is about."

"Then what?"

"The Guild. I want to meet whoever wrote that letter."

Zane nudged me, and I slowly crawled off him and stood. His knee was scraped up, bleeding, but he didn't seem to mind. He brushed himself off, grinned at me, spat. "I wondered what happened to that."

I dug in my pocket and pulled out the letter.

He began to reach for it but paused, pulled back his hand. "I don't care," he said. "Keep it. It's all bullshit anyway."

"What do you mean?"

He seemed almost sad, though between his exhaustion and tattoos I couldn't be sure. I put the letter back in my pocket, and Zane picked up his bicycle. He looked it over, saw that the chain had come off the front sprocket, and squatted to replace it.

"Hold the bike," he said.

I turned briefly and looked north through the trees. I didn't often look this direction through Ballard, and I had the sensation that something had changed in what I saw rather than in my perspective. The mostly empty houses were larger and more undone by time; the sky was smaller. Several blocks away, a man stood on the peak of a roof and turned to look in all directions. Then he looked directly at me.

"Okay," Zane said, "all set."

"What?"

"You coming?"

He pointed to pegs on the rear axle before straddling the bike himself. I looked back for the man I'd seen and, not finding him, grabbed Zane's shoulders and stepped up on the pegs.

———

We turned right on the far side of the bridge, down into the old fishermen's terminal. It was an industrial part of town, and like most of them it looked least changed by the loss of people. Not much had grown in the polluted soil, so the buildings looked locked up rather than abandoned. We rode along slowly, hugging the waterline, but as the road was in disrepair we had to swerve and even stop to avoid potholes and fallen poles. We entered a residential neighborhood, and soon the street became narrow, became a dead end, and finally stopped before a modern gray house facing Puget Sound. I could see the water beyond a small lawn to the left, a wind kicking whitecaps up like cowlicks, and everywhere the Sound's shush muted the call of gulls into a dull caw. It was fresh, bracing even in the heat, and I inhaled sharply through my mask, wishing desperately I could take it off.

Zane seemed to wait patiently for me, as though knowing my need, and I thought about what he'd said upon seeing the letter. It sounded like he'd lost faith in the resistance, if that's what it was. I couldn't say I blamed him. Our own country had abandoned us—what could a small group of locals accomplish? Still, it was disappointing. Though I lacked faith personally, I found it a comfort knowing the faithful were among us.

"Come on," he said, and nodded toward the door.

Inside I counted over two dozen men and women Zane's age or younger lolling around on filthy high-end furniture, napping and chatting and flirting and staring at one another with unreadable eyes. A fat older man was standing on a chair and playing a simple, sad melody on a ukulele, while at his feet four women played a game of Monopoly. They all had short-cropped hair and multiple piercings, and one rocked a sleeping child in her lap. As we passed by she leaned in excitedly and whisper-shouted, "Three and seven! Three and seven!" and the girl to her left moved the shoe and went to jail.

Zane looked at me and shrugged. "No dice."

"But—"

He pulled me down a hallway that opened onto the second-floor balcony of a large, two-level room. The far wall was home to floor-to-ceiling windows, beyond which lay the Sound. Flooded with light, the room was much hotter than the last, and despite its size contained far fewer people. I was immediately drawn to a girl wrapped in bright orange muslin. She was curled up on a circular rattan chair, reading a large and unwieldy book with a broken spine. A section of it slid down toward her from the loose yellow cover.

"Aya," called Zane.

The girl looked up and, seeing me, dropped the book altogether.

"Whoa, seriously? You bring him here now?"

Her face, though distorted in anger and astonishment, could not hide its ethereal beauty. She was young, much younger than Zane, but she was obviously in charge. How did she know who I was? I turned to Zane for an explanation, but he'd already begun heading back down the hall.

"Not my problem anymore," he called over his shoulder. "He wants to see your father."

Amazed, I stared at the girl. Could this be the daughter of Dale Cooper? He'd never mentioned having a daughter. Then an idea was born in my brain and spread out into my tingling body and limbs like ice: this was a child he'd had with Blake. I searched her expression for a flicker of Blake's wit and wisdom. The girl looked up at me and frowned, but she wore her expression lightly, floating on the surface of her unfinished face, and it quickly changed to one of inquiry.

"Who," she asked, "cleft the Devil's foot?"

I thought I'd missed something until it became clear that I'd missed everything. "Is this a riddle?"

"It is what you want it to be."

"Is *that* a riddle?"

Aya rolled her eyes and began to gather up her book. I walked down the steps.

"Honestly," I said, "I don't know anything about the history of religion. I mean, the obvious answer would have to be God, right? Didn't God kick Satan out of Heaven? He was an angel, and he, you know…rebelled."

A couple lay in each other's arms on a mattress that had been pulled out of the sunlight to the back of the room, and when I got to the bottom of the stairs one of them sat up, a young man with long blond hair. He rubbed his eyes.

"This is the quiet room, dude."

Aya nodded toward a sliding-glass door leading to the rocky waterline, and I followed her out. Her wrap, already bright inside, now fairly caught fire as it writhed and fluttered and flapped in the breeze. Outside Aya looked older—too old to be Blake's—but still she couldn't have been more than twelve. Her stick body moved to stand close to the edge of the water, where it seemed in danger of being blown up into the air. A feast for the raving gulls, I thought. She watched as I fidgeted, sweat running down my face inside the plastic hood. There was going to be no easy way, I realized, to answer the question burning in my mind other than to ask.

"Is your father Dale Cooper?"

Aya smiled. "My father is busy at the moment, but he's been expecting you. You'll need to stay here until he returns. Please let me know if there's anything I can do to make your stay with us enjoyable." And with that she walked back inside.

Expecting me?

I sat down to consider this statement. On all sides hilly land rose and curled around the Sound like an ear—it funneled the noise of waves and birds and the occasional punctuation of cracks toward me as though asking for interpretation, but I sat there dumbly, the sun setting dumbly, the night dumbly coming down. In the growing darkness across the water rose Sunset Hill, once a higher-income area west of Ballard and now home to a small enclave of Latter-Day Saints. Not many houses were still lit, and since only a few scattered streetlights remained, the impression was of a weak constellation, as though stars that had begun close together had drifted apart, losing interest. It brought to mind an exchange I'd had with Blake on one of our high school excursions into Discovery Park. It was nighttime, and we'd been there since the afternoon, long enough to have talked ourselves out. We were lying on our backs, stargazing. Blake began to weep. And because everything was always, in those days, precarious; because I expected to be told that something good would end, or something bad begin; because I was always, in short, prepared for the worst, I remember feeling that she was about to leave me. The tears were the kind just shy of resignation, when you're at the far limit of tolerance and your body gives, the acceptance rushing through the ruptured spirit like air from a pressurized tank.

Trying to come up with some way of gracefully accepting my fate, I reached out to my side and felt for her hand, and to my surprise she grabbed it, squeezed it.

"The universe is expanding," she said through stifled sobs.

Wisely, I remained silent.

"The universe is expanding, and everything is moving away from everything else. Galaxies are moving away from other galaxies, the Milky Way is becoming diluted, and if we wait long enough we'll only see part of what we're seeing now, and then less, and then nothing at all. If the Earth lasts long enough without being swallowed by the Sun, and if we haven't killed one another off yet, if we're still here to see it, people will lie here where we're lying and look up and there won't be anything beyond our Solar System. It will be a night sky with no stars, and all the dreams and stories we have about traveling to other planets, other galaxies, or about not being alone, will be pure fantasy. Eventually we'll forget that there was ever anything to see, or that we ever dreamed about what it meant. Isn't that terrible? Isn't that tragic? We won't even know we'd ever known anything else."

At which point she'd turned to me, putting me on the spot, and I said the first thing that came to mind, something I should not have said at that moment.

"Well," I said, "I don't think we'll be around that long."

"I'm glad you've come."

I started, sat up, and frantically felt my suit for openings. It was an automatic response. I didn't have any reason to believe my suit had been punctured, and I immediately regretted the impression it must have made. Sure enough, the man standing over me saw my floundering and laughed in a deep, good-natured way.

"I don't think you have anything to worry about," he said.

I wished I could rub my eyes. It was now well into the evening, and I felt distinctly as though I'd lost time. Cursing myself for having squandered the hours in reverie instead of poking around, I tried to compensate for my flummoxed state by looking this man over as though tasked with his approval. He was large and wore loose white clothing, his shirt open around a big white belly. His hair, too, was long and white, and he presently pulled it back into a ponytail and bound it with a rubber band from his wrist. This left his face round and red, like an overripe fruit.

"I was looking for Dale Cooper," I said.

The man laughed again, not mean-spirited but insulting, as though no one could blame me for my ignorance. He turned then, toward the Sound, and in the relative silence I could hear water lick the big rocks along the shore.

"I always dreamed of owning waterfront property," he said finally. "Especially on saltwater, somewhere with a tide. Somewhere with waves. There are plenty of handy metaphors for the cycle of life, aren't there, but for my money not even our path around the sun does the thing justice like a tide. In and out and in and out, all that water…"

He turned around and smiled. "Come to think of it, it's more like fucking, too, which always tips the scales for me, I suppose."

With that, he held out a flask he'd been concealing in his waistband.

I took the flask, pulled my mask up over my head, and had a long pull of scotch. The fresh air felt good on my face and immediately improved my mood. I passed back the booze, and he took a drink, held it in his mouth for a moment, then swallowed. He held out his arms like Jesus on the cross, and in a deep, dramatic baritone offered, "I'm a sick man. I am an angry man. I am an unattractive man. I think there is something wrong with my liver."

"And yet," I said, "you don't know a damn thing about your illness. You don't even know what's wrong with you!"

The big man beamed and held out his big, meaty paw.

"I'm Russell," he said. "Russell Jonskin. And it is truly an honor to meet you. I followed your articles with great relish."

I shook his sweaty hand. "Always nice to meet a fan of Fyodor."

"Who?" he said. He looked at me in a way only someone who legitimately didn't know what I was talking about would look at me. His face was a bass drum.

"Where did you live before?" I asked.

"All over! The city was my home. To say I was homeless would be a complete mischaracterization of my state, but there you are: I was without a fixed position. I had no mortgage. I paid no property taxes. Frankly, I was a bum. A liberated man, but a bum all the same. No ambition but to be a sponge of all things. I could be found most days in the public library, the downtown location, where I in fact made friends with a man whose position entailed cleaning the floors every night, and by knowing this man I was able, should I choose, to remain in the building all night. He went by the rather remarkable name of George Washington. It was George who—"

"I know George! He led us to the—"

"Indeed. The very same. I was the one who sent him there."

Russell waved his arm in the direction of the house, and we went in, where he handed me the flask again and begged my pardon: he had something to attend to upstairs, but would promptly return. I watched his big body lumber up the stairs to street level, and then I finished the whiskey.

DAY 38

As I waited for Russell to return, I considered his quote. Had Russell truly forgotten that he'd read those lines in *Notes from Underground*? I'd read some time ago that Helen Keller had been accused of plagiarism, that certain descriptive passages in her memoirs had been lifted word for word from other books. She'd gone to the Grand Canyon, and, of course, instead of seeing the view for herself, she'd read someone else's description of it in Braille. When it came time to recount her visit, the words she'd read had been internalized to the degree that she was unable to distinguish them from her own experience.

An argument had erupted in another part of the house, or at least a side of one. A young man—judging by his high voice—was expressing some dismay about being asked to fulfill a task, the description of which I hadn't caught. Between his outbursts nothing could be heard. How long had it been since Russell left? It felt too long, like I'd been forgotten. I went to the bottom of the stairs and waited for a pause in the argument. Light spilled down the staircase and curled inward, against the back wall of the large, open room, and in the light I saw a door I hadn't noticed before, a door not hidden but unannounced, built into the wall with a small depression in lieu of a handle or knob, just something to slip fingers into and pull. It opened easily.

Behind it was a long, dark hallway, nearly parallel to the one on the floor above, but longer it seemed. A light switch just inside turned on a series of bulbs running along the ceiling, and it became clear that the hall extended farther than the front of the house. It was not contained by a foundation, but more akin to a bunker, a structure in and of itself on which the house sat, connected but distinct. I stepped inside. The passage was entirely cement, with no doors but the one in which it terminated, and as I moved the sounds of my steps were amplified, loud and hollow howls of fabric and sole. I inched forward and the air grew closer and damp, as though victim of a long-standing leak. I reached out to touch the cement. It was hard, grainy, and cool, and it quickly sucked the heat from my hand.

The metal door at the end of the hall was not locked, and opened easily, silently, into a large, square, empty room, the far wall of which was not a wall at all but one side of an enormous bolder. As my brain adjusted to the sight of the room I realized it was not empty after all; in the middle of it stood a single chair facing the door, and in the silence its worn wooden slats called to me. I'd sat on that chair before.

The realization of where I was crashed over me in waves, and I froze as though waiting for a punishment I deserved. The damp air filled my lungs—air that with each breath became earthier, smelled more of minerals and mud. And in part because I was concerned about my ability to stand, but also because it was where I belonged, I stepped forward and sat again in the chair.

Standing in the doorway where I'd just been, Russell smiled warmly. He was barefoot.

"When I was a child," he said, his voice booming through the room, "there was a large black dog that lived down the street. This was in eastern Washington, mind you—very rural—and though we lived in town the yards were large, there were no sidewalks, and what you'd call a *block* might stretch for a quarter mile. Are you feeling okay?"

I don't know whether or not I nodded. Russell's smile had broadened somehow, deepened, had become his entire face.

"This dog, Ramen—like the noodles—was always chained up in the front yard. It was a well-known terror. No fence, you understand. All the kids in the neighborhood were afraid of it. It would growl, bark, lunge. It was a big black hole of a thing.

"To get revenge on this beast, a friend of mine, Joey, would stand at the far edge of Ramen's tether and throw a stick beyond the dog's reach in the opposite direction. The stupid animal would run after it, only to be jerked back violently when it ran out of chain. The dog would let out a high-pitched whine and skitter back to its place beneath a rhododendron it used for shade. It was a cruelty, I knew, though I didn't stop it. Joey was something of a bully, and I enjoyed the opportunity to be on his side, to share in his dark jest rather than be the bare, willing butt of it.

"But one day on the way home from school, Joey offered me the stick. I remember looking down at the pale, barkless thing, a stick you might whittle into a point. I didn't want to do it, but I couldn't let Joey know that. I took it from Joey's hand, held it by one end, and reached way back. I was terrified that I wouldn't be able to throw it far enough, that I'd be laughed at for being a weakling. But the stick went sailing out into the next yard over, far beyond the chain's length.

"Joey was impressed—he whistled as it landed on the far side of a big hedge, and Ramen went after it as usual. Only this time the dog didn't stop when he came to the end of his tether. He just kept going. He'd broken free. Joey turned and ran in the other direction. I, on the other hand, remained standing. I remember that my mind was blank, and that inside me were two conflicting emotions, both of which result in immobility: absolute terror, and resignation in the face of fate.

"Well, I didn't have to wait long before the beast came bounding back around the hedge, stick in mouth, and I closed my eyes. I was dimly aware of someone shouting at me to run, but I could no more run than fly at the moment, and in that very last instant I become entirely slack. I thought for a moment I'd died, perhaps, that I'd somehow transcended the pulpy mass of my flesh as Ramen tore me apart, and it was a supreme act of courage, I felt, to open my eyes and witness the massacre.

"But when I finally opened my eyes, I saw only a dog sitting in front of me with an enormous smile, mouth open, panting through its yellow fangs. The stick was at my feet. Ramen gave me a friendly bark, and I picked up the stick, and I threw it again, and I tell you this story to illustrate another interesting element of living with the tide. Occasionally the ebb is severe, a larger wave gaining mass out at sea, and the water pulls back, it pulls back to expose the sea floor, and when it returns it can bring with it all manner of unexpected things."

I was nowhere near able to process this story. Most of what I was thinking while watching Russell speak to me could not be accurately recounted in words. There were words, but they coursed through my mind haphazardly, a *might* making way for a *worry*, a *pain* being spun off axis by *another*. *Escape* came to mind. But like Russell with Ramen, I was held invisibly in place, and with what I could only assume was reverence for this man's ability—because it did seem, at the moment, like an ability rather than some peculiar accident of echo and rhyme—to spin his story into my own, found my head nodding assent. Whether or not I actually agreed was irrelevant. My muscles, my body, my being was connected to his words as though tethered, and I could feel his satisfaction as he saw me concede.

"I want you to stay with us," he said. "I want you to join us."

"Us," I managed to say.

"The Guild, the movement. Like everyone else, I read your articles in the beginning. I read your translated missives from the front line. Cooper's missives. They were crucial for the powerless citizens given very little in the way of explanation for the goings-on around us, which explanation, when it did come, was contradictory at best, and very frequently overtly manipulative and sad. So now we're on the verge of something significant. The Lights are weakened, they're desperate, and they may well do something catastrophic. Do you know what would happen if the Ross Ice Shelf were dropped into the Southern Ocean? The Lights apparently either do not know or do not care. So it is time to act—it is time to send out a beacon to those still out there willing and able to rise up against the tyranny of Illumination. Know this, my friend: you're needed again. Your voice is needed. Don't worry, Blake, you'll be safe here."

Here he stopped, stood to one side, and nodded back down the hall. He wasn't keeping me, his gesture seemed to mean. There would be no repeat of what had happened before.

Russell had released me, but I still found it difficult—no, impossible—to move. I tried to recall the first step of standing and remembered that it was a forward motion of the torso, a swinging forward of mass that upset the balance of being seated. I willed my head forward, not sure whether it was responsive, willed my

head and shoulders and chest into the vacuum before me. Was I
falling? Teetering? I could not be sure. Russell was now beckoning
to me with his left hand, a soft patting motion of encouragement,
something he might offer a child suspicious of his motives. Did he
think I was simply reluctant to follow? I was struck by the idea that
this could be it for me, that I had simply come to a halt, my struggle
to act becoming manifest in a ludicrously literal interpretation, a
parody of itself. No sooner had I thought this, however, than an
abrupt ripple of half-laughter shot through my body, causing it to
list forward, and before I knew it my legs responded by shooting
out to prevent me from spilling to the floor, and all of a sudden
I was standing. It was more like a crouch, really, but I was on my
feet, and Russell seemed satisfied.

"Yes!" he said. "Yes! Come!"

I stood slowly, took a step, and Russell, seeing my difficulty,
offered his arm. Together we walked back to the back of the
house while he excitedly described what the future held. He'd
planned the major actions, he explained—he just needed me
to write articles from the front line, articles about Cooper's
activity with the Guild, about how we were a growing army of
resistance.

When we emerged from the hallway, the room was lit, and
because it was still night the floor-to-ceiling windows wore our
reflections, a double of ourselves in a mirror world, and in this
mirror world I saw Aya, and because I hadn't seen her in the first
world, I turned and there she was.

"You've met my wife," Russell said.

"I—" I said. "I—"

"Aye aye!" Russell said, chuckling. "Good. She's been what I'd
call the moral compass of our mission."

"How do you do," said Aya, and she gave me a polite curtsy as though being shown off in company.

I was still trying to accept what I'd heard: that this child was this man's *wife*. But being a coward, I dared not ask for clarification lest I insult either or both of them. I thought my position too precarious for any overt judgment or sudden conversational moves, even if I'd been able to author them. And there was still the issue of Cooper. Where was he?

Feeling a little more myself, I took a brief circuit around the room, which was full of discarded projects involving a variety of media—torn paper, glue, shoelaces, small stones. It looked like nothing so much as a nursery school during recess. Surely, I thought, Dale Cooper had not just let this ragtag group run amok with some half-articulated goals of civil disobedience. Surely there was a master plan. I felt eager to hear it.

"So," I said, playfully holding an unpainted papier-mâché mask before my face, "will Dale be joining us tonight, or…"

I lowered the mask to see neither Russell nor Aya was amused.

"Oh, come now," Russell said. "You can dispense with the theatrics. I must say I admired you sticking to your guns during our interrogation—that's the kind of caution we'll need should you *actually* be questioned by Weyerhaeuser. But you're among friends, truly you are."

The energy of the night had changed. I thought of Dale's process of attaining clarity, and I wondered if that's what was happening. Perhaps this was being staged in order to open me further to the possibility of a truth I was not yet ready to understand. All these small tactics meant to careen me off course, to upset some natural equilibrium that on some level resists, has always resisted, would always otherwise resist an acknowledgment of my role, my duty.

And yet.

And yet Russell seemed entirely sincere. He seemed to be at once confirming and abdicating his association with Cooper's Guild. It didn't make sense. And the kidnapping. Doing so to determine whether or not I knew what was going on made sense, I supposed, but why then ask me whether *I* was Dale Cooper? Did they think I was insane? Aya, sitting in a Papasan chair, had gone back to reading her big yellow book, and between it and her orange dress she looked like a bowl of fruit. Ignoring us both, Russell shuffled around the room, kicking pathways through the detritus of ill-executed hobbies. I looked back and forth between them, and I looked around at the disarray of craft materials, and I thought about the room we'd walked through on the floor above and I thought about Dale Cooper, and when the question came to me I felt as though I'd been circling it ever since coming back down the hall. Where were the clocks?

The thought that Cooper wasn't a part of what was going on here, that he'd never been, came to me slowly and without emotion. The fact that they didn't even know who Cooper was, that they thought I'd invented the whole thing—the thought that they thought I'd invented Dale as a source for my journalism, that they now wanted me to reinvent him, not as a witness but as an active agent, as a freedom fighter—all this bloomed in my mind like mold, growing imperceptibly until it stank. I watched Russell's reflection in the bay window until, with dawn on its way, it grew dim and it grew dimmer and it finally disappeared.

"Is there any more bourbon?" I asked.

Puget Sound was truly beautiful, even through my mask in the flat light of midday. It was made stark and lonesome, satisfying, by the absence of human activity, and it triggered a sense of haunted, soulful completion I associated only with water or great distances. Aya was napping inside, but Russell and I had gone the distance ourselves—whether out of obstinacy or true belief didn't seem to matter at this point—and together we sat on the craggy shore and stared forward, stared at the depth as though at a wall, a painting with brushstrokes we'd leaned forward to admire. I liked him despite what he'd put me through, and despite my unwillingness to help him I found our exchange strangely encouraging. Our argument.

The basic disagreement was not over whether or not Dale Cooper was real—Russell very plainly thought not, and there was nothing I could do to convince him. At issue were the ethics, whether or not the man existed, of using his name in service of activities of which he may or may not have approved, and of using the fourth estate, moreover, to broadcast and enlarge those activities. My case was that this was unethical. That it was *wrong*. Russell's view was more complicated.

"Truth," he said with a straight face, "is a narrative."

"Truth is truth," I said.

"And I'm not concerned with that narrative. I don't want that story anymore. I'm bored of that story. I'm bored of being trapped by it."

"No."

"It's a means of control, is what it is. It's how the conversation is controlled. You're raised to respect the truth so you can be easily controlled, and soon enough you're bound to this discourse you didn't author, nor did you authorize, revolving around an arbitrary value with an inherited priority that leaves you helpless in the face of authoritarian rule."

It had been like this for hours and both of us were drunk.

"So all this," I waved my arms around, "all this is the result of my naïve assumptions about truth."

"You're thinking too narrowly. Don't fall into another narrative without a plan, is what I'm saying."

"That's not what you're saying."

"Think about action. Once you've dispensed with truth, what you're left with is an empty prohibition."

"Okay, okay, okay," I said. "I know you don't believe me about Cooper. But just tell me, honestly, if he was real. I mean really real. If I knew him, okay?"

"If."

"Yes, if. If he'd been real this whole time, and maybe he's disappeared now. Maybe he's dead! Say he's dead. Wouldn't it be better to honor his memory? Like a martyr! Every cause needs a martyr."

"Every cause needs action. How it gets there is beside the point."

"God damn it. Shit. What I should have done, you know what? I should have taken a picture of him. Simple as that! That's what I should have done. I should have—"

Suddenly Aya was standing behind us. "What might have been is an abstraction remaining a perpetual possibility only in a world of speculation."

"That's—" I said.

"That's my girl," said Russell. "Always with the *bon mot.*"

"No, but that's…that's someone."

I collapsed backward and lay against the hot stone. I was terribly hot myself, sweating in my suit, dehydrated and exhausted, and it was all I could do to keep my simple argument straight, let alone field the mysterious parables of a child bride. I looked up at her gently rippling wrap, envying her fresh air, and for the first time thought of why it was possible. I raised my finger into the air, making a point.

"Aren't you worried that the Lights inside you know what you're doing? I mean, we don't know whether they transmit stuff. I mean, my mother says we don't know much about...you know what I mean?"

Russell looked up at Aya and nodded.

"Actually," he said, "we're quite certain they know what we're doing."

I laughed. "Oh, right, of course. Actually, let me guess, you're working right alongside of them!"

I reached over and gave Russell a friendly pat. I felt we'd reached the stage of friendly pats. But Russell wasn't laughing, or even smiling. Instead he flicked his eyes up at Aya in a motion that meant, *Pay attention.* I tilted my head back so that I was looking at her upside down, a bright orange wedge in a big blue pie. Her young face was still free from the careful sculpting of time that trims in the features and flaws that become true beauty. I suddenly had the thought of taking her away from this place, from this man. Of protecting her. Though she might not know it for lack of experience, surely there were other options she'd prefer. As I was envisioning my heroic duties toward this odd baby bird, she looked down at me quickly. Then her face contorted. Her eyelids fluttered and her eyes narrowed, her chin pulled back grotesquely and her mouth opened. My first thought was that she was having a seizure.

"Aya," I said, and spun around onto my knees.

Russell put his hand on my shoulder, holding me down.

The girl began to heave, blowing forcefully from the back of her throat as though trying to clear it, until a glow became visible inside her mouth. I watched in horror as the glow became brighter and the brightness became defined, a single point. The Light emerged slowly from her mouth and hovered inches from the fleshy cave. I'd never seen one so close before, and I was terrified, appalled. No bigger than a pea, it seemed to be spinning, seemed to be composed somehow of even smaller swirling lights. I leaned away from it, from them, and looked over at Russell, whose entirely flat affect made me wonder if I was hallucinating.

"You see?" he said.

The Light receded back into Aya and disappeared, and within seconds the girl had closed her mouth and opened her eyes, and she stood there as though nothing had happened. I looked back at Russell. Everything had changed.

"They came to us," he said. "They are detractors, and they're on our side. We're working together, do you understand? They're risking everything to be here, and we let them in willingly. I have one inside me too."

"Prove it!" I shouted.

"I wish I could. They won't emerge until they trust you'll let them back in. Children are easier to trust, it seems. Mine has not yet left me, but I'm working on it. I think we're close."

I stood up too quickly and felt lightheaded.

"You're crazy," I said. "You're both crazy!"

I crouched down, steadied myself with a hand on the ground. And that's when I saw them. All the kids I'd seen the day before now standing inside the room, some crowded at the door, watching. It was silent except for the birds, the water, the sound of a braking car.

"Please don't be upset," Russell said. "You're with friends."

I looked at the dirty children. I looked at Aya, at Russell. I looked across the water toward Ballard, toward my mother's house, toward the writing room where I'd spent so many days staring out the window, daydreaming. My eyes filled with tears. My entire body was filled with a cold, clammy hatred, and on its heels an acute sense of relief flooded through me, flushing out the anger I'd felt a moment before. A prick of heat was born in my chest, a disturbance that vibrated muscle and bone, breathing life into me, whispering and whirring inside me like a tiny engine. It was keeping me alive. I was dead, and it was keeping me alive. Alice had been right. Fearless as a ghost, I reached up and began to unzip my mask.

A murmur swept through the crowd inside the house. Then shouts could be heard. A moment later, people were spilling out of the door and filling the yard, and from their midst emerged a man, spinning slowly, a pistol in his hand.

It was Mitch.

"Stay the fuck back, you vampires!" he yelled. "I won't fucking hesitate to blow you cocksuckers away."

Russell leapt up and grabbed Aya, pulling her behind him and taking a step back.

"Please don't shoot," he said. "We're peaceful."

Mitch walked up to Russell and put the gun in his face. "Peaceful people don't kidnap, and they don't fucking force aliens into other people's bodies. I should blow you away." But he didn't. Instead, he looked at me and said, "Did you see a Light enter you?"

I was so startled it took me a moment to understand that he wanted a response.

"Did you actually see," he said, "a Light physically go into your body?"

"No," I said.

"Then don't take off your suit."

I dropped my hand.

"Now come with me. We're getting out of here."

I looked at Russell, whose face was still prepared to take a bullet, then took a step forward, stumbled, and Mitch reached out to offer me his arm. I grabbed it and walked with him through the throng and into the house, then slowly up the stairs and out front, where his car was still running. He opened the passenger door and helped me in. Moments later we were speeding back along the narrow roads leading to the Ballard Bridge.

Though alcohol pumped through my veins, I was buzzing from the terror of what I'd been through, the shock at realizing how close I'd come to surrendering myself. How quickly and easily I'd fallen under Russell's spell, and under Aya's—his secret weapon, his muse and perhaps even master. I felt profoundly embarrassed. What I'd mistaken as inevitable only moments before had been revealed to be nothing more than a cheap trick, and I had not even been involved in the revelation. I was as much a victim of salvation as I'd been of imminent demise. I rolled down the window and tried to vomit, but nothing came.

"Where are we going?" I managed to ask.

"Your mother will know what to do," Mitch said. "She's beyond the reach of those limp-dick hooligans, trust me."

My mother. I thought of the sacrifice she'd made to get me in to see Blake and felt a swell of anger. Had I once, I wondered, been anything other than a nuisance to her since the evacuation? Had I done anything other than be another thing to worry about, to take care of? As we got closer I tried to picture her expression as I entered the house; I pictured her looking us up and down, noting Mitch's lack of protection, noting my drunkenness; I saw her reaching for her phone to call in another favor. We turned onto 64th Street and in the distance I saw someone standing out front of my mother's house. He was fully suited up but I could tell right away it was Kent.

"Stop the car," I said.

Mitch pulled over. "Who is that?"

"It's my brother. God damn it! My mother asked him to come rescue me."

"Well, you could probably use the—"

"Let me think."

As we sat there, some words from the poem I'd heard in my hallucination came back to me, came to me with a force I hadn't felt when first hearing them through the liquid door: *Words of the fragrant portals, dimly-starred.* Yes, I thought, but to what did these portals lead? Did they lead to revelation or to destruction? And as one came closer to understanding their nature, was there still time to decide, to reverse your passage? My mother, I realized, was wrong. The power here was not in the not knowing, it was in the potential for action. Mitch was undoubtedly right: she *would* know what to do. My brother, too, would know what to do. But I was suddenly determined not to ask either one of them.

"I don't want to get them involved," I said. "Don't you know anywhere else?"

Mitch looked at me askance.

"Well," he said. "I'm headed north. But I can't promise it'll be safe."

"Perfect," I said, and I leaned my head against the window.

We drove through Ballard and through more remote Seattle neighborhoods and then suburbs and then exurbs and finally we were in farmland. Mitch was keeping off the highway, though it would have been faster, and I wondered if people would actually be looking for us. Did Russell have that much reach? Or was he working with Weyerhaeuser after all? I thought about our conversation, his insistence that we could escape the truth, the certainty in his voice, but before long the booze and the heat and the exhaustion caught up with me and my thoughts turned to images, and the images became indistinct, became colors, impressions, the soft sounds of the road. The important thing was that I was getting away from the Lights, away from Russell and his child wife, away from Alice and Zane, away from Blake, away from my mother and Kent—the important thing was that I was getting away from Seattle.

DAY 39

MY MASK WAS OFF when I woke up. We were driving through mountains. It was dawn. I hadn't been this far from Seattle in years, so long that it seemed amazing to me that it was even possible. That you could simply decide to leave. I'd expected barricades, border control, a wall. To be turned back. A road like a Möbius strip that led to the underside of itself, until you traveled it again to arrive where you'd begun. Instead the city had released us, and this filled me with optimism about the journey ahead. Mitch too seemed to be in a good mood—his window was rolled down, his elbow jutting into the cool, thin, high-elevation air—and in the pregnant silence I even had the notion that he'd only moments ago been whistling. Sensing me awake, he looked over and winked.

"It stirs!" he said.

"Where are we?"

"Cascades. Well, Rockies? No, Rockies are farther east. We're still in Washington. Way north. We should be closing in on the border now. We drove through an actual town called Twisp not too long ago. Twisp! That's not a town, it's a candy bar. Anyway, place seemed a little overgrown, but from what I could tell it was a normal town. Normal people there, all that. Well, semi-normal. There was not one, but two antique trucks held twenty feet in the air by telephone poles. Some kind of billboard gimmick. Point is, and I say this to reassure you, mask-wise, we're out of danger."

"Yeah," I said. "Lights don't travel far from their food source."

Just having my mask off in a car was astounding; to have the windows open was revelatory. I poked my head out slantwise. It was still cool, and I gulped the moist morning air in mouthfuls, our speed making my eyes water.

"That must feel good!" called Mitch.

I pulled myself back inside and exhaled sharply. "You have no idea."

He smiled, but the comment was probably unfair. We drove for a while in silence. The morning was clear, and though the sun wasn't yet visible it cast a soft gray light that egged the trees, the shoulder, the smooth black road. Objectively, the man beside me had very likely saved my life, or at least saved me from being Lit, if I wasn't already. He deserved my gratitude, not my gratuitous displays of selfish abandonment.

"I haven't thanked you," I said, somewhat sheepishly.

"No need. Had to be done."

Did it? I considered this. What difference did one Lit person make, more or less?

"Anyway," he said, "I need you!"

"You do?"

"I do."

"I don't actually know much about anything. I have no idea where Cooper is."

"There's a cathouse just across the border called One Eyed Jacks, and I have it on good authority that he's been seen there within the month."

"A brothel?"

"Could be nothing, of course, but I'm optimistic."

Though my first reaction to this was disbelief, after what I'd been through I was open to the possibility that disbelief was just a habit.

"What do you need from me?"

"I've been thinking about that, and I think what I need from you is simply to be there with me. If we find him, you're the one who knows him."

"Mitch," I said, "why are you looking for Dale Cooper?"

Mitch began to answer, but the car suddenly lurched, slowed violently, and came to a stop. My organs throbbed as they relaxed back into their appropriate places, and the seatbelt, having pulled my body back from oblivion, now eased. We'd merely braked, but I had the feeling that we'd somehow broken from where we'd been just moments before. Across the road was a diner tucked back into the trees. The sign above it, in neon, displayed an enormous white chicken roosting, then, in animated frames, leaping from its nest and letting fall an egg, which cracked in midair and landed in a frying pan.

"It's a sign!" he said.

"Can't argue with that."

The diner had just opened, and the early morning customers— all loggers and laborers of one kind or another—were quiet but content, the spare clatter of silverware and swinging kitchen doors the only sounds save the waitress's soft call and response. It was an old-fashioned place, with a counter in the center of the room and booths to all sides with red plastic seats and glittering white Formica tabletops. We took a booth by the window, and while we waited for our food I listened to Mitch's story.

"I came to Seattle the minute I heard about the Lights," he began. "I felt called. I'd been in between things for a long time, and when I saw it on the news I knew there was something there for me, that I could help. I didn't really know how, and it wasn't until recently that I figured it out. It just felt like the place I needed to be."

"So you just drove out."

"I just drove right out. I mean, I didn't disappear or anything, but within a week I was heading through the Lincoln Tunnel. Anyway, when I got to Seattle I moved in with a few people who were staying behind—a couple photographers, a French journalist—in a house right at the inside edge of the utility zone, and just did my thing, talking to people, helping out where I could. I actually worked as a volunteer for your mother for a while early on. At least, I worked for someone who worked for your mother."

He'd made friends with people all over the city, using his PI charm and genuine warmth to establish a respectable level of insight into the workings of the entire apparatus.

"There are obviously places and people I never got access to," he admitted. But he'd proven himself gifted at knowing what to ask who, and how to frame these questions as unobtrusively as possible. Soon people were giving him tips on everything from where the Lights were likely to process next to how the City's response was slowly shifting from an entirely triage role to one of containment and systematic early notification. It had been, throughout the first years, a wholly neutral endeavor, in which he gathered information from all sides with no particular purpose in mind other than creating a kind of archive, an inside portrait of the events underway.

"But then I got Lit, and that changed everything. I'd worn a suit, of course, but a Light snuck through a zipper I hadn't fully closed. Right in front of my face! The little fucker was traveling along my arm toward my midsection—I was used to them sniffing about by then, since I spent a lot of time hanging around Weyerhaeuser vans en route—so I was just casually watching it go along, doing whatever it is they do, and then it suddenly vanished."

I'd already eaten my meal at this point, but since Mitch had been doing all the talking he'd only taken a couple bites. His eggs, over easy, had begun to congeal, and his home fries, once slick with grill grease, had become matte with the drying fat. He pushed his plate away and stared out the window. The service and work trucks had been replaced by cars and SUVs, a different crowd with different jobs, no less hungry.

"So what did you do?" I asked.

"At first I flipped out. I went dark. I stayed in my little room for months, doing basically nothing. My housemates brought me hardboiled eggs, and that was almost all I ate for the duration. But after a while my depression was replaced by anger. The anger is what finally got me out of the house."

I asked whether he'd been called to serve.

"Not that I know of. But sometimes you don't even know, you know? I mean, if your fingers aren't bloody stumps and your boots aren't muddy, who's to say? But that's not the point anyway. It's the principle. I objected. Fundamentally."

When he resumed his rounds, he did so with a new purpose. Though not letting on to anyone on either side, he began to store information in a more directed way, ask more pointed questions. Still, he wasn't getting anywhere.

"And that's when I heard about the initials."

"DC."

"Yeah. And when those started cropping up I pretty quickly realized that I'd discovered my purpose. That I'd finally figured out what I'd come here to do."

"Which is find Cooper."

"Which is help Dale Cooper lead a counteroffensive in whatever way possible! I have no idea how I'll be able to help, exactly, but I'm assuming my connections, my inside knowledge—"

My expression must have given me away, though I tried to hide it. And strangely, it was not pity for his ignorance I felt, but true sadness, as though it were me, not Mitch, who had lost something dear.

"What?" he asked.

"Shit, Mitch. Of course you wouldn't have heard this part, but everything happened so quickly I didn't make the connection until now."

"What connection? You don't think it's him up there? Maybe, maybe not, but I'm not going to give up just because—"

"No, no, it was Russell. It was Russell and his…whatever it is, cult? It was those people who've been killing rhodies and putting Cooper's initials on the stumps. They did the newsletter, the Guild letters, not him. They were actually trying to recruit me to their cause when you swooped in."

I tried to look away but couldn't, could only watch Mitch's face. But instead of the destruction I'd expected, a small twitch and glance to the left was all that passed. It was a subtle reset, a quick adjustment, and before I knew it he'd regained what little composure he'd lost and moved forward.

"But they're doing it in his name. They're building a movement that's going to need a center, that's going to need him. And he'll see that. He'll understand."

I was about to argue the point when a collective gasp shot through the diner. Mitch blanched. I followed his gaze over my shoulder to a small television hung above the cash register.

"What you're about to see," said the host, "could be difficult for certain viewers."

They cut to a reporter in what appeared to be a helicopter. They were somewhere out at sea, and presently the camera panned out the open doors and down to the ocean below. It was difficult to tell what was happening at first, but once my eyes adjusted to the blue-gray expanse of water I could plainly make out the precipitous rise of a colossal tsunami moving across the screen. The copter spun slowly to the right until the coastline could be seen, and at the bottom of screen appeared the words WASHINGTON STATE.

"Remaining inhabitants of coastal towns were alerted throughout the night," the reporter voiced over, "but it is unknown how many received the message to evacuate."

The camera cut again to footage from above Seattle: I-5, bumper to bumper with traffic. Traffic didn't appear to be moving.

"Experts are especially concerned with Seattle and other points within Puget Sound, since the water levels will rise even farther there, thanks to the narrower passage afforded by surrounding land masses."

When it cut to an animation of this principle I got up from my seat.

"Let's go," I said.

We walked outside in silence. It was getting warm already, but not too warm. At higher elevation it was cooler than I was used to, than it had been in Seattle for months. It felt rejuvenating, and since I was still new to being outside without protection I felt as though I could stand there all day. Mitch's impractical faith in Cooper notwithstanding, his story had stirred something in me, and though I couldn't quite say what it was just yet, I felt compelled to know how it would end. To be there for it.

"You know," I said, "it's interesting that if it weren't for being Lit, you might not have come to this epiphany. You might not have found this calling."

"I've thought that over and over, Blake," he said at last. "I get Illuminated, as they say, and actually find that I *am* called to serve. Even if it's not the way the Lights might have wanted."

Mitch paused. I could tell he still wasn't sure how to take what we'd seen. How I'd taken it.

"Blake, if anyone could make it out of there, it would be—"

I held up my hand.

I wanted to take what he'd said further, perhaps to reassure him that the irony of his service did not in the least sabotage the value or potential of his mission, of our mission. But this was something he already knew. What could I add? What could I say? What I didn't say was, what if, at any moment, he could be called to serve by the Lights themselves? Their reach was unknown, their intentions vague. However pertinent, it seemed too cynical a speculation for the sweet, cool heat of the morning mountain air.

We walked to Mitch's car, and before getting in he took an orange cloth from his jacket pocket and rubbed away a little smudge on the hood. The small gesture was mindless, but it occurred to me that if we were to find Dale Cooper at all, it would be in this way: through an automatic respect for the very real world around us. Standing on the passenger side of the humble gray Honda, I watched Mitch, waited for him to unlock the door. Improbably, this man had infected me with his optimism. I felt as though I'd long been underwater, deep down beyond the reach of sunlight, imperiled by my own stubbornness and running out of air, and that I was now freed by some great inner strength and guided by a friendly force, swiftly rising upward toward the surface, to a place both wonderful and strange.

ACKNOWLEDGMENTS

Thanks first to the early readers who helped me figure this thing out: Erin Flaherty, Nicholas Bredie, Matthew Simmons, Jonathan Redhorse, and, a little later, my mother Kathie Huus. You are all part of this book. Also part of this book are my awesome agent Stacia Decker and the good folks at Dzanc, especially Guy Intoci, who is one of the hardest workers I know. Thank you. Thank you.

And thanks for reading.